Brian Morrison is the author of three previous novels, *State of Resurrection*, *Blood Brother* and *A Cause for Dying*. He has spent many years in Paris, but now lives with his wife and three daughters in Devon.

Acclaim for *Blood Brother*:

'Morrison writes with authority and a compelling sense of pace... a gripping tale with a disquieting ring of accuracy' *Time Out*

'Excellent... fast-moving and pacy' *Yorkshire Post*

State of Resurrection:

'Irresistible reading entertainment... a white hot storyteller' CLIVE CUSSLER

BY THE SAME AUTHOR

State of Resurrection
Blood Brother
A Cause for Dying

BRIAN MORRISON

ATONEMENT

HarperCollins*Publishers*

HarperCollins*Publishers*
77–85 Fulham Palace Road,
Hammersmith, London W6 8JB

A Paperback Original 1994
1 3 5 7 9 8 6 4 2

Copyright © Brian Morrison 1994

The Author asserts the moral right to
be identified as the author of this work

A catalogue record for this book
is available from the British Library

ISBN 0 00 647877 8

Set in Palatino

Printed in Great Britain by
HarperCollinsManufacturing Glasgow

All rights reserved. No part of this publication may be
reproduced, stored in a retrieval system, or transmitted,
in any form or by any means, electronic, mechanical,
photocopying, recording or otherwise, without the prior
permission of the publishers.

This book is sold subject to the condition that it shall not,
by way of trade or otherwise, be lent, re-sold, hired out or
otherwise circulated without the publisher's prior consent
in any form of binding or cover other than that in which it
is published and without a similar condition including this
condition being imposed on the subsequent purchaser.

Prologue

The dark blue Mercedes swerved back onto its own side of the road, out of the path of the surge of oncoming traffic. The driver sat hunched forward, his knuckles white on the wheel, as he aimed for an impossible gap between a delivery van and a traffic island. Clipping the van, a rear wheel bucking as it caught the kerb, he sent the car barrelling through the red light.

Beneath their umbrellas, tourists spun to watch in dismay as the car sped across the square towards the Montparnasse Tower, its tyres spinning on the soaked tarmac. To the left, traffic was already accelerating hard, anticipating the green light. The driver reared back in surprise as a Citroën saloon appeared ahead and to his side, on a certain collision course. With a choking cry, he swung the wheel hard, trying to cut behind the Citroën. He shouted again, a noise that was almost a sob, as the rear wheels lost their grip on the waterlogged surface. He wrestled futilely for control as the heavy car turned a full circle and buried its nose deep into the side of a taxi. The Mercedes driver reared back in his seat, twisting to look behind him through the heavily tinted glass, as though he contemplated reversing and fleeing the scene. It was too late, already the traffic had stopped, hemming him in.

Watched by the grinning onlookers, the taxi driver was already out of his cab and strutting around towards the Mercedes, shouting and gesticulating. The Mercedes driver threw open his own door and sprang out, slinging the strap of a leather satchel over his shoulder. Slightly built, he wore cream linen trousers and a burgundy silk shirt that flapped loose around bony wrists. Globules of rain the size of cherries spattered the shirt, leaving dark spots like bloodstains. Desperation was etched deep in the fine-boned face, drawing the flesh taut, giving the already lean features a haunted look.

For a second or two the man hesitated, staring back down the rue de Rennes with wide-set, vulnerable brown eyes, oblivious to the cab driver's crude insults. The cabbie began jabbing him in the chest, sharp, painful blows. For another second the man continued staring over his shoulder. Then, he snapped his head round to face his assailant. He looked at him for an instant in silence, taking in the coarse face and the belly straining against the cloth of his creased polo shirt. Sneering, the cabbie drew back his hand to jab him again. The slim man shook his head with an emphasis that made his whole body shake and drove a bony fist into the jutting belly. With a breathy sound the cab driver sat down heavily on the wet tarmac, his legs splayed and a befuddled expression on his face. The other man sprang past him and ran.

He raced across the place 18 Juin towards the Montparnasse Tower, weaving recklessly through the thin summer traffic. As he ran, one hand clutching at the satchel, he cast constant glances over his shoulder, looking back at the gridlocked traffic in the rue de Rennes.

As he drew close to the far pavement, heading for a gap in the parked cars, his stride faltered. A policeman had let fall the pad of parking tickets he had been distributing and was moving to intercept him. He flinched as the policeman called to him to stop, his eyes flickering over the close-packed cars, looking for a way around. The policeman called again, sharper, louder, the beginning of a threat, and took a wary step towards him.

The man twisted to look back again at the rue de Rennes. As he watched, two men erupted from among the hooting cars and began sprinting across the intervening square. With a low choking sound, the man turned back to face the front. The policeman was moving watchfully towards him, talking low and gesturing at the scene of the crash.

He was three paces away, a hand extended, when the Mercedes driver, with no change in his ravaged expression, plunged a hand into the satchel. Before the policeman could respond, he withdrew the hand and stuck it out at full stretch in front of him.

The policeman's mouth was open to speak. No sound came. He stared at the weapon, as though unable to absorb what he was seeing. The man held the stub of a shotgun, the stock and barrel sawn off so close it would have fitted into a woman's handbag. The end of the gun was barely more than arm's length from his face, close enough for him to see the slightly ragged rim of bright metal where the barrel had been roughly hacksawed. With a whimper he threw himself back and sideways, into the shelter of a parked car.

The man glanced behind him. At the sight of the policeman the two pursuers had halted. Now, they once again broke into a run. Leaving the policeman shouting into a radio and struggling to free his own weapon, the man shoved his way through the panicking bystanders and into the entrance of the C&A store.

His breath coming in great rasping whoops, he ran full tilt through the store, cannoning into shoppers, sending them sprawling, several times almost falling himself. The sound of shouted protests made him glance back again. His pursuers were already inside the store, themselves impeded by the confusion he had created. Jaw muscles straining, his fingers grasped tightly around the gun, he forced himself to greater speed.

Bursting through the far door of the store he emerged into a maze of arcades lined with boutiques. He hesitated, muttered to himself, and wheeled to his left. He ran, zigzagging through the arcades, and then shouldered his way through a glass door back onto the pavement. Turning south, he sprinted the short distance through the driving rain to another door.

He found himself alone in the carpeted lobby, facing the battery of lifts. Gasping for breath, he ran to press the call button and stood waiting, his eyes flickering constantly from the indicator board to the entrance behind him.

The doors of a lift hissed open. He leapt in and jammed his finger on a button. His finger stayed ground against the button until the doors slid closed, hiding him from sight. Then, his hand fell to his side. Closing his eyes, he fell back against the wall and let out a long, moaning sigh.

The indicator stopped at the twenty-third floor. The doors opened. With a shudder, as though awakening from a dream, the man stepped out into a thickly carpeted reception area. Opposite him, a policeman slouched in a cream leather armchair, cradling a rifle. Despite the rifle, nothing had been further from his mind than trouble. The man stepped towards him, the gun held awkwardly but firmly, straight out in front of him. Slow bewilderment filled the policeman's face as his eyes moved from the wet gleam of the gun to the bedraggled figure, hair plastered to its forehead, fabric of the shirt clinging, and then slowly back to the gun.

'Take the lift, please. Quickly.' The gunman spoke with incongruous courtesy.

Nodding, the policeman let his own weapon slide to the floor and sidled to the lift, his eyes never leaving the shotgun muzzle as it swivelled to follow him. The gunman watched the doors close, heard the hum of the departing lift, and turned to stride into the room.

A handsome woman, fortyish, blonde-streaked hair held tightly in place by a dark velvet headband, sat at an impressively bare desk, looking at him in stark disbelief. One hand lay in the open drawer of her desk where she had been hurriedly stowing the remains of her lunch. Her mouth hung open, revealing a partly chewed mouthful of the food.

'Madame Massenet, I've come to see Monsieur Vadon.'

Her mouth snapped shut. The face worked beneath the perfect make-up. 'Oh, yes, Monsieur Bengana. I see.' Her normally deep, measured voice was shrill. She did not look at him as she spoke, her gaze welded to the gun at his side. 'I'm afraid he's not, er . . . He's . . .' Her voice broke off in a croak. She swallowed and tried again, forcing herself to look into his face, trying to smile. The smile came out ugly, a death's-head contortion of the taut, lifted skin. 'The Minister isn't here. He's . . . It's the anniversary, you know, the . . . arrangements.' As she spoke he watched her eyes flick to the leather padded door across the big open-plan office.

He nodded. 'I need to speak to him.' He began striding towards the padded door.

'But, Monsieur Bengana, he isn't . . .' Her voice trailed off as he continued walking, watched by the two women, younger versions of the receptionist, who had remained in the office to eat at their desks.

Reaching the door, the man paused, appearing to have a moment of hesitation. Then, with a movement of his shoulders, he seized the handle and hurled it open.

'Hello, Christian,' he said bleakly.

Across the office, Christian Vadon sat at an antique wooden desk, his back to the glass wall. A dark blue suit, superbly made, set off the blue-grey hair that lapped at his collar. He had frozen in the act of reaching for a telephone. Astonishment and then fear fought for possession of his handsome, pouchy, face. His eyes, their brilliant blue emphasized by the deep tan, darted between the intruder's face, the gun, and the open doorway. He wet his lips and tried to smile.

'Bengana, my dear fellow. Whatever is *that* thing for?' As he spoke he began rising from his chair. He fell back again as the man drew closer, raising the weapon. The visitor's desolate eyes seemed to pin him further back in his seat.

The gunman stared down at Vadon in silence, his lips working as though seeking words. Noises from the outer office made them both glance quickly at the door. As he turned back to face Vadon his eyes seemed suddenly to empty. It was as though he were no longer seeing the man cowering in front of him, but staring into the void beyond, where purple-grey storm clouds shrouded the Eiffel Tower, leaving only its top visible, as though it were floating free. From the perspective of the twenty-third floor it seemed to be on a level with them.

Running feet in the outer office seemed to bring the man to himself again. The receptionist appeared in the doorway, pointing, a uniformed policeman jostling at her shoulder. The man shot them a single bereft glance. Swallowing hard, he raised the gun and fired, twice.

The shots died away to a moment of unnatural quiet. Behind Vadon the window was opaque, the safety glass splintered into a million tiny fragments. Only the hole, as big as a barrel, blasted by the shot, allowed a stray ray of sun to stream through.

The man let the gun fall to the floor and spoke to the still cowering figure of Vadon. 'You can be free now.'

As Vadon watched, blanched and speechless, the man took two running steps and hurled himself, headfirst, through the hole.

1

'Hey! Hold it, Duvall!' The woman's voice was muffled by the pillow. Brown shoulder-length hair lay in wisps across her face. One leg protruded from the crumpled sheet that covered the rest of her, the foot already on the floor. She swatted at the hand that moved on her thigh. 'You have to get me to the office. Remember?'

Bill Duvall raised his head from the pillow and peered at the glowing numerals of the clock. 'The office?' he said, in feigned disbelief. 'It's still only five-fifteen.' He shifted his hand speculatively.

She lifted it off and swung herself out of bed. 'Right. I have a breakfast meeting for seven-thirty.'

He dropped his head back onto the pillow and winced. 'A *breakfast* meeting? What does all that bullshit get anybody, except maybe coffee stains all over the files? Why can't you Wall Street types just eat breakfast at home, and then go to the office and *work*, like anybody else.'

She nodded, heading across the spacious bedroom for the bathroom, collecting discarded clothes as she went. 'Only people who don't have to work for a living ask questions like that. The rest of us just obey.'

He watched her retreating back. 'Ho-hum. Still thinks running a gallery isn't work, huh?' He threw off the sheet and followed her into the bathroom.

She closed the shower door. 'Too right!' she called, over the hiss of the water. 'What kind of business is it that doesn't even open until after midday?'

He grunted through the lather as he prepared to shave. 'I've told you before, my clients use their mornings to select the day's jewellery. And *I* use them to catch up on background.'

She whooped derisively. 'Reading magazines! Then he breezes into the gallery, hangs around for three or four hours while his glamorous assistant makes him coffee, and who knows what else, and calls it work.'

He chuckled. 'Solange is a lot of wonderful things, but glamorous? No. And there's no "what else".' His voice dropped. 'Even if there had been, Amy, there wouldn't be now.'

She stepped out of the shower, her eyes shining. He handed her a towel, looking at her gleaming body with frank appreciation. 'You sure this meeting is all *that* important?'

She leaned and kissed him chastely, high on the cheek, getting herself a white lather goatee. 'Afraid so.'

By the time they had drunk coffee and were climbing into the car for the drive to New York, dawn was breaking. For a while they drove in virtual silence, enjoying the sun rising on what promised to be another scorching day. They were approaching the city when Bill spoke.

'Thanks, Amy. It's been a great few days.'

Without turning her head, she reached out to rest a hand lightly on his thigh. 'M'mm.'

He glanced round at her, studying her profile, his smile fading. 'Hasn't it?'

She nodded, returning his gaze. 'Yes, it has. It's been great. Perfect.' She paused. 'Bill, there's something I have to ask you.'

His eyes flicked back to her, the beginning of a frown clouding his brow. 'Ask.'

'Well, look, I've known you for three weeks now.'

He gave her a quick smile. 'Is that all? Seems like years.'

'I know. To me, too. That's the trouble, in a way. Look, Bill, you're a very attractive, clean, heterosexual male, and this is New York City, 1994. Men answering to that description just aren't, well, available.'

He inclined his head in a mock bow. 'Thanks for the compliment,' he said gently. 'What's the question?'

'Just this. Are you really, well, free?' She bit her lip. 'I know we've only been on, what, a dozen dates, but I get the feeling there's something there, deep down, that you're not talking about.' She turned abruptly to look at him. 'If you've got a secret, I have to know it. Now, Bill, before I get hurt too badly.'

He glanced quickly at her. He paused for a long moment before saying, softly, 'No secret, Amy. I'm free as a bird. I really am divorced, just as I told you the first night.'

She leaned back in her seat. 'Phew!' She mopped her brow in a parody of relief and then spoke again, serious once more. 'Children?'

He paused, longer this time. 'No,' he murmured at length, not looking at her. 'Not now.'

'Not now?' Her eyes were on his face, calm and attentive.

For several seconds he drove without responding, his teeth sinking deep into the flesh of his lower lip. 'I had a son. Tim. He died. In a car accident. Almost three years ago.'

A shadow flitted across her face. 'Tell me about it, Bill, please.'

He nodded, drawing breath loudly, his eyes momentarily squeezing shut. 'Oh, shit, yes. You're right. It's time. You have to know about it.' He let a few more seconds pass. 'Katie, my ex-wife, was driving. Trying to avoid some bastards in a pick-up, she . . . she missed a bridge. Ran into the river.' His voice caught. 'My boy drowned.'

'My God.'

He grimaced, chewing harder at his lip. 'M'mm.'

'And the divorce?' she asked, almost whispering.

'Katie's decision.' He sighed deeply. 'She couldn't get it out of her head that I was reproaching her.'

'Were you?'

'God, I hope not.' He wiped a hand over his face. 'But then, who knows? Maybe I was. *She* was, for sure.'

'Where is she now?'

'The West Coast. Portland, Oregon. She's doing fine. She's with somebody. A banker. Lives in the country, farms a few dozen acres for fun. A real solid citizen, in fact.' He rolled his shoulders. 'Which, to tell you the truth, is a big weight off my mind. There are an awful lot of assholes out there.'

She laughed aloud. 'You're telling *me*! You've just taken a big weight off *my* mind, too.'

They were by now deep in the city's financial district. Bill swung the car over and stopped. 'I'm glad to hear it, Amy. See you tonight?'

With one hand on the door handle she leant over and kissed him, a long hard kiss. 'You bet. And thanks again for four perfect days.'

It was almost one o'clock when Bill pushed aside the pile of magazines and saleroom circulars, rose from his desk, collected his jacket from the sofa and headed for the door. He was frowning as he went. Most mornings, by the time he had been through the day's slew of mail he could quote the price and the purchaser of any picture of interest to him that had changed hands anywhere in the world. Today, he barely remembered a thing. Partly, it was the glow of the last four days that still had him distracted. But mostly it was the phone calls.

He was out in the hall, pulling the door of the apartment closed, when, with another glance at his watch, he stopped short. He shook his head. 'Oh, shit!' As he murmured the words, he turned and strode back into the flat, slamming the door hard behind him.

Without bothering to sit down, he stabbed at the buttons of the answering machine. His head cocked in concentration, he listened once again to the tape.

Amid the cheerful friends with invitations, the dealers and buyers, one anguished voice stood out. The first call had come on Friday, the evening he had left for the trip with Amy. For the next two days they had continued, punctuating the tape every few hours, day and night. As the weekend wore on, the desperation in the voice grew, amplifying the troubled note he had first heard late Friday afternoon, as he closed down the gallery. He had heard the voice, even reached for the phone, and then, already an hour late for his appointment with Amy, he had turned away without picking it up, intending to call from the Cape. He had even tried, once, unsuccessfully, on Saturday afternoon. Then the sheer joy of being with Amy had driven everything else from his mind.

Throwing down his jacket, he took up the phone and dialled the Paris number. He let it ring for fully two minutes before replacing the receiver. He stood for a few seconds more, his hand still on the phone, his face clouded. Then, with a last look at his watch, he wheeled, snatched up his jacket, and left the apartment.

'Beautiful morning, Mr Duvall. Get you a cab?'

Bill gave the doorman a distracted smile, pointing mechanically at the cloudless sky. 'Thanks, Mike. I'll walk.'

He set off to walk the few blocks south-east towards Lexington Avenue. The streets were busy with a mix of the wealthy women who inhabited the smart apartment blocks and bare-legged tourists using street maps to navigate between the art collections that clustered in the area. Even the parched old widows walking the five-inch tall dogs looked glad to be alive.

On such a day he would normally have taken an hour or more to reach the gallery, strolling, loafing by other galleries to talk, storing the casual scraps of gossip in case of future need. Today, as he pushed open the glass door, shuddering at the sharp bite of the air-conditioning on his sweat-soaked skin, he was surprised to find it had taken him less than fifteen minutes.

A slender woman in her late fifties sat at a steel and glass desk at the back of the room, speaking into the telephone. She looked up as he entered, glancing pointedly at her watch.

He shrugged. 'Hi, Solange,' he muttered, crossing the room. 'What's new?'

Still speaking, she pushed a pad across the desk to him. He picked it up, perched on the edge of the desk, and began looking over the notes. By the time she put the phone down, a deep frown furrowed his brow.

Solange caught the look. 'He called half a dozen times on Monday. He sounded in a terrible state. I told him I had no number for you. I thought you would call in. I . . .'

He cut her off with a raised hand. 'It's okay. I meant to call you.' He gave her an odd, lop-sided smile. 'I was preoccupied.'

She studied him over her silver-rimmed glasses. 'Lucky you. Shall I try . . . ?' The ringing of the phone cut her short. As she took it up Bill turned back to her list of notes. Hearing her break into French, he looked up again. Solange put a finger on the mute button. 'It's a woman.'

He cocked an eyebrow. 'Who?'

'You heard me ask. She wouldn't say. She sounds, I don't know, hostile.' She cocked her head. 'You haven't been getting anyone into trouble?'

He laughed. 'Hell, no. Not for the last fifteen years or so, anyway.' He reached out a hand. 'Here.'

He put the phone to his ear. 'Allo, oui?'

Solange was watching him with the beaming, proprietorial manner she adopted whenever she heard him speak his almost unaccented French. The look faded as she saw the disquiet spread over Bill's face.

'Keltum? How are you?' He pressed the phone closer to his ear. 'You don't sound well. Are you alright? What can I . . .' The voice at the other end cut him off short.

'It's not me, it's Ahmed.'

'What?'

'He's dead. He committed suicide. Yesterday.'

Bill's face drained of colour. 'Oh, shit!' His voice was a whisper. 'Oh, shit! Oh, *merde!*' He murmured the last word several times, as though to himself. Then, with a shake of his head, he gathered himself. 'What . . . ? I mean, how . . . ?'

'He jumped out of a window. The twenty-third floor.'

'Oh, my God.' Bill slumped into the chair Solange had brought for him. He spoke in a hushed, distant voice. 'Your father? And your mother? How are they taking it?'

'My mother has had to have tranquillizers. My father's doing wonderfully, considering his condition. It's for him that I'm calling. He wants you to come to the funeral.'

Bill's head was throbbing. 'Of course, Keltum. Tell him I'll be there. When is it?'

'We don't know yet. A few days. I'll let you know as soon as I can.'

'Thanks.' He paused. 'And you, Keltum? How are you?'

There was an almost imperceptible hardening of her voice. 'You don't have to worry about me, thank you. I'll be alright.'

Bill readied himself to say something and then changed his mind. 'That's great,' he murmured. 'Take care then, Keltum. Thanks for letting me know.'

He sat for several seconds with his eyes unfocused, the phone still in his hand. Solange took it from him and replaced it gently on its cradle. 'Coffee?' She was already pouring from a jug on the table as Bill nodded. 'Bad news? You look awful.'

He swallowed a gulp of coffee and cradled his head in his palm. 'Yes, it was. Very bad. That was Ahmed Bengana's sister.'

'Keltum? The one who worked here?'

'That's right.' His voice was a mumble, barely audible. 'She was here for a few months.' He paused, his fingers and thumb kneading his temples. 'Ahmed killed himself yesterday.'

Solange's hand flew to her mouth. 'Oh, my God! Yesterday! You mean . . . but I was *talking* to him only on Monday . . . Oh, my . . .' She sat down heavily in her chair. 'How horrible.'

A shudder ran through Bill. 'It should have been me.' His voice was distant. '*I* should have been talking to him on Monday.' He looked abruptly up at her. 'Jesus, Solange, I should have talked to him on *Friday*! He was *desperate*! Beside himself. And I didn't take his call.' He dropped his head again, cupping it in both hands. 'Oh, God. He was *pleading* for help and I didn't listen!'

Bill opened his eyes once more and turned to stare out of the window. Already, in the east, ahead of the aircraft, the sky was turning pale. Since they had taken off from New York, he had been unable to sleep, prevented by the images that churned in his mind. Nightmarish pictures of Ahmed somersaulting through space to smash into the asphalt, showering blood and brain tissue over passers-by, mingled incongruously with moments from their friendship. The recurring image was of their first encounter. He had replayed it a dozen times in his mind, each detail as clear as though it had happened yesterday.

It was 1968. He was approaching the end of his year in Paris and it had been wonderful. The atmosphere in the city was electrifying. The cafés were thronged with people debating deep into the night. A feverish sense that something momentous was about to take place infected everybody. Then, in May, it had happened. In Paris, London, Prague, on campuses all over America, the dam finally broke. Barriers of class and race were all going to be swept away on the flood. It was an intoxicating time, and Paris was the most intoxicating place.

The Sorbonne had been one of the breeding grounds of the movement and Bill had hardly been able to help getting caught up in it. He had taken part in the first sit-ins, distributed handbills and helped organize marches. A feeling of euphoria reigned. The government was reeling, seemed ready to fall. Nobody worried too much about what should replace it. Change was an end in itself. And then, suddenly, it had begun to turn sour. The violence had started. The euphoria evaporated in a cloud of tear gas and baton charges.

Bill was a steward on a march. Despite the efforts of the stewards, the march had been infiltrated. Crash-helmeted anarchists had taken over its head. As they approached the Pont St Michel, a line of police, sinister and tough in their riot gear, stood silently barring their way, as though they had been tipped off that there would be trouble. Stones and bottles started to fly. A Molotov cocktail fell at the feet of a policeman and spread a quick, ineffectual puddle of flame. As though that had been a signal, the police had charged. More police, emerging from side streets, attacked the peaceable marchers at the rear of the column. People were staggering and falling as the column fell apart under the blows of the batons.

Bill side-stepped a baton. Turning to run, he saw a policeman drive a fist into a girl's midriff, knocking her to the ground. He leapt to help her, shoving the policeman aside. A baton landed across his own shoulders, pitching him to his knees. He tried to turn to reason with his attacker. Another sickening blow to his forehead drew a gush of blood. The girl had gone, losing herself in the crowd.

Ducking another blow, Bill scrambled to his feet and ran. He stumbled across the place Saint Michel, and kept running until he found himself in a quiet, narrow street lined with the blank walls and porches of eighteenth-century town houses.

He leant against a wall, fighting for breath. The sounds of the street were almost like silence after the mayhem he had just escaped. Abruptly, three men came round the corner at a trot, fanning out across the street. They wore jeans, leather blousons and crash helmets. Scarves hid the lower halves of their faces. Each gripped a short steel bar in one hand. For a moment Bill took them to be another group of anarchists on their way to the battle. It was only when one of them shouted and pointed at his bloodied face that he realized his mistake. Before he could straighten they were on him, jostling for the pleasure of hitting him. He fell back against a pair of great oak gates that separated one of the private courtyards from the street.

A steel bar bit deep into the flesh of his shoulder. He tried to raise his arms to defend himself, only to find the blow had deadened the nerves. Frantic, he lunged to his feet again, his good arm crooked in front of his face. In the same moment his vision dissolved in a kaleidoscope whirl of lights as a blow exploded onto his skull.

When his vision steadied he was on one knee. A helmeted figure towered above him, the metal bar held high. Bill tried again to push himself upright. The man seemed to sway above him as his eyes lost focus again. He pressed back into the angle of the wall, his hand extended in a futile effort to ward off the coming blow. The voices of the other men seemed to come from a great distance, urging their companion to further violence.

The man shifted his feet, taking his time. Setting himself, he raised his arm a little higher, and then, unaccountably, jerked and twisted backwards. The bar clattered harmlessly to the ground as the man spun away, pain and stupid puzzlement in his look.

Bill dashed a hand across his face, wiping away a loose strand of his shoulder-length blond hair. A slender, black-haired man of about his own age stood between him and the three men. The nostrils of the chiselled nose flared. His dark brown eyes blazed with a mixture of fear and rage as he stared defiantly at Bill's attackers.

The three of them stared back at him, their looks uncertain above the scarves. The one who had been about to hit Bill held one hand pressed to a gash in his sleeve. Blood soaked the sleeve and ran from the limp fingers of his weapon hand. All three glanced from the newcomer's face to the blade of the horn-handled clasp knife he gripped in his hand. The dark man's eyes glittered, daring them to move. The assailant's gaze dropped to where his blood was gathering in a pool among the cobbles. With a grimace, he muttered to his cronies and began backing away.

The moment the men were out of sight, the young man dropped to a crouch in front of Bill. 'You okay?' he asked, grinning.

'Thanks. Yes. I think so.' Bill pushed himself upright, trying to return the grin. The street spun. He fell against the wall, choking back an urge to vomit. 'Oh, shit,' he mumbled softly. 'No, I'm not.'

The young man smiled. 'No, you're definitely not, are you.' Leaning forward, he probed at Bill's head with his fingertips. He recoiled, drawing breath with a hiss. 'Come on,' he added, reaching out a hand. 'I think you should get to a hospital.'

Bill snorted softly. The effort sent pain stabbing through his brain. 'Sure. And get a visit from those gorillas! There's a good chance they're cops freelancing, not wanting to miss the fun.'

The young man laughed. 'Of course. And after what we did to the one that was about to break your skull, they'll be visiting every hospital in Paris looking for another chance.'

Bill nodded, smiling even through the pain at his new friend's use of 'we'. 'That's right. Hospital's are out, I guess.'

The young man looked grave for a moment and then abruptly brightened. 'You must come home with me. My parents will help us.'

Bill gestured to the row of handsome buildings. 'Here.'

The young man brayed with laughter. 'No! I live up in Goutte-d'Or.' He put an arm around Bill's shoulders, hauling him upright with surprising wiry strength. 'Come on, before any more of those bastards find us.'

To the background wail of sirens and the plop of exploding tear-gas grenades they made their way down through Saint Germain to the river. Running people passed them. Nobody took more than fleeting notice of another two bloodstained figures limping from the scene of the action.

Struggling to keep his feet, Bill leant heavily on his companion, barely able to respond as the young man talked, speaking with the unguarded, faintly feverish innocence that had infected the youth of the city.

'What's your name?'

'Bill. Bill Duvall.'

Despite the fact Bill was draped over his shoulders, the young man sought his hand and shook it warmly. 'And mine is Ahmed Bengana. Is yours a French name?'

Bill laughed softly. 'American. And you?'

'I'm French. My parents are from Algeria. I was born there. We came over in 1960. My father always thought the future would be better here. I think what's happening proves him right, don't you?'

Bill touched his head gingerly. 'If it works,' he said, smiling ruefully. 'What do you do?'

'I'm a student. Art. How about you?'

21

'I'm a student, too. Art History.' Bill faltered, the effort of speaking almost making him pass out.

Ahmed gripped him harder, settling Bill's arm more firmly over his shoulders. 'Sorry. I'm making you talk too much. My car is just across the river.'

They crossed the Seine in silence and cut up past the Louvre. Ahmed guided him towards a beat-up green Citroën Deux Chevaux, one of many cars parked at crazy angles in front of the museum railings. At any other time the cops would have been busy towing them away. Right now the Paris police had other things on their minds. Ahmed opened the unlocked door and helped Bill inside.

Bill slumped in his seat, almost passed out. In his moments of clarity he was aware of his new friend's cheerful disregard for the traffic regulations. Taking full advantage of the prevailing spirit of anarchy, he wove through the choked traffic, sailing around the wrong side of traffic islands and taking breezy shortcuts across pavements, waving happily to the mildly dumbfounded pedestrians.

By the time they stopped, Bill's head was aching fit to explode, but the rest had restored a little of his strength. He climbed unaided from the car and straightened, taking in his surroundings.

They were in a narrow street lined with dilapidated buildings four or five storeys high. Irregular patches of stucco had fallen from the facades, leaving exposed patches of fluted red brickwork and parts of the rotting wooden frames of the buildings. Washing hung drying from a maze of cords and wires strung from the pitted iron guardrails at each window. At ground level the shopfronts sported ineptly hand-painted signs, some French, some Arabic. The French was approximate. He suspected the Arabic was, too. The street was thronged. Broad-hipped North African women with over-stuffed, unlined faces chatted in front of the displays of food and textiles that spilled onto the pavements. In the poorly lit, sparsely furnished bars keening Arab music wailed tinnily from transistor radios. The men, lean, hard and hostile, in disturbing contrast to the overfed women, stood moodily drinking beer at the counters or gathered in knots outside arguing. Heads turned to watch in wary curiosity, as Ahmed, himself bloodied from head to foot, led Bill, his hair and clothes soaked scarlet, towards a double-fronted store.

Several men were busy carrying yellow sacks from the store to a parked truck. At the approach of the odd couple one of the men first stared in momentary disbelief, then gave a shout and ran towards them. He exchanged a few anxious words in Arabic with Ahmed and then, after a frankly curious look at Bill, turned and ran into the store.

By the time they got inside, a man in his late forties, wearing crumpled tan slacks and a polo shirt, was leaping down the last few steps of a worn spiral staircase to meet them. Long braided muscles slid under the skin as he threw an arm around Ahmed's neck. He laid his other hand gently on Bill's shoulder and spoke softly, questioning.

Ahmed responded, speaking French for Bill's benefit. 'I'm okay, Father. This is my friend, Bill. He's been attacked – by police, we think. He needs a doctor to look at his head.'

The older man nodded and smiled, showing no inclination to question his son's judgement. 'Then we'll get him one,' he said, smiling at Bill. 'But first let's get you upstairs.' He turned to the young man who had called him. 'Go and find Doctor Hassan. Tell him I need him here. Quickly.'

Bill's knees finally gave way. Father and son manhandled him between the ceiling-high mounds of sacks of grain and cans of olive oil and up the awkward stairs and dragged him gently into the flat above. He was aware of a close, sweet smell of perfume and spices, music, a fleeting impression of a woman reclining on a couch in front of a flickering black and white television screen, and then nothing more as he lost consciousness completely.

He awoke to find himself on a bed. Pink and blue rabbits frolicked on the wallpaper. The window was hung with extravagantly ruffled curtains. A neat row of dolls and stuffed toys sat attentively along one wall. An olive-skinned, prematurely bald man was smiling down at him. 'Good afternoon,' he said in a warm, soft voice. 'I'm Doctor Hassan. How do you feel?'

Bill tried to speak and made only a croaking noise. He tried again. 'Thirsty.' He put a hand to his head. A thick dressing was soft under his fingers. 'And this hurts. Like hell.'

The doctor smiled as Ahmed appeared at the bedside with a glass of water and handed it to Bill. 'I'm not surprised, on either count. You've been asleep for thirty-six hours. I had to sedate you. Your skull is fractured. We removed some blood, from inside.'

'You did that *here*?'

The doctor nodded. 'We talked it over. We decided you were better off here than in a hospital. After all, if the man Ahmed injured *was* a policeman of some sort his colleagues will be very anxious to meet you again.' He smiled with a trace of irony at the shadow that crossed Bill's face. 'Believe me, you really were better off here. I have done a lot of such work in much worse conditions than this. I was a doctor during the war.'

A momentary frown puckered Bill's brow.

Hassan shared a brief, faintly bitter smile with Ahmed. '*Our* war. The war of independence. I'm sorry to have to tell you that your injury was . . .' He paused, groping for the word. 'Well, trivial, compared to what the French did to some of our people.'

'Don't blame me. I'm an American,' he answered, making them both smile. He handed back the empty glass. 'But,' he went on, waving a hand at the room. 'I can't stay here.' He tried to sit up.

As the doctor pressed him firmly back down, Ahmed's father appeared at his son's side. It was the first time Bill had been aware that he was in the room. 'Of course you can.'

Ahmed placed a hand on his father's shoulder. 'We have discussed that, too. You'll stay as long as you need, or wish to.'

'But, I can't do that. I'm a complete stranger to you.' He gestured again at the line of toys. 'And you must need this room.'

The father smiled. 'Keltum won't complain. She's two weeks old.'

He had remained in bed for a week. Sidi Bey worked a fourteen-hour day in the store while Madame Bengana wafted in and out of her cramped kitchen with Keltum clasped to her breast, bringing him the endless glasses of sweet tea which seemed to be her form of communication. By day, he followed events on the portable television they provided and devoured the papers. Each night, Ahmed would come home, sometimes with a gaggle of friends in tow, bringing him breathless reports of the day which they would discuss until Bill fell asleep, exhausted.

As he grew stronger, they moved him to the sofa in the living room. Propped on cushions, a rug over him, he would hold court to Ahmed and the admiring circle of friends while Sidi Bey and his wife sat silently at the oilcloth-covered table, drinking their tea and smiling indulgently, before finally gliding silently off to bed, leaving the young people eagerly discussing revolution into the early hours.

It was almost a month before Doctor Hassan finally gave his smiling assent for Bill to leave. By then he had been virtually adopted into the family. All of them, along with various relatives and a shoal of the young men and women veterans of their late-night discussions, had accompanied him to the airport, a joyful convoy with Bill and Ahmed at its head in the battered Deux Chevaux. Madame Bengana, with no more than a few halting words of French to express herself, had resorted to a flood of tears that had left the front of her dress, and the tiny Keltum, soaked. Even Sidi Bey's shrewd eyes had glistened. Holding his own tears in check only with the greatest difficulty, Bill had embraced each member of the family, knowing that these friendships would endure for life.

'Breakfast, sir?' He started, jerking around to face the brisk voice. A stewardess was proffering a tray, smiling the faintly defensive smile of cabin crew who know people would rather be left to sleep. Bill struggled upright, trying to raise a smile himself as he reached for the tray. He squinted at his watch.

'We're right on time, sir. We'll be landing at Paris in an hour.'

2

Bill hurried towards the passport booth, shouldering his way with muscular courtesy through the knots of half-awake, disorientated tourists that blocked the moving walkway. He reached the booth fifth in line and stood watching with no particular interest as the red-eyed immigration man perfunctorily examined the passports.

Bill stepped up to the booth and slid his own passport across the counter. The official let his eyes slide from the passport to Bill's face and then, yawning ostentatiously, handed it back to him. A minute later Bill stepped off the moving ramp into the baggage claim area and strode past the conveyors, heading directly for the exit. The briefcase in his hand, with its patina of good leather ageing gracefully, held a minimal in-flight toilet kit, memo recorder and a half-dozen slim files. It was all the baggage he ever needed on visits to Paris. Everything else he kept permanently at the flat in the rue Galilée, a short walk from the Champs-Elysées.

He passed the lounging customs officials without slackening his pace. Moving with the sure purpose of someone totally familiar with the airport, he turned to make for the taxi rank, not even glancing at the cluster of people awaiting friends and relatives. At the rear of the group two men stood slightly apart. The younger one, dressed in jeans and T-shirt, was murmuring into a portable telephone. At Bill's arrival, he lowered the phone and murmured to his companion. The second man, chunky, with silver hair that grew in thick, close waves, was holding aloft a make-shift placard with a name scrawled in childish capitals. At the younger man's words, he lowered the placard and muttered a quick response. The younger man pocketed the phone and turned to stride briskly towards the lift leading to the car park.

It was a quiet time of day. In less than three minutes Bill was being ushered towards a green Renault taxi by the policeman who was supervizing the rank with a cheerful zeal completely out of synch with the hour. He lowered himself into the seat, already aware of the odour of stale tobacco permeating his clothes. He gave the address, simultaneously winding down the window, and settled back, not looking forward to the journey.

Behind him, just far enough back to be beyond the easy jurisdiction of the policeman, the heavy-set man watched anxiously as the Renault departed, all the time craning his thick neck for sight of the cars that came around the curve of the circular building. A BMW shot into view, cut across an arriving cab and bucked to a stop next to the man. Before the policeman had time to raise his whistle to his lips, the man had clambered into the passenger seat and the BMW had sprung forward again, in the wake of the taxi.

The cab driver was a thin, slack-faced man with the uneven stubble of someone who had shaved carelessly the previous evening, saving himself a few minutes before getting up for the early shift. He eyed Bill shrewdly in the rear-view mirror.

'Live in Paris, sir?' Ash from the cigarette between his lips teetered and finally fell as he spoke.

Bill kept his eyes turned to the familiar landscape of advertising hoardings and industrial parks. 'No,' he murmured, curtly enough to discourage further conversation.

'Ah.' The cabbie paused to murmur a curse at a driver who cut close in front of him, looking in the mirror again to check that Bill appreciated his wit. 'You have a room booked, sir?'

'M'mm.'

'The place is full, you know.'

Bill sighed inwardly and turned to watch the road on the driver's behalf. 'Well, I guess it is the tourist season, after all,' he said, addressing the man's dandruff-flecked shoulders.

'Hah!' The driver grinned triumphantly in his mirror. 'It's not just *tourists*! It's VIPs! Guests of our government, the bastards. For the parade.' The whine in his voice became a sneer. 'Our dear President's pet project.'

Bill's face lit up with sudden understanding. Since the call from Keltum his mind had been in such turmoil, so preoccupied with Ahmed's death, and with his own failure to respond to his friend's cry for help, he had completely forgotten. This was August 1994. Exactly fifty years since the liberation of Paris from the Nazis. 'Just what is it they're planning?'

The driver sniggered. 'Planning? You call it planning? The whole of the centre of town's been screwed up for a week already.'

'How's that?'

The man wormed another cigarette from a pack on the seat next to him and lit it from the butt of the old one, negligently steering with the heel of one hand as he wove through the traffic, thicker but no slower now they were approaching the city. 'They've closed off the whole Champs-Elysées area. Been like it for days now. A complete bloody disaster. Worse than the fourteenth of July. For "security", so they tell us.'

Bill was intrigued despite himself. 'What's so special they have to seal off the Champs-Elysées for an entire week? It must upset a lot of people. I'd have thought the same arrangements they have for the fourteenth of July would be tight enough.'

The driver squinted at him in the mirror. 'Not what. *Who*! Bruckner, of course!' The emphasis broke another half inch of ash off his cigarette.

'The Israeli Prime Minister?'

'Right!' He pawed at the ash, smearing it over his shirt. His eyes narrowed further, giving his face an unpleasantly cunning look. 'You're not Jewish, are you?' he asked warily.

For just a fleeting moment, Bill entertained the idea of saying yes. At length, in a voice empty of any expression, he asked, 'No, why?' As if he did not know *exactly* why.

The man gave a soft grunt. 'Got no time for them myself. Nor Arabs.' As he spoke, he gestured angrily around him, taking in the pavements that, even at this early hour, were beginning to be crowded. They were off the highway now, into one of the blighted areas that huddled beneath the ring road. A home to cheap clothing stores, drab cafés, broken, dog-fouled pavements and dilapidated buildings where immigrant families huddled in cramped, cold-water flats, the only accommodation most of them could afford. The faces on the pavements were immigrant faces, mostly Arabs.

Half a block ahead of the cab, a crocodile of Arab children waited hand-in-hand to cross the road. They wore neat uniforms, the boys in grey trousers and sweatshirts, the girls in grey dresses that reached to their ankles. A quartet of young women accompanied them. The women were also in plain grey worsted robes that brushed the street around their feet. Head-dresses of similar material hung close about their faces concealing their hair. One of them was veiled.

Spotting them, the driver jabbed a finger and spoke with new venom. '*Especially* those fuckers.'

Bill groaned to himself. He took a lot of taxis. Probably their drivers were no more bigoted than anyone else. It was just that, like barbers, they had a captive audience. You took a cab, or got a haircut, it was part of the price. Usually he just kept his mouth shut until they ran out of steam. This much venom aimed at pre-school kids was unusual enough to intrigue him. 'Any particular reason?'

The man twisted in his seat to look at him directly, as though he did not trust the mirror. He frowned, unsure if Bill was laughing at him or just a plain imbecile. 'Look at them,' he expounded reasonably, turning back to jerk his chin at the group. 'Not satisfied with sponging off the social security, or peddling drugs outside the schools. Now they want to turn France into a Moslem country. Running their own kindergartens.' He snatched the cigarette from his lips and jabbed with it towards a closed-up shopfront, its window blocked off with roughly mortared cement blocks. A row of identical, blurred posters was pasted haphazardly at head height. A face stared out from them, topped by a turban. Even the poor quality of the printing could not entirely disguise the sheer power of the eyes that burned out from it. Beneath the face was an inscription in flowing Arabic script.

'Know who that is?'

Bill knew perfectly. The driver did not wait to hear it.

'Bouhila!' he went on. 'Oh, no. Sorry. *Imam* Bouhila. Their leader. He's the one stirring them up. I lost a full day's work last week through that character. He had them out on a march demanding special schools for their kids. At the French taxpayer's expense, of course. Snarled up the entire town.'

Bill could barely help smiling. He sounded just as outraged by the traffic jam as by the prospect of paying for their schools.

The man swivelled to look at him accusingly. 'Would *you* stand for that?'

Bill shook his head, still half smiling. 'No,' he said truthfully, after a moment's reflection. 'I guess not.'

The cabbie nodded triumphantly. 'Hah! Me neither! If it was up to me, Bouhila'd be the first one on a plane home.' He shook his head in disgust. 'If you ask me, de Medem's right. The only one with the guts to tell the truth.'

Bill's interest quickened. For the last couple of years Blaise de Medem's neo-Fascists had been gathering momentum, mining the rich lode of anti-immigrant feeling. He was pretty sure several of the art-dealing crowd he knew might be at least passive supporters. But those people were too smart to admit it. This was the first time that he had met someone too ignorant even to know he was supposed to be ashamed of himself. 'And what is the *truth*?'

The driver snorted. 'We ought to send them back where they came from. Give French people an equal chance. These immigrants get better treatment than our own people. Priority housing! Summer holidays for their kids at the government's expense so they'll be kind enough not to start setting fire to cars again. All they know how to do for themselves is breed more kids and claim more welfare. If they want their own schools and their own religion, they're welcome. But over there, in their own countries, not here.'

Bill listened in silence to the man's almost unbroken stream of invective as they skirted the city centre, avoiding the Champs-Elysées. He let out a soft sigh of relief as the cab pulled into the rue Galilée. 'Over there will be fine.'

Bill paid the man off and swung out of the car. He slammed the door while the man was still grunting a protest that he had not given him a tip and strode the last few metres towards a pair of polished wooden doors furnished with gleaming brass. He pressed a bell-push and waited, looking around him.

Well-kept buildings that flanked the street. There was not a pedestrian in sight. The residents, and the lawyers and tax consultants who used the spacious apartments as consulting rooms, had deserted the city. If you wanted to avoid tax in Paris, August was the wrong time of year for it. His eye wandered over the parked cars. Mercedes and Jaguars were heavily over-represented, as were the Range Rovers that some of the locals apparently needed to handle the treacherous terrain of the fifteenth arrondissement. Among them the bronze BMW sliding to a halt fifty metres from him had nothing to draw his attention. At the sound of the latch snicking open, he turned from the street and pushed his way into the building.

The young man cut the motor of the BMW and turned to grin at his silver-haired companion. 'Shall I go and take a look inside?'

The other man grimaced and shook his head. 'You always want to overdo things. Just go and find a public phone instead of that toy in your pocket that half Paris can listen in to. Give him the address and see what he wants us to do. And give me the keys in case our American friend decides to leave before you get back.'

* * *

Bill let the heavy glass door from the courtyard swing to behind him, shivering as the chill of the air-conditioning hit him. He strode across the lobby, past the antique furniture with its red cloth and gilt paint, towards the counter where the jowly porter stood smiling, his hands spread wide. 'Monsieur Duvall! Whatever brings *you* to Paris at this time of year?'

Bill's own smile was brief. 'Personal matters, Michel.'

The porter's smile turned to concern. 'Oh!' His voice dropped in speculative condolence. 'Nothing grave, I hope.'

Bill gave him another quick smile and shook his head. 'A funeral, Michel. Any mail?'

The porter turned and slid a sheaf of mail from cubby-hole. He handed it over, placing a key on top of it. 'Shall I have Juliette bring you some breakfast?' He paused then added, wheedling,'Er, was it somebody close to you, Monsieur Duvall?'

Bill shook his head distractedly, already thumbing rapidly through the mail. 'Just coffee would be great, Michel, please.' He dumped the wad of junk mail unopened into a bin and walked to the lift.

The gilt lattice doors of the lift glided open with a sound no louder than a breath. Bill stepped into the corridor, strode the few paces to his apartment and let himself in. He threw aside the briefcase and headed for the bathroom, casting off clothes as he went.

It was fully twenty minutes before he emerged from the shower, pulled on the crisp white towelling robe that hung ready, and returned to the living room. A tray, loaded with a pair of thin porcelain cups, one jug of coffee and another of frothy milk stood waiting on a low table. Pouring a cupful, he settled himself full length on a sofa and took up the television control. He had been through two dozen of the channels that the flats were wired into, in God knew how many languages, before he found anything so simple as the French news. He set his watch to French time and settled back.

A reporter was speaking into the camera. As he spoke the

camera drew back to take in a wider scene. Bill felt the faint shock of recognition. The man was speaking from the tree-lined main street of Aix-en-Provence, a town he had often visited, still a favourite residence for French painters who were making some money. As the reporter spoke, Bill sat up, leaning closer to the screen. Behind the reporter, police wagons and fire engines blocked the street. Burnt-out carcasses of cars lay among them, still smoking. Firemen were playing hoses on a gutted building. The reporter disappeared, to be followed by a filmed re-run of the previous evening's events.

Marchers, wearing the distinctive red, white and blue armbands of de Medem's National Salvation League, advanced up the broad avenue, carrying banners bearing anti-Moslem slogans. Bill made a soft noise of surprise. Instead of the rabble of tattooed, crop-headed youths he would have expected, the marchers were mostly middle-aged to elderly, soberly dressed and neatly barbered. Only a few marshals on the outskirts of the march, clad in jeans and T-shirts, had the muscular look of political thugs.

As they came on, chanting slogans but calm and orderly, the camera swung to cover a sudden mêlée further back. A group of people in motorcycle helmets had burst at a run from among the spectators. Bill leaned closer, shocked. Some of them wore the ankle-length grey robes of Bouhila's female supporters. Flailing with the sticks or iron bars they carried, they fell upon the marchers.

The column swirled and heaved like a wounded serpent as more groups emerged from the crowd to attack it. There was total confusion for a minute or two and then the screen began to clear as the marchers melted away. For a few seconds it looked as though they were routed, leaving the terrain to the Fundamentalists. Then, the camera swerved again to catch a column of young men running three abreast from a side street, batons in their hands and their faces covered by scarves. Within seconds, the street was a battlefield as the Fundamentalists and de Medem's shock troops laid into each other. The battle raged for two or three minutes before the flashing blue lights of police wagons streaked into the picture. At the same moment tongues of flame erupted in the gathering dusk. A car exploded in a sheet of yellow flame.

'Oh, my God,' Bill murmured aloud to himself. Glancing at his watch, he flicked off the set and reached for the phone.

'The Bengana residence.'

Bill grimaced. The warm voice he remembered had taken on a chill, brittle tone. He guessed she had had to field hundreds of calls since the suicide. It was not surprising if the strain were starting to tell. 'Keltum? It's Bill.'

'Ah, yes.' He raised an eyebrow, disappointed that her tone had barely altered. 'You're in Paris, I suppose?'

He bit his lip. 'That's right. I arrived this morning. How are you? Sick of answering the phone, I'll bet. Don't you have someone there who could take care of that for you?'

'No. We don't want anybody here now. I can manage perfectly well.' Her voice was taut, as though tears could come at any moment.

'Well, sure, I guess you can. I *know* you can but . . .' He shook his head. 'Keltum, may I speak to your father?'

'He's very weak, you know. The doctors have told him to rest as much as possible.'

'Is he resting now? I just want a word, to say hello.'

'Oh, well, I suppose if he finds out I said no I'll only be in trouble. For my *father*, Bill Duvall can do no wrong.'

'Will you put him on. Please,' he replied, wincing at the anger that she could still summon after so long.

It was more than two years since she had returned from New York. He had understood then that she had been hurt and angry. God knew it was not hard to figure out. She had come to help in the gallery, learn English. He ought to have seen it coming but he had not. He had known her so long, taken it so much for granted that they were friends, just like everyone else in the family, that he had not seen her falling in love with him. By the time he *had* noticed, she was head over heels. He had tried his best to let her down lightly, make her see it was impossible. He had failed miserably; she had returned to Paris, heart-broken. So far, so classic. He had been certain that within six months she would have forgotten him, found a boyfriend, probably been married. Instead of that, she had got religion.

The new love in her life was Imam Bouhila's brand of Islam. Within weeks of returning to Paris she had given up her studies, her studio apartment, the clothes from the smart Left Bank boutiques, and most of her friends, and thrown herself into full-time activism for Bouhila, helping organize cells in the teeming estates around Paris.

His reflections were cut short by the sound of laboured breathing at the other end of the line. 'William? Is that really you? You're in Paris? I wasn't sure if you would be able to come.'

It took him a moment to recover from the shock of the reedy, broken voice, hardly more than a breath. 'I promised Keltum I would be here, Sidi Bey. How are you?'

'Dying, William.'

Bill swallowed, put off-balance for an instant by the man's directness. 'Is there much pain, my friend?'

'For the cancer? I can stand that. They give me drugs for the physical pain. But there is no injection against the pain of losing a son. It's against nature, William, for a man's children to die before he does.'

'I know it is, Sidi Bey,' Bill said softly. 'It's a brutal, bitter thing. For all of you. How is your wife?'

'You know, she does not say much, William. She is still shocked. Confused, more than anything, perhaps.'

'I guess that's a lot of what I feel, too. May I come over and see you, or would you prefer to be alone?'

A few years ago the question would have been absurd. Now, he felt the need to give Sidi Bey the choice, the option not to have his grief contaminated by the residual tension between himself and Keltum.

'No, no. Come to us. I *want* to see you. I need to talk to you, about . . . Ahmed. Please come.'

'Of course. At what time?'

'Not this morning – Keltum will not allow it. I must rest. Come this afternoon. At four. I am stronger then, and not too stupid from what Hassan pumps into me. Goodbye, William.'

Bill put down the phone and sat musing at the strange note of relief in his friend's voice, as though talking to Bill had relieved him of some kind of burden. Shaking his head, he threw off the robe and headed for the bedroom. A few hours' sleep would do him good, too.

3

'Shall I play it through again, Mister President?'

The President ran an eye over the men seated in a semi-circle round the vast television set and then shook his head at the uniformed flunkey. 'No, thank you. I think seeing a news bulletin like that three times is enough for all our stomachs.' The President spoke softly in a voice that was slightly blurred, a legacy of his stroke. 'Take it away, please.' He sat silently, waiting for the footman to wheel the television and the video recorder from the room. When the door had swung closed behind the man, he swivelled his wheelchair to sit squarely facing Christian Vadon. 'Well?' The immobility in the left side of his face, another legacy of his attack, made it impossible to read his expression. The only clue to his mood was the way his fingers cut deep into the padding of the wheelchair arms.

Vadon ran a palm from his brow back past an ear, smoothing the already perfect silver hair. He wet his lips and glanced around at the group of men who sat with their eyes expectantly on him. These were the men the President had hand-picked to serve on the committee that was organizing the commemoration ceremony, the committee the President had insisted on chairing despite his condition. They made up the inner core of ministers, each with his own following of a handful of top aides and the heads of the security agencies. Two of the ministers who sat silently waiting for him to justify himself were declared rivals, openly sharing his ambition to succeed the President. Behind their impassive faces he imagined an almost palpable pleasure at his discomfiture. He cleared his throat.

'Well, it *is* most unfortunate, most unfortunate indeed. I have to say I thought we had done enough. Isn't that so, Fabre?'

The man he addressed blinked. The slightly too bold pinstripes of his suit, the pasty complexion and oiled wisps of hair combed across his crown gave Fabre the air of a mayor of a small provincial town. In fact, after a police career that had taken in some of the city's toughest districts, he now headed the national police intelligence unit. 'Well, from my people's point of view, we did all we were asked to do.'

Although Vadon's expression did not falter at the non-committal reply, his eyes flicked around the row of faces, looking for a clue as to where Fabre's loyalty might lie. 'After all, the League's people *had* given us undertakings. They . . .'

The President's hoarse whisper broke in. '*Undertakings*? From the National Salvation League?' Sarcasm vibrated in his voice. His eyes glittered with fury as he glared at the group. 'Like Mister Chamberlain, accepting undertakings from Hitler? We sit through scenes like that' – he nodded to where the television had stood – 'and you have the temerity to wave de Medem's *undertakings* in our faces? Haven't you learned *anything* in fifty years, Vadon? Do you even understand the reason for this committee's existence?'

Vadon's tan darkened as a deep flush suffused his face. 'I didn't just accept them. I took them into account, that's all. The NSL have marched often enough before without giving trouble. Anyway, I had extra men in place. Those CRS you all saw didn't appear from nowhere. I had them standing by. They couldn't have foreseen what happened.'

'Not them. You!' The voice was that of Pautrat, the Prime Minister. He was a hulking bear of a man, his great rump hanging in rolls over the seat of the spindly gilt chair, threatening to engulf it. 'Foresight is what ministers are supposed to have, not policemen.'

Vadon scowled. Pautrat, with his carefully retained thick southern accent and his slovenly appearance, cultivated a man-of-the-people image. In fact, behind the stuffed face lay the shrewdest political brain in the country. He was Vadon's sharpest rival. 'And I had. Nobody could have been expected to foresee *that*! You all saw how it was. It was well marshalled. They *were* perfectly peaceful. Until those damned Arabs appeared.'

'Ah, yes,' Pautrat rejoined, with relish. 'Just walking down the main street, amiably insulting people, peaceably inciting racial hatred. How could *you* be expected to suppose the victims might take offence?'

Vadon leapt to his feet. 'You saw the video. There's no doubt about it at all. If the Fundamentalists hadn't been there, nothing would have happened.'

The President's whisper brought his head snapping round. 'Sit down!' He waited until Vadon was seated. 'For six months now something like this has been brewing. We've had brawling every time the League, or Bouhila's people, have been on the streets. Nothing on this scale, I'll grant you, but it's been in the air, hasn't it?'

'Alright, that's true. But a street-corner brawl is one thing. We could have handled that. This, however, was organized, a military operation. They must have been planning it for weeks.'

'Probably. And that surprises you, too? For months now, Bouhila's people have seen the League firebombing their schools, they've had their women clubbed on the streets. For God's sake, Vadon, Aix-en-Provence! It's the next stop up from Marseilles. They have more Arabs down there, and more right-wing nuts, than all the rest of France put together. And yet you seem to have been completely unprepared. Even if you accepted *de Medem's* assurances, you must have known that Bouhila's people were a risk.'

Vadon sat straight in his seat, a finger jabbing the air. 'No, I won't accept that I, or any of my people, or Fabre's,' he interjected, with a glance at the policeman, 'did anything less than they ought. We had all the local Fundamentalist ringleaders under surveillance. And not just in Aix. Here in Paris, Marseilles, Toulon, Lyon. By God, they're *constantly* under surveillance. As I said, this was planned like a military operation. It hit us out of nowhere. The CRS did wonderfully well to control it so quickly.'

The President snorted softly. 'Your loyalty to your services is touching, Vadon, but none of us are questioning the actions or the capacities of the CRS. They dealt with the situation they were faced with, and, as you say, did it wonderfully.' He shot a glance at Pautrat, the good side of his mouth twitching in the faintest suggestion of a smile. 'What perplexes all of us is *why* you permitted the march in the first place.'

Vadon reared back in an exaggerated show of exasperation. 'How could I reasonably ban it? De Medem promised a peaceful turn-out, and he kept his bargain. My God, you saw them. They weren't a bunch of foul-mouthed fanatics brandishing swastikas. They were ordinary men and women, exercising their rights. People are supposed to be able to do that in this country.' He looked around him at the unimpressed faces. He drew a deep breath. 'Do you know what it reminded me of, most of all?' He paused, breathing deeply. 'The demonstrations that brought back General de Gaulle.'

Pautrat gave a snort of derision. 'Ha! Come on,' Vadon. You're not trying to compare a cheap Fascist to General de Gaulle?'

'That wasn't the comparison he had in mind – was it,' Vadon?' the President said, his voice barely audible.

Pautrat laughed, a fruity, vulgar guffaw, as Vadon flushed crimson.

Vadon leapt to his feet again. 'I'm not making any comparisons at all, about people,' he spluttered. 'What I will say, though, is that you had all better expect more trouble. The police and the security services are stretched to the limit. Beyond the limit. We just don't have the manpower to watch every damned Arab immigrant in the country. Their top people are watched, and they *know* it only too well. Not one of them left his own patch yesterday. They don't even use the phone any more. They communicate by word of mouth, by messenger.'

'I notice you don't seem as exercised about the League,' the President murmured.

Pautrat laughed again. 'Arabs are what he has most on his mind just lately.'

Vadon reeled as though struck by a missile. His expression went through a dozen subtle changes. He clutched the back of his chair for support, his crimson flush deepening further as he strove to find his voice.

'I've said all I can say about that matter,' he said, managing a tone of quiet dignity. His flush subsided as he brought his face once again under control. 'That man was a virtual stranger to me. I've repeated it to all of you, to the press and to everybody else, a hundred times already. I had met him perhaps half-a-dozen times. There seemed to be hardly a charity gala or a party he wasn't at. I couldn't *help* meeting him, and the same probably goes for half the people in this room.' An odd, strained expression flickered over his face. 'You all know it perfectly. Our positions force us to rub shoulders with people we might not choose. It's our stock-in-trade. The only difference between him and three dozen other people whose hands we have to shake in the course of a day is that *he* was an Arab, an immigrant. He appeared to think it gave him some sort of leverage, as though he were a kind of ambassador for all the rest of them. He seemed to have set himself up as an unofficial lobbyist for *those* people.' He gestured again to where the television had stood. 'Of all the sleeve-tuggers I've ever had to deal with, I think he must have been one of the most persistent. He was forever trying to phone me. I wouldn't receive him at the Ministry, so he took to plaguing me at my party office. He presented himself there on several occasions, trying to plead their cause.' His mouth puckered. 'I don't know who he thought he was. Take away the hype and he was just another little Arab queer.' A sudden bitterness made one or two of the listeners exchange curious glances. 'That's all he was! A little Arab queer who couldn't handle his life!' The vehemence of his last words left him panting.

The good side of the President's face creased in one of his incomplete smiles. 'Thank you for the speech, Vadon. We already knew your views on Arabs. And on "queers", too, for that matter. Let's turn our attention to how we can ensure nothing like yesterday's fiasco happens on the twenty-fifth, shall we? After all, it would be a pity to bring the Prime Minister of Israel here to celebrate half a century of liberation from *German* Fascism, and then entertain him with our home-grown Nazis brawling in the streets, don't you agree?'

Fury flashed in Vadon's face at the President's soft-spoken sarcasm. He bit it back and reached for the file that Fabre held out to him. 'Everything is in hand.' He pulled a typed sheet from the folder, stood up and began reading from it. 'For the last five days the whole Champs-Elysées area has been closed to traffic of all kinds. This was done without warning.'

'You're telling us!' one of the men present grumbled. 'Surely you could have let *us* know. It took me two and a half hours to get to my office.'

Vadon gave the man a condescending sneer. 'Without warning to *anyone*, with the purpose of preventing terrorists from taking steps to anticipate us.'

'You think somebody here might be a member of a terrorist cell?' the man who had spoken earlier scoffed.

Vadon fixed him with a hard stare. 'You are a minister's private secretary. From a security viewpoint that makes you no more and no less likely to be a terrorist than anybody else. Does that answer your question?' He turned back to his notes. 'Since then, the only people allowed through the security cordon have been those with an official reason, approved by myself or Fabre. *Nobody* else. The grandstands are being erected by small companies brought in from around the country. The workers are all French nationals; no Spaniards, no Portuguese. Especially no North Africans! They are all from outside Paris, hard-working people who have never had anything to do with politics of any kind. I think, gentlemen, we can be confident that a person who has spent twenty years running a one-man scaffolding business on the outskirts of Brest won't surprise us by turning out to be a closet Fundamentalist. Don't you agree?' He smirked at them for approval, regaining his poise, and continued. 'The official guests will enter through a single entry point for each compound. It will be very strictly controlled, with palm-print technology. VIP guests and members of the government will be housed together in the compound at the top of the Champs-Elysées. It will be enclosed by Zenith glass.'

'What's that?' one of his listeners broke in.

Vadon smiled proprietorially. 'A new laminate, from the Army's labs. It's a sandwich of glass and some kind of resin. I won't bore you with the technicalities, but it will stop just about any projectile in the world, short of field artillery. Certainly anything a man could carry.' Growing more at ease by the moment, Vadon moved across to the ornate marble fireplace. Dangling the file from one hand he turned and hooked his elbows over the mantelpiece, propping one heel on the fender.

The President watched without expression as Vadon expanded on the measures he had put in hand, poised as an actor, his voice low and thrilling. The man was vain, with a streak of weakness, and lost his composure easily under the pressure of debate. But as a television performer he was without equal. Next to his silken glamour, Pautrat, though far more intelligent and thoughtful, came across as if he really were the clumsy provincial he liked to affect to be.

'What about our principal guest?'

For just an instant Vadon faltered, his face clouding. 'Ah, we're still in discussion with the Israelis. They're being a little, er, intransigent about it.' A twist of bitterness pulled at his wide mouth. 'We all know how difficult they can be about security. They are still insisting that *their* people keep control of him, right up to the last minute.' He pushed himself away from the fireplace and stalked a couple of paces into the room. 'How they think we are supposed to organize security for an event like this without knowing when and by what means the person in whose aid it's all being done is to arrive is beyond me. I'm having the Ambassador in again this afternoon, to make him see sense.'

'I wish you luck,' the President murmured, smiling his lop-sided smile. He turned to Pautrat. 'What's the public reaction been like? Snarling up the city for a week can't be going down very well.'

The Prime Minister shrugged. 'It's a good thing the Germans departed in August! Even with the street closures, in most areas it's not much worse than normal for the rest of the year. Anyway, I'm making sure Vadon gets the blame!' He let out a single raucous shout of laughter and was immediately serious again. 'Cab drivers are raising hell, of course, threatening a mass go-slow. But for once I'm afraid Vadon's got it right. With all that's at stake there's really no option. Not allowing the public onto the Champs-Elysées for the parade is right, too. We can't take a chance on a couple of thousand National Salvation League crackpots goose-stepping out of the crowd to lay a swastika on the tomb of the unknown warrior.' He shook with another rough laugh. 'Next thing you know, Bouhila's people would be coming out of the woodwork and we'd have a replay of Aix on our hands, this time on satellite to a hundred million homes around the world!' He shook his head. 'Let them sit at home and enjoy it on television.' He grimaced maliciously at Vadon. 'After all, don't we live in an age where image counts for more than the real thing?'

4

Bill fumbled for the phone that had woken him, mumbled incoherent thanks to the operator, and swung himself out of bed. It was three o'clock in the afternoon. Feeling the way those people who have their bodies deep-frozen when they die are going to feel when science finally gets around to reviving them, he wove unsteadily into the bathroom.

A half-hour later, another long shower, an omelette and a lot more coffee had bullied his jet-lagged brain back into normal service. He put on a fresh shirt and pale tan summer suit. After a moment's reflection he rummaged in a drawer and pulled out a dark blue knitted silk tie. Somehow, it would not feel right to stroll in on the Benganas, grief-stricken by the loss of Ahmed and by Sidi Bey's illness, looking as though he were enjoying a vacation. Fingering the tie loose at the throat, he left the apartment.

A scattering of people sat around the lobby, mostly couples in the expensive sports clothes that marked out the wealthy taking time off. A few businessmen sat hunched over the low tables, jabbing at calculators and exchanging terse comments. Several people sat alone. Three of these were attractive young women sitting with self-conscious good posture and surveying the room through their own cigarette smoke. Returning their enquiring smiles with a shake of his head and tossing his key to the deskman, who was probably trebling his wages on his cut of the women's earnings, he walked through the glass doors into the oppressive outside air. Behind him, the stocky, silver-haired man who had been sitting half concealed by a cluster of tropical plants, threw down his newspaper and strode after him.

Bill headed south, away from the Champs-Elysées and the

knot of police that lounged around the barrier blocking the end of the street. Before he had gone two blocks he hailed a cruising taxi and climbed in.

The silver-haired man made a beckoning movement over his shoulder, his eyes not leaving the taxi. Behind him, a bronze BMW that had been dawdling some distance back, accelerated hard and slid to a stop alongside him. Without hurry, the man climbed into the front. Empty cola cans rolled around at his feet, dribbling dregs onto the carpet, to the amusement of the driver. The man kicked them aside with a grimace of disgust and turned to the grinning driver. 'Follow him. And not too close. There's not enough traffic to worry about losing them.'

They followed the cab in a circle, skirting the closed-off streets at the western end of the Champs-Elysées, and then east again. The driver, Pierrot, chuckled. 'Hey, he's taking us to Barbès. We can nip back to my place for a coffee.'

'I've had coffee,' the other man said grimly. 'Just shut up and make sure you keep your distance.'

The thin traffic of the wealthier areas had thickened, the road narrowed by squadrons of parked tourist buses. Forced to close up on the taxi, they were only three cars behind when it turned left, heading north. They were still turning when it pulled to an abrupt halt, forcing them to drive on past. Stopped fifty metres ahead of him, they turned to watch as Bill paid off the driver and crossed the road, heading for the rue de la Goutte-d'Or. 'Okay, I'll see you back here.' As he spoke, the silver-haired man was already out of the car, his eyes on Bill's back.

Bill stood at the corner for several seconds, taking in the scene. The street had changed almost beyond recognition since he had been brought there, bloodied and barely conscious, a quarter of a century earlier. Even then the area had been run-down, crowded with dilapidated, multi-occupancy buildings. The native Parisians had lived in an uneasy balance with the immigrants who flooded in, welcomed by the owners of the crumbling buildings, glad to have tenants as unconcerned with the legalities as they were. As the immigrant population had grown, local resentment had grown with it, prompting many of the old inhabitants to migrate to the new, low-rent public housing projects beyond the confines of the Périphérique highway, the area Parisians now contemptuously referred to as the 'zone'. Exchanging their vibrant familiar neighbourhood for the soulless concrete desert had seemed an acceptable price to pay to be free of their unwanted neighbours. Except that the immigrants had soon moved out to join them. Now, they were stuck in their shoddy tower blocks, frightened to go out at night, with no roads, no shops, and only television and burning resentment for company. No wonder de Medem was making headway.

He set off to walk the few blocks to where the Benganas still lived, above the business Sidi Bey had somehow started when he first arrived, penniless, in France. The roar of construction machinery added to the oppressive sultriness. Dust hung in the motionless atmosphere, prickling his eyes and drying his mouth. Whole sections of the street had been demolished. Poignant fronds of cheap wallpaper hung from exposed walls. In the gaps, excavators tore at the earth, gouging pits four-floors deep for the garages of the new apartment blocks. Thief-proof storage for cars fitted with telephones, so that the owners could torture themselves calling their secretaries for the devastating news that nobody had been trying to reach them.

The remaining buildings were still occupied by cluttered shops; cloth merchants with bolts of material strewn on trestle tables, Moslem butchers and food wholesalers. The biggest of them, on a corner, extended across four shopfronts. Pallet-loads of sacks and cans blocked the pavement. Bill ducked between the pallets into the dark interior.

Despite his deeply sombre mood, Bill smiled. Exotic foods and spices mingled into a single, unmistakable scent. It was the smell of the souks of Algeria and Morocco, a sweetly spicy perfume that never failed to bring flooding back the emotions, the sheer elation, of those few weeks in the spring of '68.

He wound his way among the familiar yellow sacks of couscous and the drums of olive oil with their stained and illegible labels, until he came upon a group of men. One young man stood throwing sacks down from a heap. Below him another young man loaded them onto a battered trolley. His hair was cropped to a quarter of an inch, emphasizing the bullet shape of his skull. Sinews jutted in his arms as he manhandled the twenty-five-kilo sacks.

'Good morning. Is Sidi Bey upstairs?' The question was a courtesy. Sidi Bey had been too sick to stir from the flat for weeks. The young man looked him over with undisguised hostility. At length, he shrugged and turned insolently away, calling to his companion in Arabic. The other man smirked and resumed throwing down the sacks. Bill watched for a moment, his eyes glittering, and then let out an audible breath and turned away.

A third man, older, stood tallying the sacks. Despite the sweltering temperature he wore an astrakhan hat and a woollen scarf knotted tight at his throat, the ends pushed snugly under the lapels of his brown cotton work coat. Catching sight of him, Bill gave the man a lop-sided smile. The man glanced at the surly youth and gave Bill an uncomprehending, exasperated look.

Bill shrugged and shook his hand warmly. 'Mohand, nice to see you. Sidi Bey's upstairs?'

Mohand nodded. 'Yes, Monsieur Duvall, he is. He does not come down any more.' His eyes veiled, as though he were about to cry. 'You know the way.'

Bill was about to mount the narrow iron staircase when the sound of a door closing above made him hang back. A moment later three grave-faced men in cheap suits, each carrying a small attaché case, descended silently past him. With a curious glance after them, he mounted the stairs to a windowless landing, lit by a dim bulb under a tassled shade. He rapped a knuckle gently on the door opposite him.

'Hello, Keltum,' he said softly, extending a hand.

Keltum's face was framed by the grey worsted cloth of a head-dress that covered her hair and fell around her shoulders. The loose-fitting robe beneath was of the same stuff, reaching to the scuffed linoleum at her feet. She stared at him as if in faint surprise, neither friendly nor hostile. He looked back, smiling, attempting to disguise his shock at the sick pallor of her face and the bruised and puffy semi-circles below her eyes, telling of not enough sleep and too much crying.

She nodded abruptly, as though only just recognizing him. 'Hello.' Without taking his hand she moved aside. The smile still on his face, he let his hand drop back to his side and stepped past her.

His smile broadened into one of genuine pleasure as he entered the apartment. The cramped hallway was as cluttered as ever. The heavily carved table against the wall was laden over every inch of its surface with dolls, china, brass figurines, framed photographs and knick-knacks. Beneath a matched pair of domed-glass cases, brightly coloured stuffed birds stared out from imitation branches. Faceted mirrors threw his reflection around dizzyingly, like a fairground sideshow. And again, the smells; the coriander and cardamum, the nutmeg and cinnamon that were the mainstays of Madame Bengana's wonderful cooking, and the sweet, dark coffee that Sidi Bey preferred to the traditional mint tea of North Africa. He was still beaming as he preceded Keltum into the living room.

The room was furnished exactly as it had always been, the worn linoleum on the floor, half hidden by a few woollen rugs, the two over-stuffed, desperately uncomfortable armchairs, the brocade divan heaped with cushions. And, in the dead centre of the room, the oilcloth-covered dining table with its vase of plastic flowers and the four wooden chairs where the family would sit to eat and watch the vast television. From the wall, amid the atrocious sets of idealized landscape prints, a framed photograph of Ahmed smiled down at the room.

'Good afternoon, William. Welcome.'

Bill had thought he was prepared. Even so, the sight of Sidi Bey wiped the smile from his face. He lay stretched on the couch, propped against a pile of cushions from where he could watch the Arabic video playing on the television. A fringed tartan rug lay across his legs. His pyjama jacket was askew.

A week's growth of dirty-looking grey stubble extended far down into the open neck of the pyjamas. A few months earlier, although already very ill, he had retained much of his old physical vigour. His face had still kept the muscular, ageless look of a man taking late middle age in his stride. Now, the vigour and humour had drained away, leaving the shrunken, haggard features a cruel caricature of themselves. Choking with emotion, Bill stepped further into the room.

Sidi Bey's gaunt features twitched as he tried to smile. He stirred and attempted to raise himself. Instantly, his wife, who sat by his head, put aside the cup of coffee she had been holding to his lips and pushed him down again. She rose as Bill almost ran across the room to embrace her. He held her for a long time without speaking, both of them fighting tears. At length, he gently disengaged himself and knelt to embrace Sidi Bey.

The touch of Sidi Bey's arms around his neck gave him another jolt. A year ago, at almost seventy, he could match any of the muscular young men downstairs in their little contests, tossing the sacks of grain, or lifting at arm's length the drums of oil. Now the arms felt frail as twigs as they lay on Bill's neck. He bent lower and pressed his face against Sidi Bey's, grinding his cheek against the rasping stubble, his eyes stinging. It was several seconds before he felt controlled enough to raise his head and look into the other man's eyes. In the shrunken face they seemed bigger, with lids that had a thin, almost transparent quality. The extraordinary, delicate beauty of them struck Bill with savage force.

'Sidi Bey, it's good to be back. How are you?'

Sidi Bey's lips parted in a smile. 'As I told you, William, I'm dying.' He laid a hand on Bill's. 'And you? How is the world treating you? Are you getting ever richer, just as my son was?'

Bill smiled wryly. 'I'm fine, I guess. You know how it is, Sidi Bey, still preying on rich widows.' He gripped the older man's bony hand tighter. 'You know, Sidi Bey, the money wasn't what counted for Ahmed. All he *really* wanted was to be *somebody*, and he was. A fine designer, up there with Dior, or Saint-Laurent. Try to console yourself with that, at least. He had achieved the thing that made him happiest.'

'So happy he killed himself.' A steely shaft of the old irony flashed in Sidi Bey's eyes.

Bill's shoulders heaved. 'I've been asking myself the same questions. You know it had been a while since I'd seen Ahmed, Sidi Bey.' He paused, hearing again Ahmed's calls, their increasingly urgent, pleading tone, watching himself as he reached for the phone and then let his hand fall back, putting his own weekend before his friend's need. 'Had anything happened to Ahmed lately? Anything that might have driven him to . . . what he did?'

Sidi Bey sighed. 'Any one thing? I don't know that, my friend. But he was not himself. When he came here to see me, he would be, well, agitated, edgy. We were convinced he had started taking drugs.'

'Drugs? Ahmed? Surely not!'

'Perhaps. But I'm convinced he was taking something. Pills, of some sort. He would sit there talking to me and I could see him deteriorating, at the very edge. Then, he would disappear for a moment into his room, and when he came out he would be calm again, like his old self.'

Bill shook his head. 'I can hardly believe it. He despised the cocaine crowd. I've seen him at parties in New York where people were downing all kinds of shit. The strongest thing I ever saw Ahmed take was champagne, and even then one glass was his limit. If he was on drugs then something must have really been eating him up.'

'It was, William.' Sidi Bey nodded towards the kitchen where they could hear Keltum moving around, making herself obvious. 'Keltum felt it, too. She tried to help him. She wanted him to get away from that whole world he moved in, all those friends.' He lowered his voice until Bill had to lean close to hear him. 'You know, since, well, since her time in New York, she has become very involved with this man Bouhila.'

Bill shifted, biting his lip. 'M'mm. I'm sorry, Sidi Bey. It was a bad time for her. She was very vulnerable. I hope you . . .'

Sidi Bey smiled at his hesitation, cutting him off with a shake of his head. 'You hope I don't feel you're responsible? No, my friend. She was young, impressionable. You behaved with absolute honour. Many men would have taken advantage of the situation. You cannot reproach yourself.'

'Except that I sent her back here with a big gap in her life.'

'Please don't take offence, William, but you were incidental. The "gap" was there before she arrived in New York. It's Keltum's nature.'

'Either way, I sent her back all set up for this Bouhila character to exploit.'

Sidi Bey sighed softly. 'You don't understand what she sees in him and his movement? Perhaps I don't either. It was not the way I chose when I came here. But the younger people have no faith in my way any more. They are angry. Impatient. They are ready to try anything, follow anyone who seems to offer them a way out, or even some dignity.'

Bill nodded, flicking a glance at the kitchen door. 'And you think Bouhila does?' he asked, in a whisper.

'*I* may not, but *they* seem to, and that's all that counts. I can only tell you that since Keltum took up with this man and his ideas she has been a wonderful daughter to me. It's selfish, I know, but when she was a modern young French woman we scarcely saw her. Now she lives here, she takes care of me. Except, that is,' he added, with another flicker of irony, 'when she is out serving her admired Imam.'

'I'm glad some good comes of it, Sidi Bey. How was she helping Ahmed? Was she trying to bring him into the fold, too?'

Sidi Bey sighed. 'You are a good person, a son to us, but you are part of that world Ahmed had joined, not this one.' He made a tiny circular motion with his fingers that took in not just the room, the apartment, but the neighbourhood, the lives of every North African in France. 'In many ways Ahmed was very strong, and so ambitious to be at the top of his profession.'

'He was there, Sidi Bey.'

'We often tried to tell him that same thing.' He closed his eyes as a wave of pain hit him, forcing a stifled sob from between his gritted teeth. 'But he had weaknesses. He depended too much on flatterers. He had grown away from us, from his family. I understood that. It brought me much pain, but I know what it is to fight your way in a strange world.' A wistfulness had crept into Sidi Bey's voice. Bill gripped his hand harder. 'But Keltum, she has become, well, less tolerant. It was a matter of honour with her to save her brother from something. Himself, I suppose,' he said with a laborious effort at a smile. 'For her, his whole world was rotten. Corrupted with money and drugs.'

'Am I included in that?'

Sidi Bey's head moved in a tiny nod of apology. 'But in her heart, at least, she knows better. Still, I can't pretend I think she's mistaken about most of it, William.' With a sudden effort he raised himself onto an elbow. 'Would you like to see Ahmed?'

Bill was taken aback by the sudden change of tack. The sight of Sidi Bey's tragic eyes burned into his, left him no choice. 'Do you want me to?'

'Yes, William, I do.' With a surprising show of energy, Sidi Bey clutched his arm and swung his legs off the divan. Brushing aside his wife's wide-eyed appeal, he hung an arm round Bill's shoulders and got shakily to his feet. He paused a moment, getting his breath in short, scorching gasps, and then began shuffling towards Ahmed's old bedroom.

In the semi-darkness of the room the overwhelming scent of flowers almost made Bill gag. Lagerfeld, Lacroix, a dozen of the biggest names from the world of couture, stood out among the bouquets piled shoulder-high around the room. A simple spray of lilies bore the name of Catherine Deneuve. Bill glanced down at Sidi Bey, who shrugged weakly.

'I insisted. Keltum was very angry. I know it isn't our way, but these people were Ahmed's friends.' He gestured feebly at the flowers. 'They have a right to express their feelings in *their* way. I have too little time left to try to convert the world to Islam,' he added, attempting a wry smile. 'Let us look at my son.'

He guided Bill through the narrow corridor that ran between

the drifts of flowers to where the open coffin lay on trestles in the centre of the room, lit by two shrouded lamps.

Approaching the coffin, Bill could see that it was a plain box of roughly sawn timber, no more elaborate than a packing case. The interior was unlined, with none of the quilted satin, the make-believe bedlinen, of the Western undertaking industry. Instead, Ahmed's corpse was wound in a plain white cotton cloth, the contours of the body plainly visible.

Bill paused, holding Sidi Bey back, pondering the contrast between the simplicity of the coffin and the splendour of the wreaths, their size saying more about the sender than the deceased. The years in Vietnam had dispelled any sense he might ever have had that death was a ceremonious thing. Agonizing and undeserved or painless and timely, it was a simple and inevitable fact. The grief that came with it was real and necessary, he just did not see the point of the flowers. The Moslem tradition seemed to be about right. You wrapped them up and buried them, quickly and simply. For three days you were free to mourn. After that, life went on.

Under the soft, insistent pressure of Sidi Bey's arm, he moved closer to the coffin. It lay at an angle to the door, the head pointing to a corner of the room. Three thousand miles beyond that corner, Bill knew, lay Mecca.

The sight of dark wet patches on the floor beneath the coffin startled him, making him recoil. His revulsion died as he realized that the stains were water. The body had only just been handed over to the family. Islamic custom demanded it be washed by the men. Sidi Bey's illness left him too weak for the task. The impassive men Bill had passed on the stairs were the professional washers who had been hired to perform the ritual.

Sidi Bey's insistent grip brought his attention back to the body. Using Bill as support, Sidi Bey was stooping to reach for the cloth where it covered Ahmed's face. Very gently, the old man took a corner and pulled the shroud aside.

Bill reared away again, this time with an involuntary groan. Sidi Bey loosened his grip and, supporting himself on the edge of the coffin, stood looking up into Bill's contorted face. Tears coursed over the old man's gaunt cheekbones. 'Look at him, William. Please.'

His jaw set tight, Bill moved a half-pace forward and bent to look again at the body. He slid an arm round Sidi Bey's shoulders, holding the sick man tight against him. 'Oh, my God, Sidi Bey,' he murmured.

Below him, the features he had known so well were barely recognizable. Where the nose had once been finely chiselled, it was wide and flat, without definition. The brow, too, was misshapen. In the low light he caught the shadows of planes and angles where the pulverized pieces of bone had been put back together like an ill-fitting jigsaw. The whole face and head had lost all the fineness they had had in life. The features were blurred, as though packed out with sawdust. The thought sent a tremor through him, making his teeth snap together. They probably *had* used some kind of padding. From such a height the impact would have burst the skull apart, spraying brain tissue out of it. His face drained, he looked down at Sidi Bey. The man was still staring up at him, silently weeping. For a moment they stood looking into each other's faces, each lost in his own desolation. Bill's eyes began to burn again. He swallowed hard. 'Come, Sidi Bey.' He reached down and eased the fold of cloth from Sidi Bey's grip. He replaced it over the face and, with a tender urgency, turned and half dragged the dying man from the room.

Keltum rushed across to meet them. Her eyes flashing, she almost snatched her father from Bill's arm. He allowed her to take the weight and turned to carefully close the bedroom door. Turning back, he watched Keltum coax her father to the couch, saw the infinite tenderness expressed by every tiny gesture, heard the love in her murmured words. As she worried the rug into place over her father's legs, Bill moved a tentative pace closer.

'Sidi Bey, I think I'd better be going and leave you to rest.' He glanced at Keltum, a faintly rueful smile touching his lips. 'There is nothing I can do for you that Keltum can't do better.'

She gave him a rapid, ambiguous look, and then turned quickly away, as though he had stirred a flicker of guilt somewhere deep inside her.

Sidi Bey pushed himself onto an elbow, brushing Keltum's protest gently aside. 'No, William. Come here, please,' he whispered, gasping as the pain washed over him.

Bill glanced at Keltum. She remained tight-lipped but made no attempt to interfere with her father's wish. Shrugging, he moved to Sidi Bey's side. The old man waggled his fingers, signalling Bill to bend closer. At the same time he gave his daughter a long look. With a pout of warning to Bill, she wheeled about and returned to the kitchen.

'William.' The voice was so feeble Bill had to squat and lean his face to within inches of Sidi Bey's. 'William, I have something to ask you. A service.'

Bill nodded, his eyes riveted on the hollowed face. 'Tell me, old friend,' he answered, his voice catching.

'William, I want you to do something for me. I want to know why my son died.'

Bill frowned. 'Don't you believe he killed himself?'

Sidi Bey shook his head with sudden vigour. 'Of course. People saw it. But I want to know *why*. Do you understand me?' His fingers closed around the cloth of Bill's sleeve. 'Oh, William,' he said, as tears began once again to spill down his cheeks. 'In a couple of weeks, perhaps less, I shall be dead. I want to make sense of it. He was my only son, William. I want to know *why* he would take his own life. I want, *need* to know what drove him to it. Can you understand that?'

Bill nodded, chewing at his lower lip. 'I understand, old friend. But what is there *I* can do? The police must have at least looked into it. They don't doubt that it *was* suicide, do they?'

Sidi Bey shook his head sharply, using his grip on Bill's sleeve to pull himself further upright. His face was four inches from Bill's. 'No, of course not. Neither do I. But for the police if there was no crime, they have no interest. I am not the police, William. I am his father. I need to know *why*.' He smiled, inexpressibly sadly. 'I just want to understand. That's all.'

His eyes stinging, Bill helped Sidi Bey lower himself back onto the cushions. The old man lay motionless, looking up at Bill with his beautiful haunted eyes.

Bill returned the gaze, his head throbbing. The shrill, imploring sound of Ahmed's voice on the tape echoed around in his brain, reverberating, layer upon layer, into a crescendo until it seemed to deafen him, blotting out every other sound. He squeezed his eyes closed for a moment, banishing the sounds. 'Look, Sidi Bey,' he murmured, 'I really had better go now. You need to rest. We'll talk some more tomorrow.'

Sidi Bey nodded and sighed, his eyes already closing. Bill eased his sleeve from the old man's loosened grip and stood up. Without his having heard her approach, Madame Bengana hovered anxiously a few feet away, her eyes wet as she looked down at her husband. Bill stepped forward and hugged her tightly to him. 'I'm sorry. I tired him. He's sleeping now. I'll see you tomorrow.'

She clung to him, as though afraid to let him leave, as though her husband's spirit might leave with him. 'Yes. Goodbye. Until tomorrow,' she said at length, self-conscious in the effort to use her few words of French.

He touched his lips once more to her smooth, tear-slick cheek and turned for the door. Keltum waited in the hall, her hand on the latch. 'What was my father saying to you?'

He looked at her sharply, hurt by her curt tone. 'Didn't you hear?'

She flushed, confirming his notion that she had been eavesdropping.

He hesitated, sighing, and then spoke, keeping his voice low. 'Keltum, your father's having difficulty accepting that Ahmed simply killed himself because he *wanted* to. It's natural. He can't believe somebody as successful as your brother could be depressed.'

'But you can?'

He pulled a face. 'I've seen it happen. There's just no telling.'

She continued staring into his eyes, her look demanding more. 'Look, Keltum,' he sighed, 'Ahmed was a tough, determined man. God knows, I've got more reason than anybody to be grateful for that,' he added, smiling, using the chance to remind her of his own debt to her brother. Her face remained closed, not responding to the smile. 'Nobody could have got where Ahmed did without that. But he was sensitive, too. And you must know that he was . . .' He hesitated again. 'Well, vulnerable.' She remained silent, her lips compressed. He shrugged. 'How about you?' he asked, a little more roughly than he intended. The suspicion of accusation in her attitude was making him uncomfortable. 'Did *you* see it coming?'

There was a slight narrowing of her eyes. 'I knew he was worried. I was trying to help him,' she answered, stiffly. 'Did my father say anything else?'

He frowned. Her attitude was unsettling, as though she saw him as an interloper, intruding uninvited into their grief. The thought of the mangled corpse lying a few metres away, together with her father's frailty, made him rein in his rising anger. 'Yes,' he said, evenly. 'He wants me to try to find out why Ahmed did it.'

She looked grimly triumphant. 'And what was your answer?'

'That I'd think about it.'

Her face clouded. 'And what will you think?'

He shook his head. 'God, Keltum, I don't know. I'm not a detective. I'm an art dealer, with a business to run,' he said, glancing behind him and lowering his voice further. 'If the police are happy it was suicide, if people saw it happen, what can *I* add that would be useful? It was Ahmed's choice. I'll miss him, just as you all will, but he's gone. It's over. I'm not sure it helps to stir the mud in cases like this.'

She nodded with a sudden energy that took him aback. 'That's right. Yes. My brother is dead, he must be buried, and then it really *will* all be over.' She spoke quickly, with a faintly hysterical emphasis, as though she were reciting something she had memorized and was not quite sure of getting it right. 'You have nothing to do here. In fact, seeing you here only makes it worse for my parents. It keeps the wound open, prolongs their grief. The Koran forbids us to mourn too long.' She snatched at his sleeve. 'Please, just go home, back to your own people. And leave my parents alone!'

He stared at her, shaken by her outburst. His parents had died long ago. Since his divorce, Ahmed's parents were the nearest thing to 'his people' he had. 'Sorry, Keltum. I told your father I would think about it and that I'd talk to him some more tomorrow, after the funeral. And I will. I owe it to Sidi Bey.' He paused, his eyes no longer focused on her. 'And I owe it to your brother, too.' He stepped around her. 'Bye, Keltum. I'll be here in good time tomorrow.'

5

It was a little before nine-thirty the following morning when Bill set out to walk to the rue de la Goutte-d'Or. He calculated that, with the detour around the closed-off area of the city, it would take him a little over an hour. That would get him there nicely in time for the eleven o'clock departure of the funeral cortège, without his being in the way. He was the only person for whom Sidi Bey had overridden Keltum's objection, insisting that Bill, at least, come to the apartment, to ride with the family to the cemetery. His presence in the car was going to be enough of a strain on Keltum without his hanging around the flat too long beforehand.

He strode easily, glad of the exercise after the previous night's party at Michel Polini's studio, situated in the irretrievably unfashionable thirteenth arrondissement. Michel was someone he had been working with for the past three years and was as famous for his parties as his pictures. In any other city, an address like that for a man whose paintings sold for close to fifty thousand dollars would have been unthinkable. In Paris, the city had a policy of providing spacious flats to artists, even rich ones, at nominal rents. Well-heeled clients who liked to mingle with those whose work they bought were used to partying on the top floor of a tower block sandwiched between rail sidings. Maybe it made them feel more bohemian.

Whatever the reason, Michel's place had been packed with them, drinking the champagne Michel splashed around as though he owned the vineyard and anxious to talk art. Talk art, that was, until they had discovered that Bill was to be one of the family party at Ahmed Bengana's funeral. The news rendered Bill the hottest property in the room. The manner of his death had made Ahmed a bigger celebrity dead than alive. Bill felt as though every social climber in the place had spent the evening trying to manoeuvre him into a corner to talk up a charity dinner where they'd been seated seven tables from Ahmed into something akin to blood brotherhood. From a sense of obligation to Michel he had borne it until almost three when yet another underweight woman with overweight jewellery had buttonholed him, one hand reaching out in comradely sympathy, the other clutching a lipstick-stained glass.

'So *you're* Ahmed's American friend! You must be so upset! My husband and I were just *devastated*! We knew him so well. We . . .'

'That's nice! I'm not even sure I knew him at all.' Leaving her looking at him cock-eyed, as if he had just told her a joke she did not get, he had put down his glass and fled back to the apartment.

He slowed his pace a little. Even at nine-thirty the sun was already hot enough to lift steam from the pavements after the early morning storm. He circled to the west and north, crossing the broad avenues of the sixteenth and seventeenth arrondissements, heading for the place des Ternes.

The area was becalmed in its August torpor. Businesses and restaurants, closed for the summer break, stood dark and lifeless behind steel grilles. A few ladies in good clothes stood watching over-bred dogs foul the freshly washed pavements. Men with high-priced haircuts cruised by in quiet cars. Everything was normal for the time of year, except that each time he reached one of the wide streets leading to the Arc de Triomphe and looked to his right, police wagons blocked the road and men in dark blue overalls lounged against them, nursing firearms. He crossed the place des Ternes, enjoying the fragrance of the flower stall in its centre, and continued along the boulevards that encircled inner Paris, heading towards Barbès.

As he progressed eastward, the dogs grew bigger and nastier, the traffic thicker. Tourist buses had already begun to gather outside the narrow-fronted hotels. In place of the neat café terraces, open-fronted booths offered plastic trays of french fries and synthetic-looking frankfurters. Instead of posters offering lunchtime Vivaldi concerts, the walls were plastered with hastily pasted flyers carrying the faces of de Medem and Bouhila, the one smiling urbanely, the other with his mad, unsettling glare. There was graffiti everywhere. Even the pavements underfoot, already strewn with trash dumped by the day's gathering swarm of tourists, bore slogans in flowing Arabic script or the stencilled fleur-de-lys emblem of the National Salvation League.

Almost at Barbès, he threaded his way through the crowds jostling around the cheap clothes heaped outside the open storefronts. Among them, young women swathed in the familiar grey woollen costume stood thrusting leaflets into the hands of anyone who looked faintly Arabic. He slowed to watch. Most people crushed the flyers without a glance, letting them fall to be trodden to mush on the damp pavement. As Bill drew near, one young man showed enough interest to scan the text. The grey-clad woman looked up and gave a signal. Immediately, one of a group of crop-haired young Arab men who stood alertly in a doorway detached himself and was at the newcomer's elbow, talking earnestly. Feigning interest in a shipment of polyester shirts, Bill paused, watching.

Within thirty seconds of approaching the young man, the crop-head was leading him to the edge of the crowd where one of the robed women waited. She began asking him questions in Arabic, entering his answers on an index card. As Bill watched, he became aware of somebody at his shoulder, crowding him.

One hand flew to his pocket, suspecting pickpockets. The other closed in a fist as he swivelled. Instead of thieves, he was looking into the hard-faced stares of three of the crop-headed youths. With an ironic nod of acknowledgment, he moved on.

Turning north into the relative quiet of the boulevard Barbès, he shook his head in reluctant admiration. They combined the recruiting skills of the Moonies with the debating talents of the Nazi street gangs of thirties Germany. Already, in Algeria, Bouhila's movement had risen from nowhere to the point where it had the government frightened witless. They would never have the numbers in France to threaten the power structure the way they were doing over there, but with the President weakened by his stroke, and election fever running high, they could cause an awful lot of trouble.

Turning to cross the street, the portrait of de Medem, defaced with graffiti, smiled out at him. He had a lot to smile about. The rise of Bouhila and his movement had done what de Medem could never have dared hope for in thirty years on the political fringe; it had transformed him from a laughing stock into a potential power broker.

He turned past the heaps of cheap shoes and into the rue de la Goutte-d'Or and stopped in his tracks. Close to the Benganas' store, a crowd blocked the street, the people craning to see beyond a row of police cars with blue lights pulsing. Quickening his pace, he elbowed his way to the front of the crowd.

A line of perspiring policemen manned a make-shift barrier, good-naturedly holding the crowd at bay. Behind the police, a knot of North African youths in red armbands slouched sullen-eyed, disconsolate at being deprived of a chance to throw their weight around. What lay beyond them made Bill groan audibly.

A couple of dozen flashy cars were drawn up, parked anyhow, near the store. Clustered nearby, a group of tanned men and women stood chattering vivaciously, taking care to present their best profile to the photographers who scrambled among them. Some of the faces were familiar from parties; a few actors and actresses, the man who read the lunchtime news on Channel 2, a blank-faced Eurasian model who used the name Taya Barclay and was that year's hot magazine face, and a sprinkling of people with terrific dentistry whose principal occupation was being photographed at charity galas.

Bill leaned close to one of the policemen, grimacing at the mêlée. 'The name's Duvall. And I really am expected.'

Smirking his disbelief, the policeman spoke into a walkie-talkie and listened to the squawked reply. With a grimace of surprise he waved Bill under the barrier.

He pushed through the group of posturing 'celebrities', and made for the store entrance, blinking as a couple of photographers snapped him, on the offchance he might turn out to be famous.

He was still letting his eyes grow used to the semi-darkness when a hand struck him in the chest, sending him back on his heels. Half winded, he squinted into the dimness. The youth who had given him the silent treatment the previous day stood with his arms at his sides, looking at him truculently. He wore the same red armband as the group outside and seemed to think it gave him a lot of authority. Another youth, with the same shaven head, stood at his side, trying not to grin too openly at Bill's surprise.

'Family only in here,' the first youth sneered.

Bill looked from one to the other of the faces leering out of the shadows. 'You didn't understand your instructions right, my friend. Step aside.'

The youths did not move. Smiling, as though he were going to reason with them, he drove his fist into the face of the one who had hit him. As the man reeled back, clutching his face, Bill took a quick step, hooked a foot round the ankle of the second one and thrust his cupped hand up under the man's chin. The shaven head flew back and struck an oil drum. The sound was still echoing around the store when Bill threw a short punch at the man's undefended belly and headed for the stairs.

Surprise flashed in Keltum's face as she opened the door. Her eyes flickered from Bill to look over his shoulder.

'Don't worry. I left them minding the store. Didn't you tell them to expect me?'

She flushed deeply. 'I'm sorry. I've had a lot on my mind.' Still scarlet, she let him pass and closed the door behind him.

Sidi Bey sat on the edge of the couch. Somebody had shaved him. Whoever it was had made a lousy job of it. Patches of stubble the size of coins had been missed. Blood was caked at the corner of his mouth and beneath his jaw. He wore a white shirt and patterned silk tie under a grey pinstripe woollen suit. A tiny patch of black cloth sewn to the lapel was the only outward sign of mourning.

Anger clouded Bill's face. The clothes looked absurdly oversized on the wasted frame. The scrawny neck protruded from the shirt collar like a turtle's. Sidi Bey's appearance had always been important to him, the nearest he came to vanity. Now, sick and helpless, he was being made to look ridiculous, too. He strode across and sat down next to the old man, putting an arm gently over the rounded shoulders. 'How are you feeling, old friend?' he murmured.

Sidi Bey looked slowly around at him. His eyes were enormous in the shrunken face. 'Sad, William. And disappointed.' Almost involuntarily, he turned his eyes towards the doorway of the room where the coffin lay. Keltum stood with her back to them, the strain palpable in her stance, giving terse instructions. 'Everything I have done was for my children. Everything. I had such hopes for them. I wanted them to be something, to have opportunities in the world, to be, well, modern.' He gave a sudden glowing smile. 'Not like their poor father, a prisoner of the old ways, eking out his living in the ghetto.'

Bill returned the old man's smile, sharing the self-deprecating joke. For decades Sidi Bey had invested everything he earned in property around Paris. This feeble old man, with his bad shave and ill-fitting clothes, could have bought and sold three quarters of the inhabitants of the posh apartments of Saint Germain des Prés or Neuilly, Hermès scarves, good family furniture, and all. 'Ahmed *was* something, Sidi Bey. Remember that, please. You'll see the crowd out there for yourself. People are fighting to be able to say they were friends of your son. Believe me, Sidi Bey, Ahmed took the chances you gave him. He *counted*.'

Sidi Bey shook his head. 'And Keltum? So close to the end of my life, William, it gives me pain to see her like this.' He fluttered his fingers, indicating his daughter's robed back. 'For me, for their mother, it was different. We were brought up in another age. We knew nothing else. But these are different times, William. The modern world needs modern ways. That's why we chose to come and make our lives in France. It was very hard, especially for their mother, but we did it for their sake. A young woman can choose now, she can have a future. And to see Keltum turning her back on all we have fought to offer her . . .' He paused, his heaving ribs barely moving the cloth of the suit as he regained his breath. 'As I told you, in some ways – selfish ways – it has been a good thing for me and my wife. But we won't always be here.' As he paused again, breathing hard, Bill's arm tightened round his shoulders, the imminence of the old man's death filling the air. Sidi Bey sighed. 'The answers Keltum seeks won't be found in the past, William. She *must* look to the future.'

'She doesn't see it that way, Sidi Bey.'

He shook his head. 'That's true, William. But in many ways Keltum is still so young. She is very vulnerable.'

'I know that, Sidi Bey,' Bill interjected softly.

The old man paused and put a hand over Bill's, the huge eyes sad and gentle. 'Yes, she is a good girl, full of ideals. Not everyone is like you. There are always people who will take advantage. Do you think perhaps even this Bouhila may be doing that? Using her?' he asked, sudden disquiet giving him the energy to raise his voice.

Keltum walked quickly across to them, shooting Bill a furious glance. 'You're exciting my father!' She dropped to her knees and snatched her father's hand from where it lay on Bill's, clasping it in hers. 'They are ready, Father. Shall they bring out the coffin?'

Sidi Bey cast a desolate look at the open door and nodded.

With a last caress of his hand, she crossed to the bedroom door and spoke in Arabic. A few moments later four of the armband-wearing youths emerged, bearing the coffin. They carried it across the room and into the hall. A bang and a sudden gust of quarrelsome voices sent Keltum rushing to direct them down the stairs. Next to Bill, Sidi Bey clapped both hands to his face in an effort to hide the fresh distress that was etched in it. Tears seeped between his fingers.

White-faced, Keltum hurried back and spoke softly to him in Arabic. Leaving him, she bustled to the kitchen and emerged with her mother. Madame Bengana was dressed from head to toe in white. The flesh round her eyes was swollen with crying. Keltum murmured to her and returned to her father's side. 'It's time to go,' she said abruptly, speaking French with exaggerated reluctance, a concession to an unwelcome guest.

Bill and Keltum helped Sidi Bey down the narrow stairs and almost carried him through the store, under the vengeful stares of the young men Bill had hit. Out on the street a barrage of flashing cameras made Sidi Bey stiffen and recoil, as if he would return to the shelter of his store. At once, the young men in armbands, responding to a command from one of their number, formed a protective wedge around them and shouldered a way to the edge of the pavement, the hardness in their eyes pushing back the photographers. With Keltum flashing looks of burning contempt at the rubber-necking crowd, they helped the old man into a dark blue Mercedes. Madame Bengana and Keltum slipped in beside Sidi Bey, while Bill, in response to Sidi Bey's hoarsely whispered words, climbed into the front. He nodded affably to the impassive driver, another of the hard-faced youths, while, behind them, the little throng of celebrities scrambled for places in the waiting cars.

A smile brushed Bill's lips as the car bucked away from the kerb. Today was probably the first time the youth would have been allowed to drive it. The Mercedes was another of Sidi Bey's surprising weaknesses, to which his simple way of life gave little clue. For business he had always used an ancient

Renault that fitted his shrewdly maintained poor-but-honest image. The Mercedes only came out of the garage for special occasions. Like today. The thought made Bill swallow and glance over his shoulder at the shrunken figure sandwiched between his wife and daughter. The next special occasion for the Bengana family would be Sidi Bey's own funeral.

They passed a knot of people gathered at the gate of the Moslem burial ground. Down-at-heel men, old women with shopping bags, and mothers pushing strollers in which food-stained toddlers sucked on feeding bottles, all gaped at the tinted windows, straining for a glimpse of a face they might recognize from television.

They drove on at walking pace until Bill saw a cluster of young men grouped round a figure in a dark robe. At the approach of the cars, the young men spread to form a loose cordon encircling the grave. The moment the Mercedes had passed through into the circle, two lean young men closed up behind it, halting the following limousines. As Bill watched, the celebrities began climbing from the cars to collect in a muttering group, eyeing the young men. One of the group, a tall television presenter with a mahogany tan, detached himself and walked towards the young men, visibly swelling with indignation. More of the lean youths drifted to join their companions. The tall man hesitated, glanced around him, and fell back to join his tastefully distressed girlfriend.

The Mercedes lurched to a halt. Bill sprang out to open the door for the family. As he did so, the black-robed figure, attended by two of the young men, moved to bar his way. For a moment Bill stood his ground, his fists bunching. Then, with a glance at the opaque glass of the car window, he stepped back, his eyes on the robed man's face as he reached for the handle. The black eyes glittered like a stage hypnotist's, making the bearded, muscular face unmistakable. These were the features he had seen staring from a hundred posters.

Keltum climbed from the car, her face strained but blank, with no trace of tears. The Imam Bouhila drew her away from the car, murmuring softly in her ear, and then moved to help

Sidi Bey. Bill remained expressionless as Sidi Bey batted the offered hand angrily aside and called Keltum's name in a sharp, peremptory voice. Flushing, she turned and ran to assist her father to his feet. Brushing aside Bouhila's fresh attempt to help, Sidi Bey beckoned Bill and gripped his arm, calling in French to Keltum to help her mother. Flushing deeper under the stony intensity of Bouhila's gaze, she did as her father bid her.

They moved towards the graveside in a loose group, Sidi Bey leaning on Bill, and Madame Bengana, tears streaming down her cheeks, clutching at her daughter's arm. Bill could hear the soft footsteps of Bouhila and his assistants, or disciples, or whatever they were, a metre behind them. As they went, Sidi Bey craned to look back at the group of onlookers. He turned his wet eyes to Keltum and made as if to speak, and then shook his head and closed his lips, as though he had already exhausted the subject he had in mind.

They stood waiting at the graveside, with Bouhila close enough behind Keltum that she must almost have been able to hear him breathing. The four bearers lifted the shrouded body of Ahmed from the coffin, carried it to where the family stood, and began lowering it into the grave. As they looked on in silence, one of the bearers shifted his position, allowing the body to tilt and the feet to touch the ground. For a grotesque and shocking instant the corpse was in a perfectly natural half-sitting position, with the white cloth of the shroud pulled tight against the contours of the face. Madame Bengana clawed at her face and broke into a high-pitched wail. Tears welled again from Sidi Bey's eyes. He stood motionless, staring into the pit, the tears flooding down his eroded cheeks and onto the lapels of the over-sized suit. Bill put his arm round the old man's shoulders. He tried to speak and failed, his own throat too constricted to allow words to pass.

For the first time he understood the Western tradition of burying corpses in coffins. Not to protect the corpse from contact with the earth. The corpse did not care. It was to cushion the mourners from the bleak implications. Here, there was no room for illusion. Two metres from him, Ahmed Bengana's body was being laid directly against the earth. A simple, necessary disposal. This was not an anonymous, flower-strewn piece of furniture. What Bill was seeing were the broken remains of the man to whom he owed his life – and whose life he might in his turn have saved – the crushed face outlined against the straining cloth of the shroud, being put away to rot.

Seeking relief from the sheer emotional weight of it, he let his eyes shift to where Keltum was trying to comfort her mother. The flesh round his eyes puckered. In stark contrast with her mother, whose tortured face was streaked with mingled blood and tears where she had torn at her flesh in her grief, Keltum wore a tight-lipped frown, as though ashamed of the older woman's emotion. Turning, she bent her face close to her mother's and spoke in a low, urgent voice. Her hands rested on her mother's shoulders, as though about to shake her. As Bill watched, he saw her flick a glance at Bouhila. It seemed a strange look for the circumstances, a mixture of apology and exasperation, as though she were asking him to forgive her for some kind of failure.

He looked at Bouhila's impassive face. Sensing Bill's gaze, the Imam slowly swivelled to let their eyes lock. Bill stared back at him, keeping his own face as blank as the other man's. Despite himself, his contempt was tinged with reluctant acknowledgment of the man's skill. Being held in that unflinching gaze was like being scalded. Slowly, still holding the man's stare, he let his lips curve into a thin, sardonic grin. The grin widened a fraction as he saw something that might have been anger flicker in the man's face. He let the smile fade and turned back to the grave.

The short burial ceremony over, they returned to the car. Bill and Keltum helped her parents into their seats and for a moment they found themselves alone together on the pale gravel of the avenue. Bouhila and his henchmen hovered a few metres from them.

'You didn't cry,' Bill said softly, making a question of the words.

She looked quickly at Bouhila before straightening a little and shaking her head vigorously. 'No.'

'I thought Ahmed meant more than that to you. He used to.'

She gnawed at her lower lip. 'He was my brother.'

'And sisters don't cry for their brothers any more?'

The muscles of her face twitched, pulling her lips out of shape. 'I did while he was alive. It's too late now.'

'Too late to *grieve*, Keltum?'

She nodded, nervily. 'Ahmed killed himself. Suicide is a mortal sin for us.' Her mouth worked as she gulped for air. 'My brother is in hell!' With the rush of the last words the tears finally came. She threw herself into the car and the shelter it offered from Bouhila's implacable eyes.

Bill closed the door behind her and turned to look from Bouhila to each of the scowling youths that flanked him. He let his gaze settle on Bouhila. 'Feeling good, asshole?' he said distinctly. Turning on his heel, he climbed into the car and slammed the door.

They drew up in front of the store to find the crowd and the police had gone. Young men once again hurried between the store and the vans at the kerbside. With the celebrity corpse gone, the crowd had gone too, making the minders' posturing ridiculous. With Bill helping Sidi Bey and Keltum supporting her mother, who still emitted the grieving wail she had not stopped since the burial, they climbed the narrow stairs. Keltum unlocked the door and preceded them into the flat. Bill was still on the landing when she screamed. He squeezed past the wheezing Sidi Bey and ran to join her.

Keltum stood on the threshold of the living room. The fingers of both hands were on her lips as she stared, white-faced, into the room. The place had been torn apart. Bill exchanged a look with Keltum. Without a word, she nodded and turned to run back towards her parents. She spoke quickly to them, an imploring note in her voice. Sidi Bey replied in French, his voice finding another of those sudden reserves of firmness. 'No, Keltum. Let me pass. I must see what they have done.'

He came to Bill's side and together they stood contemplating the damage. The old sofa on which Sidi Bey passed his days had been gutted, the worn brocade in shreds. Stuffing had been tossed in mottled grey drifts around it. The curtains were strewn in tatters among the upturned drawers discarded on the floor. The television lay face down, its innards spilling out. The scarred lino had been torn up, exposing the boards.

Sidi Bey broke his silence with a strangled sound and stepped into the room. Stooping, he picked some pieces of paper from among the wreckage. Whimpering softly, he began clumsily trying to fit together the pieces of Ahmed's photograph. Bill swallowed and put a hand on his friend's sleeve. 'Come away, Sidi Bey. Come to my place. Please.' He spoke softly, giving no clue to the fury that was boiling inside him. It was plain that this was not the work of ordinary burglars. Somebody had been searching for something. 'There's room for all three of you at the apartment. I can move to a hotel. I . . .'

Sidi Bey's look stopped him short. Tears stood in the corners of his eyes again. He shook his head, looking down at the pieces of the photograph. 'No, William, thank you. This is our home. We have people to help us. We can clear this up.' He took Bill by the arm and fixed him with a long look. 'William, will you say you'll help me now? Will you stay and try to find out who drove my son to his death?' He brandished the pieces of photograph. 'Who could have done a thing such as this to us?'

Bill glanced from the old man's pleading eyes to Keltum. She hovered fretfully, two paces from them, as though she were desperate to contradict her father but could not bring herself to dare it.

He looked back to Sidi Bey, probing deep into the man's moist, desolate eyes. 'I'll try. For a while anyway.' He turned to Keltum. 'Do you have a key to Ahmed's house?'

She frowned, nodding. 'Yes, there are keys here. Why?'

'I want to go over there.'

'What on earth for?'

He gestured at the destruction. 'To see if the same thing's happened there.'

6

Keltum swung the Mercedes into the narrow, leafy private road and drew up in front of one of the imposing town houses that flanked it. As she pulled the key from the ignition, Bill touched a hand to her sleeve. She snatched it away as though it had been hot metal. He drew breath loudly through his nose. 'Keltum, please, can you stop it?'

'Stop what?'

'The silent treatment. You haven't said a word all the way here.'

'Do I have anything to say? I did as my father asked and drove you here. What else do you want from me?'

He examined her profile for a moment as she sat staring straight ahead, the full lips pursed. 'For you to treat me as what I am, a friend who wants to help.' Swallowing, she continued to look ahead. Bill sighed. 'Let's go and look at the house.'

He mounted the front steps a pace behind Keltum. As she fumbled with the lock, he looked up and down the street. It was lined on both sides with handsome, identical houses, each of four storeys set over a basement apartment. Ahmed's was one of the few with a single bell-push set in the pale stone of the doorway. Most of the others had been divided into apartments that were still big enough to satisfy the bankers, film producers and international swindlers who had been his friend's neighbours. He found himself smiling wryly at the thought that if anything happened to her parents Keltum would inherit this place. She would probably hand it over to

Bouhila for a school. Which would delight the neighbours. He turned sharply as Keltum made a little bark of exasperation.

'What's up?'

She flapped a hand petulantly. 'I can't open it.'

He moved alongside her and tried it, his pulse already racing. 'It's bolted.' He touched a restraining hand to her arm. This time she did not recoil. 'Wait here.'

He turned and leapt down the narrow concrete steps to the basement. The window was solidly barred. He ducked under the stairs to the basement door and let out a soft groan. A hole big enough for a person to clamber through had been neatly cut out of the armoured door, enabling an intruder to enter without triggering the alarms. Charring around the neat hole indicated an expert using cutting gear, probably a virtually soundless thermic lance. 'Keltum!' She ran down the steps to join him and stood looking wordlessly at the door. 'Do you want to wait here?'

She shook her head. 'After what happened back at my father's I think I can stand this.' She followed close behind as he dropped to his knees and slid through the hole.

Bill surveyed the wreckage of the living room with Keltum, frozen and white-faced, at his side. 'Shit,' he breathed, stepping into the room.

The basement, with its torn-up carpets and smashed partitions, had partly prepared them for it, and yet still it came as a shock. The curtains, the pale yellow silk wall-covering, the carpet, all lay in ribbons on the broken floor. Amid his anger Bill could not help the wry thought that Ahmed had such excellent taste even the *wreckage* of his decor looked good.

He moved into the room, stepping carefully among the smashed floorboards, and crossed to the door that led off to Ahmed's study. The story was the same. The desk drawers had been turned out and the desk itself, a fine eighteenth-century piece, upended and knocked apart. He stood for several seconds on the threshold, studying the chaos, and then stepped inside and crouched to rummage quickly through the jetsam.

Sifting through the papers he unearthed a pair of exquisitely carved figurines, two tiny statuettes that Ahmed had kept on his desk for years, using them as paperweights. He picked them up and examined them. Their fall had not damaged them. He rose to his feet, sliding the figurines into his pocket, and turned to rejoin Keltum.

She stood as he had left her, her face deathly white, staring silently at the destruction. He tugged tentatively at her sleeve. 'Come on,' he said softly, letting his hand drop to his side. 'We'd better go home.'

At his words her head jerked up. Her eyes fixed on his, gleaming with a feverish intensity in the pallid face. 'Yes! Bill, please. Why don't you do exactly that? Why *don't* you just go home? It would be better. Why don't you go away and let us deal with all this by ourselves? It isn't your business.'

Frowning, he shook his head. 'Because I was asked not to, Keltum, by your father. That made it my business.'

A tremor ran the length of her body. 'But *why*? What's the purpose? My father's so sick, he has to have so many drugs, he hardly knows what he's saying any more. He . . .'

Bill held up a hand. 'Don't say that, Keltum! Stop it! There's nothing the matter with your father's judgement. However terrible his pain may be, his mind's as sharp as ever, and you know it.'

She flung out a hand in a violent gesture of frustration. 'Oh, you . . . you still talk to me as if I were a little girl. But I *know* I'm right. You don't understand. You *can't* understand. You can't see that you're part of the problem, you are one of those people Ahmed was trying so hard to be accepted by. You despised him, just as you despise us all. You were tearing him from his roots. And he couldn't stand the pain!'

He stared at her as she stood, panting after the vehemence of her outburst. When he spoke his voice was very low. 'I deserve an apology for that, Keltum, I don't care how much strain you're under. Your brother was the nearest thing I had to a brother of my own.'

For several seconds she stood looking down at the ground,

trembling. 'I'm sorry,' she murmured, almost inaudibly. 'But still you should go. My father's dying! He should be at peace.'

'And he won't be, Keltum. He *can't* be, not without knowing.'

A sob wrenched at her. 'But, it's so distressing. He's in such *agony*!'

'I know your father well enough to understand that not knowing hurts him more than any physical pain ever could, Keltum.'

She shook her head, the violence of the gesture taking Bill by surprise. 'There! You think you know us all better than we know ourselves. He's *my* father.'

'And he's my friend. He asked me to do something for him before he dies and if I can, I will.' He pointed at her robe. 'You have your religion now, you have Bouhila to tell you what's right. Well, personally, I've never had a religion. I just try to do what I can for people I care for. And I care for your father, as if he were my own. Now, if you'd prefer I took a taxi, just say so.'

They reached the flat without exchanging another word. As they entered, a man in a creased summer suit, a black leather briefcase in his hand, was just leaving. At the sight of Bill, a fleeting, brilliant smile lifted the deep frown from his face.

'Monsieur Duvall! How are you?'

It was with a jolt that Bill recognized the thick-waisted, bald figure as the athletic, slightly dangerous-looking young revolutionary who had treated him twenty-six years earlier. He shook the man's hand vigorously. 'Doctor Hassan. How are *you*?'

The doctor shrugged. 'I'm fine.' His frown returned as he shot a glance over his shoulder. 'Our friend is not, though. This business has been another terrible blow.' He turned and murmured a few words to Keltum in Kabyle. Keltum responded speaking quickly and urgently, glancing at Bill. Hassan nodded and turned back to him. 'He is very, very sick, Monsieur Duvall. You must be sure not to tire him, not to do anything that would shorten the little time he has left.'

Bill glanced at Keltum. She stood looking at the ground, her face flushed. 'I'll remember it, Doctor.'

In their absence the flat, with the help of the employees from the store, had been put back into shape. New linoleum covered the floor. A sleek new television set, switched on but with the sound turned down to a murmur, dominated the room. Hearing them enter, Sidi Bey tried to push himself upright, fumbling to button the top of his pyjamas. His wife leaned over him, cajoling the cushions into place and draping the worn velvet jacket closer round his shoulders. Satisfied he was decently presentable, Sidi Bey beckoned them to approach the couch. The look in Bill's eyes gave him the answer to his unspoken question. He shook his head. 'My son's house, too, then.'

Bill looked down into the desolate face. Stubble had begun to push through after his morning shave. White webs of saliva gathered at the corners of his mouth. 'I'm afraid so, Sidi Bey. Just like here.'

For several seconds Sidi Bey stared blankly into space, his eyes unfocused, as though revisiting in his mind the exquisitely decorated house. Abruptly, his reverie dissolved and he turned glittering eyes on Bill. 'Why, William? Just to steal? They didn't take anything from here, you know.'

Bill sat down in the chair Madame Bengana had pushed close behind his knees, looking around for Keltum. She had retreated across the room and stood gazing at them with an odd, pleading look in her face. He turned back to Sidi Bey and shook his head. 'I don't think so, my friend. Not valuables anyway.' He reached into his pocket and pulled out the figurines. He placed them in the old man's outstretched claw. 'Do you recognize these?'

Sidi Bey looked at them and nodded. 'They're Ahmed's.'

'That's right. Do you know anything about them?'

Sidi Bey looked perplexed. 'They were on his desk,' he said tentatively.

'M'mm.' He leaned closer. 'Sidi Bey, these things are worth a *fortune*.' He took one from the old man's crooked palm and held it up. 'They're pre-Colombian. Not my cup of tea, but there are collectors who would kill for these.' He looked into Sidi Bey's puzzled, lost eyes. 'Both burglaries were done by experts. These would have been the first things a pro would have taken.' He shook his head. 'I think they were looking for something specific.'

'And they didn't find it at Ahmed's, so they came here?'

'That's how it looks to me.'

As Sidi Bey nodded, a bolt of pain made him clutch at his chest. His face contorted in a grimace, he waited for the pain to ebb sufficiently for him to speak. Then he reached out and took Bill's sleeve, pulling him down until their faces were inches apart. 'William, I know my son *did* jump from that window. But I cannot call it suicide. Something, somebody *pushed* him to it.' He winced again as more pain flooded through him. 'Excuse me, William. It will soon pass,' he gasped. He flapped a hand at the door. 'Hassan just gave me my injection.' His face cleared again as the pain subsided. He gave a lop-sided laugh. 'It stops the pain here. But not here.' He tapped a finger to his temple. As he did so, Bill shot a glance at Keltum, reassuring himself that she had caught her father's gesture. 'I must endure it until I die – for the next few weeks, or perhaps only days, that is – unless I can know who or what it was.' His voice dropped to a rasping whisper. 'Oh, William, old friend, you knew Ahmed in the old days, when he was, well, a normal young man.'

'Normal?'

The old man smiled wearily. 'Don't bother playing games with me, William. You know what I mean. You were a *real* friend. Not like the . . . the *sharks* in that circle he had become mixed up with, with their bitchiness, their cocaine. You were his friend, and ours too, before fame took him from us. You were the one he knew he could always trust.'

The man's words made Bill want to speak out, to reveal how he had failed his son. Sidi Bey's innocent, unquestioning faith held him back. To destroy one of the last things the man had to cling to would be worse than useless.

Sidi Bey went on speaking, saving him from finding words that would have rung false in his own ears. 'I want you to talk to those other friends.' The old man gripped his sleeve and pulled himself closer, his hot eyes drilling into Bill's. 'I want you to find out everything you can. I want to know everything that my son did, all that he *was* during his last days. You can do that. You are part of that world.'

Bill laughed softly. 'Thanks!'

Sidi Bey gave a ghostly smile. 'No, you are not like them, but you are at ease with them. You can speak their language.' A sudden look of misgiving came into Sidi Bey's eyes. His grip tightened on Bill's sleeve. 'Am I asking too much? Asking you to neglect your business? I can pay, William, to compensate you.' Bill shook his head, preparing to speak. Sidi Bey's grating whisper cut him off. 'I'm sorry. I used not to be like this. It's what my son's death has done to me, it has me thinking so much of my hurt, I forget that you have your own life. Perhaps there is someone waiting for you . . .'

A sudden image of Amy, her hair spread on the pillow, flooded his mind. He reached out and, very gently, touched the other man's lips. 'I'll stay,' he said, speaking as softly as Sidi Bey. 'For a while, anyway. God knows what I can find out that the police couldn't, but if it eases your mind, my friend, I'll try. Have you any idea where I should begin?'

Sidi Bey did not seem to hear his last question. The moment Bill had said he would stay the old man's head had sunk back against the cushions. The faintest of smiles touched his lips and then his mouth fell open and he began snoring in a soft, wheezing rhythm. Bill took the eroded hands and arranged them tenderly on the heaving chest. With a long look at the sleeping man he pushed himself to his feet.

'Keltum,' he called softly. 'I need to talk to you.'

They faced each other from opposite ends of the oilcloth-covered table. Bill sipped at the glass of sweet, scalding mint tea Madame Bengana had placed in front of him, his eyes on Keltum. She sat straight-backed, looking down at her tightly clasped hands.

'How much of that did you hear?'

She raised her eyes. They were glowing with anger. 'Enough. You don't intend to leave us alone, despite what Hassan asked you.'

He shook his head, blowing out air with a hiss. 'I'll say this for you, you don't give up easily. Look, you heard what Sidi Bey asked me. And you know I can't refuse. He needs it too much. Now, will you help me?'

Moving uneasily, she shot a look at her father. His breathing seemed to fill the room. 'I have no choice,' she murmured.

'Good. So, can we start with Vadon, since he was the last person to see Ahmed alive. Did your brother know Vadon?'

She stared blankly down at the table, saying nothing.

Bill drew a long breath. 'Keltum, you *must* help me. Did he, for God's sake? Or was it just a conveniently high floor?'

His impatient tone stung her. She looked at him sharply, her eyes blazing. 'Yes, he did.'

'Well?'

'It's hard to say. He certainly *talked* about him a lot. But you must remember, though Ahmed seemed very successful, at heart he was terribly insecure. It was childish, really. He was so *flattered* when someone with a famous face, an actor or something, actually spoke to him. He might be more famous, more talented, richer even, than they were, but in his own eyes, he was still just a humble Arab boy they had permitted into the magic circle. I don't think he ever stopped being afraid they might throw him out again.'

Bill nodded, smiling gently. 'I know what you mean. He never could get over the fear that being Algerian made him an outsider, that he might somehow be . . . discarded. It's the kind of fear that makes a lot of people turn to drugs. I guess his drug was fame.' He shrugged. 'It was a way of outrunning his past. What do you know about Vadon?'

She spread her hands. 'Not much. Nothing that everybody

doesn't know.' She tossed her head contemptuously. 'A self-serving opportunist. Like all politicians.'

He nodded. 'Or the leaders of religious sects?'

She bucked angrily away, half rising from the table. 'No! I won't listen to that! You have no right . . . The Imam isn't like that . . .' She broke off, choking on the strength of her emotion.

He waved her back into her seat. 'I'm sorry, Keltum. That was cheap. Forget I said it. Please tell me all you *do* know about Vadon. Forget that I've ever been in France. Assume that I know nothing.'

She spread her hands and blew out her cheeks in a gesture so French, so totally ill-matched to her outfit, that he had to contain a smile. 'He's been Minister of the Interior for the last year or so. He heads his own party. Right-wing, although I couldn't tell you exactly what they believe in, apart from him. That's typical of the rotten politics here,' she added, her anger welling again. 'No ideas any more, just personalities. And slogans. Nothing thought through . . .'

His eyes flicked over the head-dress and robe. 'Uh-uh. Go on.'

Missing the hint of irony, she just looked disappointed that he did not want to argue about it. 'There are several like him, mayors of big cities, just as he is. He runs Narbonne, or somewhere down there. That's his power base. Mayors here have tremendous power,' she said emphatically, genuinely forgetting how familiar he was with the French scene. 'It's the huge budgets they control. It gives them so much patronage, if that's what you call it.'

'What do *you* call it?'

'Corruption. As soon as they decide to try for national office all the old favours are called in. They use their networks to get a few deputies elected as their puppets. As soon as there are a dozen or so of them, they form a group, dream up some ludicrous name for themselves, and offer support to whichever main party makes them the best offer.'

'Is that all there is to Vadon? He comes across as more than that.'

'On television, you mean?' she snorted. 'Oh, yes! He's great at that. He's got the looks, and the voice. Oh, and of course, his heroic Resistance record. He wouldn't want us to forget that,' she added, with a brief scoffing laugh.

'You don't believe it?'

She laughed. 'Have you heard of a French politician of that age who *wasn't* a Resistance hero? Considering the number of our leaders who were "heroes of the Resistance", it's a wonder they needed the Allies to join the fight at all. You'd think they could have talked the Germans out!'

He laughed. 'Do you know how old he *is*?'

'Not exactly. In his late sixties.'

'How did he react when Ahmed jumped from his office?'

'Publicly? What would you expect? You realize a lot of changes are expected here?' She waited for his nod. 'He seems to have a pretty good chance of being the next president. So, of course, he claimed he hardly knew Ahmed.'

'The public swallowed it?'

She shrugged. 'Why shouldn't they? It might even have been true. All I know for sure is that Ahmed *said* he knew him well.'

'Do *you* believe he did?'

She bit her lip. 'Yes,' she said huskily.

'But nobody challenged Vadon's version?'

She tossed her head. 'Challenge Vadon? He's Minister of the *Interior*. He runs the police, for heaven's sake. Ahmed killed *himself*, in front of witnesses. What policeman would start trying to make trouble for Vadon? After all,' she went on, veering suddenly back into bitterness, 'he was only an *Arab*!' Without warning, she began sobbing.

He reached across the table and laid a hand on hers. She did not snatch it away. It was a kind of progress. 'Look, Keltum, I'm sorry to put you through this, but I'm an art dealer, not a detective. I haven't done anything like this since I was in the military. I really *need* your help. Do you know if there's any way I can contact Vadon? A phone number, maybe? And the police – they must at least have looked at the case, if only to make sure there *were* witnesses. Do you know who was in charge? Surely *someone* from the police spoke to you? Did they leave a name, a card?'

With a visible effort of will, she stopped crying and sat erect, withdrawing her hand. She nodded, sniffing back the tears. 'The policeman gave us a card. And I have a number for Vadon, too.'

He raised his eyebrows, surprised to be saved the chore of finding it out for himself. Catching the look, Keltum gave a contemptuous laugh. 'The Minister phoned here, after it happened. He wanted to offer us his condolences!' She said the last word as though it soiled her to utter it.

'Was that all?'

'I don't know. My mother took the call. You know how her French is. She managed to take down a number. I presume we were supposed to call him back.'

He laughed. 'I'm starting to admire him. He may think you're only Arabs, but he doesn't let himself forget that you're voters, too. Did you call him?'

She shook her head. 'No. He called again, though. Several times.'

'Really?' Bill sat forward. 'What did he say?'

'Nothing. I hung up on him.'

7

Tight-lipped, still blanched beneath the tan, Christian Vadon stalked straight through the domed ante-room into the inner office, not even glancing at his secretary or at the chief of staff, who sat hitched on the edge of her desk, talking quietly. With a glance of private amusement at the secretary, the chief of staff rose and followed Vadon into the vast, elegant office.

'A difficult meeting, Minister?' he asked languidly, as he carefully closed the door.

Vadon was standing behind his desk staring out at the chestnut trees and immaculate striped lawns of the ministry garden. 'That bastard,' he said at length, as much to himself as in answer to his aide's question. 'He treats me like a child!'

'The President?' the chief of staff asked, drawling.

Vadon spun from the window. 'Yes! The President!' he hissed. His eyes burned into the other man's face, evaporating the lingering trace of irony in it. 'He talks to me as though I spent the war years running errands for the Germans. Well, I have nothing to prove, to him or anybody else.' He paused, his chest heaving. 'He doesn't know who he's dealing with.' He dropped his eyes from his aide's face. 'None of you do,' he added in a murmur. Abruptly, he looked up again and sat down behind the ornately decorated desk. 'Have you spoken to the Ambassador?' he snapped.

Sitting, the chief of staff grimaced. 'Still nothing, Minister. They refuse to give us a serious response.'

'Damn!' Vadon rose again and turned back to the window, his mobile face twitching with anger. 'The President is enjoying this.' He plucked cruelly at the flesh of his lower lip. 'He *wants* to see them make a fool of me.'

The chief of staff leaned back and crossed his legs easily. 'It seems rather unfair,' he mused. 'If the Israelis *won't* tell us I don't see how we can make them. Perhaps *he* would like to try talking to them.'

Vadon turned from the window with a short laugh. 'Yes! Can't you imagine it?' He sat down at the desk, resting perfectly manicured hands on the fresh blotter. 'It's almost beneath his dignity these days to talk to a *prime minister*, let alone argue with an *ambassador*.'

The aide smirked, taking his cue from the Minister's tone. 'One has to admit that this fellow can be particularly trying,' he drawled. 'But then so have his predecessors. It does seem to be a particularity of, ah, theirs.'

Vadon pursed his lips and wagged a mocking finger. 'Tch! People will be taking you for a racist. Don't you know that the Israelis are our *friends*.' He grimaced. 'I suppose I'd better talk to him,' he added in a tone of distaste. 'Have the girl call him.'

Half a minute later one of the phones on the desk burred softly. As Vadon took it up, his scowl was replaced by a broad smile. 'Ambassador?' Warmth flooded his voice. 'How are you?'

'Fine. What can I do for you?'

Vadon's smile faltered momentarily at the Ambassador's frigid manner. 'Well, ah, I've just been seeing the President. Obviously, he's eager to know the Prime Minister's, ah, plans.' He paused. The Ambassador made no effort to fill the gap. Vadon swallowed. The bastard always made him feel uncomfortable. He continued, his voice catching as he sought the right pitch. 'You'll appreciate that the President is very anxious that I should be able to finalize the security aspects. So, it's, ah, crucial that I should know his movements, when he'll arrive, how we get him to the compound, and so on. After all,' he added, with forced geniality, 'Prime Minister Bruckner is one of our very top priorities.'

'He's our *only* priority,' the Ambassador replied levelly. 'Please feel free to make whatever arrangements you want. If you just let us know where you want the Prime Minister, and when, we'll deliver him. I guarantee it.'

Vadon's free hand clenched. 'Look, Ambassador, it can't work like that. Your Prime Minister will be *our* guest. We shall be responsible for his security while he's here. We *must* know his movements.' His voice rose. 'I'm instructed by the President to insist that . . .'

'Don't worry. Bruckner will call the President directly. They're old friends. I'm sure the President will understand our thinking.'

Vadon slammed his fist onto his desk. 'But this is nonsense! Impossible! How can we ensure his safety if we don't even know where he's going to be, or when he's arriving? There's the *airport* to organize.'

The Ambassador spoke in the same even tone. 'There's nothing to organize. Minister, take my word for it. If you can just confirm that there will be suitable provision for the helicopter to set down, as we asked, we'll do the rest.'

Vadon's knuckles were white on the phone. 'This is totally unacceptable! Unthinkable! You seem to be saying we are incapable of . . .'

The Ambassador's voice sliced in, still even though it had taken on a hard edge. '. . . of maintaining order? Look, Minister, let me remind you of a few things. In the last seven weeks there have been twenty-six serious anti-Jewish incidents: graves desecrated, businesses firebombed, the synagogue in Dijon destroyed. And, in the last week alone, three families attacked in their own homes by neo-Fascists. And the police, for which *you*, Minister, are responsible, stand by helpless.'

'Stop!' Vadon leapt to his feet. 'I won't tolerate your insults. I was risking my life to fight the Nazis before you were born, Ambassador! Those were attacks on *French* citizens, on French soil. They aren't your concern. The police are doing all they reasonably can.'

'Rubbish, Minister,' the Ambassador said curtly. 'Don't waste your campaign speeches on me. Jewish people being attacked by Fascists will always concern us, and you're old enough to know damned well why. Anyway, getting back to our immediate problem, it's Daniel Bruckner we're talking about, remember? The man who ordered the Gaza intervention.'

'Some people here called it a massacre,' Vadon retorted, with a hint of a sneer.

'Whatever anyone calls it,' the Ambassador replied coldly, 'the fact is that ninety-one Palestinians died. For the mass of Arab peoples Bruckner is the devil himself. They *hate* him as they've never hated any of us. There's a two million dollar price on his head. And these days there are as many Fundamentalist fanatics in France as in Egypt.' The Ambassador sighed. 'Look, Minister,' he went on, in a more conciliatory voice, 'we have no argument with you or your government. Quite simply, there are things going on in this country that neither you nor we can understand or control. As long as that's so, we intend to handle security in our own way. Either that or you can tell the President that he can celebrate the defeat of the Nazis without the help of Dan Bruckner. Do I make myself clear?'

Less than an hour later the black ministerial Peugeot drew into the underground car park of the Tour Montparnasse, stopping by an empty sector closed off by a row of cones. Vadon strode across the vacant space towards a door flanked by two uniformed CRS with guns cradled across their chests. Too preoccupied to respond to the men's salute, he pushed a plastic card into a slot and waited while the doors of the private lift slid open.

He stepped from the lift into the spacious reception area of his party's office. He grunted a greeting to the receptionist and strode on past the rows of eager young men and women busy at phones and word processors and through the padded leather door into his own office. The big desk held nothing but a clean blotter and three telephones. Behind it, on the window that filled almost the whole of the wall, a careful observer could just distinguish vertical lines running at intervals down the newly installed armoured glass, the seams between the strips of transparent film he had insisted on as an additional precaution, lest anyone else should take the notion to dive through it. He sat down at the desk and pressed a button on one of the phones. 'Madame Baudet,' he said briskly into the intercom, 'Come in now, please.'

The secretary, a perfectly groomed woman in her late thirties, closed the padded door, cutting out the brief murmur from the outer office. She stood hesitantly inside the door. Vadon gave her a reflex smile and waved impatiently to a chair. 'Sit down, Madame. And go on, please.' His curt, overbearing tone contrasted sharply with the quick movements of his fingers as he fidgeted with the heavy gold signet ring on his left hand.

The secretary bobbed her head and sat down, knees clenched tight together. Donning the glasses that hung from a gold cord round her neck, she laid a folder open on the desk. 'It's mostly routine calls, I think.' She began reading down a list, using a slender gold pencil as a pointer.

Vadon sat impassive as she went through the list, showing no response as she catalogued the usual favour-seekers and manipulators. Then, abruptly, he stopped fiddling with the ring. *'Who?'*

She flicked a nervous glance at him over the glasses, as though she feared she had committed an error. 'A Monsieur Duvall, Minister.'

'Yes, I heard. An American?'

She frowned, trying desperately to recall the voice. 'I don't *think* so. The caller certainly spoke excellent French.'

Vadon scowled. 'And just what did he have to say in his excellent French?'

She glanced at her notes, a touch of panic in her manner. 'Nothing, really, Minister. He just left his name and a number. He wanted to speak to you personally.' She flashed him a discouraged smile. 'Did I do something wrong, Minister?'

He ignored her question. 'Was that all he said?'

She looked at him through widened eyes, surprised by a new unease in his manner. 'Yes, Minister. I *tried* to ask him what it was about. He simply . . .'

'You have the number there?' he interrupted, thrusting out a hand.

She wrote the number quickly on a fresh sheet of paper and pushed it into his outstretched hand. 'Did I make a mistake, Minister? Is he somebody I should have known?'

He remained silent for several moments, his eyes resting on the number. Then, shaking his head, he slid the paper into a drawer. 'I doubt it, my dear,' he said, mechanically. 'Please go on.'

Relieved, she continued reading. Vadon sat with his chin sunk into his chest, the fingers of his right hand again twitching at the signet ring. Without warning, he cut into her reading. 'Thank you, Madame Baudet. That will be all.' She looked up at him, frowning, hesitant. 'Didn't you hear me? That's all! You may leave now.'

Open-mouthed, the woman snatched up her file and hurried pale-faced from the room, biting her upper lip as she fought back tears.

The instant the door closed behind her, he dropped his head into his hands. For more than a minute he sat like that, massaging the flesh round his eyes with his fingertips. Then, drawing in breath sharply through his nose and inflating his chest, he reached for the telephone.

'Mister Duvall?' The voice oozed urbanity. 'This is Christian Vadon.' At the sound of the name, Bill's clenched fist punched the air above his head. His call to Vadon's number had been a flyer. He had deliberately not mentioned the name of Bengana. Realistically, the chance of a man in Vadon's position replying to a call from a complete stranger was zero. And yet, here he was. Not a secretary or a go-between, but the Minister. In person. Which told Bill that he was not that much of a stranger, after all. Vadon continued speaking. 'My secretary informs me that you wish to speak to me. Do I know you, perhaps?'

Bill grinned. A minister of the interior, covering his rear while he squashes a potential scandal, would have ordered phones to be tapped as a matter of routine. He had probably seen the text of Keltum's call to New York, and every call since.

'I do want to talk to you. As to whether you know me, I'm not sure. Maybe you know of me.'

'Really? I rather believe you have the advantage of me. What is it you were wanting to tell me? Is there something I can do for you?'

Through the impeccable courtesy, the easy authority of a man who chose whom he spoke to and when, Bill caught in the last question the distant perfume of loathing, as though the possibility of his wanting to do something for Bill lay far beyond the frontiers of his imagination.

Bill smiled to himself again. 'As a matter of fact, there is. I'd like to meet and talk to you.'

'Really? I'm sorry to repeat myself, but as you have agreed, we don't seem to be acquainted. May I ask what we might have to talk *about*?'

'A mutual friend.'

'Do we have mutual friends?'

'We had. Ahmed Bengana.' He waited for a reaction. Vadon gave none. Bill broke the silence. 'His family have asked me to talk to some of his friends, to help them understand more about why he died.'

'You've been informed that *I* was a friend of this, er, Bengana?' Vadon's voice brimmed with scornful incredulity.

'I'm told you knew him. He certainly claimed to know you.'

'Ah, I see,' Vadon drawled. 'A lot of people do, I'm afraid. It isn't always true, though.'

'But it was in Ahmed's case, wasn't it?' The affability had gone from Bill's voice, replaced by something steelier. 'Listen, Ahmed Bengana's father is close to death. He's got a week or two left, maybe less. He needs to know exactly what happened. All I want is fifteen minutes of your time.'

'M'mm, yes, a great many people do, I'm afraid. And you have had five minutes already. Which is more than most of them ever get.'

'I want it more than most of them, Monsieur Vadon.' Bill spoke now with a rough, almost jovial confidence. 'It could be helpful. For you as well as me.' He paused, just long enough to let his words sink in. 'It concerns something Ahmed gave me to take care of. Some documents,' he added, and fell silent, his senses straining for Vadon's reaction.

'Documents? What kind of documents?'

Bill nearly exclaimed aloud. There had been an almost imperceptible change in Vadon's voice, a haste in the way he said the words. Bill injected the faintest wheedling note into his voice. 'Monsieur Vadon, I don't feel this is the sort of thing we ought to discuss on the telephone, do you? Can I see you?'

He thought Vadon had rung off. He was about to hang up himself when the voice, a little hoarse now, came on again. 'Well, look, Monsieur, that young man's family is, er, North African, I believe. Those people are, well, very close-knit. The loss of a son must be . . . I suppose I *could* make myself available for a few minutes, if it would help the family come to terms with their grief . . .'

And if it will reassure me that no one knows anything which might upset my election chances, Bill thought, smiling. 'When?' he asked briskly.

'Can we say six-thirty this evening? Here at my party offices? Do you know where to come?'

'Sure I do. I've just been reading last week's papers. See you at six-thirty, Monsieur.'

Vadon sat for a few moments longer, staring into space, a deep frown on his brow. Then he pressed the intercom button. 'Madame Baudet! Come back in here, please. With the book.'

She hurried into the room clutching the red leather appointments diary. Her eyes were blood-shot behind the glasses.

'What do I have between six and eight this evening?' He listened, his eyes fixed on a point on the wall, as the woman listed the meetings. When she had finished he went on staring at the wall. 'Cancel them,' he said irritably, still not looking at her.

'All of them, Minister? Including the television?'

He dropped his eyes to her face and gave her a look of indignant disbelief, as though she might have been daring to mock him. 'No! Of course not the television. But those other idiots can wait,' he said unpleasantly. She went on sitting, looking into his face. He looked away, dismissing her. 'Do it, Madame, please. Now.' She snapped the book shut and walked stiffly from the room.

Bill stood with his hand still on the receiver and laughed out loud. Suddenly he stopped laughing, rose, and walked over to stare from the window.

Something was seriously bothering Vadon. It would have taken a single phone call for him to have Bill run out of the country. Instead, he, a minister, had not only returned a total stranger's call, he had agreed to a meeting the same day.

Bill gazed down at the empty street. The blackmail hint

had been a spur of the moment invention. It had come to him from the way the documents in Ahmed's house had been disturbed. A burglar turned out drawers, he did not go through them, scattering documents the way they had been at Ahmed's. Vadon had swallowed the bait whole. Something was making him extremely nervous, and it was connected with Ahmed.

The phone rang several times before the familiar voice answered, thick with sleep.

'Hi. No breakfast meeting?'

'Bill!' The pleasure of hearing him brought Amy wide awake. 'We had one yesterday. Where are you? Are you back?'

'I wouldn't be calling, I'd be ringing your doorbell. I'm still in Paris.'

'Oh! I thought the funeral was yesterday.'

'It was.'

'Ah-hah. Did it go okay?'

'I guess so. It was weird. I'll tell you about it in a couple of days.'

'A couple of *days*! You expect me to last out another couple of days!'

Bill smiled. There was real disappointment behind the light-hearted tone. 'I'm afraid so, Amy. Sidi Bey's torturing himself over Ahmed's death. He's asked me to stay on for a while, to see if I can find out why Ahmed did it.'

'Don't think I'm being hard, but what is there to find out? People commit suicide because they're depressed. If there was anything more to know, wouldn't the local police have found it out?'

'Maybe. If they'd looked. Anyway, it's not quite that simple. Ahmed was Algerian. Kabyle.'

She laughed. 'I think that's what made me fall in love with you. When *you* wake me at six o'clock in the morning you contribute to my education. Bill, I know it makes me look small-town, but I've never met an Algerian. Never even heard of . . . Kabyles. What are you telling me?'

'Only that their culture's a hell of a lot different. To a Kabyle there are other reasons to kill yourself than depression. Shame, for instance. Family honour. It's another world, Amy.'

'Well, please don't stay in it too long. I need you badly in this one.'

'I need you, too, sweetheart. More than I ever knew I could. But I owe it to Sidi Bey to try to find out what he wants to know.' He paused. 'I owe it to Ahmed, too,' he added, almost inaudibly.

'Whatever you need to do, Bill. Just get back as soon as you can. Please.'

'M'mm, you bet. There's one other thing, Amy, connected with all this. I've got an appointment this evening with a man called Christian Vadon.' Amy made no sign of recognizing the name. 'He's the Minister of the Interior.'

She laughed again, and then stopped laughing, her voice dropping. 'Bill, are you serious? What's going on? I know you've got contacts, but the Minister of the *Interior*? Whatever has he got to do with what you're doing for Sidi Bey?'

'That's what I'm going to ask him. In fact that's the real reason I woke you up.'

'The mystery really does deepen.'

'Not too much further, I hope. But in case it does, mention to a few friends that I had an appointment with Vadon.'

'Bill?' she said, alarmed by the sudden earnestness in his voice. 'What's going on? You're not going to get into trouble, are you?'

'I sure hope not. But stranger things have happened in this country. If you don't hear from me soon, promise me you'll stir up all the shit you can for Vadon.'

There were fifteen seconds to go to six-thirty when Bill stepped from the lift. He was warily surveying the vast, deserted office when the door at the far end of the room swung open. The big, tanned actor's face, silver hair and superb tailoring looked almost as impressive in the flesh as they did on television. Teeth gleamed briefly amid the tan as Vadon strode forward to greet him. 'Monsieur Duvall, no doubt?'

Bill nodded, noting the same mixture of courtesy and contempt that he had heard over the phone. Without offering his hand, Vadon stepped past Bill and flicked a switch, locking the lifts.

'This way, Monsieur.'

He walked at Vadon's side through the silent outer office, warily eyeing the open doors of side offices. The sense of surprise that Vadon would receive him without even a token bodyguard was swept away in a sudden realization. Vadon knew more about him than he could have learned from transcripts of his phone calls alone. As Interior Minister, Vadon would have access to the police and intelligence records of friendly countries. Checking Bill out would have been routine for him. Bill's service record, his intelligence background, would have been enough to reassure Vadon that he was not keeping a date with a psychopath. A brief chill ran through him, an eerie feeling, accentuated by the echoing emptiness of the offices, that he was no more than a puppet, a victim of forces manipulated by Vadon. Shaking off the sensation with a roll of his shoulders, he passed into Vadon's private office.

His eye ran over the interior taking in the thick quilting of buttoned leather that covered the doors, the bare desk, the deep, creamy carpet, the tremendous view. Everything conspiring to remind a visitor that he was in the presence of power. Vadon indicated a seat and strolled round the desk.

Bill watched in silence as Vadon unhurriedly took his seat, snaking his arms away from him to bring his shirtcuffs just the right half-inch below his jacket sleeves. He sat back against the expensive, worn leather of his chair, crossed his legs and arranged his fingertips meticulously together beneath his chin. The tip of the Eiffel Tower showed over his shoulder.

'Well, Monsieur Duvall, now that you're here, perhaps you would like to make it a little clearer to me just *why* I've cancelled some important meetings.'

Bill could hardly keep from smiling. Vadon's was a great act. In a good year, Bill was declaring taxable income of over a half a million dollars. He bought his clothes in the best stores in Paris and New York. He dealt every day with some of the richest, most successful people in New York City, and yet the man across the desk almost succeeded in making him feel like a truck driver.

He smiled and nodded. 'Okay. As I told you, I'm a friend of the Bengana family. They've asked me to try to find out *why* Ahmed killed himself. What was on his mind.'

Vadon's face remained immobile. 'You say you were a friend. Don't *you* have any ideas?'

'I hadn't spoken to him for a while.' Despite himself, a shadow flitted across Bill's face. Forcing the thought back below the surface, Bill fixed his eyes on Vadon's face. 'His family seem to think he'd been, well, disturbed about something just lately.'

'Perhaps your friend was seeing a psychiatrist. You might be better off finding out and talking to him, instead of me.'

'Perhaps. It's one of the things I wanted to ask *you*, since you were a friend of his, too.'

Vadon remained quite motionless, except for a tightening of the muscles beneath his eyes. 'You do cling to that idea, don't you? May I ask the source of it?'

'His sister. She says Ahmed was very proud of the connection. He talked about nothing else.'

Vadon was silent for a moment, his only movement a brief flicker of his tongue across his lower lip. Then, he laughed, a stagey, deep-throated sound. 'Monsieur, er, Duvall, that's a professional hazard for someone in my position. I shake a lot of hands. People remember that. They like to, well, talk it up.' He made an expansive gesture that took in the office, the view, and a lot else besides. 'It goes with the territory. Monsieur Bengana was a man who liked to be seen with well-known people. He had met me perhaps half-a-dozen times, at galas, charity functions, that kind of thing. I'm sure his death was very upsetting for his family. Perhaps they're reading too much into things, not seeing matters plainly.' He cleared his throat. 'But, you indicated on the phone that you had some, er, document that your friend had entrusted to you.'

Vadon spoke the last words lightly, almost chuckling, but his eyes never left Bill's face. Without responding, Bill rose and walked to the window where he stood for several seconds, staring out. A purplish haze almost blotted out the sun, bringing the promise of more storms. A ribbon of fog was strung between the two top floors of the Eiffel Tower, so that the tip seemed to be floating on nothing. He leant close to the window, and looked down, running a finger along the join of two strips of safety film. 'I knew Ahmed Bengana for a long time,' he said quietly, still gazing down. 'He wasn't a liar, Monsieur Vadon.' He turned to look at the man. 'If he said he was a good friend of yours, I think that's how it was.'

Vadon's brow had creased. Bill watched his Adam's apple saw against the flesh of his throat as he swallowed. 'Well, I'm afraid you're sadly mistaken.' He let his eyes drop, not holding Bill's gaze.

Bill shook his head slowly. 'Are you?' He turned again and looked down at the traffic a hundred metres below him. 'Have you ever thought what a fall like that must do to a human body?' he mused, softly. 'Can you imagine the speed at impact? Heart and lungs torn adrift. Head bursting like a melon. Brain tissue spraying all over. I saw his body, you know.' He twisted his head to look again at Vadon. His tan had taken on a sick, greyish tint. The blue eyes were watery. Bill shrugged. 'But, still, what is it to you? You hardly knew the fellow.' He smiled, his eyes once again locked onto Vadon's.

Biting at his lip, Vadon shifted and drew himself taller in his seat. He made a business of looking at an over-engineered gold watch. 'Monsieur Duvall, I agreed to see you because you gave the impression that you had, er, something to offer me. So why don't you show me what it is and let us conclude this disagreeable encounter. I have to be at the television studios in less than forty minutes.'

There was something pathetic in the words, as though the fact he was appearing on television, and Bill was not, seemed to reassure him, to remind him how significant he was. Bill's first impression had been incomplete. When the going really got tough this was a man who could easily crack.

Vadon stuck out a hand and waggled the fingers peremptorily. 'So come on, let's see what it is?'

Bill smiled slowly and spread his hands. 'I was lying, Vadon. Just to see if you'd take the bait. And, by God, you did.' He moved closer, leaning over the seated man. 'What are you afraid of, Vadon? Why did Ahmed choose *your* office to destroy himself?'

Vadon flushed deep crimson. He propelled himself out of his seat, bringing his face within inches of Bill's. 'You cheap con man!' His voice caught in a sound like a sob. 'You bastard! Get out of here!' His voice breaking completely, he grabbed Bill by the sleeve and made to drag him towards the door.

Bill slapped the hand away with just enough violence to serve as a warning and strode into the outer office. Vadon followed a pace behind, still muttering insults. They were almost at the lifts when Bill turned to face Vadon. 'One more thing, Minister. Have you ever been married?'

Vadon's head jerked back sharply, as if he had been struck. For a second or two he stared at Bill with a look of undistilled venom. Then his eyes went blank. He shut and then slowly reopened them, as though just awakening, and then his teeth shone as he gave Bill a slow, unexpected smirk. 'No. But then, I don't have to tell you, do I? Nice-looking men of our age, successful, the trappings of power . . .' he left the sentence uncompleted, giving Bill a surprising slap on the arm instead. Turning away, he took a hurried step to the locking switch and flipped it. The lift doors slid immediately open. As Vadon turned back to face Bill, his composure had returned. He spoke softly, measuring his words. 'And now, adieu, Monsieur Duvall. Please take this advice. Remember who I am. And go home. It will save you a lot of grief.'

Bill's eyes puckered shrewdly at the heavy-handed threat. Both tall men, their eyes were almost on a level. 'You prick,' he said conversationally. He turned and stepped into the lift.

By the time Vadon emerged from another lift, Bill was

already at the kerbside flagging down a cab. Vadon watched the taxi pull out of sight before hurrying to a bank of public telephones.

He hunched close over the phone. 'It's me,' he said, speaking in a murmur even though the foyer was deserted. 'I need to see you.' He paused, listening. 'No, tonight. It's the American. I think he may be about to cause some trouble.'

8

The sound of the doorbell made Blaise de Medem look up sharply from his desk. With an air of surprise, he checked the time on a wafer-thin watch, absurdly frail amidst the hair that covered the thick wrist, and stood up. He was a thick-chested man, with a short neck and heavy, sloping shoulders. It was the physique of a nightclub bouncer, giving ample clue to the reserves of energy and sheer doggedness that had enabled him to struggle on, leading the National Salvation League through the years of ridicule, waiting patient decades for the tide to turn in his favour. Stretching to relieve muscles cramped from too many hours spent at the cluttered desk, he lifted his jacket from a sofa and pulled it on. Moving with a surprising, careful grace, he ambled towards the door.

The bell was chiming for a third time when he pressed the button on the entryphone. The musing half-smile on his face widened into a grin as the tiny screen came to life, revealing the face of Vadon staring at the camera, his hand reaching out again for the bell-push. De Medem leaned his lips close to the grille. 'Patience, old boy, patience,' he murmured, pressing the button to release the door. Still grinning, he watched Vadon bull his way into the lobby, then he straightened his tie and settled his jacket before opening the door onto the gleaming parquet of the landing.

Christian Vadon stepped from the lift, his head bowed as he glanced nervously at the doors of the two apartments that shared the landing. De Medem let out a booming laugh. 'Relax!' he told him, with a trace of mockery. 'This is August. There won't be a soul in the building until the end of the month.' He placed a blunt-fingered hand behind Vadon's shoulder and guided him into the apartment. 'Come in, old boy, please.' Despite his own reassuring words, de Medem turned back to the landing, his head cocked to catch any sound on the stairs. Satisfied, he closed the door, slipping a sturdy chain into place.

Vadon preceded him into the living room. As he went, the movement of his own reflection in the gilt-framed mirror over a console table made him start. De Medem gave another booming laugh. 'My God, Vadon. You need a drink. You look as though your own police were at your heels.' He raised his eyebrows in amusement. 'They aren't, are they?' He spoke in a low voice, a suspicion of seriousness in it. After an instant's pause, he laughed again. 'Scotch?'

At Vadon's quick nod, de Medem crossed to a low table and picked up one of a pair of decanters. 'I watched you on television just now.' He spoke with his back to Vadon, hiding his smirk. 'You really were magnificent. Just magnificent!'

Vadon's pinched expression compressed further. He stared through narrowed eyes at de Medem's back. 'Keep your sarcasm to yourself, de Medem,' he said bitterly.

Smiling serenely now, de Medem turned and handed Vadon a tumbler half-filled with whisky. He took up his own glass from among the papers on the desk and tilted it at Vadon. 'Cheers.' He sipped the drink. 'No, I mean it. You really do it beautifully.' He nodded at a portable television set that stood on a low table. 'You impressed *me*.'

Vadon was silent for a moment, eyes half-closed as he tracked the descent of the first big swallow of whisky. 'M'mm,' he said, sulkily. 'I can imagine! Anyway, it wasn't you I wanted to impress, was it?'

De Medem inclined his head. 'True. But you did it anyway.

The way you contrive to condemn my people's excesses without quite going for *me*. Very clever. You're a master, old boy, an absolute master.' He jerked his chin at the handwritten sheets on the desk. 'You make *my* efforts look amateurish.'

'You *are* a bloody amateur,' Vadon blurted, venting his fury at de Medem's mocking undertone.

De Medem smiled suavely. 'Well, but then I don't have access to your resources. Not for a little while yet, anyway, h'mm?' He paused to pick a cigarette from a pack on the desk and lit it, blowing smoke fastidiously away from Vadon. 'Although, I must say, I'm rather proud of *that* one,' he added, jerking his chin at the papers on the desk. 'For tomorrow night's rally, up in Lille.'

'Congratulations. Can we get to what brought me here?'

De Medem smiled dreamily, ignoring Vadon's question. 'You'll be glad to know your broadcast has already done some good. Persuaded by your very responsible pleas, I've toned down the anti-immigrant elements of my address.'

'I'm pleased to hear it. Frankly, a little restraint just now wouldn't hurt anyone.'

De Medem inclined his head in ironic confirmation. 'Of course,' he added, gravely, 'it means that to avoid disappointing my supporters I'm going to have to go a little heavier on the anti-Semitism.' He watched the expression on Vadon's face, saw the confusion he was looking for, and threw back his head with a guffaw. 'Oh dear! My friend, you really *do* take me too seriously.'

The muscles of Vadon's face twitched. 'Listen to me, de Medem,' he said sullenly. 'I didn't come here to hear about your speech. No doubt it will be very similar to the last one, and the one before that. And the next one, for that matter.' De Medem smiled modestly, as though accepting a compliment, and blew out a long thread of smoke, waiting for him to go on. 'I came because there's a problem brewing and we need to talk about it before it turns into something serious.'

De Medem's face shifted. He was still smiling, but the light of it had changed. 'Tell me about it,' he said with a soft intensity.

'Bengana's American art-dealer friend came to see me today.' He paused to gulp another mouthful of whisky, a smaller one this time, as though the first taste had taken the edge off his thirst.

'What?' De Medem's eyes were fixed on Vadon's face.

Vadon nodded, spilling a little whisky with the violence of the movement. 'He came to see me at my office. I was alone, of course,' he added hurriedly.

'What the hell did he want?'

'Apparently Bengana's family aren't satisfied about their son's death. They asked him to look into it. He phoned me, wanting to . . . talk about it.'

'What is there to talk about? He jumped out of your window, in front of witnesses. Nobody's suggesting you *pushed* the little faggot.'

Vadon flinched. 'Don't use that gutter vocabulary to me.'

'Sorry. Pederast. Will that do? It's not your fault he jumped.'

'No, but it appears Bengana had been telling his family he and I were . . . friends.'

De Medem stared at him, his face white with fury. 'And on the strength of that you gave him an *appointment*?' De Medem's voice rose in disbelief. 'You're a *minister* for God's sake!'

Vadon shook his head as though coming up from under water. 'I *had* to. He made some insinuations on the phone. He pretended he was holding some sort of . . . documents.'

The words brought de Medem to the edge of his seat, his eyes narrowed to slits. 'What *kind* of documents?'

'He didn't say.'

'But what *were* they, when he turned up with them?' de Medem hissed. His face was deadly pale, even the lips drained of colour.

Vadon swallowed. His eyes flickered around the room, as though seeking an escape route. 'There were no documents,' he muttered, his eyes watering as though he were about to cry.

De Medem fell back in his seat with a sigh. He wiped a hand slowly over his face. 'You fucking idiot,' he said at length, almost in a whisper. 'No wonder you came in here looking like a survivor of a train crash.'

Vadon pouted. 'What could I do? He said he had something that Bengana had given him.'

De Medem gave a soft, sneering laugh. 'You little prick. You thought you were off the hook, didn't you? You so *needed* to hope he had something that you agree to see a total stranger. If he didn't know there was something wrong before, he does now, doesn't he!'

'What would you have expected me to do? Was I supposed to ask him to spell it out over the phone?'

'No, I suppose not. What did you tell him?'

'That I hardly knew his friend Bengana.'

De Medem bared his teeth in a sardonic grin. 'And?'

'I don't think he believed me.'

De Medem threw back his head and laughed. Recovering, he stared pityingly at Vadon. 'Thirty years in politics and you still haven't understood, have you? Television's your medium. That's where it all works; the haircut, the tan! But that's your trouble – in real life, you look too much like an actor.' He broke off, sneering at the silent figure of Vadon, and then went on, brusquely. 'What did you talk about?'

'He tried to ask some questions about my . . . private life.'

'Which you, naturally, didn't want to go into.'

Vadon gulped some more whisky. 'I brought the conversation to an end. It's not his business. Or yours. What *is* your business, and mine, is that I had him checked out. He's got a background I don't like.'

De Medem looked at him intently, the sneer gone. 'What?'

'Intelligence.'

De Medem's eyes narrowed further. 'A few minutes ago he was an art dealer.'

'He is, now. He was in military intelligence in Indo-China.'

De Medem brayed with sudden laughter. 'Indo-China, he calls the place! My God, to think that an hour ago you were on there,' he gestured at the television, 'berating *me* for living in the past.' He sighed. 'It doesn't necessarily mean anything.

You know as well as I do that in Vietnam any American with a dozen words of French ended up in military intelligence. *Somebody* had to tell all those innocent villagers to stand in line so they could be shot tidily,' he added, sniggering. 'Do your sources say he's still involved?'

'No. He's out, as far as anyone ever is once they've been in the intelligence business. He even wrote a magazine article that trod on a few toes, around the time of My Lai.'

De Medem grimaced. 'I imagine that would have been enough to get him off the books!'

'Perhaps. That's not what worries me. He wasn't just an interpreter. He was an investigator. According to the file he was a good one, too; tough and awkward. He stirred up a lot of things his superiors would have liked to see left alone. They ended up shipping him home before his time.'

De Medem gave another sudden laugh. 'And we don't want men of principle getting in our way, do we? Will you deal with him?'

Instead of replying, Vadon rose and strode across to the table where the whisky stood. The decanter rattled hard against the glass as he poured. As Vadon raised the glass and downed an inch of the whisky, de Medem watched his back with an expression of undisguised loathing.

'I see,' de Medem said softly. 'We mustn't ask the Minister to soil his hands, huh?' He stood up and refilled his own glass. Grinning, he touched his glass to Vadon's and, gripping him by the arm, led him back to his seat. 'Okay. Just so long as I understand the situation. Now, what about Bruckner? Is he here?' He spoke the name of the Israeli Prime Minister with a venom that sat oddly with his air of languid command.

Vadon shook his head. His tanned face was a lifeless tint, like dried mud. 'I don't know. They refuse to tell us anything at all.' He spat the words, his voice rising with an almost adolescent frustration. 'They seem to think they're going to produce him out of thin air on the night, like a bunch of damned illusionists.'

De Medem smiled. 'In other words, you're still letting that

bastard of an ambassador give you the run-around? It doesn't matter, as long as he *does* show up on the night. They've approved the security arrangements?'

'Oh, yes. It's just that since the Gaza business they're terrified, scared to death of an Arab suicide squad. This is the first time he's even been out of Israel since then.'

'I don't blame him. Still, as long as there's nothing to stop our people doing their job.' He leaned forward. 'But they accept the arrangements? There's no change to the enclosure security?'

Vadon shook his head. 'No.'

'Good.' De Medem stooped over Vadon. 'Then there's nothing to stop you playing your part, is there, old friend?' As he spoke the last words, he cupped his free hand and brought it hard against the side of Vadon's face. It was the affectionate pat a father might give a child, but delivered with enough force to jerk Vadon's head to one side.

Stung by the humiliation, Vadon sprang to his feet, rounding on de Medem, his nostrils flaring. 'Don't strike me, you uncouth swine!'

With the cold smile unchanged on his face, de Medem stood his ground, so that the two men were toe to toe. Vadon's fists bunched. Coolly, de Medem sipped at his drink, the glass inches from Vadon's face. At length, de Medem laughed through his nose and turned away, shaking his head. 'It's time you learned that it's bad for a man to want something too much. It gives people a hold on you.' Archly, he looked sideways at Vadon, who still stood rooted to the spot, breathing heavily. 'Get out of here now, I've still got work to finish. And don't worry about the American. I'll set the dogs on him.'

9

Bill approached the Alexandre bridge, walking slowly in the clammy heat, past the glass-roofed bulk of the Grand Palais where the flags hung in limp contrast to the vigorous bronze horses and bare-breasted charioteers. To his left yet more of the dark grey vans clustered by the barricades that closed off the avenue Franklin Roosevelt where it intersected the Champs-Elysées.

He had decided to walk the couple of kilometres up to Montparnasse, killing the hour to his appointment. It had taken a dozen calls before Inspector Lantier, the policeman who had handled Ahmed's death, had agreed to talk to him. He had been brusque and dismissive, hostile even, making it plain he thought Bill was wasting his time. Only Bill's insistence on Sidi Bey's imminent death had finally won enough of Lantier's sympathy for him to agree to a meeting.

Bill understood the man's attitude. In a city the size of Paris the police were busy enough with people who had died at the hands of others without having to worry about deaths which had been self-inflicted. Ahmed's choice of Vadon's office was a curiosity, but did not change the fact that it was a case of suicide. It might have been of fleeting interest to the media, but to a working policeman, whose career prospects were in Vadon's hands, it was a poisoned apple.

He turned onto the bridge. Across the Seine the gilded dome of the Invalides shone with a sudden gold flame as the sun found a gap in the thick haze. After a quarter of a century the sight still sent a thrill through him.

His mind returned to the previous evening's encounter with Vadon. The man undoubtedly had charisma, a sense of his own powers, and yet he had clearly been uneasy, off-balance. Bill's experience as an interrogator had taught him something every policeman and court-room lawyer knew: very few people make good liars.

Vadon's claim that he had hardly known Ahmed was transparently false. The lie disturbed his physical and mental balance, making him fractionally mis-time the easy gestures and the man-to-man smiles. On television afterwards, free from the pressure of questioning, he had been a model of assurance and charm. Not a facial expression, not a hand movement that wasn't perfectly calculated. He had delivered his message superbly, every confident, resonant word perfectly weighted, immaculately timed.

Something stank. Vadon was a man with a lot to hide and serious doubts whether he would get away with it. It would be interesting to keep up the pressure and see what broke.

As Bill reached the Left Bank, a bronze BMW eased onto the bridge. Behind the tinted windscreen the driver held a telephone to his lips. The car was at the middle of the bridge, cruising at a jogging pace, when Bill reached the far side, dodged among the thin traffic, and set off past the Air France terminal and across the open space in front of the Invalides. The driver spoke sharply into the phone and dropped it onto its hook.

A green Renault saloon turned onto the bridge behind the BMW, accelerating to pass it. As it went, the driver of the Renault grinned and nodded. The BMW rolled slowly off the bridge and continued south, the driver watching the strolling figure of Bill.

The Renault headed south for two blocks, turned left into the rue Saint Dominique, and stopped. Two of the four young men inside got out and strode across to a nearby newsstand. The two remaining men emerged from the car, spread a map on the roof, and began studying it. As the BMW driver looked on, Bill reached the Renault. One of the young men turned and addressed him, gesturing at the map. Bill smiled and nodded. He was reaching out to point to a spot on the map as the other two men returned from the newsstand. One of them raised what looked like a rolled-up magazine and brought it down hard on the back of Bill's head. The weight of the iron bar concealed inside it sent Bill staggering. Instantly all four of the men were upon him, throwing straight, quick punches and kicking with the economical sideways motion of trained kick boxers. Bill crumpled to his knees, his arms raised to cover his face, helpless under the hail of blows.

The attack lasted no more than eight or nine seconds. As though at a signal, the four men sprang back into the car and sped away, leaving Bill to collapse backwards into the gutter. Still smiling to himself, the BMW driver brought the car to a stop and sat watching as the newsvendor and a gaggle of tourists ran to Bill's aid.

'Damn!' Blaise de Medem muttered. He hesitated for a second or two, as though debating whether to answer the phone or let it ring, and then disentangled himself from the sharp-boned, handsome woman in his arms and rolled across the bed, reaching for the handset.

'Hello. It's me, Saïd.'

De Medem gave the woman a grimace of distaste.

'No names, my friend, please,' he said into the phone, speaking sharply. 'What's the news?'

'It's been done.'

'Good. How, er, serious is it?'

'I wouldn't say it was *serious*. But it was persuasive. He'll have got the message.'

'I hope to God you're right, my friend. How did he react?'

'Well, he's on his feet, if that's what you mean. In fact he's just about to get into a taxi – to take him home to bed, I should imagine.'

'Don't try imagining things. It's not your strong point. Just stay with him and make sure. And keep me up to date.'

'Whatever you say, my friend. You're paying the wages.'

De Medem's expression hardened at the insolent tone. 'Yes, I am. And for what I pay I expect to see the job done properly.

Call me here.' He put down the phone and lay propped on an elbow, his face pensive.

'That ghastly Saïd man, I suppose. Is there trouble?' the woman asked huskily. The skin round her eyes, already taut from cosmetic surgery, was drawn tighter by concern.

He shook his head and drew the back of his hand gently down her naked breast. 'I don't think so. Not yet. We'll see. So far they just hurt him a little.'

Her frown deepened. 'You didn't want them to do *more* than just hurt him, did you?'

'What I want is for him to go home, no more and no less. Especially no less. We'll see whether they did enough to persuade him.' Sighing, he rolled towards her. 'For now.'

Bill paid off the cab and climbed laboriously out onto the pavement. For a moment the ground spun beneath his feet, making him catch at the roof for support.

'You sure you're alright, monsieur?' the driver asked, leaning across to hand him some change.

Bill nodded. 'Yeah. Thanks. Getting better all the time.' He handed a couple of coins to the driver, checked the name plate of the narrow side street, and set off along it towards a brick building where a French flag dangled from an iron bracket over the entrance.

He walked gingerly, stopping every few paces to rest, one hand on a parked car to support his weight, the other gently massaging the sore and bloody spot on the back of his head. Outside the building a line of unmarked cars obscured the painted 'no parking' sign. Alongside them a row of old-fashioned black bicycles stood reared on their back wheels in a rack. He paused once more to gather some strength and turned to mount the three concrete steps.

It was the first time he had been in a police station for twenty years. Nothing had changed. The room was high and bare with small windows covered in a close steel mesh that cut out most of the daylight. Overhead a faulty neon strip cast a palpitating white light. The air smelled faintly of vomit. Five damaged chairs were ranged around the walls. A middle-aged man who looked as though he had had a very bad night sat in one of them, staring blankly in front of him. Behind a counter that ran the width of the room a uniformed policeman tapped laboriously at a dusty manual typewriter. Hearing Bill enter, the policeman looked up distractedly. 'Yes?' He spoke grudgingly, like a man who would rather be speeding to the scene of an armed robbery than helping out with the insurance formalities for another victim of the city's pickpockets.

'My name's Duvall. For Inspector Lantier. He's expecting me.'

The policeman looked at Bill more closely, interest flickering briefly as he noticed for the first time Bill's sickly pallor. He reached for a phone and pushed a button. 'Somebody here for you. A Monsieur Duvall?' He pronounced the name on a rising note, looking at Bill as though he suspected it might be an alias. Bill met his gaze levelly. He could already feel the muscles round his eyeballs beginning to ache as they struggled to synchronize with the pulsing neon.

The officer put down the phone and jabbed a finger towards a door. 'Through there. Fifth door on the left.'

The door gave into an uncarpeted corridor lined on both sides with offices divided by cheap partitioning; green-painted plywood to waist height with glass above. Cigarette ends and gum wrappers were strewn on the tiled floor. He limped along the corridor, peering with frank interest into the offices. About half of them were occupied, mostly by men. None of them seemed to even notice the near-hysterical young woman with unwashed hair who sat in one of the offices, her head in her hands, screaming something unintelligible about her baby. A uniformed policewoman and a detective in designer dungarees stood over her, both wearing the bored but almost kindly look of people who spend part of every day trying to get sense from shrieking junkie mothers who love their babies just as much as anybody else.

He counted to the fifth door. Here the glass in the partitions was frosted. That, together with the pale rectangle that showed through the frosting indicating a window on the far wall, looked like evidence of status. A metal holder on the door contained a crumpled card with Lantier's name on it. He rapped on the glass, heard a grunt from inside, and pushed open the door.

A chunky, deep-chested man sat hunched at a paper-strewn desk, studying a thin sheaf of documents. The cuffs of an out-at-elbows grey cardigan were pushed back, revealing powerful wrists. At the sight of Bill he frowned, hesitated and then rose, shuffling the documents he was reading into a brown folder and tossing it, face down, onto the desk. 'Monsieur Duvall?' He reached across the desk. 'Inspector Lantier. Good morning.' They exchanged a perfunctory handshake and Lantier sank back into his chair, waving to Bill to do the same. For a second or two they sat in silence as Lantier looked Bill over in a frank examination. At length, he gave a quick grimace, looking into Bill's face. 'Are you alright? You look sick.'

'Not sick, exactly. But I'm not really okay, either.' He put tentative fingers to the back of his head and winced. 'I just got beaten up.'

Lantier's brows knitted. 'Beaten up? Just? When do you mean?'

Bill jerked a thumb over his shoulder. 'A few minutes ago. On my way here.'

Lantier's eyes glittered. 'How did it happen?'

'How does it ever happen? One of them distracted me, the others jumped me.'

Lantier shook his head. 'Oh, shit! Did they do much damage?'

Bill dipped his head, showing Lantier the wound. 'Depends on your standards. I could have been killed, I suppose.'

Lantier had risen and was moving round the desk. 'Very funny. Let me look at it.' He stepped behind Bill and touched a hand to the wound.

'Ah! That hurt!' Bill shouted, jerking away from Lantier's hand.

'Okay, I see.' Lantier strode back to his chair. He touched

a button on an intercom and spoke into the dust-caked grille. 'Lantier. Is the doctor still here? Good. I've got another patient for him.'

For the ten minutes it took the police doctor to examine Bill, confirm that his skull was intact, and dress the wound, Lantier stood silently at the window, staring at the blank brick wall three metres away. As the door closed behind the doctor, he turned and strolled back to his desk. 'Coffee?'

'I thought you'd never ask.'

Lantier took a scratched flask from a table behind him. He picked up a cup, shook half an inch of dregs into his waste bin, put the cup down in front of Bill, and filled it to the brim with coffee. Bill took a long sip. 'I hope you aren't going to ask me for sugar?'

Bill started to shake his head. The pain stopped him. 'No.' He raised the cup to his lips and took a long gulp.

Lantier kept his eyes on him as he drank. 'Did they rob you? Did you check your wallet, credit cards?'

Bill waved a finger in the air. 'They didn't even try.'

Lantier pinched at his lower lip, pulling out the flesh and letting it go with a snap. 'Could you describe them? Did you by any chance get the registration?'

'The news vendor took the number.' He reached into a pocket and pulled out a scrap of newsprint. 'Here.'

Lantier studied the scrawled number. 'And the description. You must have got a pretty good look at the one who accosted you, at least.'

'I saw all of them, more or less, once I stopped seeing stars. All in their late twenties. Short, dark hair. T-shirts and jeans. Tennis shoes. I was pleased about the tennis shoes,' he added, touching a hand to his bruised rib cage.

Lantier gave a short snuffle that was nearly a laugh. 'H'mm. Anything else? Anything that might help me to know what they actually *looked* like, for instance?' he asked with an ironic grin.

Bill shrugged. 'Sorry if I let you down. They didn't think to introduce themselves.'

Lantier smiled and then leaned abruptly forward and pressed the intercom button again. 'Three-one-six E-H-G ninety-three,' he said, reading from the scrap of paper. 'Check it out for me, will you?' He looked back at Bill. 'Certainly stolen but he'll check it anyway. Smoke?'

Bill grimaced a refusal.

'No, of course, nobody does in America anymore, do they?' he said, gouging a crumpled Gitane from a pack and lighting it. He blew a cloud of smoke over his shoulder, waving the match to death. 'Don't mind if I do, do you?' he asked, belatedly. He continued speaking without bothering to wait for a response, squinting through the smoke. 'Now, Monsieur Duvall, why don't you stop insulting me and tell me *exactly* what all this is about?'

Bill puckered his eyes against the stinging smoke. 'As I said on the phone, Ahmed Bengana's suicide.'

Lantier's eyes stayed on Bill's, his expression unchanging. 'Go on.'

'Sidi Bey, Ahmed's father, has cancer. He's dying and he knows it. He's probably got no more than a week or two left.'

Lantier nodded and took another long pull on the cigarette. 'So you told me, at length, on the telephone. What is it to you? What's *your* connection to the Bengana family?'

Bill looked into Lantier's face, trying to read the eyes, narrowed now to slits against the smoke. 'How long have you got?'

Lantier's face did not change. 'As long as you want to take.'

By the time Bill had finished outlining the story, responding to Lantier's occasional gentle question, Lantier was most of the way through his second cigarette. As Bill finished, he drew the overflowing ashtray closer and ground it out. 'I see. It's a touching story.' He spoke with no trace of irony. 'I can see why the old man chose you. Apart from anything else, most of the immigrant population don't have any friends outside their own community. He probably thought you had a better chance than anyone else of getting close to the circles his son moved in.'

'Maybe he's right. Would you have seen me if I'd been from his "community"?'

Lantier smiled. 'If I were an American, like you, I would plead the Fifth Amendment.'

Bill laughed in return. 'At least I know I'm dealing with an honest man. So, all Ahmed's father really wants from me is that I spend a day or two trying to find out why his son died.'

'That won't take you long, Monsieur Duvall. His son died because he dived from a window a hundred metres above the ground.' He paused. 'A perfectly reliable witness saw him do it. Two, if you count Christian Vadon.'

Something in Lantier's last words made Bill study him more closely. Lantier's face betrayed nothing. Bill let it go. 'That's not what I mean, and you know it. What Sidi Bey Bengana wants to know is *why*. What – or maybe it should be who – drove him to do it?'

Lantier nodded. Pushing himself out of his chair he walked to the window again, his hands deep in the pockets of the shabby cardigan. 'There always has to be a who, doesn't there?' he said, speaking at the window. 'In my time as a policeman I must have dealt with a hundred suicides. And hardly a single family has ever wanted to believe *their* son or daughter, husband or wife, simply *chose* to do it because they just couldn't face it any more. People seem to think it's some kind of stain on the family.' He turned back into the room. 'Personally, I don't see why, do you? It seems a fairly tidy way of settling your problems, maybe taking a stain *off* the family, in a lot of cases. Provided, of course, you don't hurt anybody else.' He smiled wryly. 'It happened once; somebody jumped off the top of Notre Dame and landed on a couple of tourists.' He shook his head. 'That's why they had to put up the wire netting.'

'Maybe they should put some wire netting round Vadon,' Bill murmured.

Lantier gave him a strange look, made as if to speak and then kept silent.

'Look, Inspector, his father just wants to *know*. That's not unreasonable, is it? It's certain that Ahmed Bengana was under a lot of pressure from *something*.'

Lantier took a step closer. 'Was he? How do you know?'

Bill looked hard at him, trying to find in the man's eyes the hint of eagerness that had been concealed beneath his flat tone. He hesitated for a long moment before speaking. 'He called me several times.'

'When?'

'The few days before he died.'

'And what did he say?'

Bill hesitated. 'I didn't take the calls personally. They were on my machine.'

'But what was the message, then?'

Bill looked into Lantier's eyes, trying again to read what was there, to confirm his impression that this man wanted to help. At last, he spoke, very softly. 'He wanted me to call him. He needed my help. Very badly.'

Lantier's eyes were on his face, reading every nuance. 'And you didn't call him back,' Lantier spoke softly, without reproach.

Bill shook his head, ignoring the shaft of pain that the movement sent stabbing into his brain. 'No.'

For a moment Lantier remained quite still, his face pensive. Then, he reached out and touched Bill lightly on the shoulder. 'I see,' he murmured, returning to his seat. 'The calls gave you absolutely no lead as to any name, any *person* who might have been hounding Bengana?'

'Nothing.'

'So you have nothing at all to go on.' Lantier sat back in his chair, not bothering to hide his disappointment.

'Well, there's the fact he chose Vadon's office.'

Lantier held up a hand, fingers crooked, studying the uneven nails. He flicked absorbedly at one with the thumbnail, trimming a jagged edge. Then he gave up and bit at the offending edge instead. It was perhaps four seconds before he spoke, his voice a flat drone, like a prisoner-of-war reading a propaganda text under duress. 'Christian Vadon's office is near

112

the top of the Tour Montparnasse. It's the highest building in central Paris. It would have been ideal for Monsieur Bengana's purpose.'

Bill frowned. 'Come on, Inspector. I can read the press releases. If a person wants to kill himself, the fifth floor will do fine. Over that, and it's just for the look of the thing. Unless he has a point to make.'

'You think your friend did have a point to make?'

'Don't you?'

Lantier sat for a long time considering the question. Outside, the woman's discordant screams rose to a frenzy as she was manhandled along the corridor. Lantier waited for the sound to die away before he spoke, his voice barely more than a murmur. 'Listen to me, monsieur. I didn't want to receive you. I finally agreed to it, partly because you were so persistent and partly because of what you told me about Bengana's father, his health. But now I find you're abusing my generosity. You're asking me to speculate about a case involving the Minister of the Interior, a straightforward case of suicide in which there is no police interest. In case you don't realize it, Christian Vadon, give or take a few intervening layers, is my direct superior, and I didn't allow you here to give myself the opportunity to indulge in irresponsible rumour-mongering about an event involving someone he scarcely knew . . .'

'Supposing that were a lie?'

Lantier's eyes narrowed. 'What?'

'That Vadon hardly knew Ahmed.'

Lantier drew breath, glancing at the door. 'You have evidence of that?'

'Ahmed's sister claims her brother knew him well.'

Lantier sat back abruptly in his chair, raising his hands and letting them fall back flat on his desk. 'Ah, yes! Mademoiselle Bengana. Keltum!' He sighed. 'Monsieur Bouhila's star pupil. Go on.'

'There's nothing more. She just says he was proud of it, to be a friend of Vadon's.'

'There's no accounting for tastes,' he said drily. 'What do you think? You knew her before she took the veil, or whatever they call it. Is her word worth anything?'

'Why wouldn't it be? God knows, I think the whole Bouhila thing is a terrible blind alley, but she's not stupid. In fact she's very smart. I'm sure that she believes it, and that she got it from her brother.'

'Well, I wish to God she had told me about it.'

'Did you try asking her?'

Lantier gave him a long look of exasperation. 'How long would I have to sit there watching her look at the wall and refuse to talk to me before you'd call it trying? I'll admit, after a half-hour or so I'd had a bellyful of her. I gave up.'

'She wouldn't talk to you at *all*?'

'Not a word. She made me sit there, asking the same questions, over and over, and didn't open her mouth. And frankly, I doubt if I would have believed a word if she had.' He shook his head. 'To tell you the truth, they drive me nuts.'

'Arabs?'

Lantier grimaced. 'Remember, I took the Fifth. Let's just keep to the Fundamentalists for now. I'll admit I don't understand them. There's no reason why I should, any more than they have to understand why I'm looking forward to retiring so that I can go fishing. Some people like fishing, some don't. But I'll tell you, what they're about is downright dangerous. You've got enough cults in America that I don't have to tell you how it works. It's brainwashing. Take the case of Mademoiselle Bengana. You say you've known her since she was a child, right?'

Bill nodded. 'A baby.'

'Okay. So let me guess. You say she's bright. I'll bet until recently she was a nice, approachable young woman. Integrated, studious, maybe even ambitious, huh? Then she gets dragged along to a meeting by some friends. And there, up on the dais, it's Bouhila, with his hypnotist's eyes, and his message of salvation.'

Bill grimaced agreement. 'Sounds familiar. We've got a dozen cults at home like that. Don't be hard on Keltum, though, Inspector. She'd been through a hard time.'

'How's that?'

'Well . . . let's say there was a gap in her life.' He faltered. 'She . . . that's all. She had been through a bad spell.'

'Since she came back from the stay in New York you told me about?'

'Come on. It's not your business.'

Lantier looked at him shrewdly for a moment before returning to the original subject. 'Seems to me *all* religions are like that, one way or another. The problem with this one is that its leader's stock-in-trade is racial antagonism, and he's got millions of Arab immigrants out there who think they've got a grievance.'

'Perhaps some of them are right.'

Lantier inhaled deeply. 'Look, I can't help people's view of the world, Monsieur Duvall. I'm a policeman. If someone has a problem with the law, I try to deal with it fairly, whoever they are.'

'Even if . . . ?' Bill asked, with a lop-sided smile.

'Even if they're immigrants?' Lantier interjected. He put both hands to his face as though he were suddenly unbearably tired. He drew them slowly down his face. 'I could take that as a very nasty insult, but I won't. Maybe I've given you the wrong idea.' He sat back, his hands falling to his thighs. 'It might interest you to know, Monsieur Duvall, that I became a policeman for better reason than to be free to park my car where I liked without worrying about a ticket. It may surprise you, but I happen to take the institutions we have here seriously. I'm fifty-three years old. That's just old enough to remember, or think I remember, the mess this country was getting into before de Gaulle. Ever since I was a teenager I've grown up respecting what he created, respecting the Fifth Republic, if you like.' He gave Bill a fleeting, twisted smile. 'Does that sound high-flown for a copper? Well, it's true. I thought what de Gaulle had given us was worth protecting. And I still do.' He paused, letting out a long sigh. 'So, to answer your question, I have preferences, and I have prejudices, like everybody else. But I try not to let them interfere with my work. Do you understand me?'

Bill inclined his head. 'I think so. And I apologize.' Lantier shrugged the apology away. Bill smiled. 'Now let me guess something. It's because you respect the law that this business sticks in your throat. You know Ahmed killed himself, but you still believe Vadon had *something* to do with it. And you don't like the sight of Vadon manipulating the system to cover himself.'

Lantier had yet to answer when the phone buzzed. He picked it up, listened for a moment, grunted, and replaced it, looking at Bill. 'Your attackers' car. It was stolen near to la Republique this morning, probably around nine-thirty.' He tapped his fingertips on his desk. 'What time was it when I finally agreed to see you here?'

Bill did not answer, letting the implication of what Lantier had told him hang between them for a while. When he did speak, his voice was very quiet. 'Did they take you off the case?'

Without taking his eyes from Bill, Lantier fished out another cigarette. He lit it, still watching Bill's face, and then rose and stalked across to the window again. He stood with one hand thrust deep into the pocket of his sagging blue corduroy trousers, jingling coins. Several seconds passed before he spoke. 'It doesn't work like that,' he murmured, his back to Bill. 'I talked to the people involved. Nobody wanted to make anything of it. It was suggested to me that I had better things to do.'

'By whom?'

Lantier's shoulders rose and fell. 'People who decide. It isn't difficult for them to get the message over. Pressure to put time into other cases. A little harassment here and there. And I had no obvious reason to insist. Nobody pushed your friend. On the contrary, he was the one doing the threatening. He was waving a gun around, a sawn-off shotgun.'

Bill grimaced. 'I read about that. Didn't you wonder what a fashion designer was doing, carrying a weapon like that?'

Lantier threw him a glance over his shoulder. 'What kind

of a policeman do you think I am? But what does it tell you? Anyone can buy a shotgun here. They can buy hacksaws, too. If your friend was far enough off his head to throw himself out of Vadon's window, who knows what his reasoning was.'

'Wasn't the gun enough to give you an excuse to dig deeper?'

Lantier turned from the window to face him. 'I started. I talked to Mademoiselle Bengana. I've already told you how far that got me. I tried to talk to Vadon's secretary, the one who saw Bengana jump.'

'Tried to?'

Lantier bared his teeth in a grin. 'She had left. Gone abroad. After twenty years working for Vadon, idolizing the man, she decided to go off and work abroad. Within twenty-four hours of the suicide.'

'Shit!' Bill murmured. 'And Vadon? Did you grill him?'

Lantier smiled. 'I asked for an appointment.' He jerked a thumb at the ceiling. 'My boss called me in. He suggested that unless I wanted a sudden career change I should leave the man alone.'

'So you did?' There was a tinge of disbelief in Bill's voice.

'That's right. I did.' He moved back to the desk, stabbing the cigarette out among the stinking remains in the ashtray. 'Look, I told you, I'm fifty-three. I've been through a messy divorce and I've got three children who hardly talk to me, unless it's to check whether there's going to be anything for them when I croak. The divorce left me with nothing but a nice little apartment here in Paris, on which I pay a very low rent, and the prospect of a decent pension if I stick it out for a couple more years. Why should I put those at risk to fight a battle I can't win anyway?'

Bill looked up into his face. 'Bullshit!' Lantier raised an eyebrow. 'You're not staying here to preserve your pension rights.' A faint, ironic smile had crept onto Lantier's face as he listened. 'And it's not the prospect of leaving your cosy little nest. You know that if they transfer you out to the provinces you'll lose touch completely. You're just doing what you need

117

to do to stay close to the case, hoping for another chance to get a handle on it.'

Lantier smiled, shaking his head. 'You're a very imaginative man, Monsieur Duvall. It's no wonder you move in such artistic circles.'

Bill looked at his watch, ignoring Lantier's words. 'And the reason you agreed to see me today, let me talk for an hour, was in the hope that I might know something that would give you that handle – am I right?'

Lantier hitched his rump onto the desk and prospected with a crooked finger in the cigarette packet. Finding nothing, he crushed the packet in his fist and tossed it at the wastebasket. He watched it miss and roll onto the floor. 'As I said, you have a free-ranging imagination. Monsieur Duvall, you're a guest in our country. What I *strongly* suggest is that you don't do anything that might interfere with the administration of justice, or that would put you in any personal danger.' He turned to look down into Bill's face. 'This morning's incident was a friendly warning. Whoever did that to you will be prepared to go much further. My professional advice to you is to go back to America, straight away. Is that clear to you?'

'Thanks for the advice.' He laughed, his eyes on the other man's face. 'Vadon said the same thing.'

Lantier started to his feet, making the desk slip with the violence of the movement. '*Vadon* gave you a warning? How's that? You've spoken to him?'

Bill smiled. 'Yesterday evening. In person.'

Lantier squinted at him, unsettled. 'Monsieur Duvall, just what kind of connections do you have in this city?'

Bill saw the concern that shifted deep in Lantier's eyes, could almost see the man re-running their conversation, measuring the extent of his indiscretion. He laughed softly. 'Relax. I just left a message at his office. He called back.'

'Vadon called *you* back. What the hell was the message?'

'My name.'

'And on the strength of that he called back and gave you an appointment?'

'No. On the strength of that he called me. The appointment was the result of what I told him on the phone.'

'Which was?' Lantier's voice had dropped to a whisper.

'I hinted that I was holding some documents that might interest him.'

Lantier was leaning very close to Bill now, his eyes drilling into his face. 'Are you saying you tried to *blackmail* him?'

'Doesn't that mean asking for something in return? I doubt if asking for ten minutes of his time would count.'

'But what are these documents?'

'I didn't say. I only mentioned that Ahmed had passed something on to me.'

'What? What is it?' Lantier reached out a hand.

Bill raised a hand in protest. 'Hey, relax. There aren't any documents.'

The flash of disappointment in Lantier's face was followed by a grudging smile. 'Where was the meeting?'

'At his office.' He read the look of surprise, disbelief even, in the policeman's eyes. 'I told you. It was the evening. We were entirely alone.'

'What did you talk about?'

'Basically, how well he knew Ahmed.'

'And?'

'The same story. Several charity galas. Ahmed liked to be seen with well-known people, apparently. Vadon claimed they had only ever met socially.'

Lantier raised his eyebrows. 'Really? And what was your impression?'

'Keltum had it right. The man was lying through his teeth.'

'But do you have evidence of that? An outright lie.'

'No, not if you put it like that. But I've handled enough interrogations in my time to be ready to swear the man was lying.'

Lantier frowned. 'Interrogations? Have you done some kind of police work?'

'Kind of. I was with intelligence for a while, back in the service.'

Lantier looked askance. 'You're not still in it?'

Bill laughed. 'Me? They drummed me out. Unsuitable material. I objected to our people shooting villagers to encourage suspects to talk. They reacted as though I'd joined the Viet Cong.'

'So we're both civil rights freaks,' Lantier said drily. 'How did you learn about Bengana's death?'

'From Keltum.'

'How, though? Mail, phone?'

'She called me, the day after it happened.'

'From the Benganas' place?'

'I guess so.' He picked up the slight movement in Lantier's face. 'The same thought crossed my mind.'

'There must be some compelling reason why a *minister* would return a total stranger's call. He must have started having their phone tapped the same day.' He paced the room restlessly, his brow furrowed. 'And then they stole that car right after you made your appointment with me this morning.' He sat down heavily in his chair and leaned forward. 'You had better be very careful indeed. No dark alleys.'

Bill touched his fingers to his scalp. 'They don't bother with dark alleys.'

Lantier smiled grimly. 'Right. Next time they might not bother with iron bars, either. It might be a blade in the ribs. You may think you owe the Bengana family a lot, but if I were you I would go home to your own family. On the first plane.'

'Thanks again. I don't have one.'

'You might want one, some day. Those people might arrange it so that you can't.'

'I appreciate what you're saying, Inspector. I promise I will leave soon. I have to. I've a lot to get back to,' he added, smiling to himself. 'But I'm not leaving before I talk to that bastard Vadon again. I don't take it kindly at all when people start sending hired goons after me.'

'You're very brave. Don't let it make you stupid though.' He reached into a drawer and pulled out another pack of Gitanes.

He looked down at the pack, fiddling it open. 'They're going to ask me what you were doing here all this time. I'm going to tell them I was persuading you to leave. That I tried hard to convince you that Ahmed Bengana's suicide was just that.' He lit the cigarette and drew deeply on it. 'As far as the police are concerned, it's a closed book.' He stood up, gesturing towards the door. 'Now, I think it's time you were on your way.'

Bill rose and followed him to the door. 'Okay. Thanks for your time. If I turn up anything, I'll let you know.'

Lantier stopped, a hand on the doorknob. 'What makes you so sure I want to?'

Bill grinned at him. 'Come on, Inspector Lantier. Isn't that what this whole conversation has been about? You hope I'm going to stir something up, make somebody do something stupid.'

Lantier had begun opening the door. On an afterthought, having cast a brief look along the deserted corridor, he closed it again. Leaning his back against the door, he stood staring into Bill's face, as though pondering something. At length, he placed a finger on Bill's chest. 'Look, since you insist on going on with this, despite my advice, there's one other thing you might as well know.'

Bill waited, watching the man's eyes. They were unblinking on his face, as though Lantier were sizing up something about him. 'There's a strong chance that your friend was being pursued when he entered that building.'

Bill stared back at him, incredulous. 'My God!' He paused, considering the news. 'But wouldn't that make it police business?'

Lantier nodded. 'It would. If I had any evidence.'

'How do you know it was happening, then?'

Lantier looked pensively at him. 'I'll tell you some other time,' he murmured. He pulled open the door, speaking at normal volume again. 'Now, I'll tell you one last time, monsieur. Your friend killed himself, unaided and unprovoked. Please make his father believe that. And when you've done so, I suggest you take the first plane back to America. Do I make myself clear?'

'Perfectly,' Bill said cheerfully. 'Thanks for your time.' He stuck out a hand. Lantier shook it, with more warmth than he let show in his face. 'And for the advice, even if I don't take it.'

10

'God, I'm going to catch my death of cold in here. It must be pushing forty outside.' Ari Levin, the Deputy Director of Mossad was perched on the edge of a side table in the windowless room, massaging the goose-pimpled flesh of his muscular arms. He was dressed as though he had just come from the beach, gaudy Bermuda shorts and a T-shirt promoting a brand of American cigarettes stretched over his thickened waist. His sockless feet were shoved into scuffed sandals.

The eyes of Daniel Bruckner, the Prime Minister, were humorous behind the thick spectacles. 'It's you people that insist on meeting down here, not me.'

'We run the intelligence services, not the air-conditioning. I'm freezing.'

Bruckner grinned. 'And this is the man who wiped out the Egyptian Air Force single-handed in the Six-day War? A bloody hypochondriac. If the Egyptians could see him now they'd demand a replay. What have you got for us, Ari?'

The Deputy Director slid his rump from the table and picked up a file. He took a handful of documents from it and tossed them onto the table. 'Here. Take a look at these. Cuttings from the French press.'

Each of the men round the table reached for one of the stapled batches of photocopies. Levin waited as they perused them, nobody speaking. Finally, they let the documents fall back to the table and looked up at him grim-faced.

'Nice, isn't it?' He looked at the ring of sombre faces, smiling coldly. 'Of course, most of it's from the crazy fringe press, but there's quite a bit from some of the big dailies, too.' He smiled at the Prime Minister. 'Sorry, Dan, but, as you can see, a lot of people aren't at all happy about your visit.'

Bruckner snorted and tossed the wad of clippings away from him with a contemptuous gesture. 'Come on, Ari. This is the kind of filth they've been hinting at for years. What's new?'

Levin's smile faded. 'What's new, Dan, is that they aren't hinting any more. They're calling you these things openly.'

Bruckner shrugged. 'So what?'

'So, now they can get away with it. Before Gaza they wouldn't have dared. That incident cost us a lot of friends, Dan. It changed the atmosphere, just the way our people warned you it would.'

Bruckner shrugged and blew out his cheeks. 'No point digging up the past, Ari.'

Levin breathed deeply. 'Not everyone sees eleven months ago as lost in the mists of time, the way you seem to, Dan. Not only did it lose us friends, it made us some new enemies, which even you will admit we didn't need.'

'What difference does it make as far as Dan's visit is concerned?' one of the seated men asked.

Ari turned to face the speaker. 'I'll tell you. There were always plenty of people in the French service who didn't like co-operating with us. The xenophobic element.'

'You can say anti-Semitic, Ari,' Bruckner murmured, smiling wryly. 'We're man enough to take it.'

'If you like. Anyway, what it comes down to is that we're getting the feeling that there are things that aren't getting through to us any more. In fact, people in the French service that we *know* are our friends have the feeling they're being frozen out, that information isn't reaching them.'

'And you think that what they *aren't* hearing concerns my visit?'

'I have no idea, which means I have to take the possibility seriously. And I take that man Bouhila seriously, too. He's stirring up a lot of trouble, and we've not been able to get anyone close to him yet.'

'So what are you suggesting? I'm not going to cancel the trip, if that's what you're leading up to. We aren't going to back down because of some jumped-up ex-waiter, or road sweeper, or whatever he was.'

'It's not what he was that bothers me, it's what he has become. But no, I'm not saying call it off. All I'm saying is let us handle it, from start to finish, not Foreign Affairs. No parties, no chance to play your old Ukrainian Resistance hero number. You'll be under wraps the whole time. We'll put you on their platform, let you applaud their parade, and then we'll lift you straight off and home again. No chance to enjoy Gay Paree at all.'

Bruckner nodded. 'You've been talking to my wife.'

'No. To mine. She's sick and tired of us holding elections. She's made me swear to keep you alive for a while.'

Bruckner laughed. 'How about the arrangements on the platform itself? Are you happy with *that*?'

Ari held out a hand, fingers splayed, and rocked it. 'More or less. After all, the President will be sitting in the seat next to yours. Anyway, our people over there are keeping very close to the French, looking over their shoulders. Nobody's going to be able to get a weapon in there.' He paused. 'Of course, somebody could always lob a mortar bomb at you, but, to tell you the truth, that's a danger I've just had to learn to live with.'

Bruckner scowled theatrically. 'You're very staunch. By the way, you know the President's very unhappy about your idea? He thinks we're giving in to extremists.'

Ari shrugged. 'That's his problem. He probably wants to use you to help put a shine back on his own image, old Resistance heroes swapping stories from their glorious pasts, and all that.'

The self-mocking twinkle went out of Bruckner's eye. 'Don't use that tone, Ari. It was all real enough. And we weren't the only ones. The French lost half a million lives, too. Don't ever forget that.'

❖

A gap in the churning purple cloud released a sudden beam of sunlight, letting it track slowly across the delicate bulk of Notre Dame. In the storm-cleansed air the detail of the stonework stood out with a dream-like clarity that made Bill stop eating, lost for a moment in delighted contemplation. It was moments such as these that had ensured that the restaurant, on the fourth floor of a building overlooking the Seine, had remained his favourite long after the standard of the food had been overtaken by a dozen others.

The cloud shifted, extinguishing the sun and casting the cathedral again into the deep twilight gloom. Returning to his present thoughts, Bill laid down his knife and looked up, ready to catch the eye of the waiter.

Despite the restaurant being crammed with tourists, most of whom had booked nine months earlier on the strength of the reputation of a chef who had been dead for the past two years, the waiter had anticipated his gesture and was already gliding towards him. With a smile that acknowledged Bill's frequent custom, but which never crossed the thin line into familiarity, the young man briskly cleared the table, whisking the last crumbs from the cloth as he noted Bill's request for coffee and some very old Calvados.

A few moments later, the waiter laid his order in front of him and melted away leaving him to the view. He swirled the Calvados round the huge glass, sniffed appreciatively at it, and then, cupping the glass in both hands, sat back to think.

After leaving Lantier, he had returned to the apartment. There, a half-hour's sleep had left him with the headache mostly gone, an urgent need to think, and a ferocious appetite. In response to both needs, he had called the restaurant, which, despite the weight of bookings, had immediately given him his favourite window table.

For almost two hours, while eating a leisurely, even if outrageously over-priced, lunch, he had been going over in his mind the events of the last twenty-four hours.

The interview with Lantier had been strange. There was no doubt Lantier was tough, shrewd and smart, and he had read Bill with a sensitivity that was unsettling. In fact, he was smart enough and shrewd enough to give the ring of truth to what he had said about himself and his own attitude to police work. Respect for the rules, plus a hearty contempt for the compromise and political in-fighting that were part of any ambitious French policeman's baggage, would explain why he was still working out of a flea-ridden dump in Montparnasse instead of a carpeted office down on the Quai.

Straight arrow or not, though, he was playing some game of his own with Bill. Seeing Bill at all, giving him the time he had, above all, his apparent frankness with a total stranger, none of that was from any particular desire to ease Sidi Bey's last days. They were the calculated acts of a man with his own agenda.

The more Bill had thought about it, the more he was convinced his words to Lantier had been true. Lantier, despite his solemn warnings, *wanted* him to stir up trouble. He wanted something to happen, anything, that would break the case open, turn it into a criminal one, one that Vadon could not easily have him pulled off. Lantier was convinced there was something more to the case than suicide, but he was powerless to do anything about it. It was not just a matter of bowing to pressure from the hierarchy. His conversation with Lantier had been more than enough to convince him it was not the man's style. Quite simply, if Lantier ignored his superiors' instructions, Vadon not only had the power to stop him, it would take no more than a word to have Lantier moved out of Paris, to somewhere that put Vadon himself, and everything connected with the case, irretrievably beyond his reach.

For some reason of his own, Lantier wanted Vadon's head.

And that, he thought, fingering the sore spot on his scalp, put them in the same camp.

He finished off his coffee and made a rudimentary writing gesture with his thumb and forefinger, signalling for the bill. The most intriguing thing about the meeting had been Lantier's mention of Ahmed being pursued. Bill had read every account of the suicide in every paper in Paris. Nowhere had it been suggested that Ahmed was being chased. If it were true, and Lantier was plainly convinced of it, not a journalist in Paris had picked it up. Once again, Vadon had shown how easily he could keep the lid on something he wanted kept quiet. If Ahmed was being hunted, it had a lot to do with his suicide, and it somehow threatened Vadon. On both counts he owed it to Sidi Bey, and he owed it to Ahmed, to find out how. He touched a hand to his head again. Already the effects of his sleep were wearing off and it was beginning to ache, a rhythmic throbbing pain that penetrated deep into his brain. Now, he owed it to himself, too.

'The House of Bengana.'

Bill pulled the padded door of the restaurant's phone booth more tightly shut, trying to blot out the Martini-charged laughter of a knot of businessmen who had waited an hour for a table. He spoke distinctly, keeping his voice as low as he could over the noise. 'Monsieur Burgos, please. My name is Duvall. William Duvall.'

Michel Burgos had been Ahmed's partner for ten or twelve years. An accountant by training, he handled the business side of the Bengana empire, keeping Ahmed's creative excesses sufficiently in check to ensure the web of enterprises turned in handsome profits. Bill had met him a number of times, mostly at Ahmed's parties. Once, when Burgos had been in New York negotiating a ready-to-wear franchise, Bill had even managed to sell him a picture, charming his way past the man's instinct for eighteenth-century Flemish masters. He had found Burgos a courteous, ascetic man, whose diffidence concealed an acute commercial mind. Whenever Ahmed's soaring imagination got the better of him, Burgos would always be there to guide him gently back to earth, the perfect counterweight to Ahmed's artistry. Over the years Bill had developed a sneaking fellow-feeling for Burgos. Like himself, Burgos worked at that crucial, fragile interface where art meets money.

'Monsieur Duvall?' The high, rather thin voice sounded uncharacteristically flustered. 'What can I do for you?'

'Give me a few minutes of your time, if you would. I'd like to come over and talk to you.'

'Oh, you're in Paris?' His voice dropped. 'Of course. You came for the funeral, I suppose?'

'Right. I thought I might see you there.'

'Oh, I couldn't. I just couldn't. Not with that horrible sister, and her ghastly . . . friends. I couldn't have borne it.'

'I know what you mean. I'm at the Colonne d'Argent. Could I come by in say, twenty minutes?'

'Oh!' The fluting voice rose higher. 'But things are in such a *terrible* mess. I'm up to my neck, without Ahmed. This place is . . .'

Bill laughed softly. 'Monsieur Burgos, I know it's a bad time, for all of us. But I just want to talk to you, not criticize your housekeeping. Shall I just jump in a cab?'

'Oh, well, if you really . . .'

'Great. Thanks. See you in a few minutes.' He put down the phone and pushed open the door. Then, on an afterthought, he turned back to the phone, pulling a thin address book from his pocket. He thumbed over the pages and dialled a number.

'I'd like to speak to Christian Vadon, please.'

'I don't think Monsieur Vadon is in. May I know who's calling?' The voice managed to be both warm and emotionless.

'My name's Duvall. William Duvall. He knows me.'

'One moment, monsieur.'

Several seconds of silence were broken by the clicks of his call being shunted through their system.

'Monsieur Duvall?' It was a different woman, cool and just possibly hostile. 'I'm Monsieur Vadon's secretary. What can I do for you?'

'Pass me to the boss,' he answered, with cheerful confidence.

There was new ice in her voice as she responded to his tone. 'I'm afraid the Minister isn't in the office today.'

'No? Well, it doesn't matter. I'm sure you'll be kind enough to pass on a message.'

'Certainly, monsieur.'

He smiled at the meticulous horror in her voice. 'Tell Vadon Bill Duvall called. It didn't work. I'm still in town. And I don't intend to let his hired help run me out. And I'm going to want to talk to him again.' He put down the phone and left the restaurant.

❖

After the sticky heat of the street, the bite of the air-conditioning made Bill hunch his jacket closer around his shoulders. A stick-thin woman who had once been Ahmed's favourite model, and who now doubled as receptionist and saleswoman, smiled in recognition as he crossed the thick beige carpet towards her desk.

'Good morning, Delphine. Monsieur Burgos is expecting me.'

She nodded towards a curtained door set in the rear wall. 'He's with a client. He asked if you would mind waiting in the workroom. Although it's a *terrible* mess, I'm afraid.'

He shrugged, laughing. Ahmed's workroom had been a legendary mess, a standing joke between them for twenty years. Nevertheless, he stopped dead in the doorway. Instead of the kind of disciplined chaos that he would have recognized as Ahmed's normal working regime, the room was a mad jumble, the trestle worktables and the huge oak partner's desk submerged beneath heaps of fabrics, sample swatches, sketches, and half-finished garments. Rolls of fabric had been dragged from their shelves and lay tangled in ankle-deep drifts on the floor.

He turned to look at Delphine, who stood at his shoulder. For the first time he noticed the puffiness under the careful make-up round her eyes. 'Is this how Monsieur Ahmed left things?' He spoke in a hushed, incredulous voice.

She nodded, her head bobbing too hard and fast, as if her grief had slightly unhinged it. 'Terrible, isn't it? We wondered, you know, with what happened, if he had gone, well . . .' She broke off, tears beginning to form as she made a vague gesture towards her temple.

'Crazy?' Bill smiled wearily. 'Maybe. Is there any coffee around?'

Sniffing to stem another tear, she turned and glided back across the immaculate carpet into the showroom. Her grief had not impaired the cat-walk perfection of her movement.

Bill stepped into the workroom. The walls were bedecked with framed pictures. Pride of place went to a cover of *Time* magazine. Bill studied it for a moment, smiling slightly ruefully. The picture had been taken a year and a half earlier. Ahmed had been forty-four. The handsome, narrow face that smiled from the magazine cover was that of a man ten years younger. Looking at the glossy black hair that framed the face, he touched a palm to the grey-flecked hair above his own ears. He had once teased Ahmed, accusing him of dyeing it. Ahmed had laughed, but the heat of his denial had been enough to ensure that Bill never joked about it again. The memory of the small, pointless vanity made Bill smile some more.

He moved on, pausing in front of each of the pictures. They were blow-ups of photographs from the French and international glossies – *Jours de France*, *Paris Match*, various editions of *Vogue* – showing Ahmed in the company of the world's glitterati. Some of them, current European royalty and the show-business clique, Bill recognized. Others were less familiar, members of dispossessed aristocracies, trading on resounding family names that meant nothing to him, although for all he knew they might still have meant a lot in Rumania. And they had meant quite a lot to Ahmed, too. The pictures made the room into some kind of shrine to celebrity. Not achievement, just celebrity.

Bill turned away, biting his lip. Ahmed's cultivation of the rich, the famous and the well-connected was a side of his friend he had always been uncomfortable with. He encountered a lot of the same people in the art trade. As far as he had ever been able to see, the only things they appeared to have more of than other people were money and an over-generous idea of their own worth. Ahmed had seen them differently. He had seemed to need them, to need the bogus hugs and public kisses from people whose attainments were not a fraction of his own. What they had, though, was that unshakeable certainty of their own specialness, a certainty Ahmed had sought in their company, as though he might somehow learn their secret.

Ahmed had never taken Bill's advice to move to America, never quite been able to break the family ties completely. In America, nobody would have given a thought to his origins. Being Arab, or black, or Eskimo, would have meant nothing. The only thing that would have mattered was his talent. Instead, he had chosen to stay in Europe, with all its barriers and its snobberies, and there to fall between two cultures. No longer at home with the old values of his family, uncertain of acceptance in the world into which he had been admitted, he sought reassurance in the company of television presenters and the empty and arrogant nonentities of dead-beat royal houses. It had been a waste.

The woman returned with his coffee in a tiny translucent cup. Holding it in his fingertips, he continued examining the room, rooting among the sheaves of sketches and riffling through the sample swatches.

It was almost half an hour before he heard voices in the showroom and recognized Burgos's voice, an unfamiliar whining tone in it. He looked up at the half-open door to see him accompanying a woman a head taller than himself towards the door, worrying at her like a solicitous sheepdog. He stood smiling a fixed smile through the glass for some seconds after she had left the shop, as if reassuring himself she still remembered how to get into her car. The moment the woman's car drew away, the smile faded, as abruptly as a spent firework. He paused for a moment and then, putting on a fresh, genuine smile, he turned and hurried in to Bill, extending a hand.

'Monsieur Duvall! So sorry to have kept you.' He rolled his eyes and flapped a hand towards the door. 'I'm not used to dealing with that side of things. Since . . . since the, er, this business, I'm having to do *everything* myself.'

'That was thoughtless of Ahmed.'

Burgos recoiled, pouting. 'Please, don't. I didn't mean anything like that. It's absolutely shocking. Tragic. It's just that these,' he flapped a hand again, '*people* are so selfish. They couldn't care less, apart from the dinner table status they get from having been Ahmed's clients! All they want to know is whether poor Ahmed finished *their* dress before . . . before it happened.'

Bill smiled. 'Yeah, well, you know I sell to pretty much the same crowd myself. Most of them are so rich that spending money's no fun. Being a pain in the ass is!'

Burgos's laugh was a strangely desolate one. 'Yes, indeed. I always *hated* having to deal face to face with the clients. Ahmed was so much better at it. He loved it. I think it appealed to the showman in him. He should have been an actor, if he hadn't had the talent for design, don't you agree?'

Bill frowned at an edge of bitterness in Burgos's voice. 'He would have been good at it, Monsieur Burgos.' He gestured at the shambles in the room. 'What do you make of this?'

Burgos's hands fluttered. 'Oh, I know, it's awful, isn't it? I'm going to have to make a start on getting it all sorted out.' He swallowed hard. 'It's been one thing on top of another, trying to keep the whole business going, these last few days. And then, to tell you the truth, I just haven't had the heart to even come in here, you know.'

Bill laid a hand on the man's sleeve. 'Don't apologize, Monsieur Burgos, please. This must have been a terrible personal blow for you. But what I meant was, I know Ahmed had a kind of disorganized way of working, but I've never seen his workroom in anything like *this* state. Have you?'

'Well, no, not like this.'

'So, what do you make of it?'

Burgos took several quick paces around the room. 'I, well, Delphine shares my opinion; we assumed Ahmed had probably gone, well, had some sort of attack, a brainstorm, if you like. Seeing what he did,' he added in a plaintive voice. His eyes had moistened at the thought.

Bill nodded. 'Did you consider the possibility that the room might have been searched?'

Burgos started and gave him a strange look, up from under his brows. 'Is that what *you* think it was, then?'

'So, it's not the first time you've had the idea?'

Burgos shook his head hard, like a small dog drying itself. 'No. Look, I wasn't here the day Ahmed died. But I spoke to him, on the phone, only an hour or so before it . . . happened.'

'And? Did he *seem* like someone about to flip?'

Burgos smoothed his tie. 'Well, no, not really, not more than other days of late. Although, to be honest, it's hard to say. He had seemed to be under a huge amount of strain lately. He had been behaving, well, oddly. Even here, in the showroom. Some of the clients had begun to, well, to *notice*.'

Bill's eyes narrowed. 'How oddly?'

The little man wet his lips. 'Well, poor Ahmed. If you ask me, he hadn't been himself for some time. You know his sister quite well, I believe?'

Bill nodded, looking hard for some background of malice in the man's eyes. He found none. 'I know her,' he said levelly.

Burgos looked at him, trying to read his thoughts. 'Yes, well, you know she's involved with that man Bouhila?'

'Uh-huh. What of it?'

'Only that he seems to be attracting a lot of the young, er, North Africans.' He paused. 'You do know about him, don't you? *Imam* Bouhila, as he calls himself.'

Bill nodded. 'I know of him,' he said wearily.

'Yes? Well, since the sister, since Keltum, got involved in that she was becoming quite an influence on Ahmed. She wanted him to abandon his career, everything.'

'And what was Ahmed's reaction, as far as you could tell?'

'Well, at first, he laughed about it. He thought it was just something that she had drifted into after . . . her . . . well, I believe she had some kind of breakdown, after she returned from America.' Burgos looked at him with a hint of a question in his eye. Bill remained impassive, returning the man's gaze. Burgos dropped his eyes. 'He thought it was a five-minute wonder. That she would soon find a boyfriend, and forget all about it.'

'And later, when she didn't?'

Burgos drew a deep breath. 'Ahmed was a susceptible man, you know. Very, very sensitive. He had lots of problems of his own. Terrible emotional difficulties,' he said, the sudden bitter force in his words surprising Bill. 'That girl . . . she was very persistent. She had taken to coming here. In the middle of business hours! I pleaded with Ahmed to stop her. She would walk in in that, that, garb!' For a moment he seemed to be more offended by her dress sense than her religious beliefs. 'She even took to bringing that man, Bouhila, in here! Can you imagine? That robe down to his ankles, bare feet, sandals!'

Bill raised his eyebrows, his mouth twisting in the effort to restrain a smile at the image, despite his curiosity. 'Bouhila? During business hours, too?' He nodded to the door, in a reference to the departed woman. 'Just her cup of tea, I should imagine.'

Burgos tossed his head and sniffed. 'At first Ahmed wouldn't have it, wouldn't let him around the place. Then, I don't know, he seemed to sort of give in to it. It was as though that man had cast some sort of spell on him. He has frightening eyes you know . . . like . . .'

Bill nodded. 'I saw him, at the funeral. They seem to be his big weapon.'

Burgos sniffed. 'He looks like a criminal to me. Anyway, it lost us at least one very good customer, I can tell you.'

'M'mm. Apart from driving away trade, what was Bouhila after?'

Burgos rolled his eyes. 'I wish I could tell you. Making a convert, perhaps? Ahmed was a very big celebrity.' He paused. 'If Bouhila *were* looking for someone to be a figurehead, some sort of advertisement for his ridiculous movement, Ahmed would have been a real catch, accepted everywhere. Frankly, there aren't many Arabs in France you could say that about,' he added, with a touch of venom.

Bill nodded. 'Almost like a real Frenchman,' he murmured, barely audibly.

'I'm sorry?' Burgos said, leaning to catch his words.

Bill raised his voice again. 'It doesn't matter. You said he was behaving "oddly". How oddly? Enough for you to think he might be planning to jump out of that window?'

The words sent a tremor through Burgos. 'Well, frankly, it seems possible.' Pale-faced, he took out a crisply folded handkerchief and dabbed at his lips. 'For the last week or so he was really strange, as though he were under some terrible duress. In fact, he mentioned you several times.'

Bill frowned. 'What did he say?'

Burgos shook his head. 'Oh, only that he had been trying to get in touch with you. He apparently wanted to talk to you. He set a lot of store by your opinions, you know, Monsieur Duvall.'

Bill flinched. 'But do you know what about? Could it have been the business? You aren't in trouble, are you?'

Once more, Burgos shook his head with the exaggerated, dog-like emphasis. 'Good God, no. Our work – Ahmed's – is, or I suppose I have to learn to say was, in tremendous demand. We could hardly keep up. No, no. Nothing in the business could have been worrying him.'

Bill caught the way Burgos leaned on the word business. He looked at him, waiting for the man to tell him more. Instead, Burgos turned away from him, throwing out a hand in an abrupt gesture. He gave a sudden strained laugh. 'I suppose it will all go to the sister, by the way. To dear Keltum,' he added, his voice almost breaking.

'I guess so, eventually. Who knows, she may even come around to enjoying it.' He paused. 'Monsieur Burgos, there was *something* wasn't there? Apart from business. Something in Ahmed's private life. Do you know what it was?'

Burgos shook his head, his back still to Bill. 'Not some*thing*,' he murmured, so low Bill had to step forward to hear it.

'Some*one*, then? Is that it?' Bill asked, his voice almost as low as Burgos's. 'Who was it, Monsieur Burgos?'

The man's shoulders heaved. 'I don't know. I begged him to tell me. He just wouldn't.' Burgos spun to look into his face. His eyes glistened. 'The poor boy. For these last ten days or so, he was absolutely *tortured*. He was so depressed. Just anything, the tiniest little matter, and he would break down in tears. Whoever it was, he was just tearing him to pieces.'

Bill reached out and touched the man's sleeve. 'Look, I know this is a painful question for you to answer, Monsieur Burgos, but just when did you lose Ahmed?'

Burgos stared at him. 'You know quite well when it was he jumped from that window! He . . .'

Bill shook his head gently. 'No. When did *you* lose him, not the rest of the world? When was it you first knew, for sure?'

Burgos went on staring at him for a moment longer and then sank among the skeins of tangled fabric that almost hid a cream leather sofa. Tears streamed down his polished cheeks. Bill stepped past him and quietly closed the door. He turned back to look at the sobbing figure.

'A month ago. Although things had been going wrong for weeks. He had stopped talking to me, except about business. He had just cut me out of his life. It got so that I couldn't stand it any more. I confronted him about it, here, in this room.' He choked back a new fit of sobbing. 'It was an awful scene. Awful.' He broke off, his fingertips pressed to his eyes, momentarily overwhelmed at the memory.

'And he never gave you any clue who had taken your place?' Bill asked gently.

Burgos dropped his hands and sat with his head hanging, staring at the floor. 'No,' he whispered. 'I asked him, over and over. It was important to me to know,' he added, casting an appealing look at Bill. 'He just refused to discuss it. He wasn't horrible about it, really. Just secretive. Said he simply couldn't tell me, and that was all.' He dropped his head into his hands, sobbing silently, his shoulders heaving.

Bill stood quiet for some seconds before dropping to a crouch and putting his face close to Burgos's. He spoke in a whisper, his hands on Burgos's shoulders. 'I'm sorry, Monsieur Burgos, I really am. I know what he meant to you, and I understand. Ahmed had his weaknesses, but we both owed him a hell of a lot. I know it's hard for you to talk about it, but I need to ask you a few more questions. You would like to see them pay for it wouldn't you, whoever drove Ahmed to do what he did? And to help his father die decently, too?'

Burgos's head dipped as he muttered indistinctly behind his hands. Taking one more gulping breath he dropped his hands from his face and looked, watery-eyed, at Bill.

'Please try to help me then.' Bill stood up. 'You said Ahmed was here the day he killed himself. Did any of your staff see him?'

'Not exactly. Delphine was at lunch. She goes every day from twelve-thirty till two.'

Bill smiled. 'Vive la France! Do you close the store?'

'The showroom?' Burgos corrected mechanically. 'No. There was another girl here, Florence. But she was in the stockroom virtually the whole time Delphine was out. She heard him arrive.'

'Was that the first time he had shown up that day, at lunchtime?'

'Ahmed often did that, you know. He would start work in the afternoon and work through until two or three in the morning. He always said he couldn't create in the mornings.'

'Right, I'd overlooked Ahmed's Mediterranean schedule. You said she heard him. Did she see him, too?'

'Apparently not. She heard the bell, looked out, and saw nobody. She assumed it was him. It was his normal pattern, after all.'

'Was his door open or closed?'

Burgos recoiled a little at the question. 'Well, as a matter of fact it was closed. Which was a bit strange, because he hardly ever closed his door once he was at work. He liked to feel that he was available, for the staff as much as for clients.'

Bill frowned and nodded. 'Would the girl have heard anyone else come in?'

Burgos moved uncomfortably. 'Yes. Normally.'

'Normally?'

Burgos made a face as if what he was about to say had a bitter taste. 'The buzzer works on a pressure pad. You *can* avoid it, if you know where it is. But you would have to want to. I've tried it. Since Ahmed . . . went,' he added, answering Bill's look. 'There's very little here to steal. We've always resisted the mania for security that seems to afflict everyone these days.'

'I'm glad there are a few of us left. So somebody *could* have got in and been waiting for him in his office when he arrived?'

'Well, yes, I suppose so. You mean, you think there might have been men in here, searching for something, when he came in?' He cast a quick, nervous glance round the room as though to reassure himself the intruder was not still there.

'I don't know. It seems possible. You know he was carrying a gun when he went to Vadon's office? He threatened Vadon with it.'

At the mention of the gun a shudder of real horror shook Burgos. 'Yes, I'd seen it. I actually walked into his room and found him sawing the thing down, with a hacksaw blade! I nearly died at the sight of it.'

'Didn't you ask him why he wanted it?'

'Of course!' His eyes clouded at the thought. 'He told me it was none of my business, that I should forget I had seen it. He made some remark about the National Salvation League, how as an Arab he didn't feel safe on the streets any more.'

'You don't sound convinced.'

Burgos made an attempt at a smile. 'Ahmed, on the streets? Really, the idea is absurd. He never walked *anywhere*. He either used the Mercedes or took a cab. He would call a taxi to go from here to Fouquet's.'

Bill smiled wryly at the recollection. 'I've argued with him about that myself. Just another part of the cultural heritage, eh, Monsieur Burgos? If you're an Arab and you strike it rich, it just seems silly to walk when you can have somebody drive you. So why do you *think* he might have wanted to be armed?'

Burgos shrugged. 'Because he was afraid. Not of street gangs, but of something.'

'Did he keep the gun here?'

'No, of course not. I wouldn't have been able to stand knowing it was around. They terrify me. He carried it about with him.'

'In his pocket? Even sawn-off, a shotgun would make a hell of a mess of the line of a jacket.'

'He kept it in his bag.'

Bill nodded. For years Ahmed had carried that same shoulder bag. It served as a wallet, a briefcase, almost as a desk, always stuffed with sketches and scraps of fabrics. 'So, if anybody *was* in here, he could have given them a nasty shock.'

'Scared the life out of them, I should think,' he said with another tremor.

Bill made a sucking sound. 'Guns scare the shit out of me, too. But some people are used to them, I guess.' He paused. 'The girl, Florence, did she hear anyone *leave*?'

'She says not.'

'Isn't that odd?'

'Not really. There's the back door, through the kitchen,' he said, waving a hand vaguely at the door. 'It was open.'

'Unlocked, you mean?'

'No, open. Hanging open. Delphine found it like that when she went to make me some coffee, after she had returned from lunch.'

Nodding, Bill turned away and let his eyes roam over the mess in the room, musing. 'What did the police make of what you've just told me?' he said, at length.

139

Burgos looked at him curiously. 'The police? Apart from a phone call they haven't shown the slightest interest.'

'What was the phone call for, then?'

'An Inspector Lantier called to say he wanted to come and talk to us.'

Bill gazed at him. 'And?'

Burgos made a little flapping gesture with his hands. 'He never came. I suppose it was a clear case. After all poor Ahmed really *did* jump.'

Bill turned to face him. 'He jumped,' he said, his voice distant. 'No question about that.' He held out a hand. 'I guess that's all for now, Monsieur Burgos. Thanks for your time.' Burgos sat as though stricken, lost in a memory, not seeing Bill's outstretched hand. Bill let it drop back to his side. 'Goodbye, monsieur.' He began making for the door. An afterthought brought him back. He put a hand on Burgos's shoulder. 'I'm sorry. About you and Ahmed, you know. That must have been very hard, after so many years.' Under his fingers Burgos sat motionless and silent. Tears began running down his face again. Bill gave the man's shoulder a squeeze and withdrew his hand. 'It's a shitty business, Burgos. A lot of people seem to be getting hurt.' He touched his hand to his own head. 'Until now it's been all the wrong ones.'

11

Bill let the showroom door swing closed behind him and waited at the top of the marble steps, scanning the avenue Marceau, ready to dart back into the relative protection of the showroom at the first sign of trouble.

The conversation with Burgos had left him angry, and warier than ever. Burgos's account virtually confirmed what Lantier had said about Ahmed having been pursued. Somebody had almost certainly entered the showroom during the lunch break and had searched Ahmed's workroom. Maybe they had waited for him, maybe he had surprised them. If he had pulled the shotgun on them, he would have surprised them even more.

He smiled despite himself at the memory of his first ever sight of Ahmed, holding off the masked attackers with a kitchen knife. Those men had looked into his eyes and they had known beyond any doubt that he would use it. He hoped the searchers had at least experienced that look, that they had known a moment of real fear as they looked into the snout of the weapon.

His hand went automatically to his head, the fingers probing speculatively at the scalp wound. The intruders had very probably armed themselves. But even if they had, they would not have dared make a move against the sawn-off shotgun, not in the confines of the workroom. Shooting Ahmed was not what they had come for, anyway. They could have done that from a passing car. It was more likely that they were looking for information. If they had been planning to beat it out of him, the shotgun would have changed their minds. It left the question of why they had pursued him, instead of getting the hell out of the place. Maybe Ahmed had recognized them and they needed to silence him. Or perhaps he was carrying something they wanted.

He was still pondering these questions when his eye alighted on a grey Citroën, parked fifty metres back up the road. He could just about make out the silhouettes of four men inside. Four men whose idea of the place to enjoy a stifling summer afternoon in Paris was inside a car with all the windows up. He mentally kicked himself for not thinking of it sooner. They had probably been following him since the beating, checking whether they had succeeded in running him off.

Still standing on the top step, as though unsure of his next move, he watched a taxi round a corner two blocks away and stop, letting off a passenger. The cab drew forward again, gathering speed. It was practically alongside when Bill leapt onto the deserted pavement and ran into the road, waving it down. It had still not quite stopped before he was inside.

Reaching for the meter, the driver eyed him peevishly in the mirror. 'You could get hurt doing that. Where do you want to go?'

Bill had twisted round in his seat. The Citroën was nosing away from the kerb, forced to dawdle in the thin traffic to let a few cars move into the gap between them. Bill turned back to the driver. He thought for a moment before announcing 'rue Beaubourg. From the top.'

Three hundred metres back from where the Citroën had been parked, Saïd watched as it edged out into the traffic. Grinning, he spoke a few further words into the car phone and slapped it back onto its hook. Taking his time, he twisted the rear-view mirror, pulled out a comb, and ran it through the thick silver waves of hair, patting it into final perfection with his palm. Satisfied, he put away the comb, gave a quick wrench at his tie, and climbed out of the BMW. Moving in a slow, head-forward shamble, arms curving out from his sides like a wrestler about to engage an opponent, he set off towards the Bengana showroom.

❖

Ten minutes after leaving the showroom, Saïd loped up the steps of a well-kept building on the avenue Montaigne. He was reaching for the bell for the fourth time when he heard the voice, the surprise and distaste in it clear even over the distortion of the entryphone.

'You! Whatever do you want?'

Saïd smirked up at the lens. 'I was in the neighbourhood, so I thought I'd drop by.'

Blaise de Medem's voice was stiff with incredulity. 'Drop by? There's no reason in the world for you to come here like this. Get out of here, you idiot!'

Saïd's smirk stayed on his face. 'Oh, yes there is. We need to talk. Now.'

De Medem was silent for a moment, weighing the insolent confidence in Saïd's manner. He spoke again, his voice still contemptuous. 'M'mm, really? You'd better come in, then. Quickly!'

De Medem was waiting at the open door of the apartment. He wore a shirt and underpants, and socks. One cuff link was fastened, the other he held in his hand. 'What do you mean by coming here like this, without an appointment? I've told you before about that.'

Saïd grinned unpleasantly. 'I know. I was two minutes away. There was something I thought you'd like to know. It didn't seem like something we ought to talk about on the car phone.'

De Medem nodded, frowning. 'Come in here.' He stepped aside, allowing Saïd to precede him into the living room. 'Do you want a drink?' Saïd shook his head. De Medem shrugged. 'So, what is it?'

'Well, it's your friend, the American.'

'What about him?'

'Doesn't give up easily, does he?'

De Medem's eyes narrowed. 'What do you mean?'

'I stayed with him after his, er, trouble this morning.'

'And? Has he gone?'

'Gone? Home, you mean? Back to America?' Saïd grunted with laughter. 'Look, after the boys hit him he went on to keep his appointment with the policeman.'

'That doesn't worry me too much. They wouldn't have had anything to tell each other.'

'Okay. Try this. After lunch he went over to the Bengana showroom. He talked to Bengana's partner.'

'You sure?'

'Of course I am.' He showed his teeth. 'Right after the American left, I dropped in to see him myself. A few minutes ago.'

De Medem frowned again. 'Did you hurt him?'

'T'ch. Of course I didn't *hurt* him.' He leered at de Medem. 'What do you take me for? A cheap thug? I gave him a good *talking* to, that's all.' He laughed aloud. 'I thought he was going to shit himself, right there in the showroom! It seems Bengana's friend was asking questions about the little faggot's suicide.'

'What kind of questions?'

Saïd snorted. 'All sorts. How he was acting before he jumped out of Vadon's window, whether the police had taken an interest – all kinds of crap. Anyway, he seems to have made a big impression. The way it came across to me, our Yank didn't act like somebody about to run away.'

De Medem screwed up his face. 'Didn't he?' For several seconds he stood musing, fiddling with the cuff link. At length, he motioned Saïd to a sofa. 'Sit down. I think we'd better talk about this.'

❖

Bill sat staring through the windscreen, too deep in thought even to hear the driver's incessant grumbling. The whole ethos of post-war political life in France had been forged by men whose ideas had been shaped by the war. Urbane, apparently civilized men, respected pillars of the political scene, could be as ruthless as Corsican gangsters the moment they sensed a threat. At least since General de Gaulle and his personal struggle against the OAS, a twilight world had existed where gangsters, police, secret services and politics merged. A murky, obscure world where deeds too dirty for government agencies could be contracted out to pimps and drug-traffickers on the understanding that their own activities would escape close scrutiny. The men that attacked him could as easily have been policemen as pimps. Setting up his beating would have been simple. Any one of dozens of highly placed people could have done it. The phone taps left him without a shadow of doubt it was Vadon.

For the Interior Minister, it would have taken no more than a phone call to the listening centre deep under the Champs-Elysées to set up the wire-taps, and to ensure that he received immediate transcripts of the calls. The same went for having Lantier pulled off the case. Nothing in writing. Just a phone call to his superior, the promise of a future favour, would be all it took.

He stroked the back of his head. Whatever it was Vadon wanted kept quiet, he was ready to get very rough about it. The blow to the head could have killed him, instead of leaving him with a sick headache and a lump that felt the size of a lemon. He doubted it would have mattered to Vadon one way or the other. It would have been just another police enquiry to stifle, another call to a senior officer with ambitions.

Bill squirmed around once more to look back through the window. The Citroën was a hundred metres behind, separated by a handful of cars and a bus. He had long since concluded that its passengers were pimps, not police. Or, at least, not on-duty police officers – they would have had the resources to do the job properly, using several cars. The only question was whether they were planning an encore or just out to frighten him.

He turned to face the front. His promise to Sidi Bey, his sense of obligation to a dead friend, had been powerful reasons to try to discover what lay behind Vadon's fears. The beating had made it personal, strengthened his resolve to flush Vadon out. Meanwhile, if Vadon's hired help was planning another ambush, there was no point in making it easy for them.

'Five hundred francs to jump the light,' he said to the back of the driver's head.

They were already descending the rue Beaubourg. Ahead and to the right rose the Centre Pompidou, its external service shafts and steel skeleton reminding him as always of the slightly neglected engine room of a super tanker.

The driver skewed his head around, sneering. 'What do you take me for? There are cops everywhere.' As he spoke, he jerked his chin at a group of heavily armed police lounging at the foot of the building, joking with the drivers of the parked tourist buses.

'A thousand. Go left. Take the rue Rambuteau. They're looking for Fundamentalist death squads, not cabbies obliging a fare. You'll be a block away before they know what's happened.' As he spoke, he pulled the money from his pocket and waved it next to the man's face.

The driver looked sidelong at it, stupid cunning seeping into his face. 'Fifteen hundred?'

Bill pulled more money from his pocket and dropped it all on the seat next to the cabbie. 'There you are. That takes care of the fare as well.' The driver glanced down at it and grinned. 'Slow up to make sure we hit the red. When I give the word, go through and make that left turn, fast. There's a supermarket immediately after the turn, on the left. Let me off there. The moment I'm out, drive like hell to the end of the block.'

'Then what am I supposed to do?'

'After that the rest of the day's your own.'

The driver gave him a cock-eyed look, as though he were about to speak, and then shrugged and lifted his foot off the throttle, coasting to the light.

Bill looked back and smiled. The Citroën had remained at the rear of the bus. They stopped at the light. Bill waited a few seconds until all the traffic behind had closed up and stopped. 'Go now!'

The driver let up the clutch and took the turn with a squeal of rubber, sending startled pedestrians scrambling for the kerb.

'Okay. Stop!' he yelled again, the moment they were clear of the protesting crowd. The driver stamped on the brake. Bill sprang out and ran into the open front of the shabby all-hours supermarket, laughing to himself at the sound of the cabbie burning rubber again, anxious to be away before the police could get a sight of his number.

He stood in the back of the store, watching the street. It must have been ten or twelve seconds before the Citroën screeched into view and raced past after the cab. With a wave to the Arab manning the checkout, he walked from the store and across the road, mingling with the still-muttering pedestrians. Safely hidden by the glass wall of a café terrace from the view of the occupants of the speeding Citroën, he ran.

In a half-dozen strides he was squeezing into the shelter

of the clustered tour buses. He sprang up onto the raised pavement, elbowed his way through the knot of drivers and police, and plunged through the rear entrance of the building. Hardly slackening pace, he jumped down a flight of stairs to concourse-level and sprinted through the throng to the main doors.

He did not stop running until he reached out to flag down a taxi from the northbound flow of traffic on the boulevard Sebastopol. Still panting, he gave the driver the address in the rue de la Goutte-d'Or and sat back to try to get the thing in some kind of perspective.

Vadon was not kidding. Sending men after him in broad daylight once was intended as a clear signal to Bill that he was above the law. Doing it twice, having him openly followed, almost certainly knowing he had been to a meeting with Lantier, was meant to tell him that anything was possible, that Vadon could do what he wanted, without regard for the consequences. On the one hand it was scary, on the other, the speed, and the crude brutality of his reaction, smacked of panic. Vadon wanted him out of it, and he wanted him out of it fast. Once word got back to him that Bill had persisted, going to see Burgos, there was no telling how he might react.

The thought sent a faint frisson running up Bill's back. It was not exactly fear. It had not been *exactly* fear in Vietnam, either. Just that strange kind of knowledge that, in a village full of smiling people, you could walk into one of the picturesque huts and find that one of those smiling, grateful people had rigged a booby-trap to blow your throat apart. He had never been one of the crazy ones who had thrived on it. Getting back at Vadon for the beating, helping Sidi Bey die at his ease, paying his debt to Ahmed, were things he intended to do. But from now on he needed to be very careful of the booby-traps.

He climbed out of the taxi in front of the Benganas' building, looking warily around him. He had a moment's unease as a youth, standing aloof near a cluster of down-at-heel men, stared hard at him with dark, hostile eyes. His apprehension faded as the youth decided he was not a policeman and nodded to a skinny black man standing behind an up-turned carton. At the nod, the black man produced the three crumpled playing cards he had been palming and replaced the cards face-down on the carton. As the punters craned forward, mesmerized by the black man's rapid patter, money clasped tight in their fists, Bill moved across the pavement and entered the warehouse.

The young man Bill had hit on the day of the funeral was stooped over a stack of cans. In response to Bill's breezy greeting he turned to look sullenly after him, his eyes blazing with hatred. As Bill disappeared up the narrow stairs, the man murmured something to his companion and slipped out of the store. He crossed the road and hurried towards the peeling facade of a gloomy café. Inside, he tossed a coin onto the bar and murmured to the owner, who stood playing a cheerless game of dice with the solitary customer. Without turning his eyes from the dice, the owner slid the money off the bar, reached beneath it and placed a cracked telephone noisily down in front of the young man. The youth dragged it to the limit of its lead and began dialling, hunched with his back to the dice players.

❖

The murmur of children reciting drifted up from the cavernous auditorium of the old cinema. At the sound, Imam Bouhila stepped from the old projection room that now served as his office and walked to the edge of the balcony. Standing with his thighs pressing against the rail and his arms folded into his armpits, he stood looking down at the scene below.

The auditorium had been stripped of its seating. The resulting space had been partitioned into rooms, the dividing walls a little taller than a man, leaving the area open to the air above. Most of the rooms were occupied. In some, men and women sat at word processors. In others, groups of men in cheap clothes sat around tables, bending earnestly over open books as younger, robed men chalked flowing Arabic characters on old-fashioned blackboards, encouraging the men as they laboriously deciphered the sounds. Separate from them, groups of women in traditional North African clothes sat in similar postures, their classes fronted by young women in the grey woollen robes adopted by Bouhila's female followers. At the furthest end of the auditorium, groups of twenty or so boys or girls in neat grey uniforms sat on low benches or cross-legged on the floor. Although aged only from around four to seven, they, too, were strictly segregated. Perfectly behaved, they listened attentively to the young women teachers or eagerly chanted back at them the Arabic phrases the teachers recited.

Beyond them, a stream of people, mostly young, hurried in and out of the street entrance, purposeful as ants. As they entered, blinking from the brightness outside, athletic young men in jeans and T-shirts with red flashes sewn onto the sleeves, scrutinized them discreetly from their places in the shadows.

The telephone trilled softly three times in the room behind him. Bouhila did not turn round until a bearded man in a dark robe and turban came from the office and approached to a respectful few feet from him. He made a soft sound in his throat. 'There is somebody on the telephone for you.'

Bouhila continued staring down, as though he had not heard. 'Who?' he said, at length, still not turning.

The man shifted uneasily. 'He refused to tell me. He said you would wish to speak to him.'

Bouhila turned with theatrical slowness. 'And you imagine I would speak to somebody who will not even announce his name?' His contemptuous eyes played like a torch on the young cleric's face.

The man gulped and shuffled, as if resisting an urge to step back a pace under the scorching beam of the stare. 'He said it concerned the Bengana family.'

A barely perceptible frown flitted over Bouhila's brow. For another second or so he continued looking at the man, but with a changed light in his eyes. With no further acknowledgment, he swept past the cringing man and disappeared into the office, closing the door firmly behind him.

He reached the phone in three swift strides and snatched it up. 'This is Imam Bouhila.'

He stood in silence for a few seconds, the flesh of his brow puckering into a deep vertical furrow. 'When was this?' He listened for another few seconds and then, without a further word, he put the phone down. He stood for a moment, his hand still resting on it, and then turned and strode out of the office and back to the balcony. 'Mademoiselle Bengana!' The boom of his voice filled the auditorium, making the children glance up with awe in their faces. 'Would you come up here please?'

Below him Keltum had been stooped over one of the girls in the senior class. At the sound of her name she looked up sharply, her face shining. She caught Bouhila's eye and nodded, at the same time flexing a leg in a movement that hinted at genuflexion. With a quick word to the class she hurried from the room.

❖

Sidi Bey's breath came in rattling gasps, making the saliva at the corner of his mouth foam and begin to run. Bill leaned forward and gently wiped the tiny trickle away with the tissue he held ready.

Sidi Bey's wife came to his side, her slippers, out of sight beneath the floor-length housecoat, making a soft scuffing sound on the linoleum. She handed him a tiny glass of tea, the third in the twenty-five minutes he had been sitting there, silently waiting for Sidi Bey to awaken from his drugged sleep. Trying to smile, she reached out and touched his wrist-watch with a plump finger. 'Soon,' she murmured. 'Awake soon.' With an apologetic expression she made a motion of injecting herself and rested her head on her hand, miming sleep.

Bill nodded and touched her hand. 'I know. You must try to rest a little, please. I will wait here with Sidi Bey. I have nothing else to do.'

Understanding his tone more than his words, she patted him affectionately on the shoulder and smiled. As she did so, the twenty years of ageing that her husband's illness and Ahmed's death had laid on her face were for an instant swept away. For just a moment her smile shimmered with the radiance he had first known twenty-six years earlier. Then, abruptly, it was gone and again he was looking at the hollows and lines that grief had etched. Impulsively, he stood up and folded her in his arms. 'Believe me, I've nowhere more important to be just now than here with you and Sidi Bey.'

She nodded shyly, smiled another fleeting smile, and withdrew into the kitchen, as though not wanting to intrude on men's affairs.

It was several more minutes before the rasping breaths died away and Sidi Bey came slowly awake. He opened his eyes and lay still as Bill sat smiling down at him. Bill turned to take the tea and sip it. As he did so, Sidi Bey frowned as though he were experiencing pain. He dragged an arm out from under the plaid rug that lay over him and reached up. His bony fingers were ice cold as they gently probed the back of Bill's head. His eyes burned into Bill's. 'They hurt you,' he breathed.

Bill shrugged, shaking his head. 'It's nothing. A knock.'

'Because of Ahmed?' He kept his eyes on Bill's, studying his expression, watching for a hint of prevarication. 'Wasn't it?' His head strained upward, a painful inch off the cushions. 'Somebody hurt you because of what you were doing for me? Because you were taking an interest in my boy's death?'

Bill hesitated, looking for a way to respond. Sidi Bey's questions had been expressed in a tone of simple certainty. He nodded. 'Yes, I think so.'

Sidi Bey's hand fell to his side. His head dropped back. 'It's my fault. I should not have asked.' Tears moistened his eyes. 'I should have let them tell their lies.'

Bill leaned closer to the old man. 'No, you shouldn't have. You are right to want to know. It's natural, Sidi Bey. The most natural thing in the world.'

Sidi Bey was breathing hard. His eyes seemed to have sunk further back into his skull. 'And *will* I know? Have you been able to find out anything, in exchange for *that*?'

He made a faint movement of his head, indicating Bill's injury.

Bill hesitated for a long time. Sitting there, watching the old man sleep, hearing the rattle of his breathing, he had considered fobbing Sidi Bey off, concocting a story that might alleviate the man's pain. Confronted with the sheer presence of the old man, his simple dignity in the face of imminent death, a lie was impossible. 'Nothing concrete, yet. Except that I'm certain that Christian Vadon was deeply involved in it.'

Sidi Bey blinked. 'The Minister?' His thin voice was tinged with contempt. 'Keltum says he and Ahmed were friends. Do you think she's right, then?'

Bill nodded. 'Yes. I'm quite sure he and Ahmed were much closer than Vadon's prepared to admit.'

Sidi Bey scowled. 'I've watched him often, on television. To me he seems a nasty, vain little man.'

Bill fingered the tender spot on his skull. 'Nasty, certainly. And they don't come any more vain. But I wouldn't be so sure about the little. It's strange, but he struck me as a very determined man. Flawed, sure, but with a lot of power in him. Except that I got the feeling of power fettered, as though he were under tremendous pressure.' He shrugged. 'Anyway, I guess all of us are flawed.' He touched the old man's hand. 'Our friends don't always see it, or don't choose to notice it. If Ahmed found things he needed in Vadon, he wouldn't necessarily have seen what you see.'

Sidi Bey sighed and gave a wounded, wistful smile. 'I know. There were many things we disagreed on.' He gave a barely perceptible shrug. 'My own father thought I was mad to come here. Worse, he thought I was betraying my own people.'

'Perhaps his grand-daughter has inherited something of him,' Bill said, smiling gently.

Sidi Bey smiled, too, his smile a wan reflection of Bill's. 'Don't be hard on Keltum. She has her reasons.' Seeing Bill drop his eyes, the old man laid a hand on his knee. 'No, I didn't mean that. Of course she was hurt, and perhaps it made her vulnerable, but no one is to blame. It happens to many young women. It's part of the price they pay for living the Western way. In my time, our young women did not have the freedom to choose, but then they did not get hurt.' He shook his head. 'Not in that way, at least.' His voice dropped to a whisper. 'My wife and I were very lucky, William. Believe me, it did not always work out as it did for us.' He sighed. 'Frankly, I don't know which way is better. And it's the same with Keltum. Who's to say that what she has found with Bouhila is not the right way for her?'

Bill's eyebrows twitched. 'You really think it could be?' He shook his head. 'I've seen enough Fundamentalist religion of one sort or another at home. It frightens me.'

'Me, too, in a way. But we both have to try to understand the context. Bouhila did not appear out of nowhere, William. Arabs here *do* feel despised, feel that they aren't given the same rights as the others. I don't mean the immigrants, like me, William. I mean the ones born here, French people. Like Keltum,' he added, in a whisper.

'You *really* think that Keltum felt that? With so many friends? God, Sidi Bey, *none* of her friends were Arabs.'

Sidi Bey sighed. 'No, but for a woman perhaps it's different, the prejudices don't work in the same way. Perhaps that was even part of the problem. I think maybe one day she felt she was turning her back on something. Perhaps the way her brother was treated contributed to it.'

Bill bit his lip. 'You think she saw it, too?'

Sidi Bey, paused, getting his breath, tiring now. 'She is such a bright young woman, so perceptive. She saw beyond the money and the photographs in magazines. She might even have seen more than was really there. But she had her own experience to guide her. You know, she was very sensitive about the way Arab men were treated at the university, the way the women shunned them. She is convinced it was partly that which had made Ahmed what he was.'

Bill looked into the old man's face, unable to conceal his surprise. It was the first time he had ever heard Sidi Bey acknowledge his son's homosexuality. He was looking for a response when Sidi Bey grasped his sleeve with a surprising wiry strength. 'You were there with Ahmed, William. Tell me, is it not so? Did the women even speak to him?'

Bill paused, thinking back to the encounters with girls, the cafeteria queues, the cafés, the parties crammed into the tiny studio apartments. He shook his head. 'Not the French ones, anyway,' he murmured. 'Hardly ever.'

Sidi Bey's head sank deeper into the cushions. 'So, be kind to Keltum, William. Try to understand her. Try to see beyond the personality of Bouhila, to the good things she is personally involved in: the education, the work with young people, keeping them off the streets. It's there, you know, whatever you think of the rest.'

'It's hard, Sidi Bey. To me, Bouhila's just another in a long line of unscrupulous bastards, exploiting vulnerable young people for his own ends.' A smile lit his face as he leant close to Sidi Bey. 'But I'll try, I promise you, I'll try!'

Sidi Bey smiled a ghostly response. 'Thank you, William,' he murmured, his lips hardly moving. His eyelids had begun to droop.

Bill craned forward, his face inches from the old man's. 'Sidi Bey, listen to me, please. Did Ahmed ever talk to *you* about Vadon, or to his mother? Did he say *anything* about the man, something that I could use as a starting point, leverage, to confront him?'

Sidi Bey moved his head a fraction on the pillow, the better to look into Bill's eyes. There was something in the gaze that impelled Bill to silence. He sat, staring back into the ravaged face. The cancer had gnawed away the flesh from beneath the skin, leaving it draped tight over the bones. Below the emaciated brow the dark brown eyes burned beneath translucent, almost purple, eyelids. Bill swallowed, battered by the physical shock of the realization that he was looking, quite literally, into the face of death. As he looked, tears flowed from the glittering eyes. 'Never, William. In these last years he never talked to us about his life out there.' His gaze flickered for an instant to the door, indicating the world outside it, the mysterious, unknowable Parisian life beyond the confines of his own, immigrant world. 'Not to us.'

The effort of straining to hear the barely audible voice had drawn him closer to Sidi Bey, so that their faces were almost touching. They were still in that position when the door was thrown violently open. Keltum rushed across the room to them, leaving the door swinging back on its hinges. At the sight of her father's tears, her face, already angry, contorted in a flash of fury. She grabbed at the cloth of Bill's jacket, yanking him aside. 'Get away from my father! Leave him alone!'

As Bill reared back, shocked at the force of her words, she fell to her knees, forcing her way between him and her father. Laying her cheek against Sidi Bey's, she began stroking his hair with an open palm and speaking in a low, crooning voice, repeating the same sounds over and over.

Bill stood quite still for a moment, letting die the spark of real anger that had ignited in him at the way she had thrust him aside, then, pulling the cloth of his jacket straight, he strode across to close the door. Madame Bengana stood in the kitchen doorway, looking from him to Keltum with an expression filled with pain and confusion. Bill moved across and put an arm round her shoulders, giving her a brief, reassuring hug.

She returned his smile with an uncertain, shy one of her own. Then, to alleviate her sense of helplessness, she disappeared into the kitchen to prepare more mint tea. She emerged a moment later and handed Bill a glass. They stood side by side in silence, Bill sipping his tea, Madame Bengana smiling in apologetic embarrassment, watching the scene at the bedside.

It was two or three minutes before Keltum raised her head from her father's and turned to look at Bill. The lovely calm that had settled over her face was shattered as her anger flooded back. She got to her feet, already talking. 'You have no right to do that! You mustn't keep coming here, upsetting my father.' She advanced across the room to him, her eyes blazing. 'You have no business interfering here. My brother's death is family business. Not yours.' With an angry toss of her head she brushed aside her mother's nervous attempt to speak. In full flood now, she jabbed a finger at him.

'This is a matter for us, for our own people! We can solve our problems ourselves. We don't need help from *you*.' The last word was emphasized by a horizontal slashing motion of the extended finger, the universal sign of uncompromising rejection.

Bill watched for a moment in silence as she stood trembling, her chest heaving, on the edge of tears. She had spoken in a rush, on a high, unnatural note. It was as though the words had been somehow learned and she was nervous of forgetting them. And she had seemed to be talking not just to him, but to a whole culture, a whole hostile world. Abruptly, the pent-up tears began to flow.

'Oh, hell,' he whispered to himself, putting down his glass on the shiny sideboard that had replaced the one damaged in the burglary. Briefly touching the arm of Madame Bengana, who stood wringing her hands and looking from one to the other with a grieving expression, he moved towards Keltum.

'Look, Keltum,' he said gently, making as though to take her by the arm. She shook him off with a violent spasm, as though his hand were some loathsome parasite. He dropped his hand and began again.

'Look, Keltum, Your father needed to talk. If I let him go on too long, if I tired him, I'm sorry. It won't happen again.' He glanced down at Sidi Bey. The old man was already asleep. He went on, his voice a whisper. 'But as for what you said about Ahmed's death not being my business . . . well, heaven knows I respect your feelings about that . . . but you're wrong. It is my business, for a lot of reasons. Some of which you know.' He dropped his voice. 'And some of which you don't.'

At his last words she looked at him sharply, wary and expectant, demanding more.

'Look, you know the story, how Ahmed and I met. He quite probably saved my life.'

She dropped her eyes. 'Of course I know. It's part of our family folklore. Although I think you and Ahmed probably dramatized it. You can't *really* have thought those people were going to *kill* you.'

He shook his head. 'All I can tell you, is that I saw the look on the face of the one that hit me. And so did your brother.' He spoke very quietly. 'And I've seen it again since. In the service. Always, and only, on the faces of men who *were* about to kill. You haven't seen it, Keltum, I have. You cut people adrift from the law, from any rules, and you find out the world is full of people like that, waiting for their opportunity. Well, for a few days back then, there were no rules. And there were plenty of people ready to take their chance.' She remained silent, her eyes cast down. He went on speaking. 'Ahmed took a very serious risk to help me. And, to answer the question your eyes were asking, I let him down when he needed help from me. As badly as I needed it then. I want to put that straight, Keltum, if I can.'

'What do you mean?'

He looked into her drawn, aggressive eyes and shook his head. 'Maybe I'll tell you all about it someday. For now, just let me do what I have to do for your father's sake.'

She shook her head, her eyes closed, her hands clenched into tight fists. 'No! Please, do as I ask you.'

He tried to take one of her hands. She withdrew it, holding her clenched fists hard up against her chest. With another quick glance at Madame Bengana, he went on talking. 'I can't, Keltum. Please believe me. Your father asked me to do what I'm doing, to set *his* mind at rest. It isn't that he, or I, don't think that *you* care deeply, too. God knows, we all understand that you do. But his needs come first. They have to.' With a glance down at Sidi Bey, he moved closer to her. 'Your father's dying, Keltum. I *have* to keep my promise to him. I'll try as hard as I can not to hurt your feelings, but his wishes are what count most. If he asks me to stop what I'm doing, then I'll stop. Until then I just can't, Keltum. You understand that, don't you?'

She stood quite rigid, staring into his face. Muscles worked in her face as she fought to control the turbulent emotions that were etched into it. It took a few moments before she felt ready to speak. 'You just haven't understood anything at all, have you, Bill?' she said with an incredulous, intense bitterness that rocked him. 'We just don't *want* your help. You were part of what was wrong for Ahmed. Even my father doesn't understand that. There's no need to look any further to know why Ahmed was so lost. Your very presence here. Now!' She gestured angrily, stabbing a finger at the floor at his feet. 'It's wrong! You think you belong here. You just can't seem to comprehend how wrong you are, how out of place you are here.'

For a moment he stared at her, dumbfounded by the bitterness of her words. Then, he shook his head. 'That hurts, Keltum. But, if that's how you feel, then okay, I won't come back.'

Her eyes lit up. She was about to speak when he cut in again.

'*After* I've done what I have to do for Sidi Bey. After that I'll be out of your life for good, if that's what you want. Meanwhile, though, I made a promise to help, so I . . .'

She broke in, anger flashing in her eyes. 'A promise to *help*!'

He shrugged, nodding. 'I guess that's about it.'

'Hah!' she exclaimed, as though she had caught him in a lie. 'You people! You're rich, you've been to the best schools, above all you're white, and yet you all believe that you understand. Bill, can't you get it into your head that one of the things we've been doing wrong has been listening to people like you? We've waited, *believing* that somebody, somewhere, was going to help. And what did it ever get us? Nothing!' She made another of the slashing movements with her finger, as though she were practising disembowelling him. She was panting with emotion. When she spoke again her voice was softer, faintly mocking. 'And yet you even want to help us with family problems. Well, we're tired of depending on outsiders . . .'

He raised a hand in protest, patting gently at the air. '*You*, Keltum,' he said softly. 'Not *we*. What you think of me is your business. Don't speak for your father like that, though. He's not dead yet.'

She blinked away a fresh surge of tears. She shook her head violently, looking down at the floor. 'He ought to trust us. If he wants to know what Ahmed was really going through, he should ask the Imam.'

'Bouhila?' What started as a derisive laugh died away as he looked into her eyes. 'You mean that? Bouhila knew Ahmed that well?'

'Of course. He tried to help my brother. He understood. He wants to help us through this. He would help my father, if only I could persuade him to agree to see the Imam. He warned me that you would try to interfere, to come between me and my father.'

He shook his head, understanding dawning in him. 'Bouhila sent you here,' he murmured. 'Isn't that right? He knew I was here and he sent you to get rid of me. That's why you sounded so unlike yourself, wasn't it? Those were his words, weren't they?'

She flushed, her eyes on the floor. 'No! That's not true . . . I . . .' She broke off, floundering and confused.

'Oh, my God, Keltum.' As he spoke he glanced behind him at Madame Bengana. She remained in the same position, her hands clasped, an apprehensive half-smile on her face, waiting for some good news. Relieved that she did not seem to be following the exchange, Bill gave her a quick smile of reassurance and turned back to face Keltum.

'You know what *really* bothers him, don't you? He wants control. Of you, of everybody he has dealings with. All that nonsense at the funeral, his kids strutting round in their armbands, playing at policemen, it's all part of it. He knows I'm out of his reach, so I'm a threat. It's as simple as this: your father listens to me, and Bouhila's afraid you might, too, afraid of losing you.' His face softened into a self-mocking smile. 'After all, you used to listen to me, even if it seems a long time ago.' The smile faded again as she went on staring at the floor. He sighed. 'Well, he's right about one thing, Keltum. He *doesn't* control me. I'm sorry, I know it will be hard for you to do it, but you're going to have to tell him I wouldn't listen to you. That I plan to stay as long as Sidi Bey wants me to.' He paused, watching her face. Her eyes were still cast down, her face pinched and pale. The tears had stopped. 'And that if I find out he was hounding Ahmed, and that it had anything whatsoever to do with his suicide, I'll make myself a *hell* of a nuisance.'

For a long moment there was total silence as they stood facing each other, Keltum still staring down, her face blanched and tense, Bill half smiling, watching for some sign of the old warmth.

'William!' Sidi Bey's breathy rasp made them both turn, startled, to face him. He still lay deep in the cushions, as though asleep. Only the glitter of his dark eyes told them he had been listening. With an exclamation, Keltum made to drop to her knees. His fingers fluttered in a tiny, but unmistakable gesture. 'Please, my dear. I need to speak to William.' She hesitated, her eyes on his face. He watched her, waiting. At last, darting a glance at Bill, she spun and hurried away to her bedroom, slamming the door behind her. Sidi Bey moved his fingers again, calling Bill closer. Bill knelt. As he did so, Sidi Bey's hand closed round his, once again surprising him by the unexpected reserve of strength in its grip. The old man's eroded face lit in an effortful smile.

'Don't be angry with her, William, please.'

Bill laughed softly, shaking his head. 'Not angry, old friend. Worried. I'm afraid for her. It all has too many ugly echoes of our own cults. It frightens me to see Keltum sucked into anything like that.'

Sidi Bey's head moved a fraction. 'I know. Perhaps she'll get over it, though, in her own good time.' A distant look came into his eyes as he spoke. In the look was the knowledge that Keltum's time would not be his. He had lost his son, and now his daughter had gone, off into a world where he would never be able to follow her. 'Promise me you'll always be kind to her, William.'

Bill nodded, squeezing the brittle fingers. 'I will, Sidi Bey. I promise you, I will.' He stood up. 'Goodbye now. Keltum's right, I've tired you more than enough for today.' With a wave of his fingers, he turned away, making for the door. As he did so, Madame Bengana gave a soft sob and stepped forward to enfold him in an embrace. She clung to him for a long time, the desperate force of her embrace expressing all the emotion her poor French prevented her speaking. At length, he kissed her cheek and gently disengaged himself. 'Goodbye. Take care of him.' He turned away, his eyes stinging, and moved towards the door.

As he let himself out a sound made him turn. Keltum stood behind the door of her bedroom, which opened off the cramped hall, watching him. She stared back for a moment, her face defiant, and then abruptly wheeled and disappeared into the bedroom. In the moment she turned away he caught the shine of fresh tears starting from her eyes. 'Be gentle with them, Keltum, please,' he called softly at the slamming door. 'Don't ask too much.'

Emerging from the twilight of the store into the sunlit street, he paused. Squinting, as if to let his eyes grow accustomed to the brightness, he surveyed the area. Satisfied there was no immediate danger, no loitering men, no parked car with its engine running, he set off, striding briskly. The image that kept coming to mind as he walked was the expression on Keltum's face as she had torn him from her father's side. It had been a strange, disturbing look. Her eyes had held something that wasn't quite hatred, nor even contempt, which almost denied his existence. He realized with a sinking heart that what he had seen were the eyes of a zealot.

Without slowing, disliking himself for it even as he did it, he side-stepped into an open-fronted cloth merchant's store, pushing through a group of women that browsed among the garish swathes of cloth that hung suspended from rolls overhead. Pivoting, he looked back through the skeins of material, examining the street. Nobody moved for cover, nobody turned suddenly to the windows of the dilapidated stores, discovering a sudden passion for cheap kitchenware. He was not being followed. He stepped from the store and went on walking, slower now, his eyes peeled for a cruising cab.

12

With the detours it was almost an hour later when the cab drew up in the rue Galilée. In that hour he had gone over his situation a dozen times in his mind. And it had left him with his senses reeling, as though he had blundered into somebody else's nightmare. Sidi Bey's request was one he could not contemplate turning down. His debt to the Bengana family, his failure to respond to Ahmed's cry for help, made a refusal impossible. And yet, it meant that, single-handed, he was up against powers he could not measure, powers that had been able to subvert the entire press corps as well as the police. They'd had his phone tapped. They had been able to have him followed by thugs and beaten up in broad daylight. They could just as easily choose to have him killed, with the same impunity. But the people who could have helped him most were Keltum and Lantier, both of whom had some agenda of their own. Keltum, under Bouhila's influence, wanted nothing better than for him to take the first plane home. Lantier was using him as a pawn in some personal chess game.

He paid off the driver, taking plenty of time to check carefully around him, examining cars lest there was one with its engine running in readiness to mount the pavement and mow him down, scanning the sprinkling of pedestrians for any that looked athletic enough to give him trouble. Satisfied, he jumped from the cab and strode the few paces to the entrance. As he went – an innocent man in an almost deserted Paris street, within sight of half a dozen policemen, and yet with his senses strained to snapping point – he was struck by a sudden haunted sensation. It was the feeling that he had somehow fallen through the looking glass, back into the distorted world of the intelligence professionals he had once worked among, the crazed half-children for whom life was not worth living without a diet of intrigue and subterfuge.

He stepped inside the glass doors and stood panting, letting his nerves slacken. He had the Charlie Brenner show due to open in eight days. He should be there now to begin preparations for the hanging. Solange would already be going crazy. She had no objection to being left to deal with the insurance widows and the Wall Street wives. She knew she was good with them, a gentle marvel at deluding them into believing that her sure tastes were their own. But the prospect of organizing a show single-handed sent her into the early stages of paralysis. Two more days would be as much as he could spare, and as much as he could stand. After that, he would call Lantier, tell him everything he had been able to learn, and go home.

'Monsieur Duvall!'

He looked up sharply to see one of the porters, a burly, short-breathed man whose cheeks were purple with broken veins, grinning suggestively at him and holding up a sheaf of mail. 'Messages for you, Monsieur.' He brandished the papers. 'There's one caller very anxious to speak to you. Very persistent.' There was a smirk in his voice. 'She must have called a dozen times already.'

Bill plucked the wad from the man's hand, smiling mirthlessly at his wheedling tone, and headed for the lift, sifting the messages as he went. Two of them were faxes from Solange. He glanced quickly through them and smiled. It was definitely time to call and soothe her, persuade her to hold the fort for a couple more days. The next item was an envelope, in the familiar livery of the DHL courier service. He read it while waiting for the lift. By the time the lift arrived, he was laughing aloud, startling the elderly American couple who stepped out. It was a letter from Amy detailing what she had in mind when they finally did make it out to the Cape. No wonder she had used the courier service. Apart from the fact it could take a letter a week to travel from one end of Manhattan to the other, it would have been a federal offence to send it through the mail. He shuffled it to the back, intending to read it again inside the apartment, and stepped into the lift, looking through the remaining message slips as he went. They explained the porter's smirk.

There were eleven in all, timed at ten or twenty minute intervals throughout the last two and a half hours. The most recent had come only a few minutes earlier. Frowning, he flipped through them again. The message was the same each time. Somebody called Virginie had been trying to reach him. The last message announced that she intended to try again in twenty minutes. He glanced at his watch. He had a little under a quarter of an hour to decide whether to leave the phone off the hook.

He stepped out of the lift and slid the key into the lock of the flat, still trying to think who he knew by the name of Virginie.

'Monsieur Duvall, do you have a minute?'

He spun to face the voice, his fists already up in front of him, his knees flexed. He remained in the same posture for a moment before slowly unwinding. 'God, it's you. You gave me a shock.'

Lantier laughed. 'See how edgy you are? I told you you should go home.'

Bill shrugged, loosening his shoulders. 'Yeah, I remember that. As you see, I didn't take you up on it, though.'

Lantier nodded. 'No. I didn't think you would, really. I'd like to talk to you for a few minutes. May I come in?'

Bill closed the door behind them and walked ahead of Lantier into the room. His shirt and jacket, soaked from an hour spent leaning against the plastic upholstery of the taxi, were chill against his back. He stripped them off. 'You won't mind if I take a shower?'

Lantier inclined his head. 'Make yourself at home.'

'I'll try, although home never feels quite *like* home with a policeman in the living room. Want a drink?'

Lantier smiled. 'A cold beer?'

'Help yourself. I'll have one, too, while you're there.' Bill stepped out of the rest of his clothes. 'What is it you want to talk to me about?' he asked across the counter of the kitchenette. 'I thought we'd been over the ground pretty thoroughly already.'

Lantier came back round the counter, swigging from a bottle of Kronenbourg. He handed another opened bottle to Bill. 'Tell me about your meeting with Vadon,' he said quietly.

Naked, Bill gave the bottle a distasteful glance and pushed past Lantier into the kitchenette. He found a glass and poured the beer carefully into it. 'I already told you about it, didn't I?' he said, taking a long draught and moving towards the bathroom, carrying the glass with him.

Lantier ambled to the door behind him and leant against the frame. 'Tell me again, from the beginning. As near verbatim as you can do it.'

Bill looked out at him, frowning, from the shower. He was reaching for the tap when the phone on the wall rang. He hesitated for a moment and then stepped out again and unhooked it.

'Bill?' The voice was harsh, uncultivated, the accent on his name strong enough to make it rhyme with 'peel'.

He screwed up his face, scanning his memory for the sound and not finding it. 'That's right. This is Bill Duvall. Who are you?'

'Virginie, of course! And you're a *horrible* man.' She spoke with clumsy coquettishness. 'You've been in Paris for *days* and you've never even called me! You're a monster!'

He winced at the leaden gaiety of her tone. 'I'm sorry, this is Bill Duvall, but you must be confusing me with somebody else. I don't believe I know anybody by the name of Virginie. Goodbye, madame.'

He had begun taking the phone from his ear when she attempted a little laugh. It came over as a cackle. 'Oh! Bill, you absolute beast! How can you pretend to have forgotten me so soon, after, well, everything?'

He shook his head, grimacing at Lantier, who was grinning at him from the doorway. 'Look, Miss? Madame? I got your messages. You'll have to excuse me, but I really don't have a notion who you are or what you're talking about. I'd appreciate it if you would believe that and just leave me alone. Would you mind?' He hung the phone back onto its rest, giving Lantier a mystified shrug. 'Who the hell was *that*, I wonder? She's been calling all afternoon.'

'A prostitute, probably. They've got a lot of competition these days from amateurs, housewives, a lot of them. They work through the minitel system, over the phone.' He gestured with the beer bottle. 'No pimps to pay, so they can be very competitive. The old-fashioned professionals can't afford to hang around the streets any more. They have to take their trade to where the business is. That's one of the tricks they're using. Probably got your name from a porter. Calls, strikes up a conversation, gets herself invited up.' He laughed as Bill reached out and unhooked the phone again, letting it dangle against the tiled wall. 'Don't let me stop you.'

Bill scowled. At the same time a frown shadowed Lantier's grin. 'How long did you say she's been calling?'

Bill stepped back into the shower and turned on the water. 'Since the middle of the afternoon,' he shouted from behind the glass.

Lantier's grin disappeared completely. He took another slow swig of beer. 'Okay,' he said at length. 'Where were we? You were going to tell me about your talk with our highly respected Minister.'

By the time Bill stepped from the shower, he had gone over once again the whole of his meeting with Vadon. Lantier was chewing at his lip, dangling the empty beer bottle from a finger thrust into its neck. 'So all you *really* have is a conviction that he was lying?'

'Christ, Lantier, he was lying in his *teeth*. Without a shadow of a doubt.'

Lantier stood musing for a while as Bill towelled down. As he made to pull on a thick white robe, Lantier waggled the bottle, indicating the purple bruise the size of a man's hand on Bill's thigh. 'And the people who did that, you're *absolutely* sure that those people weren't just trying to rob you?'

'Ah, come on. If they had wanted my wallet one of them would have just shown me a knife. There would have been no need to beat me up.'

'It doesn't necessarily follow. Some of those thugs *enjoy* hurting people. Maybe something frightened them off before they finished.'

'Come on, Inspector, this happened in the middle of the Esplanade des Invalides. You've got half a dozen ministries, the Invalides itself, all within two minutes' walk. If they wanted to mug someone, the Métro corridors are thick with defenceless tourists. That area must be crawling with police.' He shook his head. 'Those characters *knew* they didn't have to worry about that.' He took his beer from off the sink unit and drank off a draught. 'Shit, for all you or I know, they might have *been* police.'

Lantier screwed up his face but made no answer. Bill led the way out of the bathroom and went to get two more beers from the kitchenette. He watched Lantier across the counter as he opened them. 'And there's more. This afternoon I went over to the Bengana showroom.'

Lantier took a pace closer and leaned on the counter, his eyes narrowing shrewdly. 'Go on.'

'I spent a while talking to Ahmed's partner – his ex-partner, that is.'

'Monsieur Burgos?' Lantier said ruefully.

'Right. He told me you had been in touch.'

Lantier ignored the trace of irony Bill allowed into his voice. 'M'mm. What did he have to say?'

Bill slid the a bottle across the counter. 'That Ahmed seemed to have been coming more and more under his sister's influence. And he had been acting strangely in the days before he died, as though he were under tremendous strain.'

'People don't usually commit suicide because they're so pleased with the way things are working out.'

'Come on, Inspector, no wisecracks. Ahmed Bengana was a friend of mine.'

Lantier inclined his head. 'Sorry.'

Bill shrugged. 'Okay. Anyway, I'm just telling you what the man said. The poor guy was pretty cut up.' He hesitated and then went on, in a lower voice. 'They had been lovers for years, you know.'

'I didn't know, but I'd probably made the assumption.'

'I thought you probably would have. What might be interesting is that in the last few weeks Ahmed had been giving him the cold shoulder. He was badly cut up.'

Lantier sucked at his teeth. 'M'mm. Those people can be pretty . . . ah, dramatic, though.'

'I thought we were talking about whether, or maybe just *why*, Vadon's been hamstringing your police work,' Bill said pointedly. 'Anyway, I would have thought losing the person you care for most is something to be dramatic about.'

Lantier took a long draught of beer, his eyes staying on Bill's. At length, he lowered the bottle and dropped his eyes, nodding, his expression rueful. 'Yes.' When he looked up again a flicker of regret was still dying in his eyes. 'What else did he tell you?'

'He thinks someone was in Ahmed's workroom just before he took off to throw himself from Vadon's window.'

Lantier stopped, his bottle half-way to his lips. 'Ah,' he said slowly. 'Now things *are* getting interesting. What makes him think that? Did he see anyone?'

Bill strolled back into the room, still towelling himself one-handed. 'No, but the office door was closed. Ahmed *never* closed it, I can vouch for that myself. Also, the place was in total chaos. It's possible Ahmed flipped and did it himself, but I'd say it was too systematic for that. If you ask me, the room had been gone over, by pros.'

Lantier nodded. 'Anything else?'

'From Burgos, nothing in particular. But I was followed when I left there.'

'Again? Did they try to beat you up?'

'They didn't get a chance. I gave them the slip. Four clowns in a Citroën. You want the number? Three-seven-seven E-X-N seventy-five. And that one will be stolen, too,' he said wryly, as Lantier pulled out a notebook.

Grinning, Lantier snapped the book shut and shoved it back into a pocket. 'No doubt.' Turning abruptly away from Bill, Lantier took a few paces into the room and stood, still facing away from him, as though debating with himself. 'Something else has happened since you came to see me,' he said, at length, over his shoulder.

Bill watched expectantly, saying nothing, as Lantier turned to face him. 'I've been promoted.'

Bill stared at him and then a slow, ironic smile spread across his face.

Lantier's grave expression gave way to a sudden grin. 'Yes. Subtle, aren't they? I was given the news a couple of hours ago.'

Bill glanced automatically at his wrist, where his watch would have been. 'Just about the time I left Burgos.'

Lantier gave a slight bow of acknowledgment. 'The call came from the Prefect of Police, in person. A considerable honour, you understand. I'm seconded to the Ministry of Transport. They have a major traffic study in hand. I'll be helping to take the city into the twenty-first century,' he added, in a toneless drone.

'I've been in cities that are there already. Paris is better off in this one. Did you accept?' There was a hint of derision in the question.

Lantier shook his head. 'You think I should refuse and stay where I might still get a chance to poke around this case? Don't delude yourself. This isn't Hollywood. If I refuse I'll find myself transferred to some crummy spot on the Belgian border, freezing my ass off all winter, pissing with rain all summer. And their idea of a crime wave is an outbreak of rooster rustling.' He shook his head. 'This way I at least get to stay in Paris.'

'And I can look forward to improved traffic flow. How much do you know about traffic, anyway?'

Lantier snorted. 'Nothing. But you've tried to leave town on a Friday afternoon, haven't you? Could I do worse?'

Bill laughed. 'You'd have to work at it.' His laugh died. 'But look, are you telling me that you're no longer involved in any kind of serious police work? To tell you the truth, I can only afford to be around for another couple of days, but in case I *do* turn up anything really concrete, who am I supposed to tell?'

Lantier gave him a grim smile. 'Me. That's the other reason I came here.' As he spoke, he reached into an inner pocket and pulled out a card. 'I'm moving to the Ministry as of tomorrow morning. I'll have to start dressing like a civil servant,' he said, gesturing at his stained linen jacket, 'but I'll still be a policeman. If anything comes up, anything at all you want to tell me about, call me on this number.' He stooped and wrote a number next to the one printed on the card. 'It's my home number. I'll be working regular hours now, so you'll get me most evenings from around seven, or before eight in the morning. And do yourself, and me, a favour. Remember we may not be alone on the line.' He handed over the card. 'Of course, my official advice to you is still to go home. Today.' Bill took the hand Lantier offered. The warmth of the handshake took him by surprise. 'Goodbye, Monsieur Duvall. And please take very great care.'

❖

It was almost two in the morning when Bill's taxi once again drew up in front of the building. After Lantier's departure he had slept for three hours. He had woken sore and stiff and with the head wound still blindingly painful to any but the tenderest touch. Nevertheless, he had felt well enough to take up the invitation to attend a cocktail party in honour of Carl Unger. Somebody had handed him the invitation during the evening at Michel Polini's studio. He personally regarded Unger's pictures as derivative, untalented daubs. However, they hung in every major museum of modern art in Europe and America. And, anyway, the point of these functions was not the pictures but the people. He had been certain that the reception, at the Museum of Modern Art, close by the Trocadero, would attract a high-powered guest list of influential collectors.

He had been right about the pictures, and right about the guests, too. Considering it was August, he had been able to talk to a surprising number of useful people. Maybe they had been attracted by the presence of Jacques Chirac, the Mayor of Paris, himself breaking his vacation for the forthcoming parade.

By a quarter to midnight, after several hours of too much champagne and too little food, he had been about to leave, prompted by the persistent throbbing in his skull. He was on his way out of the door when Michel had insisted that he join a group he was inviting to a restaurant. By the time Bill had managed to extricate himself and clamber into a cab, he was almost fainting with fatigue and the delayed reaction to the day.

He fumbled money from his pocket and thrust it into the driver's hand. Too tired to wait for change, he waved away the cabbie's thanks and climbed out. Despite the fatigue and the alcohol, he studied the shadows carefully before striding the few steps to the door. The usual sprinkling of late-night people sat among the plants in the lobby, the men in small groups or alone, the women conspicuously alone except for their trademark packs of extra-long cigarettes and designer lighters. Bill was half-way to the lift when one of the women sprang up from a sofa and stepped into his path.

'Bill Duvall!' she cried, speaking louder than necessary, as though she, too, had been drinking. She stepped towards him, her arms outstretched.

Realizing a fraction too late that she intended to throw them round his neck, he recoiled, half-laughing in his surprise, only partly fending off her lunge.

'Bill Duvall,' she shouted, giggling, 'Do you know you're a bastard? An absolute bastard!' As she spoke she kept coming at him. Her face, big-boned and coarsely handsome, surrounded by a frizzy mane of vividly dyed red hair, was eighteen inches from his.

He stepped back, no longer laughing, his arms raised, elbows into his sides, keeping her at bay as she threw herself forward again. If she had been a man, he would have jabbed an elbow into the exposed midriff. As it was, he grabbed her by the upper arms and shoved her away from him, stumbling a little as he did so.

A frown flitted across her face at the pressure of his fingers, but still she came crowding back, obviously bent on embracing him.

She was a big woman, hard to stop without coming close to violence. Still reluctant to use too much force, he gave a little ground under her weight. She laughed, loudly. 'I've been trying to call you all day.' With Bill's fingers still biting into her arms, she suddenly bent forward from the waist.

Fatigue and champagne had blurred Bill's reactions just enough. He jerked his head back a fraction too late. The kiss brushed his lips, catching him low on the side of the jaw. Exasperated, and revolted at the tang of lipstick, he thrust her roughly away from him, making her stagger.

'Sorry, madame,' he said, through gritted teeth. 'You must be confusing me with somebody else. We've never met.'

Recovering her balance, she threw back her head and looked around in stagey disbelief. Every eye in the room was on them. Behind the desk the two night porters stood shoulder to shoulder, trying not to grin too openly. He made to step past her. As he drew level she reached out again, taking hold of his sleeve. 'Oh, please, Bill,' she said pleadingly. 'Don't be mean. I've been sitting here for absolutely *ages*.' She half turned, her hand still extended, as though to accompany him to the lift.

Genuine anger flashed in Bill's face. He took hold of her hand and lifted it from his sleeve, squeezing the knuckles hard enough to make her face pinch. 'Sorry, madame. I told you, you're making a mistake. We don't know each other.'

As he shoved her hand away from him, she looked round at the porters, trying a mischievous grin. The pressure of his fingers had squeezed some of the sparkle from it. She tried to put her hand back on his arm, but with less conviction now as she saw the anger that flashed dangerously in Bill's eyes. 'Please, dear, don't be like that,' she said, affecting a parody of a little-girl voice that sat embarrassingly with the hair and the coarse make-up. 'Not with little me.'

With a glance at the grinning onlookers, he took hold of her wrist and drew her towards him. 'Look,' he muttered, his lips hardly moving. 'I've had a long hard day and I'm tired. I don't need your services, and I don't want you pawing me. Have you got that?' He tightened his fingers, making her give a soft moan of surprise. 'Now, please get out of my way and go find yourself another punter.' Dropping her hand, he brushed past her and entered the lift.

She stood watching him go, trying a desolate smile as she fingered her wrist. His last impression as the lift doors slid shut was of the smile dissolving into a very public fit of tears.

He closed the door of the flat with a deep sigh and fell into a sofa. He sat motionless for a full minute, his face in his hands. In the hotels where he spent much of his time prostitutes were part of the furniture. They knew their market well enough. A glance was sufficient to tell them he was a waste of time. Yet, he'd almost had to hit the woman before she would back off. Either times were as hard for them as Lantier had suggested, or the whole screwy business was getting him down so much he was completely off his stride. With another long sigh, he rose and walked slowly into the bathroom, casting off his clothes as he went. He ran a deep, hot bath and lay down in it, letting the heat dissolve away the aches. A quarter of an hour later, he towelled off and went to bed, dog-tired, depressed, and looking forward to the moment when he would be telling Sidi Bey he was calling the whole thing off. Within seconds, he was deeply asleep, his breath coming in slow, even rasps.

◆

He sat up with a start. Wide-awake and listening hard, he strained to pick out images in the faint glow of streetlights that filtered through the curtains. The silence was so total he could almost hear his head throbbing. He turned to the bedside clock. Four-thirty. He groaned and sank back onto his pillow, chewing at the stale taste of the champagne. He hesitated for a few seconds, torn between the desire to sink back to sleep and the need to drink some water. Sighing, he threw back the quilt and walked to the bathroom. The windowless room was pitch black. He reached out and flipped on the light.

'Oh, God!' His stomach churning, he staggered a step back into the bedroom. He gagged, forcing back the first bitter taste of vomit. Shaking himself like a dog, he stepped forward again, gripping the doorframe. 'Oh, my God,' he repeated, his voice barely audible. He kept on whispering the words to himself, over and over again. The red-headed woman gazed at him from where she sat, slumped on the toilet. The scarlet grin of her gaping mouth was mimicked by the red crescent of her slashed neck.

He stood rigid and silent in the doorway. The woman was propped against the tiled wall, naked to the waist. Blood from her neck and from a dozen deep slashes on her breasts had run down over the thick roll of fat at her belly and into her lap. It lay in a pool where the leather mini-skirt had rucked up over her thighs. Her tights were ripped, as though in a struggle. Around her, the whole room was awash with blood. The marble surfaces, the shower door, the towels, the bath, everything was streaked crimson. Even the ceiling was spattered.

Numbed, Bill let his hand fall from the doorframe to his side. A stickiness made him look blankly down. Blood had smeared from his hand onto his thigh. He stared down at himself in mute dismay. More blood matted the hair on his chest. He looked dumbly from his bloodied hand to his chest, struggling to concentrate on his movements of the last few seconds. He could not remember touching his chest. A shudder of revulsion shook him, making his teeth click together. He spun from the doorway and flicked on the bedroom light. The bed was bloodied. There were stains on the carpet, already turning brownish over the dark green pile. He moaned aloud as realization hit him. He sprinted to the living-room door and switched on the light. A heavy armchair lay on its back. The woman's blouse, jacket and brassiere lay scattered. A shoe protruded from beneath the sofa, a broken gold necklace lay tangled among the cushions. A half-smoked cigarette smouldered in an ashtray, the lipstick stains visible from across the room. There was no sign of a weapon. He knew, with absolute, freezing certainty that it was there somewhere, pushed out of sight to be found later. His mind racing, but already cooler as he emerged from the first shock of it, he turned and ran the few strides to the bedroom closet. He snatched a clean quilt and hurried for the bathroom.

This was without a doubt the work of the people who had tried to run him down. It was their way of expressing their disappointment that he had not taken their hint and left the country. He hurled the quilt down onto the blood-soaked floor and walked across it to the shower.

He showered in less than twenty seconds, removing every trace of blood, and returned to the bedroom. He dried himself perfunctorily on a corner of the sheet and pulled on some clothes.

The twenty seconds in the shower had been all he needed to figure out his options. There were only two of them. He could call the police, or he could run. Except that whoever had done this, whoever had just left this room, was probably calling the police for him, right now. He grabbed his wallet and left the apartment.

Even in his hurry, he took time to notice that the lock showed no sign of damage. It meant nothing. Anyone with an ounce of ingenuity, or a couple of thousand francs to spare, could have obtained a key, or an impression of one, easily enough from a maid or a porter.

He hesitated on the landing, turned towards the lift, and then spun on his heel and ran to where a dim orange light glowed above a fire-door. He opened the door, grimacing as the hinges squealed, and passed through into a bare concrete stairwell. He leapt down the stairs four at a time, his rubber soles almost soundless on the cement, until he reached the door at the bottom with its crush-bar handle.

He paused to quickly examine the door. The fine wires of an

alarm ran from the door jamb to a junction box high on the wall. He waited for a few more moments, one hand resting lightly on the bar, recovering his breath. Then, he shoved down hard on the bar and went through at a run, the nerve-jangling clamour of the alarm bell at his back.

He was in the courtyard, enclosed on three sides by the building, with the passage through to the street and the main entrance off to his left. Opposite him, a three metre wall divided the courtyard from that of the building facing onto the next street. He looked quickly around him, fighting to think coherently against the head-splitting racket of the bell. A moped stood propped in a corner, its wheel secured with a heavy, plastic-sheathed chain. He hauled it over to the wall, placed a foot on the saddle, and leapt for the top.

The machine fell away under him, the noise of it covered by the alarm, as he grappled his way onto the wall and half jumped, half fell to the far side.

He ran across a darkened courtyard, into the passageway and to the front gate. In the concierge's lodge a dog began yapping wildly. He dragged open the inset door and went through into the rue Vernet, letting the door swing shut just as light flooded the passageway behind him.

13

Blaise de Medem awoke at the first ring of the telephone. He rolled away from the warmth of the body that pressed against his, and sat up. 'Hello,' he said, eagerly.

As he listened, the expectant smile that lit his flat, square face faded and died, replaced by a look of furious disbelief. He hunched forward, cupping the receiver in both hands. 'What!'

The force of the surprise and anger in his voice made the woman stir. He glanced down and saw the shine of her eyes as she lay looking up at him in the darkness. 'Wait a moment,' he snapped into the mouthpiece. Swinging himself off the bed, he hurried to the door. 'Hang up when I pick up the extension,' he said curtly, over his shoulder.

He strode, almost ran, to the telephone in the living room and snatched it up. In the light filtering in from the street his heavy haunches glowed palely against the tan of his back. 'Now, what the hell's up? What's gone wrong? Did you get it done?'

'Yes, of course we did. Only . . .'

The sneering cockiness in Saïd's voice fuelled de Medem's anger. 'Only?' he shouted. 'Only what? A problem, you said. Have you screwed up?'

'It's just that our man left the building.'

'Left? What do you mean, *left*? Before the police arrived? Where did he go? Have they got him?' His voice was breaking with barely controlled rage.

'Not yet. He got out through a back door. The alarm had half the neighbourhood hanging out of their windows.' He sniggered. 'They were probably disappointed nothing was on fire.'

'But *he* got away? Where were the police? Were they even called?'

Saïd's insolent drawl did not change despite the icy disdain in de Medem's voice. 'Of course. A helpful guest reported noises. They were there in under two minutes. They're *still* there, swarming all over the place. It's just that he isn't.'

'You let him get out,' de Medem hissed, still grappling to keep his growing fury in check. 'You pricks!'

'And you're an asshole, just so we understand each other. Don't talk to me like your servant. I'm the best at my trade, and you know that. It's why you like to work with me, remember? Because you can count on me to do the job *and* to keep my trap shut. Pierrot, too. That's the hardest part, isn't it, finding someone who can keep quiet when he knows there are big names involved?'

De Medem breathed deeply, willing himself to check his

anger. 'And the woman? Can you rely on *her*? Will she stick to the story?'

The man sniggered. 'That's one thing you definitely *don't* have to worry about. I guarantee *she* won't be touting her story to the papers.'

'But, can you be *absolutely* certain of her? If she knew I was involved, if she guessed what was at stake, she . . .'

'Absolutely,' Saïd broke in softly. He gave a short bray of ugly laughter. 'I said don't worry,' he went on, speaking slowly, as if de Medem had been a child. '*I* thought about her beforehand, not afterwards, like you. Pierrot took care of her.'

The man's meaning hit de Medem like a blow. His mouth was suddenly parched. He ran his tongue over his lips and spoke, his voice a rasp. 'But I never asked you to . . . to . . . Not *that*!' He paused, trying to force saliva back into his mouth. 'Damaged, yes. You told me she had agreed to that. That's what she was to be paid for, but not . . . not . . .'

Saïd laughed again. 'Forget the money. I gave it to Pierrot. After all, he did a very nice job.' He paused for a moment as de Medem stammered, searching for a reply, then continued, his voice low and emphatic. 'Look, don't worry about it. You know the way I work. The American will take the rap, anyway. It's better this way, believe me. She would have been too dangerous. Take it from me, a weak link like that is just what nobody needs.'

De Medem fought to recover his composure, angry at himself for letting Saïd wrong-foot him. Already, the man spoke to him totally without respect, with the arrogance of someone too aware of his own value. It was no help at all knowing that what the man said was true; knowing how to keep quiet was the rarest of qualities. Being able to keep his mouth shut was the thing that set Saïd apart from the usual run of pimps and part-time robbers that were for hire. That, and the fact he had at least *some* brains. Even so, after what had just happened, it was as well that his mouth would soon be sealed permanently. 'So, let's agree it was good planning,' he said, sarcastically. 'But whatever may have happened to *her*, you still let *him* get clean away.'

'What's the difference? They'll soon pick him up. Unless he gets out of the country. Either way, he's out of your hair, isn't he?'

'Yes, no doubt. Goodnight.' He put down the phone and stood motionless, staring blankly into the dimness. He had been that way for almost a minute when the touch of a hand on his arm made him start.

'Something's gone wrong, hasn't it? That was that vulgar little Saïd man. He's the only person in the world who would dare phone you at such an hour.'

He looked down at her for a few moments, as though not even recognizing her. Then his shoulders rose and fell in a slow-motion shrug. 'Yes, it was.' His sigh turned slowly into a curious lop-sided smile. 'And he's much worse than vulgar. He's dangerous.' He put an arm round her and tried to steer her back towards the bedroom.

She pushed his arm off and turned to face him. 'Blaise, look at me.' He bent his head mechanically, the smile still on his face. 'Do you actually think this is all going to work?'

He stared at her. 'Work?'

She flapped a hand impatiently. 'Do you really think you're doing the right thing, working with people like . . . him,' she shuddered as she spat the last word. 'Do you really need the help of people like that? Do you even believe the whole thing can work, that they will ever let you have the *real* prize? You know I adore you, I think you're saying things that nobody else has the courage to say, but even *I* can't believe France is quite ready for you.'

He went on staring down into her eyes, shining in the half-light. Then, he reached out and took her head between his hands, furrowing his powerful fingers through the blonde hair and cradling her skull in his palms. 'The real prize? To be president, you mean?' Slowly he began to laugh. 'You haven't understood, have you?' His laugh grew louder, and unpleasant. 'That's for Vadon. He can have that. He'll be good at it, too.' He chuckled. 'He'll love all the crap that goes with it: the state banquets, the foreign trips, waving at crowds. The vain side of him *craves* all that shit.' Abruptly, he released her head, dropping his arms to his sides. The woman frowned as a look of unconcealed malice contorted his face. His voice had grown husky. 'I haven't struggled in the wilderness all these years because I wanted *trappings*.' He wiped his lips with the back of his hand. 'For years the bastards laughed. Well, they won't be laughing now. Because I'm going to have the power.' He gripped her hand hard enough to make her gasp. 'I'll have *control*,' he whispered. 'Vadon can be up there where the people can see him. He's welcome. Where I'll be is out of sight, directing his moves. Vadon can be the puppet, my dear, so long as *I'm* the puppeteer!'

❖

Bill ran, plunging headlong across streets, hardly even seeing the cars which bucked and swerved around him, conscious of nothing but the need to put distance between himself and the dead woman. He was almost at the river before he stopped, panting hard, in the shadow of a parked van. Away to his left the wail of sirens grew louder as more police sped to the scene. An unmarked police car careered off the Quai and hurtled past, sending him deeper into the shadows. As it went, an arm reached from the open passenger window and planted the magnetic blue flashing light on the roof. In the steely glow of the lamp he caught a glimpse of the occupants, laughing together at something, their relaxed faces a startling counterpoint to the wail of their siren and the screeching tyres.

The car was out of sight before his breathing was even again. Stepping from the shadows, he strode to the cab rank at the corner. Walking round the leading car so as to be on the driver's side, he climbed inside. He was seated, well out of the driver's direct line of vision, before the man had fully emerged from his doze, revived by the slamming of the door. 'The Gare du Nord.'

Only when the car pulled away and turned to follow the Seine eastwards did Bill let out a silent sigh and fall back in his seat. He closed his eyes and the ghoulish image of the dead woman flooded immediately back, filling his mind. Forcing it aside, he began going over the facts of his situation.

They were simple enough. He had come in a little drunk. In front of a dozen witnesses he had become involved in an argument with a woman who had given a reasonably convincing performance as a spurned lover. Two hours later the same woman was sitting in his bathroom, dead and savagely mutilated. Her blood was all over his bed, her clothes and jewellery scattered on his floor. It was a safe bet that the murder weapon, most likely a knife from his own kitchen, was hidden somewhere in the apartment, waiting to be found by the police the killers had taken the precaution of calling.

According to the book he should not have run. He should have called the police, told them the truth, and sat back to let justice prevail. Sure. He should have told them that he was as surprised as they were to find a butchered woman in his apartment. That she had chosen him to kiss in the lobby by mistake. That whoever had brought her to his room, killed and mutilated her and left him to take the rap, had acted on the instructions of the Minister of the Interior. And why would the Minister do that? Because I suspected him of upsetting a friend of mine!

He opened his eyes, almost smiling at the absurdity of it. His story made no sense. There was not a lawyer in the world that could save him. The instinct for self-preservation left him with only one option. The option to run.

The taxi turned away from the river and began heading north. What started as the driver's apology for the detour soon turned into a diatribe about the government and its policy of inconveniencing cab drivers. Bill cut him off with a curt word and let his eyes close again.

His story did not make sense even to him. He had nothing on Vadon. Ahmed had killed himself. Whatever his reasons, nothing changed that. There was no evidence of any crime being committed. Vadon had ridden out the initial wave of publicity with his reputation intact. Bill had found out nothing that would give Vadon a reason to go to such terrible lengths as having that woman murdered. If Vadon had left him alone, refused to see him, stonewalled him, the chances were that Bill would have been forced to give up, just as the press had done. Despite that, the woman had been done to death, for no more reason than to neutralize Bill.

He opened his eyes, gnawing at his lip. The only thing that set him apart from the press was that he had been a friend of Ahmed. Vadon would know that Ahmed had called Bill's number several times in the days before he died. If the phone-tapping had started only after the suicide, Vadon had no way of knowing the content of the calls. He sighed deeply. The woman's murder had been the act of a desperately frightened man. Whatever Vadon was afraid of *could* have been conveyed in the calls.

Once again, the image flashed across his mind of the youthful Ahmed, knife in hand, facing down the gang of thugs. For all Ahmed's over-developed taste for fame, nothing in the intervening years had dimmed his courage or tempered his inclination to face his problems squarely. It was impossible to imagine him committing suicide to escape a problem. Unless he had been left without a choice.

Ahmed was a Kabyle, one of that mysterious, proud breed from the remote mountain areas of Algeria. For all his Parisian veneer, he remained rooted in the vengeful, implacable code of his people. And for them there were acts which made death not a choice at all, but a simple necessity, the only possible atonement. If Ahmed had felt he had somehow brought shame on his family, then he would truly have seen no alternative.

A recent case had made the front pages. A young Kabyle woman, a student in Grenoble, had become pregnant by her French boyfriend, a capital offence against the tribal code. After a family discussion in one of those distant mountain villages, two of her brothers had been despatched to Grenoble where they had bludgeoned her to death, kicking her in the stomach to ensure that the baby, too, would not survive to stain the family honour. Arrested, they made no attempt at denial. Instead, they had patiently explained their position to the astonished French police, convinced that they would be released promptly once the police understood the *necessity* of their act.

The more he thought about it, the more certain he became that shame was the only force that could have driven his friend to his death. And the secret that had tortured Ahmed was Vadon's secret, too. First, it had driven Ahmed to his death. Now, it had driven Vadon to murder.

With the thought resounding in his head, and the first light of dawn already dimming the glare from the lights of the fast-food joints and brasseries, he paid off the cab and hurried into the station.

He paused, surveying the garishly lit concourse. The Gare du Nord at four-thirty in the morning would be no place to make a first acquaintance with the human race. In corners, derelicts slept on flattened cartons, hugging bottles with the three fingers of wine they had kept for breakfast. A group of young travellers with matted hair sat propped against the wall, soiled sleeping bags pulled up to their chests. They were passing round a plastic bottle of six-franc wine and carving sandwiches from a loaf and a piece of greasy cheese, proving you could do Europe on ten dollars a day, if you really cared to. He strode past them and joined the queue at the all-night money-changing bureau.

The queue progressed with painful slowness as rucksack toting youngsters re-checked the clerks' calculations and argued over microscopic discrepancies. Bill inched forward, uncomfortably conscious of his clean suit and expensive shoes among the tanned legs and stained T-shirts. The whole time, he scanned the sparsely peopled concourse, never looking directly at the policemen who patrolled in slow sweeps, exchanging hostile looks with the knots of lounging men and the dirty, glassy-eyed young women who loitered around them, cadging cigarettes. At last reaching the window, he emptied his wallet and passed the sheaf of hundred-dollar bills over to the clerk, asking for small denomination francs in exchange. While the clerk counted the money he signed his remaining traveller's cheques and pushed those, too, under the glass. Gathering up the pile of money under the awestruck gaze of the youth craning over his shoulder, he pushed it into two separate inside pockets and turned away from the counter.

He stood for almost half a minute, studying the departure board. Trains were already leaving. It wouldn't be difficult to evade the cursory passport checks. In a couple of hours he could be out of the country, in Brussels or Amsterdam, and on a plane home.

He let out a long breath. Home to what? To his business? With the reputation of a sex killer alongside that of art dealer. To Amy? And trying to explain to her what had happened, that somebody else had mutilated that woman, in his apartment, while he slept off a hangover. All because he had asked impertinent questions of an over-sensitive politician. Questions to which, in any case, he had no answers. She would probably believe him. Except for that dark, unvisited corner of her mind where the doubt would always live.

He sighed again. For a while he had wondered why whoever had been in his apartment had not simply eliminated him, too. Now he saw quite clearly that the way they had chosen was much cleverer.

He was a wealthy, reasonably well-connected American. His murder would have sparked an investigation that even Vadon might have found it hard to stifle. This way, he was branded as a maniac. Far from being anxious to stir up trouble, the American authorities would be on the side of the French police. Any record he might have kept of his meetings with Vadon and Lantier, any note of his suspicions, would be discredited, the deluded rantings of a psychopath.

He dropped his eyes from the board and mechanically double-checked the time on his watch. It was a few minutes before five. There was every chance the Paris police changed shift around six. Which gave him a little over an hour before his description would be the freshest thing in the mind of every policeman in the city. Walking quickly but without hurry, like a man nicely on time for an appointment, he strode out of the station and turned north up the rue Maubeuge.

The prostitutes' pouting smiles flickered briefly and then died as he passed by without seeing them, all his attention on the street as he watched for a police uniform or prowling vehicle. Hemmed in by the hospital on his left and the station on his right, the street offered few options if he had to make a run for it. He covered the half-kilometre to the end of the road and emerged, relieved, onto the boulevard de la Chapelle. He paused for a moment, scanning the light traffic, and then hurried across and plunged into the maze of narrow streets north of the boulevard. A minute later he was sheltering in the littered doorway of a failed bakery and watching the unlit facade of the Bengana premises.

He watched for fifteen minutes. Nobody loitered nearby or sat too long in a stationary car. No vans were parked where they would give a view of the entrance to an observer hidden inside. His senses vibrating, ready to run, he moved out of the cover of the doorway and walked quickly to the side door of the Bengana building. The clamour of the bell ringing inside the darkened store made him spin to look anxiously around at the deserted street. Nothing but a scavenging dog moved.

He was preparing to ring a second time when he heard movement inside. A hand pressed against the window and, below it, the face of the elderly worker frowned out through the grimy glass. Recognizing Bill in the half-light, his frown gave way to a surprised smile and he began drawing back the bolts.

For a few seconds Keltum stood staring at him, paralysed by surprise. Coming to herself, she snatched at the neck of her kaftan, hiding the inch of flesh that showed at her throat. 'You! What do you want? It's only . . .' She glanced at her wrist and gave a little mew of vexation as she realized she was not wearing her watch.

He smiled. 'Only five in the morning? I know. Can I come in?'

For another moment Keltum held her ground, and then, with an irritated flounce, she stepped aside to let him pass. 'Don't go in there,' she hissed, indicating the living-room door. 'My father is asleep.' She shook her head, frowning. 'What on earth do you want here, at this hour?'

He turned and looked into the clouded, hostile face. 'Help,' he said simply.

She squinted back at him. 'Help?' she said dubiously. She gave a tentative, scornful laugh. 'From us? What kind of help can *you* want from *us*?'

He spoke very quietly. 'I don't know, exactly. I thought maybe you could suggest somewhere I might stay for a while.'

Her eyes narrowed further, searching his face for signs of mockery. Before she could speak, Sidi Bey's grating whisper reached them from the living room. 'Keltum? Who is it?'

She looked hesitantly past his shoulder to the half-open door. With a warning glance at Bill, she opened her mouth to respond.

Bill laid a hand on her arm. 'Please, Keltum. Let me speak to him.' As he spoke he reached out a hand for the doorknob.

She hesitated for another moment, her lips working as though rehearsing a protest.

'Keltum?' Her father's voice came again, a little louder, wheezy with the effort.

She made a small groan of resignation. Flushing, she gave him a violent nod. 'Oh, you'd better go in, I suppose. But you mustn't tire him. You *mustn't*.'

He laid gentle fingers on her sleeve. 'Believe me, I'll try not to.' He walked into the room with her close at his heels. An empty chair was drawn up close to Sidi Bey's couch and on it stood a bowl of mush from which a spoon protruded. Bill knelt and embraced Sidi Bey, pressing his own cheek lightly on each of the old man's stubbled cheekbones, and then stood and moved to let Keltum resume her place. 'Please, finish eating. I can wait.'

Sidi Bey's feverishly bright eyes followed him as he withdrew across the room and sat in one of the hard chairs set round the table. He continued to watch Bill as Keltum spooned him the food, oblivious to the dribbles that slid down his chin, and which Keltum mopped away with a kind of guilty haste, as though she were ashamed of him. He took another two or three spoonfuls before murmuring to her. Stiff-backed, her lips tight together, she mopped his mouth once more and carried the bowl to the kitchen, not looking at Bill. Sidi Bey crooked the fingers of one hand, motioning Bill to take her place.

'You won't mind if I just lie back like this, William?' Bill smiled and grasped the sick man's fingers. Sidi Bey examined his face, his brow furrowing. 'What has happened? What have they done to you?'

Bill laughed softly. 'Does it show that much?'

Sidi Bey's head moved on the pillow, a fraction of an inch to each side. 'Yes, William, it does. Something terrible has happened. I can see it in your face.'

He hesitated, sensing Keltum close behind him once again. Glancing up, he saw that she had swapped the kaftan for her robe and head-dress. He met her scorching gaze in silence for a moment and then turned back to Sidi Bey and began to recount events from the time the woman had addressed him in the hotel lobby to his arrival at their door.

Sidi Bey listened in silence, his eyes half-closed. It was some seconds after Bill had finished before he opened them again. 'Why do you think they did this?'

Bill grimaced. 'My talking to Burgos, perhaps. Maybe he knows more than he told me. Or they think he does. Anyway, if it *is* Vadon that's behind this, I must be getting close to *something* for him to do anything this filthy.' He gave a short laugh. 'I wish to God I had some clue what it is.'

Sidi Bey's eyes closed again, as though he had fallen asleep. 'What do you intend to do now?' he said with sudden briskness. 'Do you want help to leave France?' He opened his eyes again. There was something that might have been a glitter of amusement in them. 'You know, I can put you in contact with people. Their speciality is bringing people *into* France but

I'm sure they could help you get out without having to . . . well, without formalities, shall we say.'

Bill shook his head. 'Thanks. I could have taken a train. There's no point, Sidi Bey.'

The old man's face clouded. 'No point, William? No point in avoiding arrest for something you didn't do? No point in going *home*? Has this got you too confused to think clearly?'

Bill gave his friend a grim, ironic smile. 'I've never thought more clearly in my life. What would I go home *to*? To be hunted down and returned here? And even if they couldn't extradite me, which for all I know might be the case, what kind of life would I have? How do you think life would be for me as a wanted sex killer? Plastic surgery and a villa in Paraguay. A new identity, on a passport bought from some sleazy lawyer in Costa Rica?' He sucked at his teeth. 'No thanks, Sidi Bey. Vadon's not going to steal my life from me like that. I'm going to go on living the way *I* choose.'

'So what *do* you intend to do?'

'Stay here. Ask some more questions. Talk to Vadon again, that's for sure.'

Sidi Bey's eyes puckered. 'How? He is such a powerful man. I don't see how you could even telephone him without the police finding you.'

Bill bared his teeth. 'Ronald Reagan never moved without a squad of armed bodyguards. He still got shot by some nut with a mail-order pistol.' He leaned his face to within inches of the old man's. 'Listen, Sidi Bey, after all that's happened I'm *absolutely* certain of one thing. Vadon is as responsible for Ahmed taking his own life as if he had killed him with his own hand. He took Ahmed's life, and now he's tried to take mine in the same way, by proxy. I'll ask some more questions, get some straight answers, and then, when I'm ready, believe me, I'll find a way to talk to him again, police protection or not. Just him and me.'

Sidi Bey's voice had weakened until it was a sigh. 'No, William. Please let me help you to return home. It's too dangerous for you here. It just makes more grief for me to see you in so much trouble, just for your kindness to me. Go home. From America you can fight this thing. They are your people. You understand how things work there.'

Bill tightened his grip on Sidi Bey's fingers. 'I told you, Sidi Bey, I *can't* go home. Don't you see what he's done to me? That woman's death leaves me no choice. I *have* to get the truth out of him.'

'You'll never do that, William. He can laugh at you. The death of that woman has made sure of that. Anything you say, even if you got the chance, would be the word of a madman. And don't forget, he controls the police. If they catch you it's far from sure you will ever get the chance to speak out at all. He has won, William. People like us cannot fight him.'

Bill leaned closer still. Above him Keltum gave a cry of protest as she stooped over them, reaching out a hand to pull him away, to protect her father from the intrusion. Not even seeming to feel the pressure of her hand on his shoulder, Bill spoke again, his voice low but slow and distinct. 'I'm going to try, Sidi Bey. I'm not letting him destroy *my* life, too. Not without a fight. Not if you'll help me.'

Sidi Bey's smile was distant, as though he were thinking of something else. 'How can we be of use, William? Do you need money?'

'No.' He touched a pocket with his free hand. 'I have plenty of that, for now, anyway. But I need a base, somewhere to stay.'

'You can stay here as long as you wish.'

Bill shook his head, glancing at his watch. 'No, I have to leave, and soon. They'll be looking for me here. I need a room somewhere that isn't connected with you. And a car, if you can.'

Sidi Bey did not respond at once. His eyes flickered to Keltum and stayed on her face. Bill heard the soft swish of the robe as she shifted under her father's gaze. 'Keltum will help you,' he said at length.

Bill looked up sharply at her intake of breath. She was staring at her father, pleading. Sidi Bey raised a hand, the palm flattened towards his daughter, stilling her protest. 'Yes, my daughter. You will, you must, help our old friend.' He kept his eyes fixed on Keltum's. 'There is Keltum's flat.'

'No!' Keltum could not contain her gasped protest.

Sidi Bey raised his fingers again, silencing her. 'Her brother bought it for her. It was one of the first things he did when he began to get rich.' He spoke tenderly, but with a tinge of regret. 'And he bought it the rich man's way. Through a Liechtenstein company. Can you imagine that?' He smiled as he spoke, looking at Keltum with a look of infinite tenderness. 'Her name does not appear anywhere.' Taking his hand from Bill's, he reached out to Keltum. Obediently, she laid her hand in his, closing her fingers round the eroded palm. 'He wanted her to be able to live an independent life.' He smiled again at his daughter, the tenderness tinged with regret. 'He was mistaken, of course. Keltum did not want his kindness. Not for long, anyway.' His voice had dropped so that it was barely audible. 'As you know, our daughter has chosen the old ways. Or should I say Bouhila's ways,' he added, desolately. 'She preferred to live here at home, with us.' He tightened his fingers on Keltum's, quelling her choking attempt to speak. He sighed. 'I should be grateful, I know. She takes wonderful care of me. But we came here for something else, to give our children the chance to be something different. Ahmed understood that, although Keltum tried hard to bring him, too, under the spell of this Bouhila.' Bill raised an eyebrow, but neither he nor Keltum spoke. For a moment total silence reigned in the room. Sidi Bey broke it with another long, sighing breath. 'Keltum will take you to the flat,' he went on, his eyes not leaving her face as a deep flush suffused it. 'It's in Saint Germain des Prés. A very smart address,' he said, a ghostly trace of irony flitting across his etched face. 'She will stay with you for as long as you need her.'

Keltum drew back, her free hand rising in a fist in front of her mouth. 'No! I can't do that. Father . . .'

Another tiny movement of his fingers cut her off as effectively as a blow. 'You must, my daughter.' With a tremendous effort he raised his head an inch from the pillows. The dark eyes drilled into his daughter's. 'She will stay with you, and help you in any way you wish. Please go now, Keltum, and fetch your car.'

His head sunk back onto the pillows and his eyelids dropped again. Bill looked anxiously up at Keltum. She was staring at her father in dead silence, shivering. The flesh had drained, leaving her face bloodless. Her mouth began working but no words came out. Her reaction looked so much like grief that Bill turned quickly back to Sidi Bey, checking that the emaciated chest was still moving beneath the blankets. Abruptly, white-faced and silent, she turned and ran from the flat.

She had been gone for several seconds before Sidi Bey opened his eyes and smiled wanly at Bill. 'You will see. She's a good girl, beneath all that . . . hostility. She has fallen under the influence of those people, that's all. Who can blame her, with the way things are going for us all here? Who knows? Maybe they will be proved right and we wrong. Perhaps the future *does* lie that way.' His voice dropped again so that Bill had to lean his head almost on Sidi Bey's lips to hear him. 'But it isn't the dream her mother and I had when we left Oran to come to this country, William. It isn't that, at all.'

❖

Keltum double-parked in a narrow street off the boulevard Saint Germain. Without turning off the motor, she handed him the key to the flat. 'The code is 411C. Fifth floor, right.' It was the first time she had broken her tight-lipped silence since he had clambered into the car in front of her home.

'Thanks.' He twisted to survey the street. It was not yet six-forty-five. There was only one other person on the street, a woman in a dressing gown who was watching, blank-eyed, as her dog fouled the pavement. Taking the chance that she was not a plain-clothes police officer, he slid from the car and crossed quickly to the entrance, leaving Keltum to find a parking spot.

He let the door close behind him and found himself in

a well-tended courtyard. The smell of newly watered earth rose from a flowerbed in the centre. The rear wall was almost obscured by a trellis supporting a tangle of flowering clematis. The cobbles shone from a very recent wash. He hurried silently past the concierge's lodge, grateful for the frosted glass of its windows, and entered the lobby. With the smell of wax polish faintly dizzying in his nostrils, he looked quickly about him. A well-kept staircase curved upwards, shiny brass rods holding a thick runner in place. In the stairwell nestled a tiny lift, enclosed by an ornate iron grille. Ignoring the lift, he started up the stairs, his steps soundless on the runner.

On the stairs he could turn back at the sound of footsteps, avoiding unwelcome encounters. In an up-market building like this the tenants noticed strangers. The lift, with those freeze-frame moments as the doors opened, leaving him nose to nose with a resident waiting to descend, would be tantamount to offering them his photograph.

He reached the fifth floor without seeing a soul and let himself in, the multi-point security lock opening almost without a sound. A small hallway opened onto a bright, spacious living room. He crossed to a window to check the street and made an approving face at the hardwood frames, double-glazed to keep out the traffic noise. Ahmed had spent a lot of money giving Keltum something really nice to throw in his face.

He prowled the flat, confirming the impression. Everything in the place – the polished parquet floor, the oriental rugs, the furniture – murmured money. A lot of money and a lot of taste. And total disuse. Nothing was out of place. The bathroom, with its floor to ceiling hand-made tiles, had not a toothbrush or piece of soap cluttering it's spotless surfaces. The state-of-the-art refrigerator in the kitchen was switched off and empty, its door ajar. The bed was covered with a silky bedspread but without sheets or pillows. The place looked like a speculative builder's show flat, without the homely touches.

The doorbell rang once. He went to the door and lifted aside the cover of the spyhole. Keltum stood there weighed down by plastic shopping bags. As he opened the door she swept past him into the kitchen and dumped her packages on the central island. Wordlessly, she waved a hand at them and retreated to the living room.

He flipped on the radio that stood on the window sill and began ferreting amongst the groceries, looking for coffee. While he made it he listened to the news and discovered he was a psychopath. The public were advised not to approach him, since he was probably armed.

'D'you want a cup of coffee?' he called, making his voice as unpsychopathic as possible. There was no answer. He shrugged, poured an extra cup, and carried it through to where she stood with her back to him, staring from a window. 'I brought you some, anyway. I thought maybe we both needed it. Here.' He held out the cup. She gave no indication of having heard. He shook his head and moved up behind her, stopping far enough away for his presence not to stir the air around her. 'Look, Keltum, I know how you must feel about this. And I'm sorry. I . . .'

She spun from the window. 'Do you? Are you? Then why did you let my father make me do this? Why couldn't you leave me alone?'

He looked unblinkingly into her eyes. They were reddened and moist. 'Because I couldn't see any other way to get done the things that need doing.'

She went on staring at him for a second or two, snatching at a tear that crept onto her cheekbone. 'But it's so unfair. You, and my father, are putting me in an unbearable situation. It's like a nightmare. And anyway,' she said, turning abruptly from him. 'How do I know you *didn't* kill that poor woman?'

His first instinct was to laugh. He suppressed it, chewing ruminatively at his lip. 'Well, I guess you don't.' He drank off a mouthful of coffee, his eyes on the back of her head. 'Maybe you should turn me in to the police, like a good citizen.'

She looked quickly round at him and dropped her eyes, flushing.

'Anyway,' he said, more gently, 'that's one moral dilemma you don't have to face. I'm going to call them myself.' She looked up sharply, her troubled eyes filled with disbelief. He nodded. 'That's right. I'm going to do it now.'

He pushed the coffee cup into her limp hand and walked into the bedroom, closing the door. Sitting on the edge of the bed, he fished Lantier's card from his pocket. With a glance at his watch he began dialling the number scribbled on the card.

14

At the sound of the phone, Lantier broke off from rummaging among the dirty washing in the bottom of the closet, straightened, and strolled across to the untidily made bed. He sat down heavily on the edge of the bed and picked up the phone, turning down the clock radio in the same movement. 'Hello?' he grunted, bending to pick up the mug of coffee that stood on the carpet.

'Inspector Lantier? It's me.'

Lantier stopped dead, the coffee cup just touching his lips. Two full seconds passed before he lowered the mug, spilling coffee onto the radio in his distraction. 'You!' he said, in a hoarse whisper. 'My God!'

Bill could not restrain a soft laugh. 'It sounds as though you've heard.'

'Monsieur – ' He broke off, not using the name. 'Heard? Of course I have. You've got yourself in the public eye, my friend.'

This time, Bill did not laugh. 'Look, I'll say what I have to say and get off.' Lines could be tapped, calls could be traced, and, in the electronic age, it probably would not take long.

Lantier was silent. Bill continued. 'First, let me put the record straight. What happened this morning was nothing to do with me. Or, at least, I didn't do it.'

'Who did?'

'Your guess is as good as mine,' Bill answered pointedly. 'But I don't want to talk about it on the phone. Can I trust you?'

Lantier kneaded the flesh on the bridge of his nose. 'To do what?'

'Meet me, and not put the handcuffs on me. So that we can talk this thing through.' The silence that followed was so long Bill feared the line had gone dead. 'Inspector?' he called.

'Yes, it's okay, I'm still here.'

'I thought I'd lost you.'

'I wish you had,' Lantier said ruefully. 'But, no. I was just thinking.'

'And?'

'I'll do it. But I can't give you any guarantees. If you're spotted, if *we're* spotted, I'll take you in.'

'Fair enough. Just tell me you'll come alone. And that you'll hear me out.'

Again Lantier was silent for a long time. 'Okay,' he said, at length. 'I suppose I can go that far.'

The rendezvous fixed, Lantier replaced the phone. He sat for a full minute, his hand still on the receiver, the other massaging the flesh of his lower lip. Finally, he rose to his feet and went into the cramped, dishevelled bathroom. He stepped into the bath and pulled the shower curtain round him. As he turned on the shower he was humming to himself.

❖

Christian Vadon stared out through the heavily tinted glass of the dark blue Jaguar and munched vindictively at a thumbnail. 'Stupid, stupid bastards!' He muttered the words over and over again as he ground his thumb against his teeth. His well-fleshed face was drawn and hollowed, the silver hair awry.

The car was parked in a quiet road in the Bois de Boulogne, close by a slip road onto the boulevard Périphérique. At length, the two joggers who had been conducting a conversation, bobbing on the spot as they exchanged early morning pleasantries, broke off their dialogue and went on their way. One of them loped past the car, smirking at the tinted window, supposing Vadon to be a client waiting for one of the gaudy transvestites who strutted among the trees a short distance away. Vadon let him pass on and then, with a final curse, almost catapulted from the car and half ran to the telephone box close by the spot where the joggers had been speaking. He pulled the door closed behind him and hunched over the phone, hitting the buttons with a venomous urgency.

'Hello?' he called hoarsely, as the ringing stopped.

'Yes?'

For once he did not even notice the habitual note of condescension in the Countess's cool voice. 'It's me. Is he there? I have to speak to him. Now.'

'Yes, I knew it was *you*,' she said, making no effort to conceal her contempt. 'I'll hand you over.' There was an instant's pause before she spoke again, a new wariness in her voice. 'Ah, where are you phoning from?'

'A call box, of course! Get him to the phone, for God's sake.'

'M'mm. Just a moment.'

Vadon twitched angrily. The bitch spoke to him as though he were an under-gardener on her family's estate. He chewed at his nail again, the whole time throwing anxious looks around him, haunted by the fear of being recognized.

'Hello, old boy. How are you this beautiful morning?'

The sound of de Medem's booming geniality made him start. 'How am I? How do you think I am? Did you hear what happened?'

'What was that?' de Medem asked, in deadpan mischief.

'The *American*, you fool! The woman!' He realized he was almost screaming and paused, fighting to get a hold of himself. 'Are those . . . *animals* of yours mad? I never asked for anything like this. I never intended anything so . . . so . . . brutal. I understood there would be some damage, of course. Bruises, a split lip, that kind of thing, for which she would be handsomely compensated. But . . . *this*.' He rubbed a shaking hand over his face. 'This is *catastrophic*. It should never have . . . I . . .'

De Medem cut him off. 'Grow up!'

'Huh?' Vadon stammered.

'Grow up! You're behaving like a child. What did you expect? You're a war hero, aren't you? You've done plenty of killing in your time, haven't you? You seem proud enough of that.'

'That was fighting for France! That was *war*!'

'So is *this*, my friend,' de Medem murmured icily. 'You must have understood it *had* to be this way, once she was involved.' De Medem's easy assurance gave no clue to his own reaction to the call from Saïd only a short while earlier. However, after his initial rage, he had come to see that Saïd had been right. It was better all round the way it was. He spoke again, his voice smooth. 'Sooner or later she would have realized she had a hold over us. She would have ended up trying to blackmail us.' He paused before adding, very quietly, 'I don't have to tell *you* how unpleasant that can be.' His words drew a groan from Vadon, as though he had been struck. De Medem went on, ignoring him. 'She would never have been able to help herself. Not now, perhaps, but later, when she had grown tired of her profession, the temptation would have been too much for her. This way, there won't *be* any temptation, will there?' he added, cheerfully.

'But she's *dead*,' Vadon responded, his voice rising to a whine.

'Well, you know, prostitution has always been a dangerous profession,' de Medem said with mock solemnity. He laughed out loud. 'They never know when a client might turn out to be a pervert,' he guffawed. 'Like your American friend, for example.' The laughter went out of his voice. 'Now, instead of whining about *my* people's mistakes, why don't we talk about the mess yours have been making? How come those idiots from the police haven't picked him up? They were called the moment it happened.'

Vadon's voice rose defensively. 'How could *I* help that? What did you want me to do? Tell the Prefect of Police in advance that I was *expecting* a murder to take place in the man's apartment at four this morning? Now *you* grow up! Anyway, they were there within minutes of getting the call. Your people must have woken him. And how was it they didn't see him leave? You should have had enough people watching to make sure of him.'

'Of course,' De Medem said, his voice like acid. 'And have one of them blabbing his mouth off within twenty-four hours?' He dropped his voice to a murmur. 'One loose mouth, a single misplaced boast in some bar, and everything we're fighting for would be lost. We agree on that, don't we?' Vadon mumbled his agreement. 'Good. So now it's up to *you*, dear boy, to make sure this American doesn't wreck everything.' He laughed at a sudden thought. 'After all, in your splendid television appearance, you assured us that *your* police are the finest in the entire world. Well, I hope they're good enough to catch him. And very soon. In fact, if I were you, I would have them do a little more than just *catch* him. I would emphasize just how dangerous he is, how very *unpredictable*. Instruct them not to take any chances with him. After all, he is an armed psychopath, he's already killed once, and he has nothing more to lose . . . Do you follow my meaning, old boy?'

'I don't need you to teach me my job, de Medem. We've already requested his picture from the Americans. By tomorrow every policeman in France will have it. They have been warned that he's a madman, likely to be armed and to resist arrest. It's being made clear that we don't expect any officer to risk his life trying to arrest him. You do follow *my* meaning, *old boy*?'

De Medem chuckled. 'Indeed I do. And I must say, it's so agreeable, working with someone who's on one's own wavelength. Now, have you any news on our, ah, visitor?'

Vadon glanced around him again, as though to make sure nobody had materialized in the booth with him. 'Not yet. Reports from our people over there are pretty sparse. Our friends are playing this very close to their chest. But he's expected to set off any time now. We're watching their incoming traffic, civilian as well as military, to make sure those shits don't slip him in under our noses.'

De Medem chuckled. 'Well, they're perfectly capable of it, you have to hand them that. Anyway, just so long as he *does*

198

come. It would be a shame to disappoint our little brown friends. They're so looking forward to blowing his brains out.'

Vadon shuddered. 'Please! Don't talk like that.'

'Why not?' de Medem's voice became very soft. 'This line's safe, isn't it? You've been assuring me of that for weeks. You've no reason to change your mind?' An unmistakable note of menace had entered his manner. 'Have you?'

'No, no. Of course not! I see the wiretap lists personally, every day. No number gets onto it without my signature. Do you think I'm mad?'

'No, but I think you're upset by this business. I worry that it might impair your judgement, that's all. And it would be a pity to let that spoil anything, now that we've come so far.'

'Don't patronize me, de Medem. I'll do my part.'

'Good. That's reassuring. By the way, the, er, tools have arrived. Perhaps you would like to drop by and pick them up. This evening, for instance.'

Vadon bridled. 'No, no. I don't think so. I can't. Not this evening. I shall be . . .'

'Shall we say nine o'clock?'

'I told you, I don't think I can . . .'

'Nine. It will only need a few minutes. Please don't be late. It would make the Countess nervous having them here.'

❖

'There! That's him!' Bill pointed to the glass bus shelter. 'No!' he added, hurriedly, as Keltum began swinging the wheel. 'Just keep driving.'

Lantier sat in the shelter, absorbed in a paperback book. Two women, each holding the hand of a small child, stood chatting a few feet from him. In what had already become a reflex, Bill checked the street, searching for the vans or the bogus street cleaners of a surveillance operation. 'Okay. Can you turn around?'

As he spoke, he tightened his grip on the door handle. Before leaving the flat he had insisted she change out of the robe and into conventional clothes. She had first argued, then pleaded. When he had refused to give ground she had exploded into a sobbing fury. He had responded with almost hysterical rage. Caught unprepared by the sheer passion of her reaction, he had been forced to take refuge in Sidi Bey's authority. Finally, resentful and still crying, she had disappeared into a bedroom and emerged in a high-necked cream silk blouse and dark blue skirt. And she had not spoken since, venting her simmering anger by driving with a lurching unpredictability, ignoring all Bill's urgent pleas for inconspicuousness.

Now, in response to his request, she threw the car into a forecourt, slamming sickeningly across a corner of the kerb as she misjudged the nearside. She ground into reverse, let up the clutch and shot backwards across the road, forcing an oncoming truck to a stop. She fumbled first gear, tried again, and the car bounded forward towards the bus shelter, leaving the driver of the stalled truck gesticulating angrily behind them.

'I appreciate your discretion,' Bill murmured.

She looked at him once, her eyes flashing angrily. 'You said turn around, didn't you?'

He smiled wearily. At least she was talking to him. 'That's right, I did. Can you pull in over there? Gently. Try not to run Lantier down before I get to talk to him.'

She tossed her head. 'I didn't ask to drive you. I hate driving. I haven't driven for months.'

'Since Bouhila came into your life?'

She flushed, staring ahead. 'Since you ask, yes. Isn't that one of the things everyone thinks they know about Islam, that women don't drive?' Her voice was strained, brittle with sarcasm. 'Oh, and of course, the men all have lots of wives.'

The answer that came first to his lips was another easy crack. He suppressed it, pausing. 'I'm sorry, Keltum,' he said softly. 'Really I am. I shouldn't be making you do this.'

She turned to look at him, her face clouded as she examined his expression, alert for mockery. He met her gaze. 'I know it's shitty. I need you to do it, but I truly am sorry.'

She turned and looked back through the windscreen, blinking. Her lips moved as though she intended to speak. Instead, she just gulped hard and stopped the car.

Lantier did not look up from his book until Bill opened the door and jumped out, pulling the passenger seat forward. The Inspector made no attempt to hide his surprise as he stooped and caught sight of Keltum. He glanced at her clothes and at the black hair, pulled tight into a single thick braid and pinned close to her head. He looked back to Bill with a roguish expression on his face.

'Cut it out and just get in the car, please,' Bill said, wearily. He lowered his voice. 'Just so you know, she would have torn her own eyes out rather than wear those clothes, if her father hadn't ordered her to do it.'

Pushing the book into a pocket, Lantier jutted his bottom lip thoughtfully, the smile gone. With a nod, he turned and bent to insert himself into the cramped rear seat. Bill slid back in and waved a hand at Keltum. 'Lantier, you know Mademoiselle Bengana. I want you to understand she's not involved in any of this. I just asked her to drive me to meet you, to take the bare look off me. You do give me your word you understand that, don't you?'

Lantier nodded. 'M'mm.' He inclined his head. 'It's a pleasure to see you again, mademoiselle.'

She nodded, grim faced, without turning or speaking. Lantier smiled cheerfully at the back of her head and turned to Bill. 'So, where are you taking me?'

They were on the edge of the Bois de Vincennes when Bill asked Keltum to stop. 'Will you stay here? I doubt if we'll be long.'

She turned off the motor and sat in silence, not even looking at them as they climbed from the car and began walking towards the ornamental lake.

It was an hour when the joggers had showered and gone to work, and the mothers and children yet to emerge. The only people in sight were a pair of fishermen, as still as statues, and a gardener at work on a flowerbed. Even so, neither of them spoke until they were past the lake and on the open grass. Lantier broke the silence.

'So, here we are. You a murder suspect, and me a policeman. Now, explain to me just *why* I shouldn't arrest you.'

'First, because you know damned well I didn't do it.'

'M'mm. Have you any idea who *might* have?'

'An idea? Of course. The same people that beat me up. People working for *your* boss, Vadon.'

'Do you have a shred of evidence for that? Anything you haven't already told me.'

Bill shook his head impatiently. 'No. But I know it, and so do you. And you know that Vadon's connected to Ahmed's suicide, in some way he's trying to make damned sure doesn't come out.'

Lantier made no sign of having heard him. At length, he spoke again, musingly. 'You said "first". What's second?'

Bill laughed. 'Because you *need* me out there. For some reason you want to know more about this and you think I'm going to flush it out for you.'

Lantier gave him a quick look and then looked down again, apparently concentrating on attempting to flick a discarded drink can into a bin with his foot. He missed. 'I hate to be boring, but tell me again about last night, from the moment you returned to the apartment building.'

He listened in silence as Bill described the events of the night, interrupting only to steer them away from the occasional dog-walker. When Bill had finished, Lantier put a hand on his arm and turned to face him. 'Tell me, absolutely frankly, have you *ever* been involved in anything like this before last night?' He laughed through his nose, his eyes on Bill's. 'I don't mean a murder, of course. But *anything*? Have you ever hit a woman, for example, for any reason at all? After a few drinks, maybe. Is there a woman anywhere who could testify that you had been violent, or even threatened her?'

Bill shook his head. 'I couldn't hit a woman if she asked me to. It's just not in me.'

Lantier nodded. 'Do you use, have you *ever* used prostitutes?'

Bill thought for a moment and shrugged. 'In Vietnam, I guess. Bargirls. I suppose you'd have to count that. Since then, never. Getting sex in New York isn't that difficult, you know, even in the age of AIDS.'

Lantier grimaced. 'Getting sex has nothing to do with it, believe me. You've seen enough stories of film stars or ministers getting caught with prostitutes. More often than not they've got beautiful wives, a lot more attractive than the whores their husbands go for. So, why do they do it? Why do they risk their glittering careers?' His eyes fixed on Bill's. 'Because they want to do things they're ashamed of, things they daren't ask their wives to do.'

Bill returned Lantier's gaze levelly, shaking his head. 'I know what you mean. But, no, that isn't my thing, Inspector. No tying women to the bedposts, no rubber gloves, no accessories at all. I don't want to be wrapped in plastic and put in the wardrobe. I'm not interested in being pissed on, crapped on, whipped, spanked, or anything else in the catalogue.' He smiled. 'Mind you, if I did, New York being what it is, I could probably find someone delighted to do it free of charge!'

Lantier nodded, allowing a wry smile to twist his mouth. 'Sounds like a fun place to live.'

'It is. Look, I've always taken my sex relatively straight.' The image of Amy flashed with aching clarity across his mind. 'And I sure haven't gotten bored with it yet.'

Lantier nodded and turned to continue walking. They had gone several paces before he spoke again. 'And what, supposing I don't arrest you, do you intend to do now? You can hardly stay here. But it won't be easy to leave the country. And even if you got out, every airport and airline in Europe will be on the lookout for you. You should have taken my original advice and gone straight home. Now, I doubt if you'd make it.'

'I don't intend to try.'

Lantier turned, his head cocked. 'So, just what *do* you intend to do?'

'Keep trying to find out what happened to Ahmed. Keep pressuring Vadon.'

'Ahmed jumped, as you've been told a dozen times.'

'I phrased it wrongly. I want to find out *why*.'

'Why?'

'Because that will be the reason they did this to me. I don't want to *escape*, Inspector. I want to be *cleared*. If I can give you a motive, maybe you, or somebody like you, can get a handle on this mess. Find out who hung this on me.'

'M'mm. You realize how dangerous these people are? They thought killing the woman would be enough. They slipped up. They won't make the same mistake twice. Next time it will be *you*.'

'I know.' Bill stopped and put a hand on Lantier's arm, pulling the policeman round to face him. 'Look, Lantier, do you know *anything* about Ahmed's death, or his life, that might give me a lead?'

Lantier was silent for a moment, looking into Bill's face. He seemed about to speak and then hesitated again, twisting to look all around them. The nearest human was eighty metres away, his back to them, making a German shepherd dog jump for a stick. Lantier turned back to Bill and spoke, his lips hardly moving. 'I told you that Bengana might have been pursued into the Tour Montparnasse, remember?'

Bill nodded. 'Sure, I remember. Where does that come from, by the way?'

'That's what I'm about to tell you. A traffic policeman.' He broke off with a soft snort of derisive laughter, jabbing a thumb contemptuously at his own chest. 'Like me. He was outside the building. Your friend threatened him with his sawn-off shotgun. He claimed there were other men, running after Bengana. He had just finished radioing in when he saw a couple of men disappear into the building at a full run.'

'Members of the public being good citizens?'

'Yeah, maybe,' Lantier acknowledged drily. 'Would *you* run after a man with a sawn-off shotgun?'

Bill shrugged. 'Did your traffic cop get decent descriptions?'

Lantier shook his head. 'I don't know.'

Bill said nothing, waiting for Lantier to fill the gap.

'His report went missing.'

Bill took a step backwards. 'You're a policeman, for God's sake. If you were really interested in the case couldn't you have just talked to him?'

'I wanted to. But he went missing, too, in a manner of speaking.' Lantier met Bill's stare. 'A few nights ago. I took a statement from a witness.' Still Bill waited, fearing what was to come. 'A bag lady. A sober one, by a miracle. She had been about to go to sleep, in a shop doorway in Montparnasse, not far from my office, my old office, that is. A bit before one. Two men across the street were sharing a bottle. Derelicts. Like her, except that she didn't know them. She thought they must be fresh in off a train. Anyway, as she tells it, the two of them started shouting at each other. Next thing, they're on their feet and fighting. One of them went down. The other one seemed to be trying to kick him to death when a young fellow, a passer-by, tried to break it up. He grabbed the one doing the kicking.' Lantier paused, his eyes on Bill's face. 'The one on the ground jumped up and knifed him.'

'The other wino?'

'No. The young man.'

Bill stared. 'He stabbed the guy who had just stepped in to save him from a kicking?' Lantier's lips pursed in confirmation. Bill's eyes narrowed. 'That was your man, wasn't it? The traffic policeman. The one who saw the running men.'

'Yes, it was.' Lantier swallowed. 'He was just off duty, walking home. They knew his schedule. And they were pros. The woman was a good witness. She showed me how he did it. Like that.' As he spoke, Lantier stepped closer to Bill and jabbed his extended fingers into Bill's armpit, jerking them out again with a slashing upward motion. 'One wound. It cut through the axillary artery. He bled to death in minutes.'

As Lantier finished speaking there was an unmistakable tremor in his voice. It made Bill look harder into his eyes. It was a second or two before he spoke. 'This is personal, isn't it?' he asked in a whisper.

Lantier nodded. 'I'm afraid it is. Henri Delcasse, the boy's father, was a very good friend of mine. I'd known Gerard, the boy, since he was born. He only became a policeman because of me.' Falling silent, he turned abruptly and resumed walking.

Bill watched him go a few paces before hurrying to draw alongside him. They had walked another twenty metres before he spoke. 'And they wouldn't even let you look into it?'

Lantier remained silent, his face unchanging.

'*That's* why you want Vadon's head, isn't it? Why you've been ready to let me shake the tree. Finally it makes sense.'

Lantier was silent for a moment longer, then he shrugged. 'I was *ordered* to drop it. Told it was being taken over by Renseignements Généraux, the intelligence people.'

'Who don't answer to anybody, except Vadon?'

By way of reply, Lantier smiled a quick smile and looked at his watch. He shook himself and took Bill's arm, lengthening his stride. 'Come on. Let's get back to the sister.' He looked sidelong at Bill. 'She really is a nice-looking woman, by the way, out of that headgear.'

Bill screwed up his face. 'That's just the attitude that makes her wear it in the first place. Forget it. Left to herself she would rather turn me in than do this. She's only doing it because her father virtually forced her to.' He stopped and put a hand on Lantier's arm, making him face him. 'Promise me again you'll remember that, Lantier, if things get rough.'

Lantier dipped his head. 'I will. Look, if you, well, if there's anything you need, where you think I might be able to help, call me.'

Bill's brows rose in surprise. 'What kind of help are you offering?'

'Well, if you want to play policeman, the help of a real one might be useful. For some background, for instance.'

'Keep talking.' They were circling back around the lake now, their feet crunching in unison on the gravel. Mothers sat talking on benches, half smiling at the squealing children who stamped among the pigeons, sending them fluttering in protesting flurries.

'For example, if you could get a usable description of the

people that were chasing Bengana, I *might* be able to help with an identification.'

'Your bag lady didn't give you anything you could use?'

'I said she was sober at the time, not that she'd been to police training college. And they were forty metres from her.'

'Okay. It's somewhere to start, anyway. Unless you have anything I could get a handle on? Any gossip, anything off your files that might not be public knowledge?'

'Nothing specific. Bengana was well-known. He knew a lot of big names in show business and politics. In this country it's hard sometimes to tell them apart.' They had reached the car. Keltum rose from the tree-shaded patch of worn grass where she had been sitting and moved towards them. At her approach Lantier dropped his voice to a mumble. 'Actors, designers, politicians, they go to the same parties, see the same, er, women.' He glanced again at the approaching Keltum, ensuring she was still at some distance. 'Or men.'

Bill's eyes narrowed. He was about to speak when Keltum drew level with them. Lantier cut him short. 'Don't think I'm making judgements,' he murmured. 'I'm a police officer. I'm only interested in the facts, and whether they have a bearing on the case.' He glanced at his watch. 'I have to go.' He smiled, the smile taking in Keltum. She looked past him, grim-faced. With a shrug, he turned back to Bill. The smile faded from his face. 'Be very careful, both of you. And you should understand one thing. If anything happens to you, don't count on *me* being able to help. You're expendable, I'm afraid. I want to stay close to this case, and I'll do whatever it takes to make that happen. If I have to, I'll deny I ever saw you outside of my office. That is clear, isn't it?'

Bill laughed. 'As crystal. Can we drop you off anywhere?'

Lantier walked round to the driver's door and opened it, motioning in a gesture of surprising, old-fashioned gallantry for Keltum to climb inside. As she did so, he offered his hand. She ignored it. With a tiny bow, he closed the door on her, shaking his head, and strode round the car. 'Thanks, but I think I've taken enough chances for this morning.' He leaned on the door as Bill lowered himself in beside Keltum. 'Do you have that card I gave you?'

Nodding, Bill fished the card from his breast pocket and laid it in Lantier's outstretched palm. Lantier scribbled something on it and handed it back. 'It's my sister's number. I don't think it would be altogether, er, sensible for you to call me directly any more. Leave a message and I'll get back to you.' He saw the doubt in Bill's face and laughed. 'No, you'd better not use your own name.' He thought for a moment. 'Kléber. Tell her Kléber wants me. Leave a number, and say when you expect to be there.' He took Bill's hand and shook it with surprising warmth. Ducking to bow again to Keltum, he slammed the door and turned to begin strolling away towards the city.

15

She swept past him into the living room and stood by the window, staring down into the street. He closed the flat door and followed her into the room.

'Look, Keltum, I'm sorry. I think I hate this as much as you do, but no.'

She turned to look at him, her lips clenched and pale. Her dark eyes glowed with a feverish light. 'But I'm begging you. Please! You *can't* make me go on doing this.' She gestured helplessly at her clothes. 'I *mustn't*! You can't abuse my father's wishes like this.' She gestured again at her clothes. 'They make me feel like a . . . a prostitute!' She spat the word with a kind of angry daring, her face flushed except for white spots on her cheekbones.

He stared back into the face, ready to be angry in his turn, looking for a hidden accusation in the word. Swallowing hard, he reined in his anger, reminding himself of the strain he was putting on her. 'Please, Keltum, try to understand,' he said softly. 'Look at me, my hair, my eyes. Could anyone take me for an Arab? If we went out together with you in those other clothes we'd be the oddest couple in town. Surely you see that? I'd be picked up within minutes.'

She looked down at the floor. 'You should have taken my father's offer and let him put you in contact with the people who could have got you over the border. You can't do any good here.'

He shrugged. 'Maybe you're right. But, I'll say it again, even if it bores you: I made a promise to your father.'

She tossed her head and spun again to face the window. 'Stop it, please! My poor father's dying. He's so upset by what happened to Ahmed, he's not thinking rationally. He can't see that when you first agreed to help him you were patronizing us again.'

For a moment he stared at her, too shocked to speak. 'He seems pretty rational to me,' he said quietly.

She turned, colour suffusing her face. 'Of course. *Because* he wants you to help him. You think trusting you is normal.' The hint of sarcastic humour in her voice was a welcome change. 'It's your role, isn't it, as a good Christian? You're here to show us all how good life could be, if only we would learn to live like you. Well, you saw where it led Ahmed, trying so hard to be one of you.' She paused. When she went on, her voice was lower. In place of the mockery there was a distant, tragic note. 'If he had only been able to put his trust in his own people, if he could have been more open with me, and with Imam Bouhila, we could *really* have helped him.' She broke off, her breath coming in noisy gulps as though she were once again on the brink of tears.

Bill swallowed, taken totally by surprise by the abrupt change in her voice. He moved a half-step closer to her. 'More open? With Bouhila?' He watched her face work as she fought against the turbulence of her emotions. 'Keltum,' he said gently, 'just how well did Ahmed know Bouhila?'

She stared at him blankly for a moment as though she had forgotten he were there. 'It was strange,' she said, as though to herself. 'Quite early on he came with me to some seminars. The National Salvation League, de Medem's people, were really beginning to make headway. De Medem had discovered that we were just the target he had been waiting for all these years. He found that every time his thugs attacked us, burned one of our creches, his poll ratings rose. It was manna from heaven for him. The more violent the attacks, the more his support seemed to rise. Ahmed was worried sick about it, like a lot of us.' Her eyes focused suddenly on his face, her expression softening. 'You know, despite the fame, the wealth, the . . . superficiality of his life, politics, *ideas*, had always fascinated him.'

Bill smiled, remembering the discussions in the Bengana apartment, the arguments that had gone on from late in the evening until they had ended with Madame Bengana appearing laden with trays of coffee and croissants for breakfast. 'Yeah, I know.'

'He *hated* all that de Medem stands for. He despised racism. It made him so angry to see people picked on. Ahmed always wanted to help the underdog.'

Bill touched his fingers to the narrow indentation almost concealed in his hairline, a memento of the beating so many years before. 'You're telling me!' he said, smiling. 'You said something was strange. What?'

She shook her head. 'Well, at first, he seemed really drawn to the Imam's ideas. It was just like when I was a girl. He would come to my room, we would talk about it for hours. He agreed with me that the Imam's way was the only way for our people. That we have to take control of our own destiny, be true to our own culture.'

'Something changed his mind?'

'He seemed to . . . I don't know, to withdraw. For a while he and the Imam were quite close. Ahmed seemed to accept the Imam's teachings, to really want his guidance. But then, suddenly, he just broke away. He wouldn't even hear the Imam's name spoken.'

'When did this happen?'

'Very recently. Only a few days before he . . . before he killed himself.'

'Do you know why? What changed his mind?'

She shook her head violently. 'He wouldn't talk about it at all. He seemed to just change completely.'

'How?'

'He became depressed, nervous, paranoid, as if he were terrified of something.'

Bill grimaced. 'So much for Bouhila's spiritual guidance.' He raised a hand hurriedly as her eyes flashed. 'I'm sorry. That was cheap. He never gave you *any* clue what was on his mind?'

She shook her head again. 'No,' she said emphatically. 'As I said, one moment he seemed ready to join our movement, the next he wouldn't stay in the room if I so much as mentioned the Imam's name. He hardly spoke to me at all. He said I should get away from the Imam. He claimed to know that he was a fraud.' She spoke the last words in a barely audible murmur, as though she were blaspheming.

Bill raised an eyebrow, surprised at her even allowing herself to say the words. 'I guess they all turn out to be in the end,' he murmured, almost to himself.

She bridled, inhaling loudly through flared nostrils, warning him. 'You see! You can't help sneering, can you? It's easier than trying to understand that what Imam Bouhila is doing *will* change things. He sees the truth. For years we have been told we should make an effort to integrate. Well, we tried it. And when we tried we found out that *that* was the fraud. He makes us see that integration is an illusion, it's running away from the real problem. We will always be Moslems, and we should act like Moslems, not try to impersonate Christians.' Her eyes met his and locked onto them, searing him. 'We found out that, when it comes to it, the people we were trying to integrate with didn't *want* us!'

Bill shifted, hardly able to stand the intensity of her gaze. He was still searching for a response when she went on talking, sparing him the need. 'Western society only wants to take away our self-respect. The Imam gives it back to us.' In a gesture that took him totally by surprise, she reached out and touched his sleeve. 'You *can* see that, can't you, Bill?'

He nodded, swallowing. 'Yes, I guess I can.'

Gratitude flitted across her face. 'That was Ahmed's problem, I'm sure of it. For some reason he hated himself.'

'How did Bouhila react to his change of heart?'

She looked down at the floor, as though embarrassed at revealing Bouhila's response, as though it were a form of treachery. 'He was angry. With himself. He felt he had failed us.'

Bill nodded. 'Anything else? Was he content to let Ahmed just slip from his clutches?'

She looked sharply up at him, her face strained, once again somewhere between anger and tears. 'He tried to *help*. Ahmed was behaving very strangely. He lost a lot of weight. He seemed to be about to break down completely. The Imam did his best. He tried every day to phone him. I know he went to his showroom more than once. Ahmed threw him out.' The tears came now, darkening the creamy cloth of her blouse. 'Oh, Bill, something, I don't know what, guilt, maybe, or shame, was just eating him away. Something inside him.'

Her last words were almost lost, sucked away in the first gulping sob. For several seconds Bill remained still. Then, he placed his hands on her shoulders and pulled her towards him. He did it with a careful, gentle wariness, expecting her to flare into anger. Instead of shying, she allowed her head to rest on his chest. He looked down at the top of her head, feeling the warmth of her tears through his shirt. He let her cry, not daring to shift his position, resisting the instinct to slide his arms round, until the movement of her shoulders slowly subsided. Then he said softly, still not moving, 'Please say you'll help me find out what it was.'

❖

The Israeli Ambassador was seated among the people crowded into the cluttered office, facing the blonde woman who sat hitched inelegantly on the edge of the desk. He raised a hand to catch the woman's attention just as one of the phones on the desk began to ring. With a nod of apology she reached for the instrument.

The card fixed to the office door gave her title as Assistant Cultural Attaché. In fact, there was hardly enough cultural work to occupy the Chief Cultural Attaché, a languid young man who worked from the adjoining office. The woman was head of the Paris bureau of Mossad.

She held the phone to her ear for a few seconds, smiled, and put it down again. 'Ariel? You wanted to say something?'

'I certainly do! You're setting all this in motion, getting everyone excited, and we don't even know for sure if he's *coming*. I've had no confirmation at all. I . . .'

The woman flicked a finger at the phone. 'I'm confirming it now. He'll be here in fifteen minutes.'

'A quarter of an hour!' The Ambassador was almost choking with indignation. 'And I'm sitting here listening to you.' He looked busily at his watch, already rising. 'There's not even time to get anybody to the airport! How can you people . . . ?'

'Relax, Ariel.' The woman broke in, laughing. 'He'll be *here* in fifteen minutes. In the building.'

The Ambassador swivelled to face her, his eyes wide. 'You mean he's *already* in France?'

She glanced at her watch. 'He's been here over three hours.'

The Ambassador continued staring. 'That's impossible. He wasn't on today's special care lists.'

The woman smiled. 'Paris has softened you up, Ariel. How secure do you think those lists really are? We brought him into Lyon, not Paris.' Her eyes twinkled at the Ambassador's frown. 'On an Orion Oil company plane.'

The Ambassador looked dazed. 'Orion?' he said weakly. 'For the love of God! You shipped Dan Bruckner in on a plane belonging to a *Libyan* oil company?'

The woman nodded happily. 'Neat, huh? At least it would have fooled *you*.' Shedding her smile, she turned her attention back to the rest of the room, effectively dismissing the

Ambassador from any further participation. 'He boarded the plane at Malta. The only member of the crew that saw him is one of our own people. He came in on a Belgian passport. With a hat and contact lenses in place of those bullet-proof glasses he insists on wearing, the passport officer didn't give him a second glance. Outside this room there isn't a soul in France knows of his arrival.' She looked around at the dozen men and women seated in front of her. 'Keep it that way, please. No pillow talk to girlfriends or boyfriends, even if they work here. Is that clear?' She looked at each in turn, eliciting their individual acknowledgment. 'Good. Now, here's what we've worked out. He'll stay at the embassy. On the evening of the twenty-fifth, at four minutes to nine, he'll be lifted out by helicopter and set down right inside the secure compound, no more than a few metres from the podium. The moment the parade ends, it will take him directly to Le Bourget, where we'll have a plane waiting to fly him home. He'll almost be able to finish the night in his own bed.'

'Make a change,' somebody murmured.

The woman beamed. 'You've been reading the files! Anyway, that's it.' She looked at her watch and grinned at the Ambassador. 'Ariel, if you really want to impress him, you've just got time to put on a tie.'

❖

Bill sat hunched down in the front passenger seat scanning the subterranean gloom of the car park for Keltum. She had been gone for over half an hour and he was beginning to get nervous. At every movement, every sight of a car prowling the alleys in search of the perfect parking spot, his hand sought the door latch, ready to make a run for it.

His hand leapt for the latch once more as a figure erupted from a door fifty metres from the car and began hurrying towards him. He let his hand drop back, sighing, as he recognized Keltum, still unfamiliar in the modern clothes.

She wove between the rows of cars, bouncing off them in her haste, and snatched open the door. She threw in some packages and dropped into the driving seat.

He smiled, retrieving a bag from the floor. 'I was beginning to wonder if you'd given up on me. Did you get everything?'

'Shopping always takes longer when you're actually doing it than you think it will.' She gave him a quick, thin smile. 'It's one reason I'm glad I don't have to do it much any more. I hope the stuff fits.'

He sat up, rummaging in the plastic carrier bag. He pulled out a spiral-bound notebook, a felt-tipped pen, a light blue poplin blouson and a red cotton baseball cap with a ten-centimetre peak. He pushed the notebook and pen into an inside pocket and held up the cap and blouson admiringly. 'They look great. Glasses?'

She reached into another bag and pulled out four pairs of sunglasses. 'Here.'

The third pair he tried, lightly tinted, with thin, black-lacquered wire frames, fitted snugly. He swapped his jacket for the blouson and put on the glasses and cap. While he did so, she fought into another crackling plastic bag and produced a leather shoulder satchel with plenty of zippers and pockets. It was the kind of bag the French call a 'reporter', under the misapprehension that journalists toted the things around. Maybe French ones did. The American journalists Bill had met were less style-conscious, relying heavily on dog-eared shorthand pads and stubs of pencil. She opened another bag and showed him a camera with a long snout.

'Great. You'll look like an ace operator for *Life* magazine.'

'What's that?'

'Forget it. It was before your time. How do I look?'

'Exactly like an American tourist,' she said sourly.

'God preserve me. Let's go.' Tossing his jacket into the rear, he climbed from the car.

After the chilly shadows of the car park, the heat of the street came as a shock. They paused, surveying the street and letting their eyes grow accustomed to the brightness. Although motor traffic was thin there were enough tourists making for the shopping centre at the foot of the tower to counter the August languor that affected most of the city. They stood for almost a minute, watching, Bill standing his ground as two policemen strolled past, studying the crowd with a lazy, professional alertness. He felt the eyes of one of the officers slide over him, and his mouth parched as he waited for the momentary hesitation that would have sent him running for the maze of the car park. The policeman's gaze moved on without showing a flicker of interest. Moistening his lips, he touched Keltum's sleeve and they set off towards the rue de Rennes.

A sudden throaty sound from Keltum brought him round in alarm, his arms coming up instinctively in front of him. She stood rooted to the spot, her hands pressed over her mouth as though to stifle a scream. Her eyes were fixed on a spot on the pavement, a patch of the asphalt very slightly paler than the surrounding area, as if it had been recently cleaned. He moved closer and placed an arm round her shoulders. The asphalt in the centre of the cleaned patch was faintly indented. He felt her whole body begin to shudder. He looked up once to the tower above them, at the reflections of the sky gleaming on layer upon layer of windows, and tightened his arm round her. 'Come on!' As he spoke he was already moving, almost dragging her with him. 'Let's get away from here, quickly.'

They began at a café a third of the way down the rue de Rennes, introducing themselves to the waiter working the terrace as journalists looking for a story in Ahmed's death. He was eager but unhelpful. He had been on duty at the time, but had seen and heard nothing. He thought he had probably been inside getting drinks for clients at the time of the car crash, making it clear as he said it that he still nursed a grudge against the customers. Keltum mollified him by holding up the camera and feigning to snap him pretending to wipe a table. Leaving him still smirking for the empty camera, they moved on.

They mounted the slope of the rue de Rennes, repeating

the same routine, looking for anyone who might have seen the events around Ahmed's crash. The closer they got to the spot where the crash happened, the more anxious people were to talk, thrilled to have been among the last ones to see somebody famous before he died. None of them had anything useful to add. Dispirited, almost at the top of the street, they moved to the sandwich stand at the edge of the terrace of a busy café.

Bill approached the stand, notebook in hand, and nodded to the youth working it. 'Good morning. We're from *Libération*. Looking into the Bengana suicide.' He jerked a thumb casually towards the tower opposite. 'The one that jumped, over there.'

'Uh-huh,' the youth said, turning eagerly from impaling bread rolls on the spikes of a hot-dog dispenser.

Bill gave him an amiable smile. 'Were you working when it happened?'

The young man nodded, jabbing a finger at the ground. 'Right here.'

'You saw the crash?'

'Heard it, anyway. I was bending down for a new can of frankfurters. I couldn't believe it when I looked up and saw Ahmed Bengana getting out of the Merc.'

'You *recognized* him?'

The young man laughed. 'Wouldn't everybody?'

Bill smiled briefly at Keltum. Ahmed was a pretty well-known name. It took a fellow North African to assume the whole world carried his face around in their heads. 'What happened, after he got out of the car?'

'The cab driver started bawling him out. He flattened him,' he said, laughing at the recollection.

'And then?'

'He ran across there, towards the tower.'

'Was he alone?'

The man frowned. 'In the Merc? Yeah.'

'Apart from the Mercedes, was there anything else. Did you see anyone else running?'

The man frowned. 'Down there.' He made a jabbing motion, using the long bread roll he still held as a pointer. 'Ahmed was checking behind him. Seemed as if he was scared, or something. It made me look down that way, to see what the score was.'

'And?'

'Two men jumped out of a car and started running up here.'

'Do you think they were chasing Bengana?'

'Sure of it.'

'How's that?'

The man gave Bill a pitying look. 'They didn't take their eyes off him. And one of them shouted to the others.'

'What did he say?'

The young man said something incomprehensible. 'Huh?' The man repeated it. Bill heard Keltum's breath hiss. He glanced round to find her staring at the man, the camera dangling, ignored, at her waist. 'What's that in French?'

'Get him, before he loses us in the tower,' Keltum responded, before the young man could answer.

The man stared in delight at Keltum. 'You speak Kabyle?'

'So he *was* being chased,' she said distantly, ignoring the man's question.

'Yeah, she does,' Bill answered for her. 'Did they say anything else?'

'No. Just that.'

'Okay.' He looked at Keltum and then back to the man. 'Did you get a look at the driver?'

The man shook his head. 'No. It was tinted glass. Couldn't see a thing.'

'Pity. How about the make of car?'

'BMW five series. Metallic bronze.' He said it confidently, a note of yearning in his voice.

Bill dipped his head in a bow. 'You seem pretty smart. Maybe you'll have one yourself some day.' He smiled. 'You're not going to tell me you got the number?'

The man grinned, flattered and pleased with himself. 'Part

of it, not all. I tried, but the driver threw it round and was gone too quickly. I got the letters: ERS. And the seventy-five, of course. By then the traffic was backed up so I couldn't see the rest. Sorry.'

'Don't apologize, my friend,' Bill murmured, peeling a hundred-franc note from the roll in his pocket and pulling it out into view. 'Can you give me a description of the running men?'

The young man shrugged, eyeing the note in Bill's hand. 'Well, I saw their backs mostly. Ordinary looking.' He looked optimistically at Bill, his hand half-extended for the note.

Bill moved it an inch further from him. 'Tall? Short? Thickset? Slim?'

The man pursed his lips, frowning. 'Sort of medium.'

Bill nodded, exchanging a glance with Keltum. 'How about their hair? Dark? Blond?'

He laughed. 'Dark.' He pointed to his own thick waves. 'Like me. I told you they were Kabyle, didn't I?'

'What were they wearing?'

'Jeans. T-shirts. Trainers, I think. Is that okay?' he added, his eyes flickering again to the cash.

Bill nodded and pushed the money into the man's hand, feeling the fingers immediately curl tight around it. 'More than okay.' He pulled out another banknote. It was five hundred francs. Smiling, he pushed it into the man's grasp. 'Here. The down-payment on the BMW. Thanks.' Turning, he took Keltum by the arm and led her away, jubilation in his eyes.

16

The purring hydraulic mechanism brought the heavy steel plates of the embassy gates together with almost soundless precision. The two CRS positioned in the sandbagged sentry posts flanking the gates relaxed visibly, lowering the barrels of their weapons. Neither of them had more than glanced at the nondescript little Peugeot. For every second the gates remained open their attention was wholly on the street, straining for the first sudden movement that might signal the start of a terrorist attack.

Inside the courtyard, the driver, six feet tall but so broad and deep-chested he looked almost dwarfish, jumped out and opened a rear door. The diminutive figure of Daniel Bruckner scrambled out and was half-way up the steps before the Ambassador and the blonde woman burst out to greet him.

The Ambassador threw his arms round the Prime Minister's shoulders and kissed him on both cheeks. Bruckner responded with a perfunctory slap to the Ambassador's ribs. 'Hello, Ariel. Nice to see you. You too, Riva,' he added, blowing the woman a kiss. 'That was a lousy ride, by the way.'

The woman smiled and shrugged. 'You're here, Dan, and nobody took a shot at you. In my book that makes it a *great* ride.'

Bruckner was already pushing through the armoured glass door. 'Is it *that* bad?'

'Yes, it is. The place is coming apart. You've seen the reports. On the one hand we've got de Medem's people on the streets pretty nearly every night now. They've attacked synagogues, Jewish cemeteries, businesses. Even schools. The last few days people have been attacked in their *homes*.'

Bruckner grimaced. 'And the Fundamentalists? I had the

driver make a detour on the way in.' He laughed at Riva's horrified shudder. 'Sorry, it's a habit that won't die. I believe in seeing for myself. The kids I saw, with the women in grey robes, were they Bouhila's people?'

The Ambassador nodded, ushering him into his office. 'Right. That's one thing that makes me shudder. They try to catch them so young.'

Bruckner threw back his head and laughed. 'Ariel! Come on. Don't try to bullshit an old bullshitter. Of *course* they do. If Bouhila were stupid he wouldn't be dangerous. He tries to catch them young, just like the Catholics, and the Jehovah's Witnesses. Just like *our* longhairs back home!'

The Ambassador looked chastened. 'They're no laughing matter,' he said sulkily. 'They're fanatics. And plenty of them would be ready to do anything to get at you. Killing you, the "Butcher of Gaza", would assure them of a place in Bouhila's version of heaven.'

Bruckner winced. 'Is that what they're calling me?' he asked, suddenly reflective. The mood lasted only a moment before he turned to Riva. 'What's all this doing to de Medem's standing?'

'It's hard to say precisely. His poll support seems to have more or less levelled off, around sixteen, seventeen per cent. Basically, every time the Fundamentalists do something stupid, de Medem moves up another quarter point.'

'Still nowhere near enough to make him a candidate, though?'

'Not if people vote the way they tell the pollsters they will. But then, a lot of people won't tell pollsters the truth.' She smiled. 'It's kind of poor taste, you know, admitting you're a Nazi. Alone with a voting paper it might be another matter. My guess is, he'll do a lot better than people think.'

Behind the contact lenses Bruckner's eyes glinted. 'Should we do something about him?' He smiled, but his eyes were steely, drilling into theirs.

Riva laughed uneasily, glancing quickly at the Ambassador. 'My God, Dan. This is France, 1994, not Palestine in '48.

Anyway, knocking *him* off wouldn't change anything. We would probably end up with something worse.' Bruckner dropped his eyes and nodded reluctantly. 'M'mm, I suppose you're right. I'm living in the past. For God's sake, I *am* the past. That's why I'm here, to celebrate it. The future belongs to you young people, not old farts like me . . .' He grinned suddenly. 'Mind you, I still think our old methods can save everyone a lot of trouble.'

❖

Keltum grabbed the phone the minute it rang. In the hour since they had left the message with Lantier's sister she had hardly moved more than a metre from it. She listened for a moment without speaking and then said, 'Just a moment.'

Bill was already off the sofa where he had been dozing, trying to catch up on sleep. As he grabbed the phone from her, she answered his questioning look with a nod. He put the phone to his ear. 'Lantier? Where are you calling from?'

'Don't worry. Not the office. My sister told me you were in a hurry to speak to me.'

'Right! Look, we were up at Montparnasse this morning, asking around. We talked to somebody who *saw* a couple of men jump out of a car and run after Ahmed.'

'Really?' Lantier said quietly. 'How could your witness be sure they were chasing Bengana?'

'He heard one of them say so.'

'What! In public?'

'Well, he spoke Kabyle. Maybe he thought he was pretty safe.'

'And your witness speaks Kabyle? Are you sure?'

'Certain. Don't forget I had an interpreter with me.' He smiled at Keltum as he spoke. 'There's no mistake.'

There was a short silence. When Lantier spoke again his voice sounded eager, but softer, as though he were hunched close to the phone. 'I don't suppose he noticed what kind of car it was? Or the number?'

Bill repeated the details the young man had given him. When he had finished, Lantier gave a low whistle. 'I'm impressed. Did he get a look at the driver for us?'

'Tinted glass, so he didn't see the driver. The runners, he did see. Late twenties, medium build, short, dark hair.'

Lantier sucked at his teeth. 'That narrows it down – to about three quarters of a million people. But these both spoke, or understood, Kabyle?'

'Right.'

'Okay. Anything else?'

'Some people are just hard to please! Isn't that plenty to get you started? If you seriously intend to try.'

Lantier's answer was low and distinct. 'I do, believe me. Can you stay where you are now?'

'So long as you promise not to send a squad car for me.'

'Scout's honour. Stay near the phone. I'll get back to you as soon as I can see where any of this is leading.'

Two and a half hours later Bill stood in the kitchen, humming to himself and chopping the vegetables Keltum had shopped for. From the corner of his eye, he became aware of Keltum hovering beyond the doorway, watching with a kind of stealthy curiosity, and he smiled to himself. Trying to reconcile his role as Western oppressor with his insistence on doing the chores was making her restless. He was about to speak when the ringing of the phone drew her hurrying out of his sight.

'It's for you!'

The knife still in his hand, he snatched up the extension that hung on the wall. 'Hello?'

'It's me.'

'Just as well. Anybody else I'd be half-way down the back stairs by now. Do you have anything?'

'A lot more than I want to tell you over the phone. Can you meet me?'

Keltum cut the motor. They were in one of the small streets of low-built old houses that formed a tight little maze in the heart of the thirteenth arrondissement. Each of the neat houses had a front garden, shielded from the street by a wall or a luxuriant hedge. The streets were as deserted, as if they had been in a dormitory suburb, a train-ride from the city, instead of less than a kilometre from the speculative real-estate disaster of the place d'Italie. And the walls, the rhododendrons and the dense and ancient wisteria meant that anyone who might be at home probably could not see the car, much less have a clear view of the occupants.

Looking in her mirror, Keltum made a warning sound. Moments later Lantier's car rolled past and turned the corner a few metres ahead.

Bill reached for the door handle. 'Are you coming?'

Keltum shook her head. In the car she had fallen back into silence. Not the angry, hostile silence of the last few days, though. It had given way to a grave and silent preoccupation, as though she were grappling with deep thoughts and emotions, realigning things in her mind. Bill nodded, touched the cloth of her sleeve awkwardly, not making contact with the flesh beneath, and got out of the car.

He waited while Lantier reached out and swept a drift of empty cassette boxes, unopened mail, crushed cigarette packets and accumulated filth off the passenger seat and onto the floor. He accompanied the gesture with mumbled apologies, as though he had just discovered a mess left by an inattentive cleaning lady. Laughing, Bill lowered himself into the seat, on top of the remaining layer of crumbs, and placed his feet carefully amidst the litter on the floor.

Lantier's handshake held a lot of frank warmth. He nodded, taking in the baseball cap and glasses. 'Not bad. I hardly recognized you. Now you know why it's hell being a policeman, when for a hundred francs France's most wanted man can make himself unrecognizable,' he said cheerfully.

Bill grimaced. 'Yeah, well, you know how it is with us psychos. Chameleons. Masters of disguise.'

Lantier grinned happily. 'It's almost uncanny.' His grin faded. 'I think I may have something on your BMW.'

'Tell me.'

Lantier pulled a photograph from a pocket and handed it over. He let Bill study it in silence for a moment and then said, 'I can't be categoric about it, not having the complete number, but this character owns the right type and colour of car. And the parts of the number fit. Be a big coincidence if it weren't his.'

Bill spoke without looking up from the picture. 'Who is he?'

Lantier shrugged. 'Saïd Khoury. A hard man. Bodyguard for crooks with more clout than he has. Some pimping. Occasional armed robber, we think.'

Bill frowned. 'Back home that description would fit two-thirds of the idiots the police have on file.'

'Here, too. The pimping to pay the rent. The armed robbery as a kind of seasonal work. These characters'll hear about an up-coming job and get themselves recruited, or not, depending if they've gambled and drunk away what they earned for the last one. But there is another aspect to this one that might, just, make him a little more interesting.'

Bill looked expectant.

'He's Algerian. He lived in Marseilles, until about a year ago.'

'What's interesting about that? There must be more Arabs in Marseilles than they have left in Tangier.'

'Not quite. It's got enough of them to people the eighth biggest town in Algeria, though. Did you know that? I got it from one of de Medem's speeches. I checked it. He's right.'

Bill inclined from the waist. 'No, I didn't know that, Professor. Thank you, and Monsieur de Medem for bringing it to my attention. What brought Khoury up to Paris, do you know?'

'Well, the funny part about him is he used to do strong-arm work for some of the right-wing groups down on the south coast.'

'I'm surprised that left him *time* for pimping.'

'Right. The point is, it would be very unusual for those people to use an Arab. It looks as if he might have a lot more brains than the average crash-bang criminal. He worked in Nice for quite a

225

while, for one of the bogus companies Jacques Palatin set up to milk the municipality while he was Mayor.'

'What kind of work did our man do for him?'

'His speciality was blackmail operations.'

Bill was thoughtful for a moment. 'Tell me more.'

'Well, it seems the kind of blackmail he was setting up for Palatin *never* led to requests for cash. They wanted people's co-operation, not their money. They were doing well enough looting *public* money. No, what mattered to them was keeping people's mouths shut. That was your man's job. Word would come down that somebody was getting too curious, and Khoury would get to work. Mostly he would just set them up with a woman, or, better still, a schoolgirl. A few photographs, and that was that. Some needed a little more finesse. Local officials, or politicians, would be invited on "study" trips. They might actually have studied something, for all I know. The way it worked, after they got back they would be allowed a few weeks of fun, showing their friends the photographs of them gorging on lobsters in beachside restaurants, film stars at the next table. Then, it would turn out the trip had been paid for by the Mafia, or a group of paedophiles, or something. It was a pretty silky operation. It kept Palatin's hand in the till for years before they slammed the drawer.'

'Do you know who Khoury's working for now?'

Lantier shrugged. 'Himself, as far as the records show. We've had nothing serious on him for quite a while. He's got a couple of girls on the rue Saint Denis. His front's a peepshow and sex shop on the same street. It saves his poor old legs when he goes out to collect.'

'Which one?'

Lantier leaned back against his door and nibbled at an imaginary spike of broken nail on his little finger, looking shrewdly at Bill. 'I'm not that certain I ought to tell you.'

'Why not, for God's sake?'

'Look, Monsieur Duvall, I've gone a long way out on a limb with you. You're an intelligent man and you guessed from the start that it's not for your beautiful blue eyes that I'm doing this. I didn't, I still don't, want that officer, Delcasse, to have died for nothing. I thought you were a resourceful man who might come up with something that would help me reach the bastards responsible. And, by God, I seem to have been right. But it's turning bad. This man's dangerous.'

Bill snorted. 'Oh, for God's sake, Lantier. I just want to *talk* to him. I can take care of myself.'

Lantier made a wry face. 'I don't doubt that for a moment, Monsieur Duvall. From the look of you, I'd say you could give a good account of yourself in a street brawl. The trouble is, a street brawl is not what we're talking about. This man might have started out along that route, but he's come a long way since then. Americans tend to have the idea that other country's criminals are second rate, not quite the real thing. A joke, maybe? Well, let me tell you, as someone who has spent a career on the streets of this city, they are not. And Khoury specially is not.' He paused, his eyes on Bill. 'If this man suspects you are a danger to him, if you even *offend* him too badly, he's capable of putting a bullet into your head.' He tapped a finger to his brow. 'Without hesitation.' He paused. 'In case you were thinking of smiling, Monsieur Duvall, he's done it before. It's in the file. We couldn't prove it, not to a court's satisfaction, but there's no doubt at all. He's done it three times to our certain knowledge. More, if the rumours on the street are true.'

'You really think he's going to risk years in gaol when all I want to do is talk to him?'

Lantier sighed and moved impatiently in his seat. 'Please, get this into your head: these people don't care about going to prison. To you or me the idea of years out of our lives is unthinkable. It would simply be too much of a waste. People like this man don't even think about it. One, because they don't have the imagination to think that far ahead, and, two, because, in a peculiar way they actually *like* it. In his world, knocking you off and doing time for manslaughter is a kind of success. Another credential. Also,' he added, breaking into a smile, 'when these people go to gaol, their social life doesn't suffer the way yours or mine would. To them, going to prison is a way of catching up with old friends.'

'How about the girls they aren't going to get, the terrific cars they won't be driving?'

Lantier shook his head, smiling. 'You know, Monsieur Duvall, you just haven't got the make-up to be a criminal. Prison doesn't change anything for these people. No women is an inconvenience, of course.' He surprised Bill by looking suddenly deadly serious. 'But then they make do with what they can get in prison.' Bill's mouth twisted at the idea. Lantier shook off the sudden moroseness, leaning closer. 'Listen. If you or I had half the money this man takes from his girls the first thing we would do is buy a terrific flat in the sixteenth. Our neighbours would be lawyers, doctors – people like you,' he added with a laugh. 'Well, *he* lives in a room four metres square in a fleapit of a hotel, a hundred francs a day, over in Belleville. That's his world. It's where he fits. For Christ's sake, prison may have less women than he's used to, but it's got better plumbing!'

'What the hell does he do with his money, then?'

'I told you. Gambling. Clothes. Those fancy cars you mentioned. Nightclubs. He has no trouble getting rid of it.'

Bill straightened, his hair brushing the ceiling of the car. 'Okay, so, all this to tell me that I ought to watch my step? It's nice of you to care.'

Lantier's head and shoulders moved in a barely perceptible shrug. 'Not necessarily about you. If Khoury did put a bullet in your head, it would play right into Vadon's hands, though. Since you've chosen to get in this deep, I'd rather it turned out to be of use to somebody.' He grinned, suddenly, briefly, and bitterly. 'Of course, it's personal, up to a point. I'd be lying if I told you otherwise. You are stirring things up, and it might mean I can end my career the way a working policeman should. Not as some minister's puppet!' he added with a sudden upsurge of resentment that took Bill by surprise. Immediately getting a grip on himself, he shrugged again, laughing briefly at his own emotion. 'Sorry.' He sat up straight in the seat and held the wheel, stretching his shoulders back. 'Anyway, I've warned you. If you choose not to listen, that's your lookout. But if you *do* come across anything, make sure you let me know fast. And keep me posted on where you're going and who you're seeing.' He grinned. 'At least if anything happens to you I'll have something to tell your next of kin.'

Bill laughed. 'I don't have one.'

Lantier jerked a thumb over his shoulder. 'She does, though,' he said, no longer grinning. 'Don't you think you're getting her in too deep?'

'I'm not sure how much influence I'm going to have either way. She's a strong-willed woman, even if she does have a lot of things to work out. She's relaxed a little, although I'm still having trouble knowing just how she'll react from one minute to the next. Basically, she thinks we're all part of a big anti-Arab conspiracy. Especially you.'

'What did *I* do?'

'Not you, personally. The police. She's convinced her brother's death wouldn't have been treated the same way if he hadn't been an Arab.'

Lantier bit his lip, musing. 'It's a point of view. If Yves Saint Laurent had jumped out of a window I guess it might have been a little harder for them to bury the case.'

'Are you saying she's right?'

'Not exactly.'

'But approximately?'

'The Bouhila connection won't have helped.' Lantier sighed. 'Look, I already told you, I've spent most of my career in this city. I've been in a housing project out in the "zone" at four in the morning, trying to arrest some kid I caught stealing a car radio, and found myself surrounded by a mob. It's happened to me in Arab areas and it's happened in French areas, if that's what I'm allowed to call them. And I can tell you, I was more scared in the Arab neighbourhoods. Don't ask me why, I just was. If you're going to have a hundred people threatening to throw bricks at you, you prefer them to be *your* people. At least you *feel* you've got a problem you can talk about. When they hate you for the colour of your skin or your religion it's hard to know where to start. Frankly, your instincts are to shoot one of them, just to give yourself time to think. Now, with Bouhila's people out there playing the vigilante with their ridiculous armbands, and the women in veils which is all you need to see to know they hate you, it's ten times worse.'

'Just what's this got to do with the cover-up on Ahmed?'

'Nothing directly. It just produces a climate that makes it easy for Vadon. Let me give you another example. My men see a nice car driven by a couple of Beurs,' he used the word the immigrants had coined to describe themselves. 'They stop it. Why? Because it's about eleven times more likely to be stolen than if the kids were . . . French. That's not my *opinion*, that's the figure, what the statistics say. Every once in a while there's a screw-up and a perfectly respectable young Arab gets hurt. The papers kick up a stink, but it doesn't last. And nobody in the administration gets excited, because they *know* the copper was just doing his job. There's this built-in bias.'

'So Beurs can get killed and nobody worries?'

Lantier looked exasperated. 'Bengana *jumped*. And, for your information, from what the bag lady said, the two men who killed that officer were North Africans. That didn't stop him trying to help.'

Something in Lantier's tone made Bill study his face, frowning. He nodded slowly. 'That killing really is on your mind, isn't it?'

Lantier dropped his voice to a whisper. 'Police work is dangerous. He knew the risks. But his family is entitled to have his death investigated, to see his killer caught. If anything that could be done isn't being done because some shitty little politician is using the police force as his personal security service it makes me very angry.'

Bill smiled grimly. 'Angry enough to use a crazed killer like me to help?'

Lantier laughed. 'Sure. You're a sex maniac. And I'm the reincarnation of John the Baptist.' He reached into his jacket and pulled out a piece of paper. 'Here. If you're really determined to ignore my advice, you'll need these.'

Bill unfolded the slip of paper and looked it over, deciphering the two addresses scrawled on it. He read them aloud, looking up at Lantier.

Lantier gave him a confirming nod and laid a hand on Bill's sleeve. 'Please, do us both a favour, and remember what I've told you about this man. Above all, don't involve her.' He jerked his head towards the corner. 'Not unless you want her father to suffer more than he has already. This character,' he tapped the paper, 'would kill her like that.' He snapped his fingers. 'And that's trouble I don't need. Remember,' he went on, smiling and wagging a finger, 'my pension's at stake here. If anyone finds out what I'm doing, I'm busted.'

'How about me?'

Lantier guffawed. 'If he shot you, he'd be a hero.' Brusquely he stuck out a hand. 'Good luck. And please take it all seriously. Be very careful.'

Bill shook his hand and returned his smile with a lop-sided one of his own. 'I appreciate your concern.'

Lantier retained his grip on Bill's hand. 'I mean it, Monsieur Duvall. I repeat, keep me informed what you're doing, and let me know immediately if you pick up anything that could be interesting.'

'Don't die taking a clue with me, huh?' Bill laughed. 'Is there anything I wouldn't do to help your faltering career?'

Lantier grinned. 'No. You've already been very kind to a man looking forward to the autumn of his years. Goodbye, and once again, take care.'

❖

The French Prime Minister craned forward so that the edge of the desk cut deep into the flesh of his belly. His untidy, stout face was blanched and quivering with suppressed fury. 'And you mean to tell me, Caillart, it's taken until now to be reported to you!'

The Minister of Defence nodded miserably. 'The raid was only discovered at six, when the fresh guard detail came on duty. According to the guard who survived, the attack took place just after midnight. He didn't see them leave, but he judges that they were only inside for five minutes. It took a while to go through the inventory, but the base commander called me less than an hour ago. Until then he had been hoping we had been lucky, that nothing had been taken.'

Pautrat, the Prime Minister, heaved upright, snorting contemptuously. 'Raiders attack the armoury of a so-called top-security military base, kill a guard, and the commander "hopes nothing's missing!" My God, Caillart, I trust you're dealing with him as he deserves.'

'I'll be taking whatever action seems appropriate, of course.'

Pautrat pushed himself to his feet and lumbered round the desk to stand inches from the other man. 'I'll tell you what's appropriate, Caillart. He should have his balls cut off and stuffed down his gullet! Does he even begin to understand what's happened? A roomful of weapons, and the whole night ahead of them, yet they took only the two Austrian carbines!'

The Defence Minister nodded miserably.

Pautrat turned to another of the men in the room, a slim grey-haired man with the rosette of the Legion d'Honneur in the lapel of his carefully cut suit. 'You've seen enough fighting, Bouillot, and you've done enough policing; what do you make of it?'

The man grimaced sympathetically at Caillart. 'Well, if I wanted to rob banks I would have settled for machine guns, something that would spray plenty of metal and scare bank clerks shitless. Those things don't even *look* like guns. If a robber stuck one of those across the counter, a bank clerk would laugh in his face, think it was a toy. He'd have to shoot somebody just to let them know he wasn't kidding.'

'So who *would* want plastic guns?' Pautrat asked sarcastically.

'Terrorists, of course. Aircraft hijackers would be my first choice, or anyone who wanted to move weapons through metal detectors. Or snipers who plan to kill and run,' he added, his lip curling in the professional soldier's contempt for the cowardice of the assassin.

'Exactly,' Pautrat barked, turning to face his audience. 'So, there we are. We have Daniel Bruckner, with a three million dollar price on his head, about to go on show for us; we have de Medem's people desecrating Jewish monuments all over France; we have Bouhila's crowd acting like an Islamic republic within France. And now we have two of the world's most advanced sniper rifles floating around loose.' He grinned coldly at his audience. 'Does anyone here think there isn't a connection somewhere?'

There was a long silence. People shifted uncomfortably as Pautrat looked at each of them in turn. He sniffed loudly. 'Nobody?' His gaze alighted on Vadon. 'Well, I think *you* had better have another look over your security arrangements, don't you?' He gave a sudden sardonic grin. 'I don't suppose anyone here would like to tell the President about this, in place of me?'

17

Bill glanced again at Keltum's broken-backed street guide and gave another instruction. He sat silently looking out as she nodded and turned into yet another narrow street clogged with damaged cars, double-parked with total unconcern for the ones they hemmed in. After all, that was what car horns were for.

This part of Paris, the warren of streets around the boulevard de Belleville, was untouched by the torpor that enveloped the rest of the city. Here, the Arab, African, Asian and Eastern European immigrants lived in a world unaffected by sixty years of labour legislation. To the sweatshop owners, or the godfathers running the 'African' artefact pedlars, the idea of giving their employees holidays would have seemed as big an affront to common sense as paying income tax. Their employment terms were exquisitely simple. Nobody putting in the ten hours a day, six days a week, fifty-two weeks a year grind behind the sound-insulated doors of the clandestine workshops should complain. If they did, they would wake up to find the police at the door of their multiple occupancy flop-house room demanding residence papers they had never owned, nor even heard of.

Now, the summer heat had driven them from the stifling squalor of their rooms to the relative freshness of the streets. Men spilled from cafés onto the pavements, drinking beer from bottles and gesticulating and laughing. Women crowded onto steps talking in a dozen unfathomable dialects while they suckled children, occasionally breaking off to shout at the laughing broods that played among the rusting cars.

They rolled along slowly, following a delivery van with a pair of grinning boys hanging from the back, their filthy T-shirts riding up over muscular stomachs. Ignoring their gesticulations, Bill kept his eyes on the shopfronts to their left. Most of them were dismal uncarpeted drinking joints, where the customers stood at the bar and swigged beer from bottles, or terminally dilapidated shops. Yet another bar slid into view. Its windows were white-washed up to head height, obscuring the interior. An old man, his face the colour and texture of tree bark, sat outside on a plain wooden chair, his half-closed lizard eyes flicking up and down the street. The name 'Belgrade Café' had been hand-painted over the facade. It was repeated, this time in dribbling cyrillic lettering, across the tops of the windows. They slowed to a crawl while the van inched through the narrow gap left by a Mercedes coupé, bristling with antennae, that almost blocked the roadway outside. The breath of white exhaust drifting from the coupé made Bill smile. The trademark vanity of pimps and dealers the world over. Leaving the keys in

234

the car was a way of advertising your invulnerability. Here was a car no neighbourhood joyrider was going to take a chance on.

Above the shopfronts greying underwear hung from makeshift lines strung across windows. Here and there a parched geranium struggled for survival, wedged behind the flaking iron guard rails. Grimy zigzags of adhesive tape held cracked panes precariously in place.

The van gathered speed again, drawing them behind it. 'That's it.' Keltum's eyes flickered in the direction of Bill's nod. A black plaque, fixed to the wall alongside a doorway bore the word 'Hotel' in chipped gilt copper-plate. The door stood ajar between a laundromat with a hand-written 'out of order' sign hanging from the dryer, and an unkempt grocery store. Boxes of fruit spilled from the store, filling the width of the narrow pavement.

'Okay,' he murmured, not turning to look back as they pulled past the hotel. 'So now I know what I'm in for.'

'Where do you want to go now?'

He smiled. 'Tati.'

She glanced uncertainly around at him. 'You're not serious.'

'I am. I need to shop for some clothes.'

She looked at him sharply, ready to be angry. 'You? You're not going to buy clothes at *Tati*.' Her jaw muscles set. 'You're laughing at us, aren't you?'

He pursed his lips, pondering her reaction. The teeming Tati stores, stacked to the ceiling with ultra cheap clothes, factory rejects and bankrupt stocks in laughably unsaleable shades, were a bigger name in tracts of the Third World than Christian Dior. Black matriarchs would get off the plane from Guinea-Bissau with nothing more than a wad of cash and the name 'Tati' scribbled on a scrap of card, confident that any Parisian with taste would know how to direct them there. To Keltum, for a North African to shop there was an act of betrayal, contributing to a stereotype she despised.

He touched her sleeve. 'I'm not laughing, believe me. This isn't part of a manifesto. I just need clothes that won't be noticed.' He jerked his head. 'You saw the dump back there where our man lives.' He touched a finger to the logo of a tiny polo player on his shirt pocket. 'Tell me honestly, did it look like a place that would draw the Ralph Lauren trade?' Her expression softened in a hint of a smile. He smiled himself. 'Except maybe for the pimps. And the last thing in the world I want is for *them* to notice me, and think I've come looking for some of their action.' He shook his head. 'I just want to be part of the landscape. Back there, Keltum, that means Tati.'

She stopped the car across the wide boulevard from the store. Bill settled the baseball cap closer on his head. 'Okay, so is that a promise? You'll wait for me at the flat, and not move until I call you. If what Lantier said is true, I may need help in a hurry.'

'To wait on men. Isn't that what Arab women are for?' Her expression gave him no clue whether he should take it as a joke.

'M'mm. And if you don't hear from me by tomorrow evening, call that number and tell Lantier what's happened,' he said, tapping a finger on the envelope where he had copied the phone number. Putting on the tinted glasses, he stepped out onto the littered pavement.

He stood for several seconds, close up against a shuttered newsstand, studying the faces of the crowd milling in and out of the store opposite, looking for the watchfulness that would mark a plain-clothes policeman or floorwalker. He focused on the relatively few European faces that stood out among the Africans and Arabs struggling with the pink-and-blue striped nylon bags that were the Tati motif. None of them wore the quick-eyed, wary look he feared. Instead, in contrast to the immigrants, successful enough people in their way, the Europeans shared the pinched, defeated look of people at the bottom of their particular heap. Head-down, his shoulders rounded into a stoop in imitation of them, he set off across the boulevard.

He pushed his way through the throng worrying at a scrambled heap of synthetic trousers piled high on an outside stall and moved deeper into the store. He paused to take his bearings. Around him, heaving knots of people attacked the bins of clothes like hyenas at a corpse, ripping items from the pile, examining them perfunctorily and tossing them aside again, so that the very air seemed filled with flying clothes. Feeling like a vegetarian shark at a feeding frenzy, he began shouldering his way through the scrum in search of what he needed.

In less than ten minutes he had collected three sets of underwear, socks, a couple of shirts in colours he could not quite put a name to, an acrylic sweater priced at a quarter of what he normally paid for socks, two pairs of brown slacks with a permanent crease conveniently sewn down the front of the legs, and a nylon zipper jacket the colour of stale mustard. He moved on to the racks of shoes. Each shoe looked as though it had been hewn from a single block of polypropylene. Abandoning them, he settled for a pair of trainers in a glinting synthetic fabric and carried his spoils to the fitting rooms.

It took ten edgy minutes before he reached the head of the file of broad-hipped Arab ladies, narrow-faced men, and statuesque African matrons in headgear that made them a foot taller than he was. He pounced gratefully on a booth, drew the curtain with a deep sigh of relief, and began changing.

He pressed himself back against the wall of the booth and stared at his reflection, smiling grimly. The shirt collar was slightly over-sized, and an authentic half-inch of sock showed between the trousers and the shiny trainers. He pulled on the sweater and the zipper jacket and looked again. The sweater was a little tight over the chest and the jacket sleeves were too long. The whole effect was just what he had hoped. The clothes were so obviously cheap that their newness was not a problem. He looked no different from poor men at big city stations everywhere, men on the very brink of destitution, arriving in their sad, best, clothes in search of the last opportunity the city would never give them.

He left the store still wearing the new outfit, his own clothes and the rest of his purchases pushed into one of the striped bags.

❖

The broken wooden stairs led to an unlit landing. At his rear another flight led off to the floors above, lit by a faint glow from a distant bulb. In front of him, a door stood open, held by a piece of twine looped from the doorknob to a nail driven into the wall. He paused, breathing deeply, savouring the acrid mixture of odours that enveloped him. Somewhere up above him a lavatory flushed, followed by the slamming of a door and slow, shuffling footsteps. Loosening his shoulders, he stepped forward through the open door.

He was in a dingy reception area. There was no furniture apart from a narrow counter and a strip of greasy carpet, worn through to its backing and scarred from dozens of cigarette burns. A thin Arab, probably in his fifties, but with a narrow, shrewd face that made him look ten years older, let him stand there for several seconds before turning from the badly tuned television set that stood on a low table behind the counter. He gave Bill a stare of open dislike. 'What do you want?'

Bill gave a tentative shrug. 'I was looking for a room,' he answered in the disconsolate mumble of somebody who expected to be rejected, even in a place like this.

The man looked at him with a smug sneer about his mouth, as if he had caught Bill trying to dupe him. 'I've only got one with a shower,' he grunted, his attention already slewing from Bill back to the cartoons, convinced he had priced himself out of Bill's bracket.

'How much is it?' Bill ventured, as though he were apologizing for interrupting the man's viewing.

The Arab turned slowly back, moving his eyes last, and squinted at Bill. A mist of crafty surprise had come over his face. 'A hundred and ten francs. Per night,' he added sharply, as though Bill might have expected full-board for a week at the price.

Bill hesitated, chewing at his lip, going through the motions of grappling with the arithmetic. While he did it, he turned over the idea of asking to see the room, and decided against it. A tourist would probably do it. People in his position would not have that kind of confidence, or be that fastidious. 'Okay,' he said, blurting it out with the emphasis of a man recklessly acting against his better judgement. 'I'll take it.'

'How long do you want it for?'

He looked helplessly at the man.

'A week? They give you ten per cent off, weekly.'

Bill nodded and smiled, grateful for the guidance, and reached into his pocket. On the way there he had taken care to transfer most of his money to an inner pocket. He pulled out the crumpled handful of notes he had left for just this purpose and counted off the week's rent, tenderly flattening each dilapidated note with the edge of his hand as he laid it on the counter, as if parting with it hurt. The man watched his hands with the hostile stare of somebody who had been losing heavily at cards. Bill pushed the money towards him, stared ruefully at the few notes left in his hand, and picked up the key which the man dumped onto the counter in front of him. The receptionist clawed the little sheaf of money off the counter and slid it out of sight. His eyes already back on the television screen, he jerked his head in the direction of the stairs. 'Third floor. Number twelve.'

'Thanks,' Bill mumbled. He hoisted his bag and trudged back into the stinking stairwell, groping in the dimness for the first stair.

18

The door was half-way down a corridor with a strip of greasy carpet running two-thirds of its length. He braced himself, took a breath, and pushed it open.

He thought he had been prepared for the worst. The sight of the room made him realize with a shock how little imagination he had. The room measured three paces from the door to the cracked and grimy window, and two and a half paces across. The walls were papered with three different patterns of cheap paper. One strip had come off entirely, leaving a patch of damp and discoloured plaster exposed. The rest threatened to do the same, fronds hanging loose in the angle of the ceiling and the walls. There were three items of furniture in the room: a sagging divan with an orange bedspread thrown over it, a painted bedside table that might once have been a fruit crate, and a chest of drawers that had originally had four drawers and now held only three. Somebody had thoughtfully pinned a piece of plywood across the bottom of the cavity to make a useful shelf.

He shut the door and began examining the room more closely. A blackened gas ring stood on the chest of drawers, its stubby feet anchored in a centimetre of congealed grease. He turned away with a shiver of disgust and moved to examine a free-standing shower cubicle with transparent plastic walls, which had been crammed into the far corner, blocking part of the window. This was the luxurious fitting that the receptionist had feared might put the room out of his class. He opened the door, making the cheap, brittle plastic vibrate noisily, and checked over the inside. A wad of scummy hair clogged the drain. Grimacing, he quickly closed the door on it and turned his attention to the window.

He wrenched it open at the third attempt, giving a gap of about twenty-five centimetres before it fouled the warped frame. The view was in the same class as the room. Two metres away, on the far side of a sunless well, he was looking at a window twenty centimetres square that was almost certainly the window of a toilet. Crouching, he could see a row of similar windows mounting the building, and alongside them, a skein of dilapidated pipes with red slashes of rust indicating persistent leaks. He closed the window and turned back to the bed.

He upended the striped bag onto it and fished out his shoes, the only items he had kept back when, on the way to the hotel, he had dumped his own clothes into a skip. Already, the seams and edges of the cheap trainers had etched red weals beneath his ankle bones. He held one of the expensive, supple loafers in each hand, looking thoughtfully at them for a moment before ripping the tassel from one of them. Turning back to the window, he wrenched it open again. He crouched to check that he was not observed from the upper windows and then reached out and rubbed each shoe in turn against the rough cement render of the wall. By the time he was finished the deep shine had gone, leaving the leather dull and scuffed. Satisfied they would no longer look too conspicuous with the Tati wardrobe, he swapped them for the trainers and walked to the door.

He stood listening for several seconds, and then turned and walked softly to the angle of the L-shaped corridor. Smells of cramped living and dirty clothes seemed to come from the very fabric of the building. He was momentarily startled by somebody abruptly beginning to snore, the sound hardly muffled by the flimsy door of the sleeper's room. He surmised that at any given moment half the beds would be filled with sleeping men. Paris was full of hotels like this, owned by unsentimental men with large German cars, who knew just how much they could wring, in exchange for exactly how little, from the very poorest workers. The French had a term for them, 'sleep merchants', and it was an accurate one. They sold little more than floor space and running water to immigrants, to the solitary men doing shifts on the Métro, or sweeping streets, people who would rent a room the size of his own between six of them, turning in when they came off shift onto beds and mattresses still warm from the previous occupant. When they were not sleeping or working, the joylessness of the room would drive them onto the streets, to the dismal, sparsely furnished bars owned by the same men.

Rounding the angle of the corridor, he found the far end of it blocked by a fire door. He stepped closer, still treading carefully, to examine it. A padlock the size of his fist held it shut. It was probably unlocked once a year, when the bribed official from the fire department called to tip them off about a forthcoming inspection. The rest of the time the owner had a choice between respecting the fire regulations – in a place where every resident had a bottled gas cooker and smoked a pack a day, or night – and the chance of someone sneaking a free night on one of his filthy floors. The regulations did not stand a chance.

He checked out the other floors, noting the room numbers on each level. The lay-out of every floor was identical, and so were the padlocks. The only way in or out of the place was down the main staircase. He descended to the reception, dropping his key noisily alongside the empty tea glass on the desk. The receptionist sat slumped in the same position, the television still on as he thumbed a catalogue of pornographic videos. Bill walked on down and out into the sunlight.

He paused, the newcomer getting his bearings, giving himself time to size up the scene around him. He caught the lizard gaze of the look-out in front of the Belgrade Café studying him with lazy interest. Their eyes locked for an instant before the man's reptile gaze slid away to flicker up the street. A BMW had taken over from the Mercedes in pumping exhaust into the lungs of the look-out. Walking with his head-down, lifeless step, Bill set off up the street, pausing to peer into two more of the uninviting bars before turning to cross the street towards a third.

He paused on the opposite pavement, one foot still in the

gutter. A crocodile of small girls, aged four to ten, filed silently past, hand in hand. The girls, dark-haired and dark-eyed, all wore identical grey skirts and tunics. They were shepherded by a pair of alert young women in robes and head-dresses. As they passed him, the women's eyes cast down, not meeting his, he studied the scrubbed faces and the clean, neat uniforms. He turned to glance at the retreating backs of the young women. Slender and upright, they might have been Keltum.

Looking at them, he felt the shock of understanding what Bouhila was offering, a realization of what had drawn Keltum, and so many other young people, to his movement. Just looking at the children, happy and healthy, but also confident and disciplined, you *knew* that they would not grow up accepting the humiliations their parents had felt forced to accept. Bouhila personally might be an asshole, but what he was doing for these kids was serious.

And it was why the National Salvation League was drawing so much support. De Medem understood more clearly than anyone that these innocent-looking children represented a threat. His message was clear, and people like the owner of Bill's hotel heard it perfectly. Once these kids grew up, with the expectations Bouhila's schools were giving them, a slum landlord would hardly be able to make a decent living any more. Resisting the instinct to continue staring after them, he crossed the pavement and shambled through the wide-open door of the bar.

The scattering of stained tables were set about with unmatched kitchen chairs. Two men with lean, seamed faces sat intent over a complicated card game. The sagging cigarettes stuck to their lips moved as they spoke. A cluster of beer bottles stood at their elbows. Two more men were at the bar. One of them was downing small glasses of white wine from an unlabelled bottle and joking with the barman. The second stood with his elbows on the bar, staring vacantly into his empty cup. Bill took up a place apart from them and mumbled a request for coffee. The barman served him without breaking off his conversation, banging the coffee onto the grey metal of the bar under Bill's nose and at the same time hoisting a bottle from beneath the counter. He cocked it over Bill's cup. Bill gave an almost imperceptible nod, like a buyer at an auction, and the man up-ended the bottle with a flourish, filling the last half-centimetre with the eau-de-vie. Bill grunted, lifted the brimming cup, sipped at it noisily, and turned to gaze idly at the street.

The spot was well chosen. From where he stood, he had a clear view of the hotel entrance. Spending the entire afternoon standing at a bar drinking was the main local pastime. He could stay there until they closed knowing that nobody would pay the slightest attention to him. He sipped again at the coffee and stifled a gag as the cheap eau-de-vie seared his throat. It would be nice if he did not have to.

He was on his third boosted coffee when the receptionist emerged from the hotel entrance with a swaying stack of tea glasses in his hand. The man turned left and began walking along the pavement. Passing the storefront, he shouted to a youth in a brown overall stooped over the display of vegetables and turned into the first of the cafés. From where he stood, Bill could clearly see him at the bar, ordering a drink and gesturing to other people in the dimness of the interior. He had just been served when the young man abandoned his vegetables and hurried into the bar to join him. Immediately, but without any appearance of haste, Bill called the barman over and paid for his drinks.

He slouched back to the hotel, passing in front of the bar where the receptionist was engaged in animated conversation with the grocery man and the bartender. Bill felt a twinge of surprise at the squat shape of the Orangina bottle on the counter in front of the receptionist. He would have taken him for another straight-from-the-bottle beer drinker. As he loitered past, the man took a swig of his drink and accepted a cigarette offered by the barman. He was settling in.

Bill shambled on into the hotel entrance. The moment he was out of sight of the street, he threw off the slouching walk and sprang up the stairs.

The register, a shabby ring-binder, lay amid the debris of bills and scraps of paper behind the counter. He scanned the tea-stained pages, grateful for the near-illiteracy that obliged the man to write in laborious capitals. It took him only seconds to find out that his target had room seven, on the floor below his. He paused, listening hard for sounds from the street, and then grabbed the key to room seven, together with his own, and sprinted for the stairs.

The room was about the same size as his. The clutter made it seem even smaller. The furniture was a little better, still cheap but not quite total junk. Tangled bedclothes spilled onto the floor, the mess half hidden by a gaudy gold bedspread thrown carelessly over them, the occupant's idea of making the bed. A deep indentation in the pillow, with an oily grey stain, showed where the man's head had lain. In place of a shower, a wash basin was fixed to the wall, thickly rimmed with grime. On the plastic shelf above it half a dozen designer colognes, worth a couple of months' rent, stood in neat alignment. A late model television and video, huge in the cramped space, stood at the foot of the bed. Video cassettes lay scattered on the bed, their covers featuring naked women or men kicking opponents in the face. Mostly, though, the room contained clothes. They were everywhere. Suits on wire hangers, still in the thin plastic sacks of dry cleaners, hung in a clump from a hook behind the door. More dangled precariously from the window frame. Neat paper packages of fresh laundry were piled on the floor and on top of the chest of drawers. Dirty laundry lay in a heap beneath the wash basin. His heart pounding, alert for the slightest sound, Bill began searching.

His movements were quick but systematic. He pushed nothing aside, but lifted each item with care, replacing it meticulously in its spot. It was not a thorough search. If necessary, that could come later, once he knew what he was looking for. Right now he just wanted to learn as much as possible about the man while leaving no sign of his passage.

The top three drawers of the chest contained more clothes. Shirts, underwear and socks were arranged with a precision that was in startling contrast to the squalor of the room. The fourth drawer was crammed to overflowing with magazines: martial arts and naked women. Turning away, he dropped to his knees and lifted the edge of the bedspread. More cassettes lay beneath the bed, amid a jumble of ten or twelve pairs of shoes. Peering deeper into the gloom, he reached in and withdrew a grey Delsey suitcase. He gave a soft hiss of surprise as the locks sprang open at his touch.

He began shuffling through the layer of papers strewn in the bottom. He grabbed a paper at random. It was a bill from a tailor. He glanced at the array of suspended suits and gave a soft whistle. Maybe that was why the man did not buy a flat. He had the price of an apartment invested in clothes. He threw down the invoice and went on foraging. With a soft exclamation he snatched up another bill. It was dated four months previously, and was for the purchase of a BMW. The bill was made out to a company with an address in Clichy. He smiled briefly at the list of cheque numbers scribbled on it. In the old days a pimp with a reputation to maintain would have walked in and paid cash. Now that cash transactions that size were illegal, pimps were obliged to launder the money they took off their women using a network of bogus companies. The address on the invoice was one. The peepshow would be another. He hesitated a moment and then shoved the document into his pocket. It might be something Lantier could work with. The cheque numbers might enable him to run down some connections.

He quickly rifled through the rest of the papers but found nothing more of interest. He pushed the case back into place and stood up hurriedly, plucking grimy fluff from his sleeve. He waited with his hand on the doorknob, listening, and then left the room, locking it behind him.

Leaping down the stairs to the deserted reception area, he reached over and replaced the key to room seven. Then, he retreated to the landing above and waited. It was a bare minute before he heard movement on the stairs below. He walked slowly back down to reception, timing it to meet the receptionist as he re-entered, carrying a glass of tea and a magazine. As the receptionist shoved past, scowling at Bill's tentative nod of acknowledgment, Bill dropped his eyes. The magazine in the man's hand was in Arabic. The face of Bouhila stared out from it. Even in a photograph, the eyes made you want to flinch. Mumbling a half-audible apology for getting in the man's way, Bill dropped his key on the counter and shambled towards the door.

Once out of sight of the hotel, he walked more quickly, winding back and forth in the run-down streets without bothering where he was heading, just putting distance between himself and the hotel. At last, satisfied that nobody was around who might have seen him leave the place, he hailed a cruising taxi.

'Rue Saint Denis.' He sank back in his seat and closed his eyes, letting some of the tension flow out of him. Normally, he would have enjoyed walking the relatively short distance. Now, just being on the streets was too great a risk. He sighed, massaging the muscles of his neck. The fear, the constant watch for the abrupt movement, the sudden shouted challenge, was draining him more than he would have thought possible.

He opened his eyes as the driver half turned to give him a leer that indicated he would not be averse to a little fun himself, if only he did not have to drive a lousy taxi on a day like this. 'Yes, Monsieur.' He let the clutch out unceremoniously. 'What level?'

'From the top.'

He closed his eyes again. If the man thought he wanted to window-shop that was fine. Cruising the rue Saint Denis drooling at prostitutes went nicely with his new wardrobe.

The cab pulled off the boulevard and into the top of the rue Saint Denis, bringing the sudden sharp odour of piss and rotting oranges wafting through the open window. The stifling afternoon heat was working on the city like a woman's pulse-points on perfume. The driver swore as he pulled to a stop behind a line of traffic. Thirty metres ahead a swarm of men were hurrying to unload a truck. Despite the men's obvious haste, frustrated drivers were leaning on their horns, filling the air with an oppressive cacophony. The cab driver joined in, leaning from his window to shout obscenities as he gave them a five-second burst. Bill sat through three more blasts before thrusting some change at the driver and getting out to walk. Walking was dangerous, but sitting in a cab with a driver bent on turning every head in the neighbourhood was worse.

He walked without hurry past the cheek-by-jowl garment wholesalers, weaving among the racks of clothes being wheeled by delicate-featured Bangladeshi illegals who scraped a living servicing the basement sweatshops with their twenty-first-century brandnames and eighteenth-century labour practices. The sweatshop-owners took the air in the showroom entrances, crocodile belts taut over larded bellies, enjoying the glint of the sun on their medallions and fat gold watches.

In the alleys and stairways between the showrooms, prostitutes killed time chatting in groups; African women in hotpants and T-shirts that strained over huge breasts and thighs, honey-skinned Arab women, and French women, some cheerily brazen, others narrow-faced and edgy, with bitten-down fingernails. Their eyes flickered over Bill for just the time it took to know he was not in the market before sliding off, no offence taken, in search of the next punter. Bill scarcely saw them. His eyes were on the street well ahead, on the look-out for a uniform or the laughing banter with the girls that would be the trademark of the local vice squad.

As he drew near to the address Lantier had given him, in the lower part of the street, the prostitutes did not appear to be operating. It was as though some unseen barrier retained them a couple of blocks higher up the street. Here the sex was not so real, but it was cheaper, catering to a clientele that could not handle the emotional strain of dealing with a flesh-and-blood woman. He strode south, past the peepshows and video parlours and the handful of restaurants and fleetingly fashionable bars, whose customers liked the safe sleaze of a street where the pimping cartels kept their own order.

The address he was looking for was next to the white-tiled facade of a Mexican restaurant he had once been taken to, run by a still famous, if no longer working, film actor. He stopped outside the brightly lit window of the shop, giving an idle once-over to the photographs and stencilled promises. He loitered for a minute or two, feigning indecision, then paid thirty francs to an empty-eyed woman cashier and pushed aside the greasy plush curtain.

He paused, letting his eyes adjust to the semi-darkness. As his vision improved he surveyed his surroundings. In front of him was a row of cubicles the size of phone booths, with their doors standing open and wooden seats built across one wall. In the far wall of each booth a twenty centimetre square aperture was closed by a shutter. A slot meter was fixed next to it. A hard-looking youth with his T-shirt sleeves rolled up above sinewy biceps leaned against a wall to Bill's left, watching him with listless contempt. Bill nodded to him, grinning, and stepped into a booth, pulling the door closed behind him. He turned a bolt and an overhead light came on, no stronger than a child's nightlight. It gave just enough light to make out the stains on the pitted floor. Grimacing, he fished twenty francs from his pocket and slid the coins into the meter. The light went out, leaving him in inky darkness until the shutter racked noisily open, revealing a rectangle of light. Beyond the smeared glass a tiny circular platform slowly revolved. As he watched, a big-boned woman with bleached hair and blackheads around her nose stepped onto the platform, and began dancing lethargically to scratchy music. She gave this a few seconds to ignite her audience, and then reached back to let her bikini-top fall to her feet. She pirouetted clumsily, showing off small, slack breasts. A moment later, a man, smaller than she was, in street clothes, stepped into view and started dancing with her. In a lethargic parody of eroticism, he began running his hands over her, squeezing the small breasts as though he were wringing out a cloth. Bill turned away and stared into the darkness until the shutter chugged closed and the overhead light came on again. He set his face, replacing the morose look with what he hoped was a smirk of satisfaction, and left the booth.

He walked past the lounging youth, and pushed through another set of curtains into a long, narrow room with waist-high racks along each side and a glass-topped counter at the far end. Another hard-looking youth, this one with his hair pulled off his face in a lank ponytail, perched on a bar stool behind the counter, overseeing the dildoes, exotic condoms, pills, and bondage gear displayed under glass in front of him. Behind him, yet another of the threadbare red curtains half masked a door with a hand-written 'private' sign tacked to it.

The two other customers in the place, each in his own private world, thumbed through magazines with urgent intensity. Assuming the rules of etiquette to be about the same as in a public toilet, Bill took up a position mid-way between them and picked up one of the thin magazines from the rack. Gloomily, he began riffing through its blurred, stapled pages. By the time he had browsed his way along the rack to stand close to the minder at the counter he had done a depressing tour of the clammiest regions of men's desires. There were women wrapped in plastic, women sheathed in latex and leather, women bound and cowed, and women being brutalized and abused by everything from gloating men to farmyard animals. For the really hard to please there was an entire shelf picturing men copulating with animals. Bill recognized one of these men from an earlier photograph in which he was beating a naked woman with a length of barbed wire. Such versatility probably helped the publishers to keep a grip on overheads.

He was almost at the end of the rack, his fingers blackened with ink and his spirits as low as they had ever been, when the sound of a raised voice made him turn casually towards the counter. The curtain was shoved aside and a shortish, deep-chested man backed out, still speaking. He wore an expensive, loose-fitting double-breasted suit that would have looked superb on one of the willowy toy-boys the designer probably hung out with. The squat body in the doorway looked like a hastily wrapped gift. The man turned to speak in slangy French to the minder, making him snigger. As he did so, Bill spun back to the racks, fighting to keep the recognition from his face. The leering features were unmistakably those in the photograph Lantier had handed him, which nestled in the pocket of his blouson.

Behind him, the minder laughed again. Bill glanced idly around in time to see the thickset man holding the minder by the throat and shaking him in what both of them seemed to agree was a hilarious parody of a strangling. As he took his hand away, he slapped his cupped palm hard to the side of the minder's face. Delivered with a grin, it jerked the minder's head aside, letting Bill see the briefest flare of resentment in the man's eyes. Still grinning unpleasantly, the squat man turned and swaggered towards the exit.

Moving purposefully but with no appearance of haste, Bill passed his handful of obscenities to the sullen minder. He dispensed the money the man asked for without even bothering to be astonished at the size of the amount. The realization that the man was not going to offer him a bag for his purchases brought a sudden revelation. The people who bought this kind of stuff were not ashamed of themselves.

People with a taste for child pornography or for fellating dogs did not see themselves as perverts. It was the others who were repressed. To them it was normal, red-blooded behaviour, delicious diversions that anyone would enjoy, if only they had the guts to give it a crack. Stuffing the magazines inside his jacket he left the shop.

The man was nowhere in sight. With a glance back to ensure that the dead-faced cashier was not watching, he sprinted for the nearest corner. A metallic bronze BMW was drawing away from a delivery bay a few metres from him, a fistful of parking tickets flapping under the wiper blade. Bill spun away to examine the window display of a stand-up snack bar, letting the car slide past his back, nosing aside the tourists that overflowed into the roadway.

He was able to keep up with the car on foot until it emerged from the pedestrian precinct onto the boulevard Sebastopol. Then, the driver stamped on the throttle to send the car screaming the forty metres to a red traffic light. Before the light had turned green, Bill had already flagged down a cab, grateful that it was August, and sunny. On a wet day the BMW could have been out of Paris and on its way to the Riviera before he found a taxi.

19

The first burst of speed seemed to have got something out of the man's system. Since then, he had been driving with a restraint that Bill had not expected, making it easy for the cab to follow unnoticed as he led them westward, following the succession of boulevards that took them past the crowds in front of the big department stores and on into the grand residential streets of the western end of the boulevard Haussmann. The traffic became even sparser, prompting Bill to tell the driver to fall further back, as the BMW made some turns and emerged onto the wide-open space of the Porte Maillot. Bill frowned as the car swung around the central island and headed south towards Trocadero and the river.

'What's he up to?' Bill murmured, as it turned left again, heading back eastward along the river. 'He's taking a hell of a long way round.'

The cabbie laughed. 'You mean *you* haven't heard?'

'Heard what?'

'Your people closed off more of the centre.' Ever since Bill had told him to follow the BMW, the driver had been assuming that Bill was a detective. The notion he knew something about the police that Bill did not made him chuckle with pleasure. 'At six o'clock this morning. Since then they've been carting in police and CRS by the truckload.' He paused. 'Still, I suppose you people know what you're doing. All these Fundamentalists, and everything,' he added hastily.

Bill inclined his head. 'You're a shrewd man,' he said admiringly. 'Our intelligence people have picked up a rumour the Fundamentalists *might* be planning something.'

The man looked back at him, thrilled to be in the know. 'I guessed it! As soon as I heard the announcement, I told my wife, "I bet there's something up".'

'Good thinking. He's turning left.'

The driver jerked round to face the front. The BMW had disappeared. Without needing to be told, the driver raced for the place de l'Alma. The BMW was vanishing through a traffic light and up the avenue Montaigne. The cabbie shot the red light, drunk with excitement at committing a violation with a policeman's approval. Bill was still searching, dry-mouthed, for sight of a traffic policeman when their quarry made another left turn into the rue François Premier. Again the cabbie drove hard for the corner. By the time they reached it, the BMW was nowhere in sight.

Opposite them, blocking the exit from the rue de Marignan, one of a pair of CRS, his gun cradled across his chest, waved them busily away. As the cab driver hesitated, Bill scanned the sloping length of the street. He let out an exclamation as an illuminated sign caught his eye. 'Over there! Quickly!' he shouted, pointing.

Responding to Bill's gesture, the driver gunned the motor, sending the car racing up the incline, past the pale stone facade of the Nina Ricci building. 'Here!' He had the door open before the taxi slid to a stop. He threw money at the driver and jumped out, slamming the door on the man's protest that it was on the house.

Fifty metres along the sloping street a ramp led down into an underground car park. A few paces further up, a flight of steps was set into the pavement. With a glance to ensure that their burst of speed had not drawn the attention of the CRS, he started down the stairs.

It took only a few leaps to reach the first level. He burst through the heavy door and stood for a count of five, listening, grateful once again for the August holiday that had emptied the city. Not a vehicle nor a person moved. He spun and raced down to the next floor.

He was on the lowest level when he caught the sound of a car. He moved into the shelter of a Range Rover as the BMW, grey under the dim yellow of the overhead lights, slid towards him, its tyres swishing loud in the silence. He kept the Range Rover between himself and the car as it cruised past and slotted into a spot eighty metres away. The driver climbed from his car and walked quickly round it, towards a yellow van. Through the dirt-streaked windows of the Range Rover, Bill could just make out the stylized sailing vessel of the municipal crest of Paris on the van door.

A workman in fluorescent yellow overalls got out and moved to greet the newcomer. He spoke a few words, inaudible at Bill's distance, and turned brusquely away. The driver fell in behind him and followed him out of sight beyond the van.

He waited for two minutes for the men to reappear. When they failed to do so, he dropped to all fours and squinted beneath the cars. There were no feet to be seen. Standing again, he pulled his soft leather key pouch from his pocket. Fumbling with the keys, an innocent motorist returning to collect his car, he stepped from cover and began walking towards the van.

Drawing close to it, he hesitated, pretending to select a key, while his senses strained for every sound. There was nothing. He stood in thought for a moment and then withdrew towards the stairs. He had gone thirty metres when he took a coin from his pocket, turned and skimmed it at the van. It struck the metal panel with a noise that echoed in the silence. The sound died away into renewed silence. He took a second coin and repeated the action. He waited for a few seconds more and then ran to the back of the van.

The door swung open easily, revealing racks of tools, and coils of cable slung from hooks. He shoved it closed and looked around him, frowning. His frown dissolved as he saw, a few paces from him, a grey-painted metal door set in the wall. He strode quickly to it. The handle did not move under his probing. He placed an ear against the metal and listened.

Hearing nothing, he withdrew to the cover of a nearby cluster of cars. Dropping to a crouch, with half an ear out for an owner returning to collect his car, he settled down to wait.

It was almost half an hour before a distinct metallic sound focused his attention sharply back to the door. It swung open and the yellow-clad workman stepped out and looked carefully around him, scrutinizing the parked vehicles. Bill dropped to the cement and looked along the ground. He could see only the yellow legs of the overalls. For perhaps half a minute the man did not move. Then, quite audibly in the throbbing silence, he said, 'Okay, it's clear.'

The tan trouser legs and glossy brown shoes came into view as the BMW driver emerged and moved close to the workman, speaking too low for Bill to overhear. After a few seconds, the workman climbed into the van and drove away. The tan legs remained motionless, as though the man were watching the van's departure. Only when the noise of its engine had died away did he move, walking to the tail of his car. Seconds later the boot lid slammed and the man began striding briskly away.

Very carefully, Bill rose into a crouch and squinted through the windows of the intervening car. The man was walking unhurriedly towards the stairs, moving with the bandy-legged gait of the over-muscled. In his left hand he carried a pale blue nylon sports bag. Reaching the exit, the man looked around him once and disappeared through the door. Bill waited, giving it a count of twenty. He had reached only nine when the door flew open again and the man burst back in, looking around for the movement that would tell him he was being followed. Seeing nothing, he rolled his shoulders and turned back to the door. Drawing a deep breath, Bill rose and hastened after him.

The broad back and bull neck were unmistakable as the man made his way, striding quickly but nonchalantly towards the avenue Montaigne. He did not glance across at the side street where the two CRS were still in position, their eyes concealed by identical aviator sunglasses.

Bill let the man reach the corner before forcing saliva back into his parched mouth and stepping out from the steps. Coming level with the uniformed men, he glanced briefly across at them. The light glinted off their dark glasses, making it impossible to judge their expressions. Casting his head down again, he shuffled on past, ready to break into a run at the first hint of a challenge.

The fifty paces to the corner under the men's gaze seemed so interminable he almost started in surprise as he turned past the Ricci boutique to find the man still only forty metres away, walking with the same unhurried pace. Bill had just begun crossing to take up a less obvious position on the other side of the road, when the man threw a perfunctory glance around him and turned to mount the steps of one of the buildings, separated from the street by a narrow strip of well-kept shrubbery. Taking no account of the stoop-shouldered figure side-stepping the traffic, he jammed a finger onto a bell-push.

'Come in.'

For an instant the smirk on Saïd's face slipped. Even over the distortion of the entryphone there was no mistaking the revulsion in her voice. 'Thanks,' he grunted, as the latch snicked open, letting him into a marble-floored hall. Striding quickly and silently on the strip of crimson carpet he crossed to the lift and punched the button.

He stepped from the lift to find the slim figure of the Countess de Bernis waiting at the half-opened door of the apartment. Her pale hair was drawn back tight and held in place by a black velvet band, giving her face a youthful look. A light green silk dressing gown clung to her body. Saïd grinned oafishly, his eyes on the spot where the neckline of her robe met the first faint swelling of her breasts. 'Hello, Countess. De Medem's expecting me.'

Raising her hand to gather the neckline of her robe, she made the faintest nod in the direction of the living room. 'Yes, I know,' she said, in a voice throbbing with disdain. 'You'll find him in there.'

He looked her up and down with frank, lascivious eyes and

slowly nodded. 'Pity.' Grinning wider, he swaggered past her into the living room.

The Countess shook from head to foot with a tremor of loathing, closed the door and strode away into the recesses of the huge apartment.

The heavy curtains were closed, throwing the living room into a deep red twilight. A shaded lamp cast a pool of light onto the document-strewn desk.

'De Medem?' Saïd called from the threshold, frowning.

He was about to call again when de Medem's voice came to him. 'Ah, my dear Saïd. How nice to hear your voice. Do come in.' De Medem's face appeared over the back of a day-bed upholstered in faded silk. 'Is it me, or are you a little early?' He grinned condescendingly. 'Not altogether what one's taught to expect of people of your, ah, well, the Mediterranean races.'

Saïd's face twisted resentfully. 'Yeah? Well fuck that.'

'And I do like the suit. The colour suits you perfectly. It must be something in the skin type.'

'Fuck that, too.' He was searching his brain for further repartee when the sight of de Medem rising from the day-bed cut him short.

De Medem stood totally naked, buckling on his watch. Grinning, he gestured down at himself. 'Sorry, old boy. No discourtesy. I was just taking a nap.' He winked. 'You know how it is.'

Saïd shot a glance towards the door and nodded, a slow grin spreading over his face.

'M'mm. Well, everything in its place.' De Medem gave a brief smile and stepped round the day-bed. 'Did you bring it?' As he spoke he reached out to take the bag. Saïd took a pace back, twitching the bag out of de Medem's reach, throwing a glance at the open door.

De Medem laughed. 'Don't be a fool. You're not worried about the Countess?' Saïd's eyes glittered, hard as rivets among the muscular planes of his face. Shrugging, de Medem gave a cramped little bow and walked across to shut the heavy double door. 'Is that better?' Returning to where Saïd stood, he beckoned peremptorily. 'Now can I see the equipment?'

Grunting, Saïd allowed him to take the bag. De Medem carried it to a sofa and unzipped it. Puzzlement came over his face. 'That? Is *that* it?' The beginnings of anger overlaid the puzzlement. 'Saïd,' he whispered, twisting to look over his shoulder, 'this isn't some sort of joke, I hope?'

Ignoring the note of menace, Saïd walked over and grabbed at the bag, shouldering de Medem aside. 'Don't be stupid! Here. Watch.'

He reached into the bag and pulled out a flat, pale grey object, about forty-five centimetres long, as wide and as thick as a floorboard, slightly concave at one end and with an indentation in one edge. Under de Medem's eager, astounded gaze, he pulled out a length of tubing made of the same grey material. Grinning at de Medem, he screwed the tube into a threaded hole in the straight end of the board. With the leer still stuck on his face, he ferreted in the bag again, produced another piece of the same material, as long as his finger, and screwed it into a slot just in front of the indentation, leaving a couple of centimetres protruding.

The puzzlement faded from de Medem's face. His smile returned, his eyes glinting with understanding and admiration. As he watched, Saïd found another, shorter tube and clipped it along the top edge of the assembly. De Medem laughed softly. At once the thing looked recognizably a weapon. He held out his cupped hands.

Saïd tossed it into them, sniggering as de Medem recoiled. 'Don't worry, it isn't loaded.'

De Medem hefted the thing in his hands. 'I've heard about these. It's the first time I've held one. It's incredible. It weighs nothing, nothing at all.' He cradled the scalloped end of the weapon against his shoulder, squinted along the sight and mimed squeezing the trigger. He lowered it, almost laughing with admiration. 'You're the gun enthusiast. Are you sure it really *works*? It doesn't seem possible. I mean, well, it feels like a toy. It even looks like one.'

Saïd snorted. 'Yeah, I know. I didn't believe it myself, to tell you the truth, although I'd read all the write-ups on it. It works alright, though. I tested it on the way back into town this morning. It's as accurate as anything I've ever handled. Over the distance, anyway. It's calibrated for eighty metres. That right?' He grinned and patted his hip. 'I'd still rather trust metal myself.'

De Medem's eyes flicked involuntarily to the point on Saïd's hip. Looking back at his face, he nodded, expressionless. 'That's right. From the top of the gantry to the microphone. What about ammunition?'

Saïd reached into the bag again and pulled out a cardboard box the size of a bar of soap. He tossed it to de Medem. 'Here. Each carbine will hold two of these.' De Medem opened the carton and pulled out an object as long as a match and about four times thicker. He held it up, studying it.

'All plastic or ceramic, except for the very tip. That's depleted uranium, or some crap like that. Anyway, the makers claim they will get through any metal detector around, with no trouble at all.' As he spoke, Saïd picked a cartridge from the box and held it to the light of the lamp, examining the tip, notched in the form of a cross, with a connoisseur's interest. 'I wouldn't believe it if I hadn't seen it for myself. It looks like nothing, but it weighs more than a normal nine millimetre. From what I saw this morning, at the range we're talking about, it'll make a hell of a mess of a skull.' The thought provoked a sudden bark of laughter.

De Medem hardly seemed to hear him. He was looking dreamily from the gun to the cartridge. 'Have you considered the implications of these things?'

Saïd gave him a cock-eyed look. 'Implications? It's a gun,' he said, shrugging. 'For shooting people.'

De Medem shook his head. 'But imagine if they fell into the hands of terrorists. God knows what hijackers couldn't do with these things.'

Saïd's silence made him look up. The man was grinning at him, as though he were a pitiful child. *'Fell* into hijackers' hands?' He broke into another short, barking laugh. 'Who do you think they're *making* them for? The Boy Scout movement?' The grin vanished. 'Don't you understand, de Medem? These things are *designed* for terrorists. And, of course, people like the Mossad. But that's the same thing,' he added, with another brief, noisy laugh. Abruptly serious again, he lowered his voice. 'Are you sure you can get them in place?'

De Medem put the gun and box of cartridges back in the bag. 'Don't worry about that. They'll be there.'

'How are you doing it? One of your police admirers taking them in for you?'

De Medem gave him a supercilious smile. 'Don't worry about that, either. By the way, as of this afternoon, police officers are being searched.'

Saïd raised his eyebrows and pulled back one corner of his mouth. 'So who *is* taking them through for you? The President?'

'If I were you, I would forget all about the subject,' de Medem told him, speaking with soft menace. 'That kind of thing can be dangerous to know. Now, why don't we run through the parts you *are* supposed to know about. Your snipers, for example. They won't get more than the two shots each, and that only if they're lucky.' He ran his tongue over his lips, betraying a nervousness at odds with the rest of his manner. 'Are you *absolutely* certain they're up to it?'

Saïd leered, catching the anxiety. 'If they are not, you patriotic Frenchmen can take the blame. They learned their trade in the French army.' He dropped his voice. 'We've been over this a dozen times. Believe me, these two are *the* top men. I don't take contracts I can't keep, you know that. You're paying me to get you the best, and that's what I've done, okay? By the way, do you have their passes for me?'

De Medem shook his head, tight-lipped. 'Tonight. I'm getting them tonight.'

Saïd's thick eyebrows lowered in a frown. 'You don't sound too sure. Something wrong?'

De Medem made a contemptuous sound. 'Pah! You're

looking for trouble again. There's no problem. I'll have them tonight. Call me at around eleven-thirty. You can come by and collect them if you wish.'

Saïd continued to look at him from under the thick black bar of his eyebrows. 'M'mm, I will. Remember, I've already put a lot of investment into this thing. You're going to have to pay me regardless, even if you don't come through with the fucking passes. You do understand that, don't you?'

De Medem's smile slipped a fraction. He put an arm over Saïd's wide shoulders and began steering him towards the door. He could feel the hardness of the man under the cloth of his jacket. 'It's all agreed, isn't it? Just relax. And don't forget to give me a call tonight.'

Saïd nodded. He smiled without parting his lips. 'As if I would.'

20

'Thank God that reptile has gone. He gives me the creeps.'

De Medem stood at the window for a few seconds more, his lip curling as he watched the exaggerated swing of Saïd's shoulders as he strutted towards the corner. At length he let the curtain fall back into place and turned to look at the Countess. She stood in the doorway, her face puckered in a look of loathing. He smiled dreamily. 'You're right, my dear, of course. The man's a snake, and a particularly venomous one. But then,' he added, suddenly jovial again, 'we have to remember that even snake venom has its uses.' She shuddered. He crossed to her and put an arm over her shoulders. 'But I do agree with you. He really does make one's flesh creep. Do you know, he threatened me, just now.'

She laughed, genuinely incredulous, and looked up into his face. 'Him? Threatening you? You aren't serious?'

He nodded. '*He* was,' he said softly. 'Deadly serious.' He shook his head. 'Our good friend Saïd is getting ideas above his station.'

'*Your* friend, not mine.'

He inclined his head. '*My* good friend, Saïd.' He squeezed her shoulders. 'You see what happens when one is too democratic with these people? It goes straight to their heads. They start thinking of themselves as equals. He spoke to me in the tone he would use to one of his prostitutes,' he added, as though he found the idea moderately amusing.

She grimaced. 'Well, don't ask me to receive him *here* too often. The place feels *contaminated* whenever he's been here.'

De Medem laughed and dropped his arm to her waist. 'Don't take him *too* seriously, my dear. In a few days from now the odious, if temporarily invaluable, Monsieur Khoury will be taking a well-earned holiday. A swimming holiday.' He grinned. 'In a disused quarry.'

As he finished speaking, the phone rang. She broke from his embrace and crossed the room to answer it. 'Hello?' She looked up, putting her hand over the receiver. 'Vadon,' she said, contempt spilling into her voice.

Raising an eyebrow, he strode over and relieved her of the phone. 'What is it?' He listened for a moment. 'Well, *what*, for God's sake? Can't you tell me on the phone?' He listened again and shrugged. 'Okay, I suppose so. If you think you really must.' He put down the phone and shook his head in exasperation.

'What is it? Has something gone wrong?'

He shook his head again, his eyes unfocused. 'I don't know,' he said pensively. '*He* seems to think there's a crisis. He wants to come over right away.' Coming abruptly back to himself, he gave the flesh of her slim buttock a perfunctory pat. 'Sorry, my dear, but I have to ask you to stop leading me into temptation and give me a little time to think. He'll be here in a few minutes.'

Less than five minutes passed before the buzzer of the entryphone sounded. Dressed now, in slacks and a cashmere sweater, de Medem walked without hurry to the door, his brow furrowed with thought. By the time he reached out for the entryphone the buzzer was sounding again, a long insistent burr. He muttered a word into the phone and pressed the button. Unlatching the door, he left it ajar and strolled back into the drawing room, wandering to the window to watch the rain that pounded against the glass.

The door slammed shut. He was still turning slowly from the window when Vadon's hurried step sounded on the parquet. 'My dear Vadon,' he drawled, beaming, as he walked across to greet him. 'How nice to see you. Here, let me take that.' He moved as though to help Vadon peel off the light raincoat.

Vadon stepped irritably away from de Medem's gesture, only snatching off the waterproof nylon hat he wore and tossing it onto a chair.

De Medem watched the drops of water make dark blobs on the silk of the cushion. 'Well, have a seat, at least.' He placed a blunt-fingered paw on Vadon's shoulder and steered him towards a sofa.

Vadon shook him off. 'Never mind all that. I need to talk to you. It's a disaster!'

De Medem smiled urbanely, his eyes on his visitor's face. Vadon's skin was sallow. His breathing was uneven. His cheeks twitched with the effort of forming words. 'My,' he said softly, 'you *do* look worried. Perhaps it's just this heat. Very oppressive. A good thunderstorm might clear the air.' He moved to a side table. 'Can I get you a drink?' Mockery and contempt lay like reefs beneath the smoothly solicitous tone. He turned his back, taking up a decanter.

'I'm more than just worried. I'll tell you frankly, de Medem, I'm afraid. We have to call a halt. Call the whole thing off. It's absurd.'

De Medem turned to face him, a crystal tumbler in each fist. 'Here. A whisky might help you calm down.' He handed Vadon a glass. 'Now, *what's* absurd?'

Vadon took a deep draught of the whisky. 'Everything.

They're asking for tighter and tighter security. It's just going to be too risky. We can't go on. We simply *can't*! I can't bear the strain any more. I can't take it. I . . .' He plunged his face despairingly into his cupped palm.

De Medem stood looking down at the bowed head. In the muted light of the lamp at his shoulder, bluish tints glinted in Vadon's hair. 'You make me sick!' de Medem said with soft venom.

Vadon's face jerked up as if on a string. His mouth working as he searched angrily for a response, he half rose from the sofa.

De Medem stood his ground, calmly sipping his drink. 'Sit down, and don't be foolish. You really do make me want to vomit.' He took another leisurely sip of his drink. 'You're the vainest man I've ever met. So vain, you've convinced yourself you *deserve* to be president. Vanity has made a whore of you. You've been ready to go along with *my* proposal because you thought you were so much the man for the job that *how* you got it didn't matter.' He gave a soft, derisive laugh. 'And it's that same vanity that's had you convinced you could handle me, isn't it? You'd persuaded yourself that, once you were up there, you would find a way to get rid of me, hadn't you? You were the man of destiny, the man who could do it all!' He gave another negligent, dismissive laugh, the middle finger of the hand holding his glass extended, aimed at Vadon's face. 'And then, at the first setback you fall to pieces. Look at yourself! Look at what you really are. A quaking nonentity. And you want to be a *leader*, for God's sake!'

Vadon stared up at him, the glass held close to his lips. 'God, de Medem, I wish I'd never become involved with this. I wish I'd never listened to you. I wish I'd thrown you out the first day you came to me.' His voice shook with the desolate vehemence of the words.

De Medem gave him a grin that almost became a snarl. 'But you didn't, did you? You wanted it so much. You didn't care what the price was, so long as you could tell yourself you would never have to pay it. Well, you're not going to cave in now, are you?' De Medem leaned closer, his eyes drilling into Vadon's face, alert for every nuance of the other man's expression. 'Not so long as I still have those pictures.'

At the mention of the word pictures, Vadon jerked back in his seat, groaning, as though he had been slapped. De Medem turned away, a private smile touching his lips. 'Don't worry. We all have an interest in keeping your precious reputation intact.' He turned back to face Vadon, the smile gone. He jerked his head at him. 'Man of honour! Devoted servant of his country, man and boy!' He laughed and drank off a gulp of Scotch, rolling the drink round his mouth as though to take away the taste of the words.

Vadon straightened in his seat again. Anger blazed in his sick face. 'I *have* served my country, de Medem. In ways you can't even begin to know. And it was always what guided me, even when I agreed to your proposal.'

De Medem guffawed, mocking the desperate ring to Vadon's words. 'Of course! Isn't that what I've been saying? Anyone but you as president and France goes to the dogs within days, isn't that it?'

Vadon gulped more whisky, spilling it on his tie. He batted ineffectually at the darkening silk. 'It's true! The country *does* need me! *Somebody* has to put a stop to what's going on. Someone has to . . .'

'God, you're mad!' de Medem said, cutting him off with an outstretched hand. 'God help France, if *I* were not going to be there to keep you in order,' he added with amused relish. 'But, mad or not, you're going to see this through, do you hear me?' Vadon's face worked but no reply came from him. 'Good. Now, since you're here, let's get down to some *really* serious matters. Look.' He stepped across to where the hold-all lay and threw it onto Vadon's lap.

Vadon reared back, spilling more whisky. 'What is it?'

'Have a look.' De Medem jerked his chin at the bag, still grinning. 'Go on. And then you tell me,' he added, sipping his drink.

Tentatively, as though it might contain a deadly reptile, Vadon opened the bag. For some seconds he stared, mute, at the contents. 'What are they?'

De Medem laughed. 'The guns, you idiot.' As he spoke, he leaned down and with a violent gesture pulled the bag open wide. 'The key to the whole damned enterprise.'

Vadon went on staring into the bag for another moment and then shuddered and brushed it off his lap onto the rug. 'No. They'll be found. We'll never get them inside. There will be metal detectors.'

'Metal detectors won't find *those*, my friend. The manufacturers guarantee it! They're ceramic and plastic. There's not twelve grams of metal in there. The machine doesn't exist that will pick them up.'

'They aren't going to rely on the detectors alone. Not since *these* disappeared!' He jabbed a finger at the bag. 'That's what's caused all the upset. They were a stupid error,' he said, finding some defiance. 'They've alerted everybody. The couriers will be body-searched. I warned you on the phone. It's unavoidable now. If you try to go through with it they'll surely be caught. And you know as well as I do, they'll tell everything to save themselves.' The sweat that had been gathering on Vadon's brow ran in a sudden rivulet into his eyebrow. He brushed it away. 'We can't go on. It's over.'

De Medem breathed deeply, his free hand clenching into a fist as he fought to control his temper. 'You're letting your emotions take over again,' he said. 'You know how *that* clouds your judgement.' At his words, Vadon quivered as though about to sob.

De Medem lowered his bulk slowly into the sofa next to him. 'Look, since your call, I've been thinking. You're right. The men can't carry the weapons into the compound. They would be certain to be caught. And, as you say, they would tell everything. Eventually the trail would lead to us.' He shook his head. 'We have to abandon that idea.'

Vadon twisted to face him, his face brightening. His jowls tightened. 'Absolutely,' he said briskly. Renewed hope had driven the whine from his voice. 'We have to. Circumstances have beaten us, I'm afraid.' He began to stand up.

De Medem put a hand on his sleeve and pulled him back down, clicking his tongue. 'Sit down. I hadn't quite finished. The couriers can't take them in. But, *you*, of course, can.'

For several seconds Vadon did not speak, as emotions churned in his face. 'You aren't serious?' he said finally, his voice a breathy wheeze.

'I'm afraid I am,' de Medem answered cheerfully. He sipped again at his drink. 'Who better? They aren't going to search *you*.'

Vadon raised his hands to his face. In the last few seconds his hair had somehow become dishevelled. His tie was askew. 'No,' he said, hoarse with horror and disbelief. 'No. Not me. I can't. It isn't conceivable. Supposing . . .'

'Supposing you refuse?' de Medem broke in, speaking hardly above a whisper. 'Don't even consider it.' He placed his hand back on Vadon's sleeve, gripping it hard. 'Let me remind you once again, my friend, that you will do as I'm asking you, and you will do it successfully. Perhaps you nurse some hope that the press here wouldn't dare to print the pictures?' he said, raising an eyebrow. 'H'mm? Well, don't forget, not for a single instant, that I have the organization. I can cover every major town in France with posters in a single night. Think of those good Catholic ladies you rely on for your support, good bourgeois matrons who *so* admire their handsome Resistance hero, the dashing Christian Vadon. How many of them do you think will vote for you when they wake up to that? And the German and Austrian magazines, the British newspapers, would pay fortunes for pictures like that.' He leaned closer. 'Look at me,' he ordered. Reluctantly, Vadon raised his devastated face. De Medem's eyes beamed into his. 'You do understand?' Vadon nodded dumbly. 'Good,' de Medem murmured. 'Then I know I can rely on you.'

Vadon's face was ashen. 'But, how can I possibly do it without attracting attention?' he mumbled. 'I can't walk in with a bag and come out again without it. Or even with it empty. The place will be crawling with security men. These are trained people, for God's sake. They *report* to me. They'll be watching my every move.'

De Medem rose, smiling, from the couch. 'Don't *fret* so much. Everything's been thought through.' As he spoke he reached down and picked up the bag. 'Look.' He drew out a handful of soft cloth and held it up, dangling it by a drawstring. 'Simplicity itself. You'll do just as the couriers would have done. You'll carry them inside these, slung round your neck.' He raised a hand, stilling Vadon's attempt to protest. 'Of course, *you* can't wear an overall, so you'll need to wear a coat, but in this filthy weather, who's going to remark on that? The rest is very simple. You will make a surprise visit to the compound – an impromptu check on arrangements, to ensure that they're on their toes.' He smirked at the humour of it. 'You'll leave the bags at the drop beneath the tower, and that's the last you have to do with the whole affair. Child's play, isn't it?' he added, patronizingly. 'They'll be collected from there.' He paused, casting a hard, questioning look at Vadon. 'Provided, that is, you've brought the passes.'

Vadon started and straightened, as though he had been in a reverie. 'Yes,' he whispered, his voice miserable and distant. 'Yes, yes.' He began feeling at his jacket. 'They're here.' He pulled out two plastic-coated cards and handed them over.

De Medem flicked them from Vadon's limp fingers. He held them up to the lamplight. A blue, white and red flash ran across one corner. Beneath the plastic coating each bore a passport-size portrait of a man, staring against the flash of the camera. Nodding, de Medem dropped them onto the desk. 'Excellent.'

Vadon spoke, trying hard to fix some authority back in his voice. 'Look, this business of the passes, it's been worrying me sick. I, mean, if they're found . . . if your people *are* caught getting out of the compound . . . Very few people have access to those things . . .'

'I've told you already, you don't have to worry about it,' de Medem said evenly, in a confiding voice. 'Providing, once again, you have done your part. The men detailed to the car park will be well briefed. They will retrieve the passes and they will be handed on to me, personally. You can have the damned things *back* if you want them. There's no question that the car-park detail will be the men whose names I gave you?'

Vadon looked resentful. 'Of course not. Two more people you have some kind of hold over, I suppose?' he went on, his voice rising once again in a sullen whine.

De Medem beamed at him. 'A hold? Not at all,' he continued cheerfully. 'Well, perhaps, in a way. But not the way *you're* thinking, old boy. They just believe in me, that I'm what France needs. Just as those ladies I mentioned think *you're* what the country needs.'

'You are what *hell* needs,' Vadon muttered. 'More Salvation League members, I suppose. I'm not surprised.'

'Nor should you be. The police, the CRS, even the intelligence services,' he added, with a gleam of mischief in his eye, 'they're almost the backbone of my membership.' He gave a short laugh of genuine amusement. The laughter subsided as abruptly as it had started and a different light came into his eyes. 'Isn't that the most natural thing in the world? That the people responsible for law and order, for preserving the civilization of France, should be the first to understand the truth I'm telling?' Vadon jerked his head away, sneering. De Medem's voice rose. 'Don't take that attitude with me here, Vadon. Keep it for the public. You ought to have thrown in your lot with me years ago. You would have, if it hadn't been for your intellectual snobbery. Even now, knowing that I *know* what a hypocrite you are, you can't help feeling superior, can you? Telling the simple truth is bad taste to you, isn't it?'

'The simple truth that you tell gets a little boring to some of us, I must admit,' Vadon said, attempting to be supercilious. 'If only you had a policy on anything *but* the immigrant question, you might get some *intelligent* people to listen to you.'

De Medem snorted. 'Bullshit! You've got policies by the truckload. Like the rest of them. So what? Everything goes on just the same whichever party's in power. When things go well you want the credit; when they don't, it's due to factors beyond your control. It's the international situation, or the unions. Or maybe sunspot activity. You know as well as I do that nobody in government has a clue what the fuck they're doing. And the public is at last starting to catch onto that. They understand that the one truth I'm telling them is the one that counts for them. They know that all I'm saying is let's start by changing what *can* be changed, and the rest will look after itself. And the people who see it plainest are not the armchair theorists, like you. They're the ones who have to deal with reality every day: the police, the security people.' He took a long gulp of whisky, emptying his glass, and turned away to refill it. 'You should get out of your government limousines and into the real world a little more, my friend,' he said viciously, over his shoulder. 'Get out and look around you, the way the police have to. Look at what's actually happening to this country. Thirty years ago Marseilles was *France*. Walk around half of the city now, if you dare to, and you wouldn't know where you were. Africans, Arabs, Albanians, Croats, Romanians; anything but Frenchmen. It doesn't look like France! By God, it doesn't even *smell* like France any more! And it certainly doesn't feel like France. Tell me straight, Vadon, was this the France you fought the war for? Do you want our children growing up corrupted by foreigners peddling drugs?' He paused, panting, and took another gulp of his fresh drink. Vadon sat slack-faced under his stare, saying nothing. De Medem lowered his voice to a hoarse, theatrical whisper. 'And now, it's not enough for the stupid Arabs to riot and burn down a few shops any more. Now we've got the Fundamentalists! They've found a cause!' His voice was thick with sarcasm. 'Their neighbourhoods are no-go areas. The police, the French police, daren't even go into them any more, except in wagons. This man Bouhila tells us they don't need *our* police on *their* streets. He tells us they'll do their own policing! We're talking about foreign republics.' He flung out a hand, gesturing to the world beyond the curtains. 'Right here! On the outskirts of Paris! It's as if they wanted war!' He shuddered with the force of his own emotions.

Abruptly, his voice lost the theatrical quality and returned to its normal pitch. He looked slightly surprised at himself, like someone coming out of hypnosis. 'But, I don't need to tell *you* all that, do I? After all, you're the minister that's supposed to be responsible for all this. God help us,' he added in a perfectly audible murmur. 'Who knows better than you what's going on? Their own schools; Bouhila's monkeys playing policeman out in the "zone" with armbands and batons. Speaking seriously, Vadon, who do you think is taking the strain? You? Me? Of course not! We sit around in apartments like this and just watch it on television. I'll tell you who's facing up to it, day in and day out. The police.' He paused, his breathing loud in the stillness of the room. When he spoke again his voice had fallen once more to a hoarse, urgent rasp. 'That's why they come to me, Vadon. That's why I have policemen, of *all* ranks, flocking to join me. Because I'm the only one who speaks their language.'

Vadon sat silently for some moments, numbed by the sheer force of the man's delivery. At length, he wet his lips and spoke, having to try twice before he found his pitch. 'Yes, well,' he said, so softly his words were almost drowned by the drumming of the rain, 'that may all be true. What worries me at present is those two officers whose names you gave me. I mean, are you *sure* they will do it? Kill them, I mean, in cold blood, the way they're supposed to.'

De Medem looked at him in genuine surprise. 'Will they? They can hardly wait. They'll cut them down the moment they come out of the tunnel. After all, they are law officers. These men will have just *assassinated* a visiting head of state.'

'Prime minister. Not head of state.'

'More bullshit. In Israel it's the prime minister that counts. We're talking about assassins, terrorists, not innocent bystanders.' He stood up, suddenly cheerful again. 'Here, give me your glass. Have another drink and stop worrying.'

Vadon rose and set down his glass. He looked at his watch and shook his head, reaching for his hat. 'No. I shouldn't really have come here. I only came because of the changes. I . . . I have to return to the Ministry.'

De Medem nodded and slapped him heavily on the shoulder, rocking his head back. 'Of course, old boy. Your devotion to the public good is a by-word. You won't forget the bag, though, will you?' he added smoothly, taking up the hold-all from where Vadon had left it on the floor and pushing it at him. 'I should keep it with you, rather than leave it in your car, don't you think? Especially not the Ministry car. You wouldn't want your faithful chauffeur finding it during a spot of cleaning.'

'I didn't come here in the Ministry car, you fool,' Vadon snapped sulkily as he fielded the bag, holding it away from him as though it would soil his clothes.

De Medem sniggered. 'Really? I thought you would enjoy being chauffeured.'

'I use the official car when I have to, for official business,' Vadon answered stiffly. 'I detest being driven.'

'Ah!' De Medem gave a mocking nod. 'Very democratic of you. Although you surprise me. A clean-cut young man in a uniform, m'mm?'

Vadon shot de Medem a look of desperate, undistilled hatred. 'God, you are a loathsome bastard,' he said softly.

De Medem smiled, with his mouth only. 'I know. But I rather think it suits me. Play your part and in another twenty-four hours this will all be over. You can even have your photographs back, as a reminder of what an attractive person *you* are.' Once more, at the mention of the photographs, Vadon's head lifted as though he had been struck. Pain filled his eyes. His lips worked for a moment but no speech came.

De Medem saw the pain and smirked. 'You'll be your own man again. Almost. Bye now.' He began reaching out for a handshake. Seeing the look in Vadon's eye, he shrugged and let his hand drop back. 'You will let me know when everything's in place, won't you?'

❖

Sweat crawled and skittered down Bill's spine. He looked again at the cheap watch he had bought on his way from Tati to the hotel. It was twenty minutes since Khoury had disappeared into the building. In that time the air seemed to have grown heavier. From where he stood at the counter of the café across the avenue, watching for Khoury to reappear, he could see that the haze which had obscured the sun, making the afternoon close and oppressive, had now thickened to become a dark, purplish mist. Outside, another convoy of dark blue CRS wagons sped by, impassive faces staring from behind the steel-mesh windows. As the last wagon swept past, Bill put down his cup with enough noise to draw a curious look from the barman. Khoury had reappeared on the steps of the building opposite. He no longer carried the blue bag.

As Bill hurriedly counted out some money, the man stood for a few moments, grinning and rolling his shoulders, like a man emerging from a successful job interview. Then he leapt lightly down the steps. Bill pushed the money at the barman and headed for the door. Khoury was making for the corner, his empty hands swinging loose at his sides. Beyond the barrier closing off the avenue Montaigne, police vans were parked in rows. Uniformed men, driven from their vans by the heat, idled in the shade of the scaling plane trees and waited to be given something to do. Bill hung back until the man was almost at the corner before slipping on the tinted glasses and setting off in shambling pursuit.

His quarry strolled up the rue François Premier, pausing to window-shop briefly at the Ricci men's boutique before disappearing down the steps into the car park. Bill had just quickened his pace when the gloom was split by a sudden glare followed instantly by a crack that shook the ground under his feet. Almost simultaneously, the first raindrops hit him, as hard as peas. Seconds later, the rain was pounding down, the noise of it a roar in his ears as the drops rebounded a foot off the asphalt. Given the excuse to run without attracting the attention of the CRS across the street, he sprinted the forty metres to the shelter of the steps.

With the rain already soaking through the cheap blouson and beginning to trickle down his back, he hurried down as far as the first level. Emerging into the parking area, he looked quickly for the main exit and began running, his ears straining for the sound of a motor. He was almost at the booth, where the lone cashier sat eating a sandwich and watching a portable television, when the roar of an engine made him draw out of sight between two cars. The BMW passed him at speed, the snarl of the exhaust reverberating deafeningly off the concrete.

Bill waited while the man paid and then, the moment he roared round a bend in the ramp, he sprinted past the pay-desk and up the slope in pursuit, ignoring the cashier's half-hearted shout.

Bill burst out onto the street, and stopped dead. The BMW was already a hundred metres away, throwing up two thick plumes of spray as it accelerated into the pummelling rain. Frantically looking around him, he ran to the edge of the kerb. A Mercedes taxi rounded the corner, its roof light glowing bright in the murk. Bill stepped into the gutter, the water lapping over his shoe, already raising a hand. Before he had completed the gesture, a couple sprang from a doorway and wrenched open the cab door. With a sharp curse, he spun back to look at the BMW. It was two hundred metres away and throwing up a great plume of spray as it took a turn and disappeared from sight. He sprinted to the next corner. Where five minutes earlier they had been hunting in packs there was not an empty cab in sight. For a moment he stood, helpless and frustrated, the water sucking at his shoes. Then, turning on his heel, he set off back to the car park, pushing raindrops off his face with the flat of his hand.

As he strode along the empty pavement, he thought again of the almost exaggerated care the man had shown when driving to the car park, contrasting it with the display he had just witnessed, the shower of spray as the man had taken the corner as recklessly as a getaway driver. The difference had to be in the bag Khoury had delivered. Whatever was in it had certainly cramped his driving style.

There was some movement in the car park now as Bill made

his way down to the lowest floor. Well dressed, satisfied looking men made for their cars, preparing to head home to their houses in the suburbs. Men who used the August holiday to pack wives and children off to the coast while they lingered in Paris pleading pressure of work, inflating the phone bill with calls to sex lines. Bill hung around for several minutes, waiting for two of them to finish a leisurely conversation and drive away, leaving a faint aroma of brandy behind them. With a last look around, he crouched to examine the door Khoury and the workman had used.

It was a single grey-painted sheet of steel with a louvred aperture pressed into the metal for ventilation. A white plaque riveted to the door carried a diagram of a jagged lightning bolt, the word 'danger' in red letters and a lot of small print advising how to revive victims of electric shock, who would have passed away while the average rescuer was still looking for his reading glasses.

The lock looked fairly primitive. Behind the plate of the door a lever would swing over into a seating in the frame, which was in turn sealed into the surrounding cement. He stood up, sighing. Back in his Vietnam days he had worked with a man who whiled away the tedium of camp life by practising the art of opening padlocks with pieces of wire. Maybe he expected to find the skill an asset back in Richard Nixon's America. For the first time in his life, Bill regretted having laughed off the man's efforts to initiate him into the art. Primitive or not, without a key it would need half a kilo of plastic explosive to find out what lay behind the door. Pushing his rain-sodden hair back off his forehead, he turned and began striding swiftly towards the exit.

He paused at the top of the steps watching the rain. It had eased to a steady, soaking downpour, falling vertically, without a breath of wind to give it a slant. Cars hissed through the surface water with their headlights blazing, rivulets of rain obscuring their side windows. He considered heading for a Métro station and discarded the idea. Summer was a season when policemen cruised the Métro in droves, boosting their arrest quotas by collaring Colombian pickpockets. If one of them recognized him between stations he would be a rat in a trap. On the streets there was at least the option of making a run for it. The CRS across the street were huddled in an entry, cradling cigarettes from the rain, paying no attention to the deserted street. Hunching his shoulders, he stepped out into the rain, not shambling now, but walking with a fast, springy stride.

He swung round the corner, back onto the avenue Montaigne, and headed for the river. After twenty paces he paused at the kerb, looking back towards the Champs-Elysées in half-hearted search of a taxi. Seeing none free, he turned to resume walking, and froze.

A man in a raincoat was running down the steps of the building Khoury had visited. His left arm, raised to hold onto his rain-slick hat, hid his face from Bill's view. Under the other arm he held a blue bag, hugging it close to his body. Bill had hardly begun striding forward when the man yanked open the door of a blue Jaguar. Before Bill had gone three more strides, the man had disappeared into the gloom of the interior, stuffing the bag in ahead of him. Bill was moving forward, almost running, as the reversing lights flickered on. He was still several metres away when the car sped away from the kerb, slashing spray across the pavement. Bill stepped into the road and watched it go, repeating the registration number over to himself several times. Satisfied he had it fixed in his mind, he continued along the streaming pavement towards the river.

21

Bill pressed the buzzer and waited. Three more times he tried without getting a response. At last, anxiety etched deep into his face, he slipped silently past the concierge's door and into the stairwell, his eyes on the frosted glass where a broad shadow moved against the glow of the television. The television on which she would already have seen his picture a dozen times that day. His senses quivering, waiting for the opening door, the raised voice of the concierge's challenge, he crept stealthily up the stairs.

For more than a minute he remained motionless on the landing in front of the door, listening hard for any sound from inside the apartment. Hearing nothing, he slid his key carefully into the lock and eased open the door.

'Keltum!' he called softly, and waited.

The silence hummed in his head.

'Keltum! It's me.' He stood for a moment, hearing only the faint sound of a car starting on the street. His brow deeply furrowed, he moved towards the half-open door of the living room. He paused again, listening to the deep silence. Then, his hands raised in front of his chest, the fingers cupped, he kicked the door back and stepped quickly over the threshold. The room was empty. His hands still raised, fingers curved, he crossed to the kitchen. He gave a low groan and stepped quickly inside.

A bag of groceries, fresh milk, butter, lay partly unpacked on the counter. The door of the refrigerator stood open, the motor humming loud in the quiet. He put his fingertips to the pack of butter. It sagged under his touch. The blood thundering in his head, he turned and began moving with rapid purpose through the rest of the flat.

Two minutes later, he sat down heavily on the bare mattress in the guest room and sank his head into his hands. Nothing in the place had been disturbed. There was not the slightest sign of a struggle. For half a minute he stayed with his head bowed, deep in thought. Then, straightening, he snatched the phone from the bedside table and dragged out Lantier's card.

'Hello.' The woman's voice was brusque, preoccupied. Somewhere in the background a child cried.

'Hello.' As he spoke Bill carried the phone to the window and leant against the frame, his eyes scanning the street. 'My name's Kléber. I need to speak to Inspector Lantier.'

The voice lost its preoccupation, became focused, but with a wariness in it. 'He isn't here.'

'No, I realize. He said I could leave a message with you.'

'Yes. Go on. I can pass on a message to the Inspector. If he calls me.'

Bill spoke quickly, urgently. 'Look, Madame, could you contact *him*? Immediately. Have him call me. Please.'

The woman spoke carefully. 'I'm not sure I can reach him just like that. I'll . . .'

'Please,' Bill cut in. 'He would want you to do it. It's very important. Vital!'

'Does he have your number?' she asked briskly.

He dictated the number written on the handset. 'Please, have him call me straight away.'

'How long will you be there?'

Bill's eyes swept the street. 'I don't know.' He watched a patrol of three CRS stroll past on the opposite pavement and swallowed. 'Until he calls me. I hope.'

Bill lowered the beer bottle from his lips and turned from the window, snatching up the phone on the first ring. 'Hello!' He spoke in a hollow, neutral voice, quite unlike his own.

'Sorry. Perhaps that's a wrong number!'

Bill almost laughed with relief at the sound of Lantier's curt irony. 'Oh, God, no,' he said, reverting to his own voice. He wiped the beer froth from his lips. 'Thank God it's you. It's over an hour since I called. I've been going crazy, waiting for them to kick the door down.'

'I was in a meeting. Devising a traffic survey.' Lantier dropped the flippant tone. 'What's this about kicking the door down? Where are you?'

'The sister's apartment.'

'Her apartment? I thought she just lived at home, ministering to her ailing dad.'

'Cut it out! The man's *dying* for God's sake! And I have a lot to tell you, and I might not have much time.'

'Sorry,' Lantier murmured. 'She got under my skin. Give me the address. And tell me what's going on.'

'Can I speak openly on this line?'

'What do you take me for?'

'Okay.' Bill quickly gave him the address.

'Right. Now, what the hell has happened?'

Lantier listened in silence as, in a few quick phrases, Bill outlined the day's events. When he came to the number of the Jaguar, Lantier whistled and repeated it slowly, as though writing it down. 'You *are* doing a good job,' he muttered as he wrote. He laughed softly. 'Have you ever thought of police work?'

'They wouldn't have me, on account of my hobby of mutilating women.'

'I've had worse working for me!' Lantier retorted, with tart humour. 'What else?'

'Keltum has disappeared.'

There was the briefest of pauses before Lantier replied. 'What? From where? When?'

'From here. She was supposed to wait for me. I went to the hotel, she was to come here.'

'And she didn't show up?'

'She showed up, all right. Then she left again. In a hurry.'

'Maybe she just went out to get some groceries.'

'We *have* groceries! She was in the middle of unpacking them.

The fridge door was hanging open. She's not the forgetful type, believe me.'

'So, you think someone grabbed her?' Lantier's voice was low, urgent.

'God, I don't know. It looks like it.'

Lantier was silent for several seconds. 'When did this happen?'

'Quite a while before I got here, anyway. The butter had almost turned to oil.'

Lantier paused again. 'And you say you've been there over an hour?'

Bill glanced mechanically at his watch. 'Right.'

'And nobody's come for you yet?'

Bill grunted.

'Alright. Here's my advice. If they haven't picked you up yet, they can't have been watching the place. She must have given them some story that's got them looking for you elsewhere. So, my advice is to stay put. It's your best bet. Every policeman in town is carrying your picture as of this morning and, as you may have noticed, there are an awful lot of them.' His voice dropped lower. 'They've been told it's open season.'

'Oh, shit!'

'That about sums it up. I'll check out this number and get back to you.'

'How about Keltum? Can you check her out, too?'

'I'll try, of course. Although, if it hasn't happened through, er, normal channels, I might not be able to learn much.'

'Try, for God's sake. I forced her into this. If anything's happened to her I'll . . .'

'I'll do my best. At least check for hit-and-run victims.'

Bill groaned. 'God, no!'

'Just try to take it easy. And don't jump to conclusions. She might have had a reason of her own to leave.'

'No. She promised me. She wouldn't just walk out. I *know* it.'

'I said the same thing about my wife. I'll get back to you.'

Bill stood for some time without moving. Then he dropped the phone onto the bed, walked into the kitchen for another beer, dragged a chair to the living-room window, and sat down to watch.

He started, grabbing at the window frame as his chair tilted and almost fell. He shook his head, fighting his way out of sleep. Only slowly did he become aware of the soft, insistent ringing of the phone. He stumbled from the chair and almost tripped over the telephone where he had placed it on the floor next to him. Crouching, he picked it up.

'M'mm?'

'It's me. Can you talk?'

Lantier's voice dragged him the rest of the way into wakefulness. 'Only just. What time is it?' He looked at his watch as he spoke. 'My God, it's almost three.' He pushed himself upright and took a few paces around the room, shaking his cramped muscles loose. 'What news? Any word of Keltum?'

'No. Which might be good news. At least she's not in the morgue with tyre tracks across her back.'

'Stop it!'

'I'm not exaggerating,' Lantier said softly. 'I'm still not sure what you've stumbled into, but it's going to get you, and me, into some *very* nasty trouble, if we aren't extremely careful.'

Bill gave a short, sardonic laugh. 'I'm a wanted sex killer, and you're telling me I have to be careful not to get into *trouble*?'

'As a matter of fact, I am. There's a fair chance I might be able to help you handle the matter of that woman's death. But not if I, or you, happened to be dead.'

'Shit!' Bill breathed. 'You aren't kidding, are you? What have you got?'

'Let's start with the car. It's the private car of the man whose office your friend chose to jump from. Christian . . .'

'Vadon,' Bill hissed softly.

'Right,' Lantier murmured. 'There's more.'

'Go on.' Wide awake now, his mind racing, Bill closed the window, conscious how far a voice might carry in the quiet of the night. He sat down, his eyes again on the street.

'I had the occupiers of the building checked out. You wouldn't have heard of most of them. Rich, influential, very discreet.'

'If I ever get out of this I'll try a mail shot. Do you know who he would have gone to see?'

'Well, there's one candidate that stands out. A woman. Aristocracy, kind of. Supposed to be absolutely loaded, most of it from her dear departed first husband. He made a pile . . .' Lantier paused, 'in industrial waste disposal.'

'The Mob? At home that's big business for them. Collect waste for the incinerators, dump it as landfill. Hell of a lot cheaper, and half of New Jersey a disaster zone.'

'I wouldn't go that far. But he was . . . colourful. Anyway, she's well enough connected, and active enough in every charity in town, for nobody to worry too much where the loot came from.'

'Sounds more like one of my clients by the minute. What makes you think she's the one?'

'De Medem.' Lantier said the name quickly, almost inaudibly.

'What!'

'I had to call in a lot of favours to get this. Does "enquêtes réservées" mean anything to you?'

'The police department that handles politically sensitive stuff?'

'That's right. Although they're police officers, the enquêtes réservées people work very closely with the Minister's office. They're almost his private police force. They had her under surveillance. Until a few weeks ago.'

'What stopped them?'

'Vadon, I think. Although there's nothing to actually *prove* that.'

'Why was she being watched in the first place?'

'She's Blaise de Medem's mistress.'

For a stunned moment Bill was silent, working through the

implications. 'First, just at the time you'd think he'd be digging all the dirt he could on de Medem, he calls off the dogs. Now, he goes visiting the lady. It couldn't be that I've mis-read Vadon, could it? You don't think he's elbowed de Medem aside and moved in on her himself?'

'Nothing's totally impossible in this world,' Lantier said drily.

'So what the hell *is* going on?'

'I wish I knew. Meanwhile, I'm going to exercise extreme caution trying to find out.' Lantier's voice hardened. 'Here's what I want from you. I have some more work to do on this that will take me a few hours. I need to see some people, have a few conversations I'd rather not hold over the phone. I want you to meet me at, say five this afternoon. Same place as last time, okay?'

'If you say so.'

'I do. And if things turn out the way I fear, I'm going to have to ask you to trust me.'

'I already trust you.'

'A lot further. I'm probably going to want to take you into protective custody.'

'Hold it. To a layman that sounds like arresting me. I thought we had a deal on that?'

'We do. Don't come if you don't want to. But it's for your own good. If this breaks open, I'll want you somewhere safe.'

'Here seems to be working okay.'

'So far, so good. I checked the records. The sister doesn't appear on the deeds. It's in the name of a Liechtenstein trust. As far as I can see, nobody could know. Unless she . . .'

'Unless she told them?' Bill intervened, his voice low.

Lantier did not answer immediately. 'Look,' he said at length, 'don't let it get to you yet. We don't *know* what's happened to her.' He paused again, weighing his words. 'But then I wouldn't relax too much. If they *do* have her . . .' His voice trailed off.

'Yeah. Thanks for the advice.'

'Sorry, but we're getting into something deeper than we

know here. By the way, this afternoon I want you to meet someone.'

'Who?' Bill asked, warily. 'Are you forgetting I'm public enemy number one?'

'No. I can't tell you who it is. Someone who has the President's ear, though. Someone that I've known for a long time, that I would trust with my own life.' He gave a soft snuffle of morose laughter. 'Maybe I already have.'

Bill was silent for a count of three. 'Okay. See you at five.'

❖

Swearing, Vadon sat up and switched on the tasselled bedside lamp. The dark satin of his pyjamas shone softly as he reached over and picked up the phone. 'Yes?'

'Christian?'

The vertical crease above the bridge of his nose deepened at the sound of the voice. 'This is Vadon. Who is this? And whatever is the meaning of calling me here? And in the middle of the night!'

The indignation was not feigned. He had awoken sufficiently to put a face to the voice. A nice-looking, blond young man at a reception given by the Prefect of Police just a few days earlier. Foolishly, he had let his upset over the suicide cloud his judgement and invited the man over for a drink. The man had turned out to be a computer bore, who spent his days, and, it seemed, his nights, and probably his weekends too, hunched over the computers of the intelligence service, the Renseignements Généraux. He had somehow been distracted enough to let the man get hold of his private number.

'I told you never to call me here. And I have a title. You may address me as "Minister". Can you remember that?'

'Certainly. Of course, Minister,' the man stammered. 'I apologize. But there is a matter I, well, I thought you would wish to know about.'

'What could I possibly want to know about from you at this hour of the night, you witless imbecile?' He spoke with deliberate harshness, hoping to check the note of wheedling intimacy that remained in the man's voice.

The man quavered. 'It, er, concerns the Countess de Bernis.'

Vadon paled. He swallowed hard, composing himself. 'What do you mean? Why would I want to know about *her*, for God's sake?'

'Her file is flagged as "state red". You are listed as the initiating minister. I just thought perhaps you would, that I ought to let you know straight away.'

'At four in the morning? Then you're an idiot.'

Even he could hear the twanging, counterfeit note in his angry tone. The man had simply followed instructions. The flagging the man spoke of was designed to ensure that whenever certain highly sensitive computer files were called up, a warning was logged. The instruction to heads of records, like this man, was clear. Inform the relevant minister *instantly*. The system had served, unchanged, since General de Gaulle had set it up in the hope of minimizing damage from whistle-blowers, giving ministers time to put a friendly spin on leaks.

'Well, I'm terribly sorry, Minister. But the procedures are clear. I thought I should . . .'

'Well you thought wrongly,' he snapped. 'You should have called my office, not the Ministry. My staff would have decided if it was worth waking me.' All trace of sleep had fallen from him. His mind racing, he softened his tone. 'No, that is, you were right to call me.' He tried a careless laugh, its hollowness ringing in his ears. 'It's just that any interest I may have been asked to take in the Countess withered long ago.' He let a second pass and then added, as though it were no more than an afterthought, 'As a matter of interest, who was the officer that called up the file?'

'Inspector Lantier, sir. Police Judiciaire. Although he's just been moved to ministerial secondment. Transport. Working out his time,' he added, with a snigger of contempt. 'He managed to persuade one of my operators to pull out the files for him. Countess de Bernis and one other. It often happens when a washed-up officer sees himself being put out to grass. They start squirrelling away information for the book they plan to write. I imagine he . . .'

'What was the other name?'

'Oh, nobody that would mean anything to *you*, Minister. A man called Khoury. Saïd Khoury. An Algerian.'

Vadon frowned, searching his memory. 'And who is *he*, if I may ask?'

'Nobody. Just a particularly nasty little gangster. Pimping, some drugs. Quite a record of violence. A man to be reckoned with in his own world, perhaps, but he's only on *our* files at all because he was connected with the Palatin crowd down in Nice, during the mid-eighties. A lot of people were, of course,' he added, with a fluttering laugh, 'but not many Arabs. He seems much more like Lantier's line than the Countess de Bernis . . .'

Vadon had sat through the man's speech pale and silent. He now spoke in a strained voice. 'It doesn't matter. Neither one of them is of the slightest interest to me.' He plucked at the flesh of his throat. 'You can just forget the whole thing.'

'Certainly, Minister. I just thought, since it was flagged . . .'

'Forget it, I said,' he shouted. 'Didn't you hear me?' He jabbed a fingertip onto the button, cutting the man off.

For several minutes he went on sitting, the telephone still in one hand while he gnawed at the thumbnail of the other. The muscles in his cheeks and round his eyes twitched and skittered. At length, murmuring to himself, he slammed down the phone, cast the quilt aside and slid out of bed.

Ten minutes later, conscious that he needed a shave, he pulled the Jaguar to a halt in a leafy avenue, across the wide pavement from a public telephone. The avenue was empty except for a runner and two black street cleaners. The lawyers, promoters, heirs and Arabs who inhabited the handsome apartments that bordered the avenue were not the kind of people to set off for the office before dawn. He sat staring into his wing mirror, watching the runner approach. The man, in the torn army sweater and heavy boots of the professional boxer on roadwork rather than the fancy gear of a Parisian jogger, loped past without a glance at the car. He let the man run on for forty metres before jumping from the car and heading for the phone booth, one hand raised to smooth his hair, shielding his face. It was unlikely that the two streetcleaners would recognize him if they were trapped together in a lift. Nevertheless, it was unthinkable that he should be seen by anyone, anyone at all.

'You fool! You absolute, total imbecile! You were supposed to have fixed him. You had had him moved out of the way, you said. Shit! Why do I have to work with such people!'

Hunching close to the phone, Vadon raised his own voice, provoked by de Medem's sibilant anger.

'What more could I do? Have him posted to the South Pacific? I did all I was able,' he added, unable to keep a note of pleading out of his voice.

De Medem's anger turned to sarcasm. 'Beautiful! So you did all *you* could. And now, *I'm* supposed to undo the damage. How? Can you tell me that?'

'Stop it. Call off the whole thing. It's not too late.' Vadon licked his lips, casting anxious looks around the deserted avenue. 'It's too dangerous. It's all unravelling. First the American, and now this. The Arab, Khoury, I suppose he's part of it. Another of your gangster friends. He's probably done something stupid that's got Lantier prying again. He'll bring the whole thing down round our ears. You should know better than working with Arabs!'

De Medem gave a sneering laugh. 'Really? Well, if we're on the subject of Arabs, let's not forget your little friend. If you had been able to keep him under control there'd be *nobody* nosing around at all.' De Medem's breathing was loud as he wrestled with his fury. Vadon was about to interject when he spoke again, velvety and implacable. 'Understand this: we've started something, and we're going to see it through. You've been blowing hot and cold like a schoolgirl from the beginning. Well, you should have known me better, my friend, and said no from the start.'

Vadon's voice rose to be almost a sob. 'How could I? You

were going to destroy me! I had no choice. You have no idea what I . . .'

'You were destroying yourself. Nobody made you fall for that little fairy. He would have dragged you down anyway. This way we both achieve our ambitions.'

'But . . . like this . . .'

'Like this? What do I care *how*?' De Medem's voice fell to a husky whisper. 'I've dreamed of this for thirty years. I've worked for it. You've never suffered the ridicule, the insults and sneers of would-be intellectuals the way I have. Even today, they treat me as if I were dirt, as though I and my people had no *right* to our opinions. Well, I've *earned* what this is going to bring me, my friend. And I'm not going to let you steal it from me by backing out now. You are going to go through with this or I'll drag you so deep in the gutter you'll never get out of it. So just concentrate on finding the American and keep your nerve for one more day.' He paused and then spoke again, his voice normal, almost genial. 'There's something I've never told you before.'

'What?' Vadon sounded defeated, uninterested.

'I think *you* deserve it, too, at bottom. You've fought long enough. The truth is, I think you'll do pretty well at it, provided you remember to let your *brain* do your thinking.'

❖

Instantly wide awake, Bill sprang from the chair, listening, seeking the sound that had woken him. He had begun to relax, deciding that it was the sun streaming through the window that had brought him out of his doze, when the noise came again, the soft thump of the lift machinery. The sound stopped, followed by the whirring of the door mechanism. In three strides he was positioned behind the open door of the living room, his head tilted to peer through the crack into the hall.

Footsteps sounded softly on the carpet and stopped in front of the door. His back tingled as sweat broke out. Metal scraped on metal. It happened again, as though someone were having trouble with the lock. Glancing around him, he reached out and snatched up a narrow-necked vase from a nearby table. Gripping it by the neck, he turned again to peer through the crack as the levers of the lock snapped back.

Bill swallowed hard, running his tongue over his lips and shifting his feet for a better balance. Sweat made his palm greasy on the vase.

His breath left him in a hiss as the door swung slowly open to reveal Keltum standing motionless on the threshold, the hand holding her keys hanging slackly at her side. Dropping the vase to the carpet, he stepped wide round the door, grinning with relief and pleasure. 'Keltum! Thank God you're back.'

Without replying, she took a listless pace into the hall. Instead of turning to close the door, she simply backed against it until the latch caught.

He took two eager paces towards her. 'Where *were* you? I've been worried sick.'

She gave no sign that she had heard, but simply stood with her head drooping, staring at the floor at her feet.

Bill's grin faded. He took another step forward. 'Keltum?' he said tentatively. 'Are you okay?'

She remained motionless, her arms limp at her sides. A tear splashed audibly on the polished wood floor. Her shoulders began to heave in slow, silent sobs. Consternation flooded his face. Taking her tentatively by the shoulders he flexed his knees, bringing his face level with hers. 'Keltum! What is it?' He rocked her gently. 'What's wrong?'

Very slowly she raised her head and stared unseeing into his eyes. Her face seemed altered, lifeless, like a waxwork of herself. Gradually, her eyes focused on his face. 'He's dead.'

Bill stared at her, incredulous, appalled. 'Dead?' he said dully.

Tears gushed, streaming over the waxy cheeks. 'My father.'

He continued staring at her in silence. 'Oh, God,' he whispered, lowering his eyes briefly, in some instinctive homage. 'When?'

She shrugged. 'Early this morning. I didn't notice the time,' she added, hollow voiced.

For several seconds he held onto her shoulders as they stared into each other's faces, numbed with emotion. Gradually, the implications crept up on him, wrestling for a space in his grief-deadened mind. 'You were there? At your parents' place?'

She gave an almost imperceptible nod. 'My mother telephoned me yesterday afternoon.'

'She knew you were here?'

She shook her head, spraying him with tears. 'No, she just didn't know where else to try. She was distraught.'

'Of course.' He nodded. 'And you came back directly from there to here?' It was not really a question.

She gave another barely discernible nod. The desolation in her face wrenched at him.

'My God.' Releasing her gently, he ran to the window. Staying as far back from the glass as possible, he peered down at the street. A delivery truck had parked at a bus stop thirty metres along the street. He could clearly see the elbow of a passenger resting on the sill of the open window. He watched for thirty seconds. Nobody delivered anything. Turning, he strode back to where she still stood, immobile.

'They're here,' he said, keeping his voice to a murmur. 'I have to go.' He took her by the shoulders and brushed his lips against her forehead. 'Goodbye, Keltum. Take care of your mother. If they'll let you. If you need help, contact Lantier. He'll do what he can. I hope I'll see you someday.'

He turned and put an eye to the spy-hole in the door. The landing was deserted. He threw the door open, his hands coming up in front of him. As he did so, she wheeled and clutched at his arm. 'No! I'm coming with you.'

He shook his head, lifting her hand quite roughly from his sleeve. 'No! Go home! They aren't coming for you. Go to your mother. She needs you now.'

She shook her own head, too hard, shaking a strand of hair

loose. '*She* made me come!' she said, her voice breaking on a sob. 'It was my father's last wish.'

Bill already had a foot on the top stair, listening. 'You *can't!*' he hissed. He caught her by the arm and thrust her back towards the door. At the same moment the clunk and whirr of the lift made him start. 'Go inside.' He pulled out Lantier's card and thrust it into her hand. 'Call Lantier!' Turning from her, he started moving cautiously down the stairs.

He had descended two floors when the sound of a voice reached him, giving instructions in a low staccato. Then the hum of the lift doors was followed by the dull crash of the hoist engaging. Hearing no further sound from below, he continued down, moving quicker now, his steps soundless on the thick carpet. As he reached the first-floor landing, the lift rose past him, two shadows against the frosted glass of its windows. Almost running now, he swung round onto the last flight. A deep-chested man was coming up to meet him, walking with a light, athletic ease.

They both recoiled, and for a single frozen moment stared into each other's faces. Then the man hit him, slamming a fist into Bill's stomach. Bill grunted and doubled over. The man's other fist crashed into the side of his head. His heels caught the step, making him stagger against the wall. The man hit him again, a short, clubbing blow that glanced off the side of his head.

Using the wall for balance, Bill lashed out, aiming for the vulnerable lower abdomen. The man swayed aside and chopped the blade of his hand down onto Bill's forearm. A bolt of pain shot up his arm, the numbed fingers splaying apart. He tried to remake a fist and could find no response from the paralysed muscle. Grinning, the man leaned in and hit him in the middle of the chest. Bill made a coughing sound and fell back, helpless, against the wall. The man shuffled closer, setting himself for the next blow. The cloth of his jacket strained over the meat of his arm as he drew back his elbow, the fist level with Bill's nose.

His eyes on the man's face, Bill stabbed out a foot, catching the top of his assailant's shin with the heel of his shoe. The man roared and bent to clutch at his leg. Bill kicked out at his attacker's groin.

Even through his pain, the man seemed to have all the time in the world. He reached out an open palm and smothered the blow, using the power of his massive arm to drain the force from it. Following through, he snatched Bill's foot towards him in an upward motion, bringing Bill to one knee. Straightening, he drove the heel of a hand into Bill's face, cracking his head back against the wall. With a sneer, he drew back his hand again.

'Stop it!'

The man's head swivelled to face the sound. Keltum stood half-way down the flight of stairs, horror in her eyes as she watched the man ready himself. He gave her a quick contemptuous glance and turned back to Bill. Pinning Bill to the wall with one great palm, he bunched his other hand into a fist and swivelled from the waist, drawing his shoulder back, loading the spring.

Still dazed from striking the wall, Bill watched with a kind of helpless fascination as the man raised the fist the final centimetre, seeking one more ounce of energy, and drove it forward.

The scene seemed to be happening in slow motion. Bill stared transfixed as the great fist came at him, knowing it would smash bones, too befuddled to respond.

Magically, the thick fingers of the fist burst apart. The open hand flew up to the man's left eye. A curious, infantile protest came from his throat as he reared back against the balustrade of the stairwell.

Bill shoved himself upright, his head gradually clearing. As he did so, the man slowly took his hand away from his eye and held it out in front of him. The uninjured right eye widened, glittering with fear and awakening pain. A pool of bright blood had gathered in the slightly cupped palm.

Bill turned to look at Keltum. She was standing motionless, staring transfixed at the man's face. The leather reporter bag hung open at her right side. The hand that lay slackly against it clutched a cheap plastic pen.

'My God,' Bill said, with whispered vehemence. 'Thanks.' He took her by the arm and yanked it hard, making her head rock on her shoulders. 'Let's get out of here.'

He drove her down the stairs ahead of him. As they went, the man's whimpering rose to a distorted, animal cry. Looking back, Bill saw the face contort as the mouth opened to form a scream. With one foot already on the top stair, Bill spun and drove his fist into the man's unguarded belly. The mouth snapped shut, cutting off the scream. Bill hit him once more, the force of it jarring his shoulder, then turned and ran to catch Keltum.

He leapt down the last stairs into the lobby and stopped short. Keltum stood, waxen-faced and immobile, a pace from the door. A wide-hipped woman blocked her way, jabbering in an accent so heavy he needed a moment to recognize it as French. He was preparing to spring at the woman when he realized she was smiling at Keltum. At the sight of Bill, her smile melted into purse-lipped disapproval. Without another word, she thrust a package of mail into Keltum's lifeless grasp. Mechanically, Keltum let it drop into her open bag as Bill jostled the woman aside and swept her through the door. In the courtyard he spun and took Keltum by the upper arms, as though she were recovering from a fainting fit. 'Where's the car?'

She stared emptily back at him, as though he were someone she had never seen before, speaking a language she had never heard. He gave her a single sharp jolt, like someone testing a broken watch. 'The car, Keltum. Where is it?'

She blinked. 'Just around the corner,' she said in a flat, dreamy voice.

'Which way?'

She gestured lethargically in the direction of the river and let her hand fall loosely back to her side. 'Down there. At the corner.'

'Give me the keys. Quickly.'

She probed in the bag and pulled them out. He snatched them and turned to the gate. 'Are you sure you want to stay with me?'

She nodded, her eyes still far away. 'It was his last wish. I told him . . .'

Bill was already yanking open the gate. He dodged through, dragging her bodily after him. 'Later! Come on!' Running, hauling the stumbling Keltum in his wake, he looked over his shoulder. A man jumped from the cab of the delivery van, his face filled with stupid dismay. He gaped upwards for a moment, towards the windows of the flat, and then, casting all pretence aside, he began shouting into a wrist microphone, as a knot of gaping passers-by gathered to watch.

They ran the thirty metres to the corner with the man, still shouting instructions into the transmitter, sprinting after them. As they rounded the corner he was still forty paces behind. The car was parked a dozen metres away. Almost throwing Keltum at the passenger door, Bill ran round the car. It took him two attempts to fumble the unfamiliar key into the lock. Sinking into the driving seat, he fell across to unlock the passenger side. The immediacy of the danger seemed to have brought Keltum out of her trance. She flung herself down beside him and he stamped on the gas. Their pursuer reached the corner just in time to see the car buck away from the kerb and speed past him.

Bill began swinging the car to his right, heading away from the van. He was half-way through the turn when a bus entered the far end of the narrow street, blocking their exit. Tyres screaming, he wrenched the car through a hundred and eighty degrees and took the only option left open, pointing the car away from the river, towards the parked van.

Amid the adrenaline rush, Bill was aware of the faintest sense of farce as their pursuer scrambled to turn and began racing back up the road behind them. The feeling disappeared as a tall man, presumably one of those who had taken the lift, burst out of their building. He hesitated for a split second, taking in the speeding car and his accomplice sprinting in its wake, and then he was racing for the van.

The engine of the little Fiat screamed in protest as Bill held the pedal hard against the floor, talking to himself, willing the car to more speed. They passed the man as he leapt for the cab of the van. For an instant, Bill was looking full into his face. The sight sent a chill through him. Neither excitement nor hatred were written there; only the calm, dispassionate purpose of the trained killer.

They sped on, heading for the next corner. In his mirror Bill watched the running man reach the van and jump inside. The van bucked into motion then, almost instantly, juddered to a halt. The bus, finding the stop occupied, had pulled up directly alongside them, hemming them in.

The tall man's mouth worked furiously as he yelled at the bus driver. Behind his windscreen the driver retorted by jabbing a finger angrily at the air in an obscene gesture. Abruptly, the van driver leaned from his cab, his arm fully extended. At the end of it, the dark shape of a gun was clearly visible. As Bill threw the car into another left turn he was unable to suppress a fleeting smile. Terror-stricken, the bus driver had twisted in his seat and was trying to bull his way backwards. Behind him, the queue of cars crowded in his wake, unaware of the existence of the gun, broke into a cacophony of hooting, obstinately refusing to give him an inch.

22

He stopped the car in a quiet street south of the boulevard Saint Germain. For several seconds he sat, breathing deeply, before sliding from the car and hurrying round to open Keltum's door. Since getting into the car she had not uttered a single word, sitting in frozen, tight-lipped silence as he had zigzagged through a maze of small streets, throwing off the van. Now, as he took her hand, it was ice cold. Leaning in, he slid an arm round her shoulders. 'Come on,' he said, his voice gentle, coaxing. 'We have to go. They'll be looking for the car.'

She continued sitting, staring mutely ahead of her. Murmuring in a soft, cajoling voice, he put his hands under her armpits and lifted her from her seat. She came to her feet awkwardly, her limbs wooden and disjointed. Supporting her weight, he looked quickly around him. At the nearby cafés waiters were only just setting chairs at the terrace tables. He glanced at Keltum's drawn, ashen face. The few customers in the bright, narrow interiors at so early an hour would be regulars, too ready to notice Keltum's shell-shocked appearance. Curbing the need for coffee, he tightened his grip round her waist and began walking her south, towards the Luxembourg Gardens.

He found a bench in a secluded spot and lowered her gently onto it, taking a place beside her. For some time he sat as silent as she, savouring the quiet and breathing the fragrance of the damp earth, giving her space. Finally, he turned and looked into her face. He rested a hand lightly on hers, pressing gently on the chill, lifeless fingers. 'Do you want to tell me about it?'

Very slowly, her eyes lifted to his, coming gradually into focus. 'It was horrible.' She just managed to speak the words before her eyes closed and tears began squeezing between the clenched lids. Her teeth gouged a white crescent in her bottom lip, with the effort not to cry aloud. As Bill cast anxious glances around them, she made a visible effort of will, recovering herself enough to continue speaking. 'It happened so quickly. I went as soon as my mother called and . . . in just a few hours, he was . . . gone. The pain had become intolerable. His heart simply couldn't bear any more.' A great shudder racked her. 'Doctor Hassan was there. He was filling my father with drugs, as much as he dared. Maybe in the end that's what actually killed him. Perhaps he should have given him *more*, ended it sooner. I don't know.' She shook again. 'It was just so . . . obscene! So *unfair*! Nobody should ever have to suffer like that. It's not . . . it's just inhuman.'

'How is your mother?'

She shook her head, moving a hand in front of her face, palm out, as if fending off a wraith. 'She was expecting it. She's very strong, under that shy facade. But it was hard, terribly hard,' she added, simply. She gulped, fighting the renewed tears. 'She knew it had to happen but still, she hoped somehow it never would.' She turned abruptly to fix him with her glittering stare. 'Can you imagine how it is, for a woman like her? Life with my father was all she knew. Since they were married he had been her whole existence. She *never* went out without him, except to shop. She has never had friends of her own. Her family, her sisters, her cousins, the people who could have helped her through this, are all in Algeria.' She gave a soft, wild laugh. 'Do you realize, after all these years, *that's* where she would be at home, not here?'

'You mean your mother's back there alone? Isn't somebody with her?' he whispered, the image filling his mind of the woman, alone with her husband's body, hardly even knowing the language. 'You should have stayed with her,' he murmured, as much to himself as to her.

She shook her head. 'I tried. She wouldn't let me. I told you, she's a very strong-willed woman. My father's word was law to her. She wouldn't allow me to defy his wishes.' He felt her grip tighten as she spoke the words, the anger that comes with grief giving a bitter edge to her voice. 'The doctor will help her, and the people who work for my father . . . Worked for him, I mean,' she corrected herself, squeezing his hand harder. 'The Imam will do all he can, too. He is already helping, getting my father's body washed and ready.'

Bill reared away from her. 'Bouhila?' he exclaimed. 'You mean Bouhila was *there* at your parents' place? Last night?'

She nodded, two burning spots on her cheekbones bright against the pallor. 'Yes. He came to see how my father was.'

'What the hell was he doing there? Did your parents ask him to come? Did you?'

The flush suffused her whole face. 'No. You know quite well how my father feels . . . felt about the Imam. But, you must understand something about him. He would not let my father's opinion of him prevent him *helping* if he could. He knew quite well what my father thought of his mission. That didn't stop him respecting my father. He has often told me how highly he thinks of . . . *thought* of my father, of what he has made of his life.'

Bill's lips twisted in a sardonic smile. 'So he and I *do* have something in common! Did he know about your father wanting you to be with me? That must have pleased him no end, the idea of one of his favourite followers keeping company with the devil.'

She shook her head with sudden vehemence and clutched at his sleeve. 'Don't talk like that! Please,' she added, her anger softening to a plea. 'You really don't know him. He doesn't deserve to be spoken of in that way.' She lowered her eyes, her voice sinking to a barely audible murmur. 'As a matter of fact, it was the Imam who made me come back. I was arguing with my mother. I wanted to stay with her. Even now I feel that's where I should be, whatever my father said.'

He nodded towards the street beyond the shrubbery. 'Of course you should. But it's too late, Keltum. After what happened back there they aren't going to leave you in peace to take care of your father's body.'

She sighed bitterly. 'I know. But I just want you to be fair to the Imam. He agreed with my mother, that my father's wish had to be respected. He made me see that it would be selfish to stay, that the best homage I could pay to my father's memory was not to leave you alone.'

Bill dipped his head. 'Alright, Keltum. Maybe I've misjudged him. I don't like his views and I don't like his style, and I think what he's doing will end in a bloodbath, but let's agree he's a saint despite that. I still wish to God he hadn't taken it into his head to visit Sidi Bey.'

She looked questioningly from red and glistening eyes. 'Why? What harm could it do?'

He smiled patiently, replacing his hand on hers. 'In other circumstances you would have seen it, too. For months now, Bouhila's had half the immigrant population practically on a war footing, hasn't he?' He sat back, spreading his hands. 'Even if they weren't already watching your parents' place, hoping I'd show up, the police would *surely* have been keeping an eye on Bouhila. One of those crop-haired kids that worked for your father probably tipped him off you were there, thinking he was doing everybody a favour. So, Bouhila was followed there. Just routine. Then, while they're sitting in the back of their unmarked van, drinking coffee, and praying for the end of their shift, *you* emerge! It wouldn't have taken them many seconds to figure out that you might lead them to me.' He smiled. 'Anyway, we survived.' He looked at his watch. It was almost eight o'clock. 'I have a rendezvous with Lantier this afternoon. There's someone he wants me to meet, that he seems to think might help get us out of this crazy mess. Do you want to come with me?'

'What do you think?'

'After this morning, I don't think you have any choice, do you? That guy lost an eye this morning, Keltum. He could even be dead.' At his words, she groaned, shaken from head to foot by a violent tremor. 'Either way, neither of us would want to be picked up by some of his pals. At least Lantier is ready to listen to us.'

She nodded. 'Alright. I'll come with you,' she murmured.

'Great.' He grinned cheerfully. 'So now we've got all day to kill in a city with five thousand extra police on the streets, every one of them bent on getting revenge for what was probably a brother officer. Any ideas?'

She shook her head, flicking the tears that hung from the point of her chin onto his shirtfront.

'Okay. Look, I've got some pretty good friends in this town. Do you mind waiting for me here while I make a couple of calls? Nobody's going to try to pick you up at this hour.'

She smiled, her first real smile, her eyes glinting with irony. 'Don't worry. If they do, they'll probably be Arabs, won't they? They'll hear things from me that they've never heard from a Swedish tourist.'

Grinning, he gave her hand a brief pat. 'Okay. I'll be back in fifteen minutes.' His grin died. 'Unless I get picked up. Then you're on your own.'

She shuddered. 'Don't say that, William, please.'

The traffic on the rue de Rennes was sparse, the shops were not yet open and it was still too early for the tourist buses. He walked briskly for three blocks before spotting a telephone booth across the street. He turned to cross, glancing off-handedly to his left, and pulled back sharply. A dark blue wagon was racing towards him, hugging the kerb. He felt the swirl of air as it passed inches from him and stopped, thwarted by a delivery van parked in the bus lane. Bill found himself looking up at the darkened glass of the windows. Behind it, he could see the shadows of the police inside. Looking away, he turned and walked to the rear of the bus. His legs felt as though they had been filled with cement. He could feel the pressure of fifty pairs of eyes on his head as though it were a physical weight, pushing him into the asphalt. Passing behind the bus, he strode quickly across the road and hurried the last few paces to the phone booth.

He let the door slam behind him and emitted a long sigh, suddenly conscious that he had not been breathing. He stood with his back to the street for a long time after the bus had raced on towards the river, letting his heartbeat subside. At last, his breathing even again, he fished out a credit card and slid it into the slot.

As he dialled he found himself gripped by a strange unease. Gilles was an old friend and business associate, a man he had known intimately for a dozen years. They had last seen each other, had drunk and joked together, only two evenings earlier, at the Museum reception. And yet, Bill felt a curious chill of apprehension, as though events of the last few hours had so altered his life, driven such a deep wedge between what he now was and all that he had been, that he no longer knew how to speak to him.

'Gilles? It's me.'

Gilles had never been a morning type. His natural habitat was a party. The semi-quaver of hesitation before he responded could have meant he was still dragging himself awake, or disentangling himself from whichever woman had stayed after last night's dinner party. 'Ah, Bill.' He spoke unnecessarily loudly, like someone on a bad line, wrongly assuming his caller has the same trouble. 'You, er, what time is it? Ah,' he sighed, apparently finding the strength to look at his watch. 'It's, ah, early, isn't it. Hah-hah. Er, how are you?' Bill frowned. When he was at home in New York they spent half an hour of each day on the phone together. He knew every nuance of the man's voice. There was something unfamiliar there, something like embarrassment.

'I'm in deep trouble.'

'Really!' Gilles laughed, a foolish, uncharacteristic falsetto. 'What kind? No, don't tell me. Woman trouble, I bet. Haven't I warned you . . . ?'

Perplexed, Bill cupped a hand round the mouthpiece, trying to cut out the clatter of a helicopter that passed so low overhead it set the litter outside skidding across the pavement. 'Gilles, I mean *serious* trouble. With the police. Haven't you heard?'

Gilles gave another strained, off-key laugh. 'Hah. Well, no . . . I . . . Is it for something you did?'

Bill's frown deepened. Gilles was one of the sharpest-minded people he knew. 'Gilles, what's the matter with you? You're acting like an utter asshole. Of *course* I didn't do anything. But they *think* I did, for the time being. I need somewhere to hole up for a few hours.'

He giggled. 'Oh, yes, I see. Er, look, Bill, you want to come here? That's fine.' The voice was strained, over-emphatic. 'You can use the spare bed.'

There was a long pause that neither of them seemed anxious to fill. Bill spoke first, his lips hardly moving. 'Okay, Gilles, thanks. But, look, I've had second thoughts. I'll find somewhere else. See you around.'

'Bill! Don't hang up. Where are you now? I could come over and give you a ride.'

'Thanks, I'll walk.' He began to hang up and changed his mind. 'Oh, and Gilles, I'm sorry.'

'What for?'

'Calling you an asshole. You're not one, and I know it.'

He turned to leave the booth, his hand flat on the glass as he checked the street. Gilles lived in his studio. He slept on a mezzanine among the insane clutter of easels, paint and half-finished canvases. He did not have a spare bed.

Hastening back the way he had come, he stopped to buy copies of the early papers. As he turned from the newsstand, a shaft of light from the still-rising sun darted through a gap in the columns of purple-grey cloud. For an instant the whole Montparnasse Tower glowed as though made of sheets of gold. At the same time that the sight made him catch his breath, Bill's thoughts went spinning, as images of Ahmed cartwheeling from one of the gold-shot windows mingled with remembered moments from their strangely durable friendship.

Just occasionally, if you were lucky, it would happen that way. A friendship formed in youth would endure for a lifetime, surviving all the influences and pressures that life brought. In those first years, Bill's time in Paris, Ahmed's subsequent period in the United States, they had been as close as the brothers neither of them had. They had done everything together: study, tennis, parties, summer jobs at the coast, girls. Bill half smiled at the thought. Ahmed had been very popular with American girls.

There had been no hint in those days that Ahmed would turn out homosexual. The shyness, his perfect manners, his readiness to listen to women and not just talk at them, had charmed dozens of women into falling in love with him. It was only after he returned to Paris and became enmeshed in the fashion world that his preferences had emerged. In Bill's eyes it had not diminished his value as a loyal, funny and wise friend.

The only one who appeared to have difficulty with his sexuality was Ahmed himself. Even as he made use of it amid the preciousness of his chosen circle he had seemed troubled, beset by a sense of guilt. He felt he had somehow let down his family, failed to give his father the grandsons he yearned for, and in so doing put an unfair burden on Keltum. It was partly to compensate for that burden that he had wanted so much to give Keltum material things, and that was why he had been deeply wounded when she repudiated them.

It was suddenly clearer why Ahmed had allowed Keltum to draw him into Bouhila's orbit. To the readers of *Vogue* and *Jours de France*, Ahmed was a man bathing in success: rich, famous, and photographed at all the parties they would have killed to be at. To those close to him it was a different picture; a fragile, sensitive man, troubled and vulnerable. It was easy to see how Bouhila's muscular brand of Islam might have appealed. It offered a chance to fill the gnawing emptiness inside him and at the same time enabled him to endorse Keltum's own choice. And perhaps win back her respect.

He turned back into the park. Keltum was still seated in exactly the same attitude as when he had left her. She looked up expectantly into his face, her features hollowed by grief and fatigue. He sat down beside her, shaking his head.

'A waste of time. They've got at my friends. Gilles wasn't alone. The people with him were coaching him, trying to lure us over there. He managed to warn me off. I hope they won't hurt him. The poor guy was scared stiff.'

She stared unseeing at the ground, biting her lip as she fought back fresh tears. He laid his hand on her sleeve. 'Keltum, I know you won't like this, but you're going to have to come with me to the hotel.'

She walked stiffly beside him, her eyes straight ahead, as they searched for a taxi. Far ahead of them, to the south, sirens began to wail. Others followed, some at first close by, fading, coming one on another until the air seemed to be filled with the cacophony of it. Bouhila had announced a demonstration for that day in one of the desolate housing developments that ringed the city. In the sultry heat, tempers had probably begun rising early. He allowed himself a grim smile. Along with the evening's parade, it would help to occupy the CRS and police that had been shipped into the city. Maybe he should be grateful to Bouhila for taking some of the heat off of them. At least until tomorrow.

'Thank God a Hitler only happens once every century or two.' The President smiled archly around at the assembly. *'Celebrating his defeat sometimes seems more trouble than achieving it ever was.* Isn't that so, Vadon?'

Vadon tossed his head. 'I'll certainly be happy to see Bruckner off our hands again. Frankly, fifty years seems quite long enough to live in the past.'

Pautrat guffawed. *'You* wouldn't dream of such a thing, of course.'

Vadon ignored him. 'I can only say that my department has enough immediate problems on its hands without devoting vast numbers of men and resources to protecting the odious Mister Bruckner. For example, there's a pitched battle brewing at this very moment, with Bouhila's crowd, down in Montrouge. And with the thousands of men we have in the city today, I'm powerless to do more than play at preventing it. Why?' he asked dramatically, turning to fix his eyes on the President, who sat smiling thinly, his eyes hooded. 'Because, in accordance with my instructions, I'm keeping all but a few busloads back to protect the parade route, and to ensure Bruckner's safety.' He paused again, his eyes sweeping the room. 'Well, I'll tell you one thing, gentlemen, I have no intention of being pilloried for anything that happens today. Once this wallowing in nostalgia is over I intend to speak out. It's time Bouhila was stopped. Now, before every public housing project in the country falls under the control of his movement. He *must* be got rid of.'

'Quite,' the President murmured. 'Why don't you tell us your solution, once more?'

'Alright, I will. Send him back to Algeria. Now, before he becomes a hero. Along with his lieutenants. That's what he wants, eventually, anyway. He knows there's nothing for him here, in the long run. He's doing nothing more than using those deluded young Arabs as a stepping stone. All this *nonsense* here is just to make himself a reputation. He's simply biding his time.' His voice pulsated with contempt. 'He has it worked out. Things are in such a mess over there he's waiting for them to *beg* him to come back and take over. They'll *love* him for the way he's doing us down, making fools of France. Take it from me,' he declaimed, stabbing a finger at the seated President, 'someday, soon, your successor is going to be shaking hands with that jumped-up kif dealer across a conference table, calling *him* Mister President.' He stopped, breathing heavily.

The President clapped his hands together soundlessly, in a parody of applause. 'Thank you, Vadon, once again for that splendid exposition of your position. A few *public* performances like that and the successor in question will very likely be you, h'mm? Now, for my own information, just how do you propose we set about deporting a group of people, half of whom were born here, all carrying French passports?'

'By force,' Vadon answered flatly.

'Brilliant, my dear man! Absolutely brilliant! Why stop at Bouhila's crowd? We've got prisons full of undesirables we could provide for your scheme. Rapists, robbers, forgers. Let me know when you find a country anxious to have them. Now, being a little more sensible, what's the latest situation on the Champs-Elysées? Are you *absolutely* satisfied nothing can go awry?'

Vadon exchanged a look with the Prefect of Police. 'Cortin here is perfectly satisfied.'

Somewhere beneath Vadon's emphatic tone the faintest suggestion of a quaver made the President's hooded eyes narrow further. 'Cortin, is that so? Is there anything more you need?'

The Prefect shook his head. 'No. Short of a kamikaze attack, I don't see what we have to fear. The compound has been gone over with a toothcomb. Since then nobody could have got inside carrying a weapon.'

'Even those plastic things that were stolen?'

Cortin shook his head. 'No. We aren't relying on the detectors. Everybody is also being given a rigorous body search.'

The President nodded, looking from the Prefect to Vadon, watching the muscles in the Minister's face twitch and slide as he smiled his approval of the Prefect's assessment. 'M'mm. You agree, Vadon?' he asked in a voice so heavy with a deep pessimism that it made one or two of the people in the room narrow their eyes and look harder into his gaunt face.

Vadon nodded, a faint flush spreading over his face. 'Yes. Although I'll be looking things over for myself as soon as I leave here.'

'Good. I think we can adjourn. Thank you, gentlemen, for all your efforts.'

He watched them file out, the remains of the smile still on his lips. He had been president for longer than had been good for him. Lately, the weight of the job had seemed almost too much. Through the thirties, still only a teenager, he had watched the rise of Hitler with France paralysed by political instability. After the war, through the forties and fifties, the Communists had often seemed on the brink of taking over, for many people the natural reaction to Fascism. He had been one of those standing out against them. Finally, de Gaulle had brought France back from the brink and for a third of a century, fleeting as it now seemed, it had been a civilized, generous country to live in. And then along had come Bouhila.

In a matter of months, the man had been transformed from unemployed motor mechanic and part-time preacher in Aix-en-Provence, to what sometimes seemed like the leader of an alien nation implanted like a cancer on French soil. And, of course, the nightmare; with Bouhila had come de Medem's opportunity.

The Fundamentalists had handed him the issue which he had been seeking unsuccessfully for that same third of a century. France, *white* France, had taken fright. Their fear had propelled de Medem from the lunatic fringe to centre stage. It had pushed his poll support up past the twenty per cent mark, only a few points behind the main parties.

The President sighed. The disappointing thing was that he had himself run out of solutions. He had words enough, until he was tired of hearing them, but deep within him he knew how futile they were. The people who were going to vote for de Medem knew as well as he did that de Medem had no programme, that he addressed only one issue. But that was the one that mattered. There were four million Arabs living in France who, as far as de Medem's voters were concerned, had neither hope nor intention of integrating. Four million people who now seemed bent on *widening* the difference, rejecting French culture and answering Bouhila's call for a return to Fundamental Islamic traditions.

He wheeled his chair round to face one of the huge gilt mirrors and stared at his reflection – the diminished body, the cheekbones thrown into gaunt prominence, the purplish lids hooding his eyes. And he thought again of Vadon's well-fleshed face. Although, lately, he had noticed a twitchy, inflamed look about it that puzzled him, as though Vadon were preparing to protest at an unspoken slur, in every other way the man was made for the television age. One-on-one, or in small groups, he came over as a blusterer, his manner over-wrought and verbose, but on television he came over as a confident, decisive presence.

Sighing once more, he turned from the mirror to stare out of the window at the palace gardens where stooping gardeners moved with slow purpose among the shrubbery. He had tried hard to make Pautrat understand that Vadon's vanity made it easy to underestimate him, that beneath the bluster he was clever and shrewd, and craving power with a genuine passion. His Resistance record, authentically heroic, seemed now like a career move, as though even as a teenage boy he had known that it would be the bedrock of his future reputation. Some of his cleverness showed in his recent speeches. He was one of the few among them to write his own speeches. Lately they had been beautifully crafted, subtle appeals to those voters who had a gut feeling de Medem was right but could not bring themselves to own up to it.

The President's mouth twisted in an expression of distaste. Neither Vadon nor de Medem had the streak of madness to make them another Hitler. But another Pinochet, maybe.

One thing of which he was certain: if anything did happen to Bruckner, those two would be the ones to benefit. He turned from the window, recalling Vadon's twitching assertion that the compound was impregnable. 'My God,' he murmured. 'I hope you're right.'

23

Keltum climbed from the taxi and stood looking silently at the chipped plaque by the hotel door. Her mouth puckered as she took in the flamboyant gold script boasting of running water. Bill paid off the cab and turned on his heel, taking her by the upper arm and hurrying her across the pavement. In his free hand he carried a plastic bag with the name of the department store he had visited en route.

She stepped aside with an ironic little curtsy to allow him up the stairs ahead of her. Above him he could hear the television, the suppressed disbelief in the voice of a quiz-game presenter gamely trying to steer a floundering contestant towards an answer.

It was not until the contestant finally gathered enough of his wits to mumble the answer that the quizmaster had been desperately trying to feed him that the receptionist finally looked up, grinning with pleasure at another victory for the little man over the system. The sight of Keltum standing hesitantly in the doorway, a pace behind Bill, wiped the grin away. His eyes narrowed shrewdly, going from Keltum to Bill and back. Bill flashed him a man-to-man grin, the half apologetic, half devil-may-care look of a man astonished at his own daring, and held out his hand for his key.

'Half an hour. No more,' the man snapped, rapping the key onto the counter with unnecessary force. As Bill reached for it, two hundred-franc notes showed beneath his spread fingers. 'Can't she stay a bit longer? She's a friend.'

To his surprise the man tossed his head, ignoring the money and turning back to the television.

'Keep it,' he said sullenly. 'Alright. But remember, ten o'clock's the latest!' He turned back to glare at Keltum, speaking directly to her, ignoring Bill. 'No overnight. No matter how much he pays you! We get enough hassle with the police as it is. Ten o'clock, or I'll be up there and you'll *both* be on the street.' Staring over the man's shoulder, as if ashamed to meet his eye, Bill took the key and started up the stairs jerking his head for Keltum to follow. The man kept his eyes on her as she passed. 'You new? Well, you'd better get someone to show you the ropes or you're going to be in trouble.' She nodded, gave him a fleeting, ambiguous smile, and disappeared up the stairs after Bill.

Neither of them spoke until he ushered her into the room and turned to close the door. She stopped dead in her tracks. 'My God,' she breathed.

He locked the door and turned to face her, smiling. 'So, you like it, then?'

She did not answer. Her eyes roamed over the room, alighting on the crust of filthy grease round the gas ring. A curious expression filled her face. It was more shock than disgust. And there was something else in it, too, as she looked up at him, shaking her head. 'It's awful. Foul.' She gestured helplessly around her. 'I mean, how can people take *money* for it? That, that man downstairs, is he the owner?'

He laughed, very gently, catching now what he had not been able to define in her expression. It was shame. Shame that the person presiding over this squalor should be an Arab. 'I doubt it. Probably just a hired hand, glad of two thousand francs a month and somewhere to sleep. The owner probably has half a dozen of these places. I've seen worse, back in New York. At least here you get *sheets*.' The beginning of a smile gave way to consternation. 'Are you okay?'

She looked up at him from red-rimmed eyes. Her skin was waxy, her breathing coming in shallow gasps. Abruptly, tears welled, accompanied by a keening, continuous moan in her throat. Startled, he reached to take her by the shoulders. 'Keltum! Stop it! Please!' He glanced anxiously at the door and then stepped forward and clapped a hand over her mouth. 'You must stop. These walls are too thin. Please!'

The noise still came, muffled and distorted by his hand. She began to tremble. The trembling grew stronger until her whole body was racked with it, quaking uncontrollably. He crushed her to his chest, his hand still pressed to her mouth. His brusque, even brutal, movement was tempered with a deep tenderness. 'Please try,' he murmured, his breath disturbing her hair. 'I know this is all a nightmare for you. Try to bear it for a while longer, please.'

The moan gradually subsided into a deep-throated sobbing. Slowly, he took his hand from her mouth and slid his arm round her, still holding her close to him.

Standing like that, she cried for several minutes, each soft, choking sob making her entire body quiver. Only very gradually did she raise her hands from her sides, first clutching at his belt and then slowly sliding her arms round his back until they were entwined. They continued standing for some time before the sobs subsided enough for her to speak. 'My poor mother,' she said, the words muffled as her lips pressed against his chest. She lifted her head to look into his face with glistening, tortured eyes. 'It must be unbearable for her, being alone. I have to find a way out of this . . . this *nightmare*! It's too much to ask of her.'

He sighed. 'I know. But there is no way out. Not until after we've seen Lantier. After that, maybe *you* at least can go home.' He disentangled himself gently from her, until he was just holding her fingertips in his. 'A few more hours? Please.'

She nodded, gouging away the traces of tears with her knuckles. 'Alright,' she murmured, 'I'll come and hear what he has to say.' She sank to sit on the edge of the sagging bed. 'I'm so confused.' Her voice was a barely audible whisper. 'So tired.' Without warning, her head fell forward, making him crouch to catch her weight. Her lips moved against the cloth of his sleeve. 'Head's spinning. I'm so . . .' the muffled, far away murmur died completely as she fell asleep.

He laid her down on the bed, pulling the bedclothes up to her waist. He waited for some minutes, reassuring himself that she was sleeping deeply, before moving to the door and easing it open. Walking with a careful tread on the ravaged linoleum, he moved to the top of the stairs.

He paused, listening, and then moved down to an unlit half-landing. While the receptionist had been threatening Keltum he had checked the key board. Khoury's key was not on its hook, indicating that the man was still in his room. It was exactly what Bill had expected. Khoury's day would begin in the early afternoon and end when he left his last drinking club at five or six in the morning. With a glance at his watch, Bill sat down on the threadbare carpet and settled to wait, his senses alert for the sound of approaching footsteps.

❖

The first barrier was on the avenue de la Grande Armée, an untidy chicane of concrete blocks. A cluster of CRS waited in front of it in their characteristic lounging but alert posture, the snouts of automatic weapons protruding beneath glistening, rain-slick ponchos. As one of the CRS moved, hard-faced towards the car, Vadon lowered the window and leaned out, removing the wide-brimmed rain hat that had obscured the upper part of his face. The officer smiled ruefully and fell back, saluting.

With the sound of his own heartbeat pounding in his ears, Vadon eased carefully through the chicane, forcing a negligent wave to the officer, and headed up the deserted avenue, the tyres hissing on the asphalt, still flooded from the latest downpour.

Even with the nerves that were making his stomach churn, he was awed. Without the distraction of traffic, it struck him with new force that the Arc de Triomphe stood on a hill, the ground falling away all round it so that it stood in majestic silhouette against the sky. The colours of the flags that bedecked it were shockingly bright against the slate overcast.

The pounding of his heart accelerated as he approached the Etoile, the very heart of Paris. On a normal day, traffic gushed into it from the avenues that formed the city's arteries to whirl and eddy in a bewildering vortex. Now, it was eerily empty, as though panic or plague had driven the population from the city. A small group of uniformed men marching in tight formation towards the arch only emphasized the emptiness.

Another CRS man detached himself from a small group standing at the junction of the avenue de la Grande Armée and the Etoile itself and waved the Jaguar down. Vadon stopped and leaned again from the window, smiling confidently. The smile felt strangely separate from himself, a mask concealing his sick apprehension.

'Good afternoon, officer,' he called, with the mix of condescension and bonhomie that served to intimidate and win people over at the same time. 'Just thought I'd take a personal look at the arrangements. Make sure everything's in place, you know.'

The CRS, a young man with a mashed, concave nose, like a boxer's, gave no sign of recognizing him. 'Your papers, monsieur,' he said, with a hint of sharpness.

Vadon laughed, a little higher-pitched than he intended. 'You're not serious, young man. You know who I am, surely?' He smirked up at the man.

The CRS man's face remained completely immobile. 'Your papers, please.'

Vadon's smirk faded. Beneath the tan two white spots appeared on his cheekbones. He opened his mouth, as though to speak, and then clamped it shut again. Tight-lipped, he fished a card from his inside pocket and thrust it through the window.

The CRS examined it carefully. Showing no sign of being impressed, he turned it over, and then back. He rubbed a speculative finger over the plastic laminate that covered it, his gaze moving from the photograph to stare hard into Vadon's face. Without taking his eyes from Vadon, he produced a radio from beneath his poncho and spoke into it, reading Vadon's name from the card and walking round to the front of the car to give its number. Vadon had the sensation of time standing still as the man stood, stone-faced, listening. Finally, he murmured something and reluctantly handed back the card. 'Sorry, sir. I wouldn't have expected a minister to be driving a private car.'

'Wouldn't you?' he answered peevishly. 'Well, perhaps you will in future. Perhaps when you . . .' He broke off, forcing a smile, angry with himself for losing his temper. 'Most of us do, you know, when we aren't anxious to attract attention. Ministers are entitled to some private life, too, aren't they?' He added, with an insinuating smile.

The CRS said nothing, waving him on with a barely perceptible flick of his hand.

His face working dumbly, Vadon ground his finger onto the switch of the electric window in a vain effort to make it close faster. He gunned the car hard, disconcerted at his own clumsiness, and raced away, leaving the CRS to pivot clear of the spray from the spinning wheels.

With a conscious effort, he slowed and rounded the flank of the arch, heading for the Champs-Elysées. Sweat chilled the cloth of his shirt. The droplets on his brow coagulated and slid in a single large drop which hung at the tip of his nose. With an angry moan, he slashed an arm across his face, wiping it away. 'Get hold of yourself, you fool!' He spoke the words aloud, rubbing a hand over his face from hairline to chin and then gripping the wheel hard. He sighed. 'You're behaving like a child.'

The vista that stretched ahead of him, sweeping down to the arch in front of the Louvre, with the glass pyramid behind it catching the dull grey light, seemed as eerily unreal as the scene behind him. The only vehicles were CRS buses, parked in clusters at careless angles, and a scattering of military trucks. The only people the dark-uniformed men who lined both sides of the street at ten-metre intervals in front of the wood and metal grandstands.

He had no time to enjoy the poetry of it. He was being waved down again. This time the CRS who scrutinized his documents was backed by crop-haired paratroops, their biceps straining against the short sleeves of their combat fatigues. The man spoke into his radio before handing Vadon back his identity card. 'Would you like an escort, sir?' he asked with cool civility.

'Of course not, you idiot. I'm only going a hundred metres!' He drove away, his fingers squeezing still tighter round the wheel in an effort to control the bout of trembling that gripped him, brought on by the strange mix of offended vanity and rank fear.

The compound was on his right. The armoured glass wall stood two-storeys high on the street side, higher on the side close to the banks and airline offices that lined the wide pavement, its height calculated to block the lines of fire for a rooftop sniper. Within the compound, workmen were busy putting the finishing touches to the VIP podium. At the eastern end of the compound wall a tented tunnel, five metres long, which Vadon knew to be lined with the same armoured glass as the walls, offered the only access. At the entrance to the tunnel, under a striped awning, a group of men, uniformed and civilian, stood talking and gesticulating. Behind them, in the mouth of the tunnel, policemen manned a walk-through metal detector.

As he watched, two workmen emerged from the tunnel and walked the few paces to their truck. They collected a couple of boxes and returned to the entrance. Without apparently needing to be told, they put down their loads and walked through the metal detector. Taking up the boxes again, they continued into the tunnel, out of his sight.

He stopped the car a few metres from the entrance. His mouth was parched. His tongue felt as though it were made of lint. Swallowing hard, trying to force saliva back into his mouth, he ran his hands lightly over the front of the raincoat, smoothing it. He touched his fingers nervously to the coat buttons, ensuring they were fastened, and stepped from the car. Dabbing a hand at the hair at his temple, he began walking towards the group at the entrance.

Sweat pricked his scalp. Droplets skated down his forehead to collect in his eyebrows. He was conscious of the way his feet struck the ground, as though he had forgotten how to walk. At a word from one of the uniformed men, a civilian in the group half turned to look doubtfully at the approaching figure. The doubt dropped abruptly from his face. With a muttered apology to his companions, he spun and hurried to meet Vadon.

'Minister! What a surprise.' The man's warm tone belied the vexation he could not keep out of his face. 'I must have a very sharp word with my people. Nobody informed me you . . .'

'They were not supposed to. I wanted to see things for myself, not what you wanted to show me.' He strode on, hardly looking at the man. The official turned and scuttled after him, a half-step behind.

By the time he reached the awning, Vadon had contrived a fair approximation of his big campaigning smile. He wiped his palm discreetly on his raincoat and started shaking hands.

He moved round the group, top police and security officials, slapping shoulders and cracking jokes. Looking into the faces as they brayed with dutiful laughter at his remarks, he felt strangely detached, as though the scene were from a half-remembered dream, or moments recalled from the depths of a bout of drunkenness.

Slowly, still with the sense of being somehow outside himself, an observer of his own actions, he worked his way closer to the entrance to the tunnel. By the time he pumped the hand of the assistant director of the internal security service, he had manoeuvred close to the tunnel entrance and the metal detector. Looking beyond the man, he could see the two workmen still in the tunnel. Their boxes stood on a long trestle table, where armed officers rooted through the contents. The two men stood with arms stretched wide, submitting to meticulous body searches. He felt a fresh outbreak of sweat bead his forehead. He grinned at the man. 'God, this weather! Unbearable.' He wiped a handkerchief across his brow as he flicked another glance at the tunnel. 'Now,' he said, drawing the official with him into the entrance. 'Why don't you come and explain to me exactly how this thing works.'

The policemen were finishing with the two workmen. At sight of Vadon, they hurriedly dismissed them and stood waiting, holding themselves to attention. Vadon watched, mopping again at his face, as the security official beckoned to one of them. 'Perhaps you would like to show the Minister the mysteries of these machines.'

The policeman nodded, expressionless. 'What would you like to know, monsieur?'

Vadon tried to cajole his stiffened face muscles into a genial smile. 'Well, how small a piece of metal could pass through here without being detected, for instance?'

'That depends on the setting, monsieur. We have it set for maximum. Let me show you.' He emptied money from his pockets onto the table, laid his pistol and belt with it, and stepped through the machine. Feigning close interest, Vadon drifted along level with him, passing outside the apparatus. Safely on the inside, he watched as the man stepped back and forth several times, without setting off the alarm. He stepped further into the tunnel as the policeman walked to the table, selected a coin, a tiny copper five-centime piece, and moved back into the machine's field. Instantly, a shrill sound filled the tunnel. The policeman stepped out again, grinning proudly, looking at the detector as though it were a pet that had just performed a difficult trick.

'Very impressive.' Vadon nodded, smiling. 'Thank you very much.' He turned to the hovering security official. 'Well, no problem there.' He gave another stiff smile. 'I'll just take a prowl, make sure everybody else is as much on their toes as you people.' He turned and swept past the trestle table towards the compound.

His heart was pounding so violently he felt the policemen must be able to hear it as clearly, too. He had a powerful sensation that he was sleep-walking. In place of the buzz of conversation, his ears were filled with only a vast, echoing silence as he waited for a voice calling him back.

'Minister!' A hand touched his sleeve.

He missed a step, tottered and spun, his face draining. The security official was beaming at him.

'Minister, there's quite a lot to see. I thought it might be helpful if I . . .'

'Get out of here, you fool.' As he spoke, he reached out a hand and shoved the man roughly in the chest. The official staggered, a look of stark astonishment on his face. Catching his balance, he stared at Vadon in blank dismay.

Hastily, Vadon stepped forward and placed a hand on the man's arm. 'Forgive me, old boy, will you?' He gave a small laugh, just between the two of them. 'Frankly, this whole thing's been a bit of a strain.' He made a small motion with his head, vaguely towards the south-west, in the direction of the Elysée Palace. 'You know how it is, with me and the President, I mean.' He leaned closer, so that there was no more than a hand's span between their faces. 'There's a lot at stake just now, as you know.' Vadon cocked his head oddly, so that for a shocked moment the man thought the Minister of the Interior was actually going to wink at him.

'Yes, Minister. I do know.'

'Good. Well, you won't mind if I prefer to just wander around on my own, will you?' As he spoke, he laid a hand confidentially on the man's arm, turning him back towards the exit and propelling him on his way with sharp finger pressure. 'There's a good fellow.' He watched the man pass back out of the tunnel before turning on his heel. With his shirt sticking to his back, he strode out into the compound.

He stopped short, gazing around him in rising horror. Workmen seemed to be everywhere, hammering, hauling wood and dragging huge rolls of red carpet into place. Conspicuously armed police drifted among them, their alert eyes watching every movement. Uncomfortably aware that he was walking stiff-legged, like someone learning to walk again after an accident, he set off to explore the compound.

The enclosure was fifty or sixty metres long by thirty deep. The front, the north side, ran along the edge of the carriageway, the rear ran parallel to the line of the buildings. On the south side, nearer the buildings, the upper section of the glass wall curved forward, forming a roof for the VIP podium that would be as effective in keeping off the weather as it would sniper fire. The podium was a raised platform some six metres deep that ran two-thirds of the length of the compound. A flight of wide steps led up to it, each with a row of folding seats ranged on it. He let his gaze roam to the gaunt shapes of the lighting gantries that towered above the dais, the scaffolding of their bases forming part of the structure. He frowned and swallowed. A figure in jeans and windcheater had swung himself off the platform of planks that gave access to the bank of floodlights at the top of the gantry and was lowering himself down the outside of the structure, moving with the lithe grace of a circus performer. With a conscious effort to halt the renewed twitching of his face muscles, he hurried through a curtained aperture into the cavity below the podium.

Men in overalls worked in the twilight, setting up rows of tables. Behind them came more men, snapping out gleaming white cloths and laying them on the tables. Others were busy sliding cases of Dom Perignon champagne into coolers. Ignoring these preparations, he hurried over to where two men stood at the eastern end of the cavity, in front of the draped French flags that masked the scaffolding. As he drew near them the flags parted, giving a momentary glimpse of a snarl of cables, and the figure he had seen on the gantry emerged. He gave the approaching Vadon a quick, appraising glance and turned away to begin speaking in a low voice to his two companions.

'Who are you, gentlemen, if I may ask?'

At Vadon's question they broke off and turned to look at him, a faint glint of amusement in their eyes. One of them held out a card. Vadon examined it, squinting in the half-light, and nodded, acknowledging the man's credentials as an officer in French counter-intelligence.

The man pocketed the card and gestured to his companions. 'These gentlemen are colleagues, you might say. Israeli colleagues.'

Vadon ran an eye over the two men. The French and British intelligence people he dealt with were mainstream civil servants, slack-bellied men whose time was spent sifting information, compiling reports. Israel, on a virtual war footing for forty years, had different needs. These people were in their mid-thirties, lithe, with the long-muscled look of athletes in the peak of condition. The typical Mossad product.

He nodded a greeting, keeping his hands in the pockets of his coat. 'So, gentlemen, checking on our arrangements, I suppose? How do you find them?'

The one who had descended the gantry smiled. 'Excellent, Minister, as a matter of fact. Provided nobody finds a way in here in the next few hours, we have nothing to worry about.'

Vadon gave the man a condescending nod. His head was spinning so wildly he withdrew his hands from his pockets, convinced he was going to fall. 'Well, good.' He wet his lips, his head throbbing. 'We may be amateurs compared to you people but we do try. And you saw the controls at the entrance?' The man nodded. 'Excellent. So you've seen all you need to see?' He had again the extraordinary sensation that he was outside himself, watching somebody play his role. His voice sounded thin and strained in his ears.

'Yes, Minister. I think we have.'

Vadon nodded and turned to the French security man. 'Perhaps you would like to escort our friends off the premises, then. Best to have as few people inside as possible, h'mmm?' He tried another condescending smile, and felt it as a mirthless, death's-head rictus. 'Good day, gentlemen.'

The three men turned and strode towards the entrance. As

they went, he took an uncertain step and grabbed at a handful of the fabric of the flags, supporting his weight. Breathing heavily, his chin on his chest, he watched them disappear back out into the daylight, the remains of the ugly grin still set stupidly on his face.

It was several more seconds before his breathing grew even again. He looked quickly around him. The contractors' men were too busy to pay him any attention. Lifting aside a flag, he slipped from sight, letting the fabric fall back into place behind him.

A violent spasm in his calf muscles forced him to lean heavily against a metal upright. For almost a minute he waited there in the semi-darkness, unable to go on. At length, trembling with the effort, he forced himself onward, picking his way awkwardly among the scaffold poles and skeins of cable, towards the stack of cable drums that stood heaped in a far corner. A spatter of rain on his hair made him look up sharply. An opening in the planks above exposed a segment of purple cloud. Against it the gantry stood outlined as stark as a gibbet. He flinched as a raindrop struck his eyeball, then went on clambering across the jumble of equipment, moving with fresh vigour.

He reached the pile of drums and for a few seconds stood looking at them in surprise, as though they had only just materialized. Then, moving with a sudden frenzied urgency, he dragged the top drum from the heap and reached for the drum beneath it. He placed both hands on the flange of the central core and yanked hard. The entire core came away, revealing a cavity inside the drum. His face glowing deathly pale in the darkness, he ripped open the raincoat.

A soft cloth bag hung below each armpit, suspended from a cord round his neck. His eyes burning as though he had gone mad, he dragged the strap over his head and stuffed the bags into the cavity. He rammed the core into place and manoeuvred the top drum back into position, skinning his knuckles.

For several seconds he stood half-collapsed against the drums, his legs jelly again. Fighting to regain his breath, he stared at the asphalt beneath his feet. He shivered as sweat broke out once more, chilling him. Supposing the escape route were not really there at all? Supposing the low-grade gangsters de Medem was relying on had let them down? The whole thing *hinged* on the assassins getting out that way, their not being caught while they were still in the compound. They *had* to get as far as the car park, to where they could be intercepted and dealt with by reliable men. If they were taken alive, still inside the compound, it would be a catastrophe. He almost sobbed at the thought. They would talk to save themselves. Connections would be made. He would be destroyed. His whole life, everything he had planned and dreamed of for fifty years would be worth nothing. He clapped his hands to his face, startled by the sting of tears in his eyes. 'God, de Medem, I wish I had never set eyes on you,' he murmured, sobbing.

❖

Bill stood up, arms raised to stretch his cramped back muscles. He looked again at his watch. It was only just gone four o'clock and already it had been a long wait.

After an initial flurry, when people leaving early for work or returning from the night-shift had forced him a dozen times to turn and pretend to shamble to his room, hardly a soul had moved. There had been no sign of a maid to trouble him. They probably paid a guest with back rent to work off to go through the place once a week with a damp mop. A dozen times, he had interrupted his vigil to return to the room to check on Keltum. Each time she had lain sleeping in exactly the position in which he had first left her.

The sound of a slamming door somewhere below brought him instantly alert. Crouched, hidden from the sight of anyone passing on the landing beneath, he heard the quick, vigorous stride approach the stairs and start down towards the reception desk. Straightening, Bill started down to the floor below. Brief voices drifted up to him from reception, too indistinct to catch, and then there was only the murmur of the television.

He walked quickly down the last few stairs and then slowed as he entered the shabby lobby. The aroma of tobacco and musk cologne hung in the air. The receptionist turned blank eyes from the children's puppet show he was watching. Seeing Bill, he cocked his head to look ostentatiously back into the stairway, looking for Keltum. He turned back to Bill with a look of insolent enquiry on his face.

Bill grinned, blowing out his cheeks in a parody of being spent. 'Back in a couple of minutes. I need a break!' He grinned some more and started down to the street, leaving the man scowling at his back.

He reached the doorway as the growl of a motor split the air and Khoury's BMW shot from its parking space and hurtled for the corner. He watched it disappear in a shriek of rubber. With its noise and the stink of burning still hanging in the motionless air, he turned and strode quickly to the store next door.

He returned past the sneering receptionist carrying a six-pack of Coca-Cola, a flat Arab loaf and a bag of groceries selected more or less at random. Grinning resolutely in the teeth of the man's contempt, he sauntered to the stairs. Once on them, he stopped grinning and started running, taking the stairs three at a time. He shoved open the door of his room, no longer making the effort to be silent.

Keltum's head jerked up from the pillow. For a moment she stared blankly at Bill, and then, with a soft bleat of dismay, she raised the sheet and looked down at herself. 'Oh!' she said weakly, letting her head drop back onto the pillow, and laughing. 'That was a bad moment.'

An answering smile flickered over his face. 'M'mm. I *did* take your shoes off, though.' His smile faded. 'Look, you had better wake up. We're going to be leaving for the meeting with Lantier.'

Her eyes widened as she glanced at her watch. 'Is *that* the time? I've been asleep for hours.'

'You needed it. But we have to be getting out of here.' As he spoke, he grabbed the plastic bag he had carried from the taxi and upended it onto the chest of drawers.

Keltum raised her head and stared at the stubby screwdriver and the short crowbar that slid from the bag. 'I wondered what you had in there. Whatever is it for?'

He jerked his chin at the floor. 'Khoury's just left. I'm going to search his room again. Properly, this time.'

Her face clouded. She swung herself off the bed, taking care to keep her knees together, and touched his arm. 'Is that safe? How do you know he won't come back?'

He shrugged. 'I don't. But what would he come back *for*? He's got work to do, like everybody else, collecting from his girls, checking stock levels on dildoes.'

'On *what*?'

'Forget it. Anyway, I want to have a good look at that son of a bitch's place before we leave. He's the key to whatever's happening to us. If there is anything in there, I want to be able to show it to Lantier.' He placed a hand on her shoulder. 'Wait here. Be ready. I should only be a few minutes. But if you hear anything that sounds like trouble, beat it. Okay?'

She nodded, gulping. Abruptly, she reached out and touched his sleeve again, looking up at him with a sudden shyness in her eyes. 'William, please be careful.'

He nodded, cupping his own palm lightly over her hand. 'Don't worry. Listen hard, though, and if there's the slightest sign of trouble, run. You've gotten yourself into more than enough danger for me as it is.' He pushed the tools into a pocket and slipped from the room.

He moved down the stairs and stopped outside Khoury's room. He stood hunched close against the door, his ear almost pressing on the wood.

A gust of canned laughter drifted up the stairs from the reception. Somewhere above him a toilet flushed, followed by a slamming door. The other noises that reached him were the faint sounds of lonely, narrow lives, the babble of afternoon television, the snores, the slow-shuffling feet. From within the room there was no sound at all.

He could feel the throbbing of his heartbeat. What he had told Keltum was probably true. The chances were that the man had left the room for the day, to spend his time drinking in the dim, curtained bars of Pigalle or be out on the rue Saint Denis, attending to his women and his sordid businesses. That did not mean he might not have forgotten something, or that there was not a woman asleep in the soiled bed, who would tear the air with her screaming the moment Bill came through the door. He took the crowbar from his pocket and held it at his side. Gripping the bar firmly, ready to lash out, he raised his other hand and rapped on the door. He waited for a count of five, his ears straining for the sound of movement, and then knocked again. He waited a few seconds more and then jabbed the flattened steel fork of the crowbar hard between the jamb and the ill-fitting door, seven centimetres above the lock. He worked the screwdriver into place the same distance below the lock, gripped the ends of both tools and jerked their ends towards him.

There was surprisingly little sound as the two short screws holding the latch tore from the softwood frame, allowing the door to swing open. He waited, listening for a raised voice, a door opening, any sign that somebody had reacted to the soft splintering. Hearing nothing, he moved into the room and pushed the door closed behind him.

The same sweet stink of cologne made him wrinkle his face in distaste as he reached for the nearest of the video cassettes that lay scattered on the bed. He ripped out the thin cardboard sleeve, with its illustration of naked women embracing, and quickly folded it into a wad an eighth of an inch thick. Bending, he jammed it under the door, hammering it into position with his toe. He dragged on the door. It did not budge. Short of kicking the door down, nobody was going to come in and take him by surprise. He turned away and began a systematic search of the room.

24

Bill's heart pounded. The ten or twelve minutes he had been in the room felt like a day. The bed was a jumble of empty drawers, ripped clothes, magazines, and spirals of tape from the gutted cassettes. The dry cleaning receipts and unpaid parking tickets lay scattered on the floor. Nothing he had found so far gave him any clue to the man.

He slid the suitcase from under the bed and dumped its contents on the heap. He snatched up a handful of the dog-eared envelopes, all with Algerian stamps, and addressed in the uneven scrawl of the semi-literate. He pulled out a couple of letters. The lined paper was discoloured, cheap, with splinters of wood that had escaped the processing pressed into it. It was covered on both sides with sprawling Arabic script, blotted with the smudges of a cheap ballpoint.

In growing desperation, he turned to take a slow look round the room. The television and video lay gutted on the floor, their entrails spilling around them. The three suspect floorboards he had lifted lay loose, exposing cavities that had revealed nothing more than a few decades of dust and insect attack. He was stepping towards the window, about to check whether anything might have been concealed on the outside sill when something caught his eye. With an exclamation, he turned to the sink.

The crazed and chipped porcelain was grey with a thick layer of grime. A wet coating of foamy grey scum lay congealed round the basin, embedded with tiny shards of black hair where Khoury had shaved. On the smeared plastic shelf above the sink a small pool of scum and trimmings had formed round an unwashed razor. The line-up of colognes from Guerlain, Dior and Ralph Lauren were incongruous in the squalor. And so was the line of shining white sealant that had caught Bill's eye, running along the back of the sink, sealing the gap between the porcelain and the cracked tiles of the splashback. He snatched the screwdriver from his pocket and gouged at it.

The material clung to the end of the screwdriver in treacly threads. It was so recently applied it had not yet had time to set. A tremor of anticipation ran through Bill as he crouched to loosen the two screws that secured the sink to the wall. Nothing else in the room indicated that Khoury was a do-it-yourself freak. Letting the screws fall to the floor he stood up, jabbed the screwdriver through the soft sealant and yanked at it, forcing the sink from the wall.

It came loose, swaying on the lead plumbing. Using both hands, he took hold of the sink and dragged it further out. He almost yelled aloud. A shallow cavity, the size of a cigarette packet, had been hacked into the plaster behind the sink. Taped inside it was a tiny package wrapped in a sheet of thin white plastic. Shoving the screwdriver back into a pocket, he clawed the package from its niche and ripped away the wrapping. He gave a soft whoop of triumph. Between his fingertips he held a miniature cassette from a personal memo recorder. Stuffing it into a pocket, he turned to prise the wedge from under the door.

He thrust open the door of his room, the cassette held aloft, beckoning her to join him. 'Let's go! I found this.'

She continued sitting on the bed, not appearing to hear him.

'Keltum! Come on! It's a tape! Let's get out of here before that bastard decides to come back and . . .' His voice tailed off. With a single stride, he was into the room and at her side, the door slamming shut behind him. 'What's wrong?'

She sat bent forward with one elbow on her knee, her splayed fingers supporting her face. The other arm hung limp at her side. Her shoulders heaved in rhythm with the dry, racking sobs that welled from deep within her. Bill dropped to one knee and took her head between his palms. 'Keltum? Please!

What is it?' He lifted a hand and slapped her, quite sharply. 'We have to leave. Now! If he comes back and sees his room, all hell's going to break loose.' Her eyes remained unfocused and lifeless. The skin of her face was the colour of dough. He reached down and took the hand that dangled at her side. It was cold and lifeless as dead meat. 'Keltum?' He slapped her cheek again, harder than before. 'What's the matter, for God's sake? We have to leave.'

She continued to sit, not appearing to see or hear him, her body still heaving with huge sobs that brought no tears. He stared around, seeking the cause of her distress. The package of mail that the concierge had given her lay strewn on the bed. Leaflets advertising tennis lessons and terrific deals on leather sofas mixed with impressively printed invitations to subscribe to book clubs. A large brown envelope lay on top of the heap, its edge ragged where she had thumbed it open. Around it were strewn Polaroid photographs, face down. He looked from the photographs to Keltum's devastated face. Frowning, one hand still holding her head up, he reached out for the pictures and turned them over, spreading them on the bed.

'Oh, my God!' His words came in a whisper. He cast a quick glance at Keltum. She still gave no sign of knowing he was there. Pulling her head protectively onto his shoulder, he stared down at the pictures.

Revulsion, shock, bewilderment, numbed disbelief, combined to send his senses reeling. Fighting down his disgust, he forced himself to look at them, one by one.

Although many of them were blurred, others taken in poor light, the faces of Ahmed and Vadon were absolutely unmistakable. His throat caught with an urge to be sick. Some were pictures of the two of them doing what he supposed were the usual things homosexuals did to each other. But there was more than that. In two of the pictures Vadon held his genitals out for the camera. His face bore an extraordinary look of sublime, unbearable pleasure as Ahmed, with a curious, fixed expression, appeared to be driving a nail through the skin of his penis. For a moment Bill clung to the idea that Ahmed's expression meant he was doing it under some kind of pressure. The hope was quickly dispelled. Other pictures showed Ahmed as the victim, trussed and handcuffed, his delicate face contorting as the naked Vadon, his features ablaze with excitement, inflicted the tortures. Deeply shaken, he pulled Keltum to him and held her tightly, his lips touching her hair.

For a long time neither of them wanted or was able to speak. Gradually, Bill felt the first numbness give way to a kind of excitement. Without a doubt, these pictures were the key to Ahmed's suicide. They were the prize Khoury and his friends had been seeking when they hounded Ahmed to his death. Whether they had been working for Vadon or intended to use them against him was an open question. His lips still against Keltum's hair, Bill reached down and took up the envelope. He fumbled it open and shook it, checking there was no note inside, nothing that would have explained Ahmed's intentions. Finding nothing, he turned it over and let it fall back to the bed. He studied the spidery scrawl of the address, frowning. 'Keltum?' he murmured, tentatively. She did not stir. 'Keltum. Please look.' He took up the envelope and held it up in front of her. 'What do you think?'

She lifted her face to look at it. Her features were as still and lifeless as though she had been in hypnosis.

'Please! Try to help me. What do you think?'

'Think?' she said in a thin, distant tone. 'What should I think? About what?'

'The writing? Do you recognize it?'

Very slowly, her eyes focused on the envelope. She looked at it for several seconds. 'I don't know. It's a scribble. It *could* be my brother's.'

Bill nodded, giving a little grunt of agreement. 'Right. That's what it looks like to me, too,' he said, softly, his mind racing. 'Ahmed, but writing in a hurry, on some kind of soft surface where he couldn't get a purchase.' He studied the postmark, his eyes narrowed as he struggled to decipher the blurred print. 'Yes,' he breathed, at length. 'Look.' He dropped the envelope on the bed and stabbed a finger at the postmark. 'Look at the time. The date! It must have been posted just about the time Ahmed fled the men searching his office.' He looked at Keltum, his eyes glittering. 'There's a mail box right there, right by the café. He would have been staring at it if he went out the back way.'

She looked at where his finger pointed. 'There was no stamp,' she intoned. 'That's what the concierge was asking for, money for the stamp.'

He snorted softly. 'First thing we do, when we get out of this, we send her the five francs. And one thing I'm sure of,' he added, dropping the envelope and scooping up the pictures. 'These are going to get us out of it. One way or another we are going to be able to use these to get Vadon to call off the dogs.'

'But why?' Keltum asked, her voice still distant, as though she had not heard his words.

'Why what?'

'Why did Ahmed post the . . . the . . . *those* to me? Why the flat? He knew I hardly ever went there.'

Bill shrugged. 'To keep them out of Khoury's hands. I guess he would have expected Khoury to keep a watch on the mail at your parents' place. Your flat was somewhere nobody knew about. He knew you were sure to go by there sooner or later. Maybe he only dropped them in the mail to keep them away from Khoury, in case they had caught him. Maybe he didn't even set out to kill himself that day. Perhaps he planned to go by and retrieve them himself.'

She shuddered, burying her head in his shoulder again. He rose to his feet, drawing her with him. 'Sorry, I know this is a hell of a shock, but we have to get out of here.'

She allowed herself to be pulled to her feet, and then stood, motionless, her arms slack at her sides. Bill shuffled the photographs together and pushed them into a pocket. 'Please, Keltum, don't think about these. Just remember what Ahmed meant to you, and to your parents. Remember how proud he made them. Only please, come now, before Khoury takes it into his head to come back. He's capable of shooting us both. And then he would have the pictures.'

She answered in an echoing, distant voice, scarcely moving her lips. 'What difference would it make?'

'I don't know, exactly. Except that Ahmed went to his death trying to keep them from him.'

'But isn't that just it? He is dead. How can it matter now?'

Taking a sharp breath, he took her by the shoulders and shook her. 'No, Keltum. Don't. That's your grief talking. You've got things to do with your life. And so have I.' He showed her the cassette which he still held in his fingertips. 'The pictures, and maybe this, are going to help me do one of them, at least.'

A faint kindling of interest flickered in her eyes. 'What?'

'Make Vadon suffer the way Ahmed did. His suicide *must* have been tied up with the pictures. You're a Kabyle too. I don't have to tell you how his mind worked. He *had* to kill himself. He was afraid these would become public. Or maybe something already *had* happened, they had been used to force him into something that would bring shame on the family.' He cupped her chin in his hand and lifted her face so that their eyes were inches apart. 'Think how it would be for your mother, in her grief, to have to cope with that. You owe it to her, and your father's memory, to help me prevent that, if we can.'

The first touch of colour returned to her cheeks. 'Yes,' she whispered. 'You're right. I have to do that.'

Smiling, he took her by the hand and began moving towards the door. 'The first thing is to get hold of a machine and hear what's on this. After that, we'll meet Lantier and lay it out for him.'

She pulled back, making him look sharply around. 'William?'

'What? We have to be moving.'

'I know. But, do you really think it's wise? To go to this meeting, I mean. This Lantier is a policeman. Is he the best person for us?' She gestured at the pocket where the pictures lay. 'I mean, those . . . the things they were doing . . . Wouldn't a policeman have to . . .' She shook her head in confusion.

'Surely what they were doing is *criminal*! He would have to act on them. It would all come out. It would be horrible.' She broke off, shivering at the thought.

His mouth twisted. 'We just have to trust him, Keltum. He's already showed that we can. Anyway, what choice do we have?'

He watched, moving impatiently, as Keltum bit at the flesh of her lower lip, as though trying to find words. Abruptly, she looked into his face, pleading. 'Imam Bouhila,' she said, in a rush.

He laughed incredulously. 'Bouhila?' He stifled his laughter, lowering his voice again to a whisper. 'Put yourself in his position for a moment. You saw how he behaved at the funeral. He was making a public show of claiming Ahmed into the movement. Your brother was Bouhila's star convert. Imagine his reaction if he were to get a sight of these pictures. He would know that they would be as bad for him as for Vadon. They would turn him into a laughing stock.' He shook his head. 'If the man's as single-minded as he looks he'd take the first chance he got to destroy them.' He took both her hands, drawing her towards the door. 'No, Keltum. Lantier wants Vadon badly, but he still strikes me as someone who would respect your family's feelings. Let's keep that appointment, at least. If it doesn't look good, we'll do it your way.' She made as if to speak again, and then shut her mouth and followed him from the room.

The cloud bank had rolled away, allowing the afternoon sun to beat down with its full force, lifting wisps of steam from the soaked pavements. They strode rapidly away from the hotel, drawing sidelong glances from the idlers who were already re-emerging after the downpour, re-settling their wooden chairs or spreading plastic bags on the kerbs and squatting with their feet straddling the streaming gutters.

Approaching the corner, Bill glanced behind them. Everything was peaceful. The old men still sat talking, the children sailed cigarette packets on the puddles. Khoury's car had not returned, the receptionist was not sprinting to challenge them.

Beginning to relax for the first time since he had entered Khoury's room, he turned to follow Keltum round the corner. He almost fell over her as she stopped dead. Fifty metres away, a police patrol was moving towards them, strung across the width of the pavement. 'For a wild moment Keltum seemed about to turn and run. Without hesitating, Bill side-stepped, took her elbow and steered her into the nearest doorway. They pushed through the doorway to find themselves in a dingy novelty wholesaler's. At the sound of the door a fat man in soccer shorts and a soiled vest waddled from behind a curtain, blowing hard. 'God, this heat!' He plucked the vest from his belly and let it slap wetly back. 'It's killing me. What can I do for you?'

Bill had already plucked a clockwork rabbit from its carton and was studiously examining it, keeping one eye on the door. He continued examining the toy for a half a minute after the shadows of the police had drifted past the door and then laid it on the counter in front of the man. 'How much?'

The man squinted at the faint and indecipherable pencil marks on the carton. 'Sixty-six francs.'

Bill raised an eyebrow. 'For this?'

'For six of them. That's the minimum.'

Shrugging, Bill counted out the money while the man shoved the rabbits into a creased plastic bag with the name of somebody else's business on it.

'Thanks.' Bill grabbed the bag and propelled Keltum back to the door.

They stepped out into the sunlight, looking around for the police patrol. Keltum drew breath in a sharp whooping sound. The policemen were loitering at the corner, no more than three paces from them. Wheeling, almost pulling Keltum off her feet, Bill dragged her away, his arm in hers, supporting her sagging weight. It was not until they had rounded the corner at the far end of the block that he stopped and turned to face her. She was wide-eyed. Her whole body was trembling, making her teeth chatter wildly. He spoke very low. 'Stop it! Pull yourself together. You look like a frightened rabbit.'

With a huge effort, she brought the shivering under control. 'I'm sorry. I can't help it. It's all those policemen. I just feel they *must* recognize us.'

He nodded. 'I know. But look, they aren't on the streets because of *us*. They're part of the whole security operation. The entire city's going to be crawling with them until after tonight. Then, they'll be gone.' He smiled. 'Most of them are probably out-of-town forces drafted in for the occasion. They're thinking more about the shopping lists their wives gave them than about us. I doubt if *your* picture would even have been circulated yet.'

'I know. It just doesn't help. I'm so *afraid*, William. I can't help myself.' As if in emphasis, she shook again from head to toe.

He pursed his lips. 'I know what you mean.' He looked at his watch. 'Lantier will soon have things in hand. Until then, though, we need to get off the street.' He looked around and tossed the bag of rabbits into a rubbish-filled box outside the entrance to a building. 'Let's go and find some transport.'

They walked in silence, Bill leading the way through more of the littered streets, picking a path along the broken, dog-fouled pavements. Taking turns apparently at random, he was careful to stay aware of the alley or store that could offer an escape route if more police appeared.

The steam from the drying streets made the heat clammier than ever, so that their clothes stuck to them as they walked. They prepared to cross the end of a narrow street, hardly more than an alley, lined with cars. Bars and cafés were ranged along each side, the clusters of chairs and chipped tables that served as terraces spilled out to fill the pavement. As they stepped into the gutter, a car swept in front of them, sending up a sheet of spray that sent them leaping backwards. Choking off the shout that leapt to his lips, Bill turned to watch the car. Silently, he motioned Keltum closer to his side.

The car, a blue Audi, had drawn up in front of a café, alongside the line of empty taxis that told the world the bar was popular with out of hours cab drivers. Bill stood looking pensively along the street. Driving a cab was a perfect cover for a drug courier.

The Audi blocked what was left of the roadway between the taxis and the opposite pavement. Bill watched, with Keltum silent at his side, as the driver swung himself from the Audi and slammed the door with a theatrical flourish. A big man with luxuriant dark hair and high Slavic cheekbones, he bent to spend several seconds running his fingers elaborately through the thick waves of his hair, using the tinted window as a mirror. Satisfied, he shrugged his jacket straight and swaggered towards the darkness of the bar entrance.

Bill smiled. Since getting out of the car, the man had not touched his pockets. And yet, as he finger-combed his hair he had clearly had nothing in his hands. He turned to Keltum and pushed the cassette and envelope of photographs into her hand. He pointed down the narrow street. 'Take these. Go down to the far corner and wait for me there.'

She frowned up at him. 'Why?'

'I'm going to try to get that car. And there's no sense both of us getting shot. If it goes wrong, don't wait. Beat it and keep the date with Lantier.'

He waited until she had reached the next corner before setting off himself, strolling leisurely towards the Audi. He was fifteen metres from the car before he could be sure. His fists clenched in anticipation. The pale skein of vapour he had been counting on rose from the exhaust.

He drew level with the rear of the car. The owner was visible, just inside the threshold, a glass in his hand. Bill moved alongside the car, advancing slowly, cramped by the tables that reached to the very edge of the pavement. He glanced again at the bar. The driver had turned and was looking at him with hard, hostile eyes, already taking offence that Bill dare walk so close to his paintwork. Bill gave him a mildly apologetic smile and snatched open the driver's door.

Impeded by an old man who sat with his back to him, intent on a game of dominoes, he was still trying to squeeze inside when a bellow of rage made him snatch another glance at the bar. The driver was already half out of the doorway, his glass still in his hand. In the instant Bill looked up, he reached out and broke the glass against the doorframe, leaving him holding a jagged stump. With another shout, he leapt into the roadway.

Bill snatched at the back of the old man's chair and up-ended him onto the cracked pavement. Hurling the door wider, he threw himself into the seat. At the same moment the man yanked open the passenger door and reached in, grabbing a handful of Bill's blouson sleeve. Bill struggled for the automatic shift, aware of the power of the man as he dragged at his blouson, trying to hold him off. The man was already half in the car. He shifted position, getting set to drive the jagged glass into Bill's face. As he did so, Bill was able to curl his fingers round the gear lever and shove it into drive. He stamped the gas pedal to the floor.

The car leapt forward with a scream of tyres. He felt the fingers lose their grip on his sleeve. He glanced in the mirror. Behind him, the man rolled, sprawling in the road. As Bill watched, he scrambled to his feet and began running after his car, one hand reaching under his jacket. After a few desperate paces, he stopped, letting his hand fall to his side. As Bill slewed to a stop fifty metres from him, letting Keltum scramble aboard, the man was still in the road, making obscene one-finger gestures and shouting in impotent outrage. Watched by the clutch of staring faces from the terraces, he made a strangely pathetic figure.

'You okay?' he asked, glancing at Keltum, as he accelerated round the corner, out of the man's sight.

She gave him a peculiar look. 'Me, okay? How about you? Are you mad? He could have blinded you with that glass.'

He laughed. 'Or worse. For a moment there he thought about going for a gun.'

'Oh, God!' she groaned softly. 'What are we going to do now?'

He glanced at his watch. 'Keep the meeting with Lantier. Except that first I want to buy a memo machine that will play that for us.' He pointed to the cassette in her hand. 'So, why don't we start by finding a store where you can buy a machine that this fits. We'll find out if the fragrant Monsieur Khoury has anything interesting to add to the photographs. Then, we'll take the whole caboodle to Lantier and see what he makes of it.'

She paused, making him look at her again. 'You still don't think it would be better to go to Imam Bouhila?'

He shook his head. 'No, I don't. At least I know where Lantier stands. A policeman got killed. He's convinced Vadon had a hand in it. So, he wants to nail Vadon. Helping us, helps him get what he wants. As for Bouhila, God only knows what *he* wants. I know to you he's special, Keltum, and I don't want to offend your beliefs, but to me he's just another politician, with his own agenda. Not that I think he wouldn't love to get his hands on it. But to get a hold over Vadon, not to help find out what pushed Ahmed over the edge.' He sighed deeply. 'Sorry, Keltum, but to Lantier this stuff is *evidence*. With this he'll find a way to get Ahmed's case opened up again, really find out what drove poor Ahmed to do what he did.'

While he spoke she had sat in fidgety silence, chewing vindictively at her fingernails. 'He's *not* like that,' she said, with quiet emphasis, when Bill stopped talking.

He glanced at her again. Once more tears rolled down her face. He touched her arm. 'Keltum, your brother *killed* himself for whatever the photographs mean. I made a promise to your father, and I mean to keep it, if I can. To me, Lantier's my best chance of doing that.' She went on crying, tight-lipped and silent. His pressure on her arm increased. 'Look, they're your pictures. Why don't we do it like this: come with me to Lantier, if you don't like whatever he offers, you go your own way, and take them to Bouhila. It'll be your choice.' She shook her head, turning her face away. 'I don't know. I'm so confused, I don't know what I want. I hardly know who I am. It's a bad dream. All I want is to be quiet for a while, to think.'

He nodded, withdrawing his hand. 'Yeah, I know. These last few days have been hell for you.' Both were silent for a few moments. Bill was first to speak again. 'Look, why don't we just get a machine and see if the tape's any help? Then you make up your mind what you want to do with the pictures. I won't try to influence you any more.'

She was silent for a long time before she looked at him and tried to smile. 'Okay.'

Neither spoke again, each deep in their own thoughts, until Bill stopped in a run-down street and jerked a thumb at an unkempt store, its dusty windows heaped with secondhand appliances. 'Looks promising. Do you want to try?'

Nodding, she climbed from the car, the cassette between her fingers.

She returned three minutes later carrying a machine no bigger than her own hand. 'It didn't have any packaging. It was a display model,' she said drily.

He laughed. 'Sure it was. Displayed on the back seat of someone's car. Does the cassette fit?'

'He says so. I didn't ask him to play it to me,' she added, coolly.

He inclined his head. 'M'mm. Better not.' He tapped the back of her hand lightly with his open palm. 'I feel a bit conspicuous sitting here like this. Let's go and listen to it somewhere this car will be a little less noticeable.'

As he drove, both of them relapsed into silence. Keltum sat rigid and upright, as though frozen by anticipation of what they might be about to learn. Bill's own attention was too much on the road ahead, and on his mirror, for conversation. Every hundred metres brought a police van speeding towards them, heading for the city centre. Conspicuously armed police were stationed at every major intersection, the radios of their motorbikes squawking with static and jabbering bursts of unintelligible conversations.

It was fifteen minutes before he reversed the Audi into a cul-de-sac, killed the motor and looked around him. Behind them the alley terminated against the high wall of the Pére Lachaise cemetery. On each side were the blank walls of buildings. The line of parked cars in front effectively cut them off from sight of any casual observer passing the end of the alley. The only person in sight was a lone child batting a ball against the wall with a piece of planking.

Beside Bill, Keltum stared sightlessly through the windscreen, giving no hint that she even knew they had stopped, worrying with her teeth at a tiny frond of skin on her lip. He kept his eyes on her for a moment, trying to read in her face the turmoil within, and then turned his eyes back to watch the traffic passing the end of the alley. 'Do you want to try the cassette?'

She whipped her head around with panic in her eyes, as if she'd been aroused from a vivid dream. She stared at him for some moments before her panic subsided. Then, nodding slowly, she picked the machine from her lap.

As she set the tape spinning, Bill leaned back in his seat, his eyes scanning the entrance to the cul-de-sac, his hand resting on the ignition key. At the sound of the voice, his brow knitted as he strained to decipher the impenetrable brew of the strong Algerian accent and the rapid delivery, peppered with underworld slang.

Khoury began with surprising formality, as though he were dictating a confession, giving his full name, the date, and the time. The tape had been made that morning, only hours before Bill had broken into Khoury's room. He shot Keltum a quick glance. Her mouth twitched in a smile, though her eyes remained blank, uncommitted.

Khoury continued for some time in the same stilted, pseudo-legalistic style, as though he were parodying the language of one of his own court appearances. He went on to give details of his own background and history, even listing his criminal activities, reeling off a series of convictions for pimping and armed robbery. Bill exchanged a quizzical look with Keltum, hardly able to believe what he was hearing. It was as though the man were anxious to establish his criminal credentials, to leave his listeners in no doubt just how dangerous he was.

Bill almost found himself smiling at the absurdity of it. It was as though he were preparing to sell a proposal to a publisher for an underworld biography. Then, abruptly, he started forward in his seat, any urge to smile gone, replaced by a dizzying disbelief. 'Shit!' His stomach churned, as though he were about to be sick. Snatching at Keltum's wrist, he leant towards the machine so that his ear was inches from it. They stared at each other in stunned silence, listening as the deformed, tinny voice related its story, each phrase larded with obscenities.

Gradually, they lifted their bowed heads to stare at each other, wide-eyed and pale with shock.

'De Medem, too!' Bill breathed, at length. 'They're in it together!'

He took the machine from Keltum's numb fingers and rewound the tape. Wetting his lips, he punched the play button again and sat listening, holding Keltum's deathly cold hand in his, the sweat glistening on his face. 'The bastards,' he whispered, as Khoury came once more to the end of his story. 'Of course. It makes perfect sense. Vadon and de Medem! Together. The pair of murdering bastards.'

Keltum's whole body was racked by a spasm that sent her arching against the back of her seat. 'Oh, my God,' she keened. 'They're going to *kill* him!'

He replayed the tape twice more, holding the machine up in front of him and staring at it, as though he wanted to protest to it, to tell it that Khoury's words could not be true. Once again, the message came to its abrupt end, leaving them in renewed silence.

Slowly, as though moving underwater, Keltum balled a hand into a tight fist, and ground it against her teeth. 'Oh,' she said in a voice that was half a whisper and half a sob. 'Oh. Oh. My God! My God! They're going to murder Bruckner. And using Arabs, North Africans, as assassins!' She stared, wide-eyed, at Bill. 'People will blame the Imam. They'll blame *us*!'

Bill squeezed her other hand hard, hurting her, trying to cut through the rising note of hysteria. Her hand was as unresponsive as that of a corpse. His own voice came out hardly more than a croak. 'Khoury's afraid they'll kill him, too. This was going to be his insurance.'

She gave no sign of having heard him, too lost in her

own horrors, as she repeated her words in an eerie, sing-song bleat.

Starting the car, he gripped her by the arm with his free hand. 'Keltum, this was it! This is why he died. Ahmed must have known. He must have found out. Maybe they . . .' He paused, seeking the words. 'Maybe they even managed to . . . involve him, in some way we can't imagine.'

She nodded hard, taking breath in noisy gulps. 'Shame,' she murmured, her voice a thin, desolate echo. 'You were right. It *was* shame that made him kill himself.'

Already nosing the car from the alley, Bill looked down at the tape machine, as though he expected it to offer more, some explanation. It hummed softly as the blank remainder of the tape ran out. 'The bastard,' he murmured. 'The vain, posturing little jerk. Vadon's been pulling the strings from the beginning. The wire-taps, manipulating Lantier, that woman's murder. It all ties together. Ahmed jumping was a message for Vadon, I'm certain of it. That's why he chose that office, to warn him off.'

'But William, what are we going to do? How do we know Lantier isn't playing some kind of game with us?'

He looked at her with pursed lips. 'Sorry, Keltum. There's no choice any more. Not now.' He turned his wrist to glance at his watch. 'Lantier's waiting for us.' He accelerated hard, slicing in front of a busload of tourists. 'Stopping the killing isn't the problem now. If we had to, we could call a television station and play this tape over. That would be all it would take to raise enough of a stink to stop them. Bruckner wouldn't go anywhere near tonight's parade. But I want Vadon's head. I want that son of a bitch to pay. I mean to see him eat dirt. And for that, we need Lantier. Bouhila's got too many axes to grind. If the Imam produced this tape, Vadon would find a way to convince the world he had made it up. Lantier has the resources. He can have Khoury picked up, keep him out of harm's way, where Vadon can't have him got at. He wants that bastard as badly for what he did to that policeman as we want him for what he did to Ahmed.' He softened his voice. 'But if you insist on taking the pictures to Bouhila, you still have the choice. They're yours.'

She looked at him with feverish eyes. 'Do what you think.' She reached out and dug her fingers into his arm, surprising him with her strength. 'Whatever you want to do, just *hurry*!' She was almost screaming.

25

Pale eddies of hailstones skittered across the roof of the Audi, whipped on the gusting wind, which had come from nowhere three seconds before the hail. Bill leaned forward, squinting to read the street name as the windscreen wipers slapped the hail into drifts at the bottom of the glass. He gave a soft grunt and sat back, glancing once more at his watch. 'Okay, here goes!' He gave Keltum a lop-sided smile. 'If you want to change your mind, now's the time.'

'No,' she said steadily. 'I don't. I just want it over with.'

He nodded. 'Me, too.' He drove on towards the corner. There was no other traffic. The only people on the street were a woman and the child she was struggling to protect from the driving hailstorm with an umbrella damaged by the wind. He took the corner at walking pace.

The pavements were deserted. The shrubs and trees in front of the low houses tossed and shuddered in the wind. Still at walking pace, they rolled along the street searching for Lantier's car. Anxiety shifted in Bill's stomach like a snake moving in its sleep.

'Can you see it?'

Keltum shook her head stiffly. 'No.'

'Me neither. Maybe they came in his contact's car.' As he spoke, a glimmer of red caught his eye. He craned closer to the screen. The momentary glow had come from the brake light of a red Renault a few car-lengths ahead of them. Whoever was inside had the ignition on and had brushed the brake pedal. He blew out air, relief oozing through him. 'There they are.'

There was a space big enough for the Audi a few metres ahead of them. He pulled past it, glancing at the mirror as he prepared to reverse into it. Behind them, a grey Peugeot 205 was turning into the street. Still with half an eye on the mirror, he looked to the front again. The manoeuvre had brought him to within ten metres of the car that had shown the light. He frowned. The flat of a hand wiped the misted rear window. Through the cleared space he could see the blurred silhouettes of not two but three people. He slid the shift into reverse, his eyes still on the Renault. As he began reversing, its front wheels turned, as though it was preparing to pull out. Anxiety exploded into fear. Swivelling, he looked back over his shoulder. The Peugeot should have closed up, pressing to pass the moment he was out of the way. Instead, it waited, stationary, at the top of the street. His eyes flickered along the garden walls that lined the avenue. One of the iron gates stood open an inch. The squally wind, strong enough to rip the blossoms from the shrubs, was not moving it. 'A trap!'

In the instant he shouted, he rammed the shift into forward and stamped on the gas pedal. The rear yawed crazily as the tyres struggled to bite in the slush. The Renault was half out of its parking slot. The front bumper of the heavily built Audi clipped its wing, shunting it against the car in front. Keltum's scream reached him above the noise of the impact.

'The bastard!' he yelled, his eyes on the mirror. 'That bastard Lantier set us up!' Behind them, the Renault had recovered and was after them, unimpeded by its mashed wing. Further back, the Peugeot was racing to catch it.

Bill slewed the car into a left turn without lifting his foot, bouncing the rear off the far kerb as they accelerated away. They had thirty metres on the Renault when it drifted expertly through the wet corner behind them. He hurled the car through two more turns, coming out of them with the back end veering wildly, threatening to swing the car round. With each turn their pursuers had closed the gap. It was down to twenty-five metres as he swung the car desperately into another corner. Unused to the Audi, he bounced it hard off the kerb again. Keltum was screaming as he fought the wheel and retrieved it. The street ran straight for several hundred metres, giving him a chance to use the Audi's power to counter their pursuers' professional driving skill. He flipped on the headlights, fingered the horn, and slammed his foot to the floor.

The few cars swerved hastily out of his way as the speedometer needle swept round the dial. It was already past the hundred-kilometre mark before he looked in the mirror again and gave a murmur of satisfaction. Their lead had widened. It was up to fifty or sixty metres and growing as the smaller cars struggled to match their acceleration. He cast a quick glance at Keltum. She was silent again, and deathly pale, staring ahead of her. He took a hand from the wheel and touched her arm. 'It's okay. They don't have the speed. We're losing them.'

Her response was to gasp and widen her eyes. His hand fell from her arm as she pointed, making him jerk his eyes back to the road. A car had pulled into view ahead of them and was turning broadside across the road, blocking it.

'Damn!' Even as he cried out, he shoved his foot hard on the brake and spun the wheel. They careered to the left, forcing an oncoming car into the gutter as they hurtled into a narrow side street.

He almost stood on the brake. The car danced and skidded on the greasy cobbles, before slamming broadside against the narrow pavement that closed off the end of the cul-de-sac. It rocked, threatening to roll over, and fell back to rest with a jolt that cracked their heads against the ceiling. Bill snatched open the door. 'Come on!'

Keltum sat motionless in her seat, too shocked to move. He ran round the car and grabbed her hand in both of his. 'Come on. You can't give up. You can't let them get away with it.'

As he hauled her from the car he was already looking around them. An iron railing ran behind the pavement, pierced by a low gate. Beyond it, a flight of stone steps led down a steep escarpment to the road below, bounded by walls twice the height of a man and topped with rusting spikes. He shoved open the gate and headed for the steps, with Keltum stumbling in his wake.

They had barely started down when the screech of tyres drew Bill's attention to the foot of the steps. Two men climbed from a car and began walking towards the steps, moving without hurry, their faces turned up to watch the running figures above them.

Bill stopped short, grabbing at Keltum as she staggered, missing her footing on the smooth ramp built into the stairs to permit the passage of children's strollers. 'Back! We have to go back.'

She looked at him in blank, exhausted bemusement.

'To the car.' He was already going up the steps at a run, jerking her almost off her feet as he yanked her after him.

They reached the top of the steps side by side and stopped dead. The three cars were ranged across the entrance to the cul-de-sac, blocking it. As they stood, frozen, at the top of the steps, several men climbed from them. Moving without haste, they spread themselves in a line across the alley, and began walking slowly forward. As they came, one of them murmured continually into a wrist microphone.

Bill scanned the walls on either side of them. Nothing, not a door or window offered anywhere to run. He spun back to the stairs. The two men were no more than twenty steps away. One of them held his arm straight down at his side, some kind of weapon pressed against his thigh.

'Quick!' Wheeling, he grabbed Keltum's arm tightly and shoved her hard into the passenger seat of the Audi. He vaulted the hood, stumbled, recovered, and threw himself behind the wheel.

The man with the microphone, seeing his move, spun to check that their cars were in place. He was turning back, grinning, as Bill gunned the motor, snatched the stubby shift into reverse and slammed his foot down.

The men scrambled aside, shouting, as the Audi screeched backwards towards them, swinging through a tight arc. Bill hit the brake, smiling thinly at the dull sound of one of the men ricocheting off the bodywork. Before the car had properly stopped, he rammed the shift back into forward, once more pushing his foot to the floor.

The powerful engine whined as the wheels kicked up spray, gripped, and catapulted the heavy car forward again. He flicked a glance in the mirror. One of their pursuers was back in the middle of the road. As Bill looked he plunged his hand into his jacket, beckoning with his other hand for his men to regroup.

'Grab something! Hold it tight!' As he shouted, he braced himself between the wheel and the seat, his arms rigid. Keltum had just time to snatch at the grab handle before the car hit the kerb and bucked over it, throwing their heads forward and then back. There was a crash of tearing metal as the front of the car sheared off the railing and plunged sickeningly onto the upper steps. Sparks flew past their windows. Keltum screamed as she was thrown to the floor, the breath slamming out of her. Bill's head struck the roof, the force of it momentarily blackening his vision.

Shaking his head clear, he found himself looking into the faces of the two men who had been coming up the steps. They were staring at him in stunned disbelief. In what seemed to Bill like slow motion, they began scrambling to turn, colliding with each other in their haste. The next moment they were leaping down the steps, trying to outrun the careering car. The gun the leading man had been carrying flew from his hand and rattled down in front of them.

Recovering from his momentary daze, Bill yanked the wheel over, bringing the nearside wheels onto the smooth ramp. With only the offside wheels taking the shock of the steps, the wild bucking subsided into a controllable, spine-jolting rhythm. He almost laughed aloud at the stark panic in the men's faces as they looked back to see the car gaining on them. Shouting instructions to each other, they stopped and turned to the wall. One quickly made a stirrup for his companion and boosted him high enough for him to curl his fingers round the ironwork on top of the wall.

'Open the door!'

Keltum stared at him, hardly comprehending.

'Hold it open, like this!' As he spoke he raised his left leg, showing her what he wanted. Without speaking, staring at the two men, she threw open the door and braced her foot against it. The metal ground into the masonry, showering yellow sparks.

Horror filled the faces of the men. The one still on the ground straightened, ran a few futile paces, and flattened himself against the wall, leaving his companion hanging. The door hit the hanging one first, swinging him up like a pendulum. In the mirror, Bill saw him lose his grip and crash full length onto the concrete steps. Looking back, the second man had disappeared. He looked again in the mirror. He was pitching brokenly down the steps, his face a bloody pulp. 'Thanks,' he said softly, as Keltum let the door slam shut. 'Maybe we finally started to get even.'

The bottom of the steps rushed to meet them. Bill began braking, very gently at first and then harder. The car yawed sickeningly from side to side as he alternately braked and released the pedal, the rear bodywork mashing into the walls on each side. As the pavement rushed closer he jammed his foot down hard, almost standing on the pedal, trying to slow their momentum. The nose bit into the asphalt with a crash of twisting metal and then they were stopped, the radiator inches from the side of the car the two men had arrived in. Without a moment's pause, he jumped from the Audi, taking the key with him, and ran to the other car, shouting for Keltum to follow him.

He gave a little yelp of triumph. In their certainty the men had left the keys in the ignition. With another shout to Keltum, he sprang inside. She dropped into the passenger seat, her face as pale and immobile as a corpse, as two of their pursuers leapt over their injured companions and began sprinting down the final few steps. They sped away, leaving the two men raging impotently by the useless Audi.

Bill drove for several minutes in absolute silence, twisting and turning at random. Finally, satisfied nobody could have followed them, he drew into the kerb close by a small park, and turned off the motor. He sat back and looked down at his legs. They were shaking uncontrollably. 'My God,' he said softly, cupping his face in his hands. 'The whole damned world's gone crazy!'

Keltum leaned across to him until her face was close by his. She laid a tentative hand on his shoulder. 'Bill? Bill are you okay?'

Slowly, he raised his head. With his hands still together under his chin, in an attitude of prayer, he turned to look at her. The beginning of a smile on his face, he placed a hand over hers. 'I guess so.' He glanced down again at his twitching legs. 'That'll pass.' The smile became a sudden grin. 'Although there's still the fact those people seem to want to kill us.'

She smiled wanly back at him, her eyes moist. 'I'm pleased to see you're human, anyway. Where did you learn to *do* things like that?'

He extended his legs and worked the muscles, loosening them. The trembling subsided. 'Vietnam, maybe.'

'You did things like *that* over there?'

He laughed through his nose. 'No. But I did learn something. When someone's trying to shoot you, don't freeze. Think.' He put a hand on the door handle. 'Will you wait here for a couple of minutes?'

Her eyes widened. 'Where are you going?'

'To give a message to that bastard Lantier.'

The phone had rung perhaps twenty times. He was about to replace the receiver when it was picked up. 'Hello?' It was the same voice but altered, somehow hollowed out.

'Hello. This is Kléber. I've got a message for your brother. I just want to tell him that his boys missed us. And that he's a treacherous, unscrupulous asshole. He . . .' He broke off, disconcerted, when the woman abruptly started to sob.

'I'm sorry, Madame. But please tell him, will you?'

She spoke again, forcing the words out between gulping sobs. 'Oh, Monsieur . . . my brother's *dead*.'

'Huh?' he said dully, as if she had suddenly spoken a foreign language.

'Yes, he is,' she said vehemently, as though he had wanted to argue about it. 'Somebody broke into his flat. They think he must have caught them. He was stabbed. Oh, Monsieur, they cut him terribly. It was horrible. As if they . . . they had *tortured* him. They . . .' She broke down, overcome. He heard soft sounds of whispering and then a man's voice, strong and authoritative. 'Who's this? Who's calling? How may I be of help?' Bill hung up and walked, head down, back to the car.

Keltum's smile evaporated as he almost fell into his seat. 'What is it? You look *grey*! What's happened?'

He sat and stared through the windscreen for several seconds before turning to face her. 'They've killed him.'

She remained quite still, looking back at him with wide, incredulous eyes. 'But, he's a policeman. He's one of them.'

'*They* must have thought he was one of *us*. Which I guess means he was.' He grimaced. 'Now all there are of us is *us*.'

'No!' she said, with startling vehemence. 'That's not true. While you were gone I was thinking . . .'

'That we could try Bouhila?' he interjected.

She nodded, her face aglow. 'I *know* he would help us. He would find a way to stop them. And he would protect us.' She leaned close, her eyes pleading as she read the hesitation in his face. 'Please.' She reached out and laid a hand on his shoulder, the fingers touching his neck. He found an unexpected pleasure in the feel of them. 'Please, William. Give him the chance.' Her eyes did not leave his as he stayed silent, still hesitating. 'There's nobody else left,' she said, in a whisper.

He reached up and lifted her hand gently from his shoulder. 'You win. Show me the way.'

26

The headlights of oncoming vehicles gleamed on Bill's face as the tension and heat squeezed the sweat from him in a glistening sheet. In a matter of minutes another cloudburst had dumped an inch of rain on the streets, bringing traffic almost to a standstill. Edging the car forward, following Keltum's terse instructions, he was grateful for the weather, for the protection the steamed-up, rain-beaded windows gave from the eyes of the police patrols. Even more than earlier in the day, the city was alive with them. Conspicuously armed, they stalked the streaming pavements at fifty-metre intervals, their eyes drilling into the faces of passers-by as though they were trying to prise guilty secrets from them. Overhead, helicopters circled, sandwiched between the rooftops and the banks of sodden cloud which had somehow aged the day, casting the city into premature evening.

He sighed audibly with relief as Keltum directed him into a quiet side street. Following her instructions, he took them through several further turns, the streets becoming more run-down at every turn.

'Okay!' she called, in a voice husky with excitement. 'Stop there, behind that van.'

He drew into the space she indicated.

'Come on,' she urged, her door half open before he had killed the motor.

In the last quarter of an hour, as the prospect of seeing Bouhila had drawn closer, her whole deportment had changed. Her face glowed with excitement, her voice had regained its old authority. Now, almost having to run to catch her, he marvelled at the new purpose, the straight-backed, confident stride.

'That's it. Over there.'

He followed the direction of her eyes to a shabby supermarket squeezed between a laundromat and a video store. 'Bouhila runs all that from a *store*?' he asked, reaching her side.

She laughed, not looking at him as her eyes scanned the street around them. 'Of course not. The offices are in the street behind this one. So is the entrance. The official entrance.'

He remained quiet, letting her lead him into the store. It was cramped and untidy, a deep, poorly lit room with a central gondola dividing it into two aisles. Produce spilled from crates on the floor, leaving a passage barely wide enough for one of the collection of rickety trolleys to pass. The only customer was a thin old man in a worn suit and a brown shirt buttoned to the neck, his lips moving as he studied the instructions on the label of a canned meal. With a murmured apology, they pushed roughly past the man and continued to a pair of flexible rubber doors at the rear. Checking quickly behind her, Keltum thrust through the doors, motioning him to follow.

Metal racks lined the room, crammed with cartons and sacks. Rice, beans, damaged cans and packets lay in drifts along the gangways. A North African wearing a brown cotton overall, thick glasses and a permanent frown, sat in a cramped office, working at a ledger. At the sound of the doors opening he glanced up once, saw Keltum, and immediately dropped his eyes again, immersing himself deeper in his ledger.

Stepping confidently amid the clutter, she led Bill through the storeroom towards a door that stood ajar, its rim encrusted with locks. They were a half-dozen steps from the door when it was thrown roughly open, making Keltum draw back with a mew of surprise. Instinctively, Bill stepped forward, shielding her. Two men, both short and dark with tightly waved black hair and wearing identical dark blue overalls, stepped into the room and moved quickly towards them, their eyes hard as glass on Bill's face. Instinctively, he crowded Keltum behind him, putting himself between her and the men.

Keltum reached round and put a hand on his arm, restraining him. 'It's alright,' she murmured, as they shouldered past. 'They know me.'

Reluctantly, he stepped away from her, turning to watch as they shoved their way out into the store. Keltum was already opening the door, urging him forward.

'Who the hell were they?' he asked, still staring at the swinging doors.

'The Imam's people. His special group. They are trained to, well . . . for protection,' she added, a touch defensively.

He glanced back once more as she pulled the door shut. He was about to speak when she put a finger to her lips.

'Be quiet now, please.'

They were in a greasy courtyard. It was ten metres square, enclosed by walls three metres high, topped with several strands of barbed wire on rusting stanchions. Newer razor wire had been coiled around the old barbed wire and continued some distance up the sides of the buildings where the walls joined them. Running the length of one side of the yard, a broken-down lean-to shed sheltered crates of vegetables, a collection of trash and broken-down trolleys, and a reeking, hole-in-the-ground toilet without door or toilet paper, just a short length of hosepipe trailing from a tap. Thin cats sidled warily away as she led him quickly forward.

Close to the back wall she turned into the lean-to. The trash had been cleared from a space in front of a door set into the wall. In contrast to its surroundings, the steel plate that covered the door was new enough not to have started rusting. Keltum raised her hands to her collar and looped a cord from round her neck. Two keys hung from it. Bill recognized them with mild surprise as being for high quality security locks.

Without fumbling, as though she had performed the operation many times before, she selected one of the keys and slid it into the lock. The levers fell back with the sweet, pleasing sound of well-engineered metal.

While she re-locked the door behind them Bill looked around him. They were in another cement-floored courtyard, three times bigger than the one they had left and completely bare. It, too, was surrounded by high walls topped with more of the thick coils of razor wire. The building in front of him was twenty metres wide, three storeys high, and completely windowless. An iron fire-escape rose to a door at second floor level. The only other aperture was another plain steel door, like the one they had just passed through, opening onto the courtyard.

'Come on.' She took his hand, hurrying him towards the lower door. She rapped on it with a key and waited.

'Is this it? Where Bouhila hangs out?' Bill whispered.

She nodded, frowning and cocking her head, listening for any movement from behind the door. She rapped again, harder. Bill suppressed a smile. He had been half expecting a secret knock. To see her just whack at the door was faintly reassuring, making the whole thing less sinister.

Once again, there was no sound from beyond the door. Plainly perplexed, she glanced back towards the gate, as though she were looking for the two men that had passed them. With a shrug, she took the second key and pushed it into the lock.

Frowning, Bill took her by the arm. 'Keltum you have the keys to the kingdom. Tell me truthfully, just how close *are* you to Bouhila?'

She flushed. 'Oh, no, I'm not as important as you think. I'm just a, a helper, nothing more.' Her flush deepened as his eyes stayed on the keys in her hand. 'The Imam gave me these, for when I brought Ahmed here to see him. Ahmed insisted on discretion. We would come when the Imam was alone, so that there would be no gossip, so Ahmed's career would not suffer. And, of course, the main entrance is *always* watched.'

'I bet.'

She frowned, ignoring his remark, as she struggled with the lock. 'I don't understand. Normally, at this time there should be someone manning this door.' The lock clunked open. She dropped the keys into her bag and pushed open the door signalling him to wait. 'Let me go first. They wouldn't know you. They're very protective of the Imam.'

A flight of dimly lit stairs led upwards from the door. She ran up to a set of doors at the top, pushed one open and looked inside. Deeply puzzled, she waved for him to join her.

'What's the matter?' he asked, seeing her expression.

'I don't understand. There's nobody here. Normally there are people everywhere.' She gave a little, apologetic laugh. 'You can hardly hear yourself speak.'

'Maybe they're all still out on the demonstration.'

She shook her head. 'No. There are *always* people here. If only for security. People like those two you saw are always . . .'

He put a hand on her arm, cautioning her to silence. 'Perhaps something's happened,' he whispered. 'Like a police raid.'

She looked incredulously at him. 'The intelligence services are watching the place, we all know that. We joke about it. But why would the police want to raid us? We have never broken any laws.'

'Neither have we,' he whispered wryly. 'But tonight's appearance by Bruckner would be all the excuse they need to get anyone with an axe to grind off the streets. Where's Bouhila's office? I want to get this over with.'

She pointed. 'Upstairs. Next to the projection room.'

'This is a *cinema*?'

'It used to be.'

He nodded. 'Okay, show me. But no noise, not until we know what's going on.'

With Keltum leading, they moved through another door onto a spiral iron staircase barely wide enough for Bill's shoulders. Reaching the second floor, a door with a glass porthole enabled them to see into the room beyond. It was lit but deserted. Soundlessly, he opened the door and stepped into what had once been the projection room. It was furnished now as an office, crowded with desks and a battery of photocopiers. Papers had fallen from the desks to the floor. 'Is this Bouhila's office?'

She shook her head and pointed to a door. 'Through there,' she said, the confidence gone from her voice now.

He strode to the door, struggling to keep his own feelings

out of his face. If Bouhila had been taken out of circulation all bets were off.

He stopped dead, staring into the office. The drawers of the desk and the filing cabinets lay upended on the floor, their contents in heaps. An old-fashioned safe stood agape and empty. A document shredder was almost buried in a drift of paper fragments. Empty binders lay scattered among the trash. He felt Keltum at his shoulder. 'Maybe they had wind of a raid,' he said, kicking up a spray of chopped paper as he moved into the office. 'Police didn't do *this*. Someone was *destroying* evidence, not collecting it.'

She was not listening. She was staring through the glass partition. Although the beginnings of tears gleamed at the corners of her eyes, a new, almost hysterical light had replaced the apprehension in them. She extended an arm. 'Look,' she gasped, her voice cracking with emotion.

In two quick strides he was at her side. The old auditorium below them had been partitioned with movable screens into a maze of cubicles. All but one of the cubicles was deserted. Bill followed the line of Keltum's pointing finger. From their vantage point a turbaned head and robed shoulders were visible beyond the partition. The sharp, prominent nose and high forehead made the face unmistakable.

'Thank God for that!' As he breathed the words, he grabbed Keltum's hand and started for the door. As he turned, Bouhila raised a hand and jabbed emphatically at the air. Bill stopped short. 'He's not alone,' he hissed, dropping to a crouch and pulling Keltum with him. 'Did you see who it is with him?'

Keltum shook her head.

'Well, is there a way we can get down there? Without any noise?'

She nodded, still almost dumbstruck at the mere proximity of Bouhila, and pointed to a double door beyond the office with an extinct 'exit' sign above it. Keeping low, out of the line of sight from the auditorium, Bill ran to the door, hauling Keltum in his wake, and pushed silently through.

They were at the top of a wide staircase. Clark Gable, Jean

Gabin, Marilyn Monroe, and an assortment of identikit fifties brunettes, all thrusting breasts and painted smiles, looked down at them from the faded black-and-white portraits that lined the walls. With Bill leading, they started down, keeping close to the inner wall, the greasy, scarred carpet muffling their footsteps.

They reached another set of doors. Bill pushed one open a crack and peered through. A carpeted corridor sloped away towards the street side of the building. They passed through and hurried down the slope to a matching set of doors at the far end.

Once again they paused, listening hard, before easing their way into the deserted foyer. A padlock and chain secured the street doors. The light from the red-glazed porthole windows of the doors cast a bloody tinge over the cigarette-littered floor. Following her pointing finger, Bill led Keltum quickly past the vandalized ticket booth to where the doors of the auditorium hung from damaged hinges, permanently open. They stepped stealthily through.

The area was sparingly lit by the few recessed ceiling lights that still functioned, as though the lights had been frozen in the act of being lowered for a show. The free-standing partitions reached twenty centimetres above Bill's head, preventing them from seeing anything beyond the gangway that sloped up, away from the rotting velvet curtains that hid the screen. Moving as fast as they dared without the risk of noise, they hurried across in front of the stage, making for the spot where they had glimpsed Bouhila.

They reached the far gangway and turned up the sloping aisle, moving ever more carefully as the sound of the voices became clearer, guiding them. They passed two empty cubicles where the screens of unattended word-processors still glowed with abandoned texts. As they reached the third cubicle, Bill tugged at Keltum's sleeve, restraining her. With infinite caution, he leaned to look inside. A space between two partitions on the far side gave access to an inner area. He drew back sharply as Bouhila strode into view, his extraordinary eyes ablaze as he addressed someone out of Bill's sight. The hidden person replied, too low for them to hear. In an abrupt movement, shockingly at odds with the characteristic harshness of his expression, Bouhila threw back his head and laughed.

Bill felt the tension drain out of him in a rush, letting relief flood in its place. A laugh so relaxed, so full of genuine amusement, was not the act of someone being questioned by a hostile policeman. Whoever was in there with him was a friend. Smiling at Keltum, he put out an arm and began propelling her forwards.

As he did so, Bouhila's companion stepped into view. For a split second Bill stared at the familiar profile, disabled by sheer incredulity. Then, stifling a gasp, he spun and threw an arm round Keltum, bundling her back from the entrance, his other hand pressed hard over her mouth, suppressing her rising cry of surprise.

He pulled her tight against him, pinioning her arms and bringing her face to within inches of his own. Above his hand her eyes were wide, filled with a mixture of confusion and indignation. He jerked his head over his shoulder at the cubicle. Then, making no sound, but shaping the syllables with exaggerated precision, so that she could not mistake it, he mouthed the name. 'De Medem!'

Keltum's eyes opened wider, clouded with dumb, uncomprehending dismay. Her head moved against his hand as she tried to shake it in denial.

He nodded emphatically. 'Yes! I saw him,' he mouthed again. He looked into her eyes, still pinning her helpless against him, needing to be sure it had sunk in, before gradually releasing the pressure on her mouth. Her face was slack with shock and disbelief. He pointed down the aisle. 'Come on,' he mouthed, making to move. 'Let's get out of here, fast.'

She made no sign she had understood, no effort to follow. Gently, he took her by the upper arms. She was as awkward and unresponsive as a dummy. He slid an arm round her waist and pulled her onto his hip, half carrying her back down the gangway. As they drew level with the entrance to the adjoining cubicle she straightened, pulling free of his arm. He looked down at her, about to urge her to more speed. She was not looking at him. Instead she was moving into the cubicle, her eyes on the far wall. Stooping, he took two quick strides and grabbed her arm. He spun her to face him. 'Keltum,' he mouthed. 'What are you doing? We've got to get away from here. To give ourselves time to think.'

She shook her head. 'I want to hear them. I want to *know*!' Shaking off his hand, she turned and continued across the cubicle.

Bill hesitated for a moment, watching her back, and then once again hurried to catch her. With a quick motion of his fingers he stilled her protest. 'Okay,' he mouthed. 'If you have to. But let me go ahead.'

He moved across to the far corner and stood for a moment, listening. Then, stooping, he slid his fingers beneath the partition and eased it noiselessly aside, opening up a gap wide enough to pass through. Beckoning her to his side, he sidled ahead of her through the gap.

Showing her by example how to place her feet, heel first, avoiding the slightest sound, he led the way across the cubicle to the remaining partition separating them from Bouhila and de Medem. Taking both her hands in his, he lowered himself into a crouch, gently tugging her with him. Her ice-cold fingers bit into his. Her eyes stared with the blank, unfocused look of a survivor of a disaster. With only a single partition to separate them, the voices were as clear as though they had been in the same room.

'Well, my dear, er, Imam, I shouldn't delay you any further, I suppose.' At the sound of the deep, rough-edged voice, familiar from a hundred radio and television broadcasts, Keltum's whole body was racked with a deep shiver. Bill squeezed her hands hard, willing her to silence. 'With the state of the traffic tonight you'll want to give yourself plenty of time.'

Bill raised an eyebrow. Behind the perfect courtesy there was something in the tone, the faintest hint of a drawing-out of the syllables of 'Imam' that hinted at a deep contempt.

'After all,' the voice continued, 'you won't want to be late for your flight.'

Keltum's hollowed, devastated face creased in deepened concentration at the words.

Bouhila gave a short, dismissive laugh. 'Think, de Medem, please. Am I some teenager from the zone? Do you suppose I have come this far to be a slave of airline schedules? Tomorrow I shall be the toast of North Africa, and you expect me to return to Algiers economy class, no smoking, on Air France?' He paused theatrically. 'No, my friend.' A note of pride quivered in his voice. 'Of course not. A private jet is waiting for me at Orly.'

'Oh,' de Medem said, still with the buried hint of disdain. 'Very nice. I'll admit you've always had some style about you, Bouhila. But you'll be arriving in the middle of the night. Won't it be a bit of an anti-climax for the, er, people, if their national saviour arrives while they're all in bed? I would have thought you'd want a real welcome at the airport, being a distinguished international figure and all, to get your campaign off to a flying start.'

'You won't give credit, will you? Of course I shan't be flying directly to Algiers. Tonight we shall fly to Tunis. My arrival in Algiers is scheduled for late tomorrow morning, just at the hour when people are leaving the mosques. By then the whole world will know that Imam Bouhila has done what no one else has ever come near to doing. Not Fatah, not Black September, none of them! Killing Bruckner will be a blow at the heart of Zion the like of which has never been achieved before.' His voice took on a shrill edge. 'Bouhila will have taken revenge for the martyrs of Gaza. The bazaars and the mosques will be aflame with the news. Those crippled old men who run my country, still congratulating themselves for things they did thirty years ago, won't have the will to contain it. I won't *have* to declare my candidature. The people will be out in the streets *demanding* it!'

De Medem laughed. 'You don't think you're, well, exaggerating the effects of this business? Now that Israel and the Arabs seem to be, well, almost cosy.'

Bouhila gave a snort. 'The Arabs! Arab governments, you mean. Egypt, with its Western puppet leaders! Jordan, Saudi Arabia, with their absurd kings! What do I care about them? They are yesterday. The future is with us, people like me. The true defenders of the faith.'

'It does sound exciting,' de Medem said, flatly. 'Don't you think you should bear in mind that you won't have shot him personally, though? Won't your *people* think more of those two poor idiots than of you?'

Bouhila's quick laugh was high and brittle. 'But they are men of my personal bodyguard, you fool. They do nothing without my orders. There's plenty of material still here to *prove* that.'

'M'mm. Of course, not *everybody* will be applauding. The Israelis, for example, won't be very, ah, pleased with you. And they do have quite a record of their own where revenge is concerned. An eye for an eye, and all that. I'm sure you've thought it through, but won't you have to watch your back, even if you are living in the presidential palace, or the Hall of the People, or whatever they call it over there?'

'And what if I die?' Bouhila's voice swelled dramatically. 'There will be others. I told you. Our time has come, de Medem. Haven't you understood that?'

'Oh, dear,' de Medem replied, sighing. 'So you really are a believer? I'm surrounded by them. Vadon's the same, in his way. He really *believes*, just like you. He thinks he's going to save the French nation. He's been planning it for years, apparently,' he added in a kind of amused wonder.

'Vadon? That vain nonentity. You think *he* would not be afraid to die?' Bouhila sneered.

'Ah, there I think you may be making a mistake. He's a strange man, more complicated than you think. He's afraid of many things; stains on his tie, being seen before he's had time to comb his hair in the morning. He'd go to great lengths to avoid looking ridiculous. But death? I'm not sure, not so long as it could be done stylishly, anyway. He really has faced death before, you know. And courage isn't something a man loses. Not like his reflexes, or his hair. Take my word for it, the threat of *death* would never have brought him to heel the way the threat of exposure has. That's why I wish you had been able to keep those photographs, my friend,' he said with sudden venom. 'I need the grip they gave me.'

At these words Keltum's face contorted as though she had been slapped. Bill snapped out a hand and pressed it to her mouth, grinding the flesh against her teeth. With the other hand he gripped her arm, willing her to control herself.

Behind the partition Bouhila barked derisively. 'Bah! He needs you, photos or no photos, as much as you need him.'

'Rationally, I'm sure you're right, old boy. I would still feel happier if I had them. Pity about your Bengana losing his head like that.' He sighed ironically. 'Another of your disciples that put death before dishonour.'

'Don't be such a fool, de Medem. Vadon fell for it once, he'll fall for it again. You can't let losing Bengana be such a setback. There are other pretty Arab boys.' Bouhila gave another guffaw. 'God knows, you spend enough time complaining that there are too many of them over here!'

De Medem guffawed. 'Not celebrities, though. For Vadon, that counts.'

Bouhila gave another sneering laugh. 'Bullshit! Bengana sucked his cock, that's all. They all . . .'

Bill's fingers gouged white channels in the flesh of Keltum's cheeks as his grip tightened across her face. He was too late to suppress the keening protest that had cut off Bouhila's words. Her face burning with shame and rage, she flailed at him, fighting free.

He was half-way to his feet when the partition came down on them with a force that sent them both staggering. Keltum sprawled full length on the scuffed carpet. Bill was on one knee, his left foot beneath the edge of the partition, where the weight of de Medem, standing on the fallen panel, held it trapped.

Bouhila stood riveted, a pace behind de Medem, staring at Keltum. Recovering herself first, she sprang to her feet and leapt at him, screaming from deep in her throat, her fingernails slashing at his face.

De Medem's eyes were on Bill. His face contorted, he stepped forward and kicked out with all his force. Bill jerked away, taking the blow on the cheekbone. The violence of the effort had drawn de Medem a fraction off balance. In the moment while he set himself for another shot, Bill curled his fingers under the edge of the partition and jerked at it. It moved only an inch or two, but that was enough to send de Medem, on one leg, hopping awkwardly backwards. With the shift of weight, Bill gave a shout of effort and lifted the partition again, enough to drag his leg clear. De Medem had already recovered his balance. His eyes blazing, he took a long stride forward, positioning himself for another kick. Bill threw himself onto his back and swung his legs towards de Medem. As the man raised his right foot to launch a blow, Bill placed his legs on either side of de Medem's left leg and snapped them closed in a scissors movement, scything away the man's support. With a look of stupid surprise on his face de Medem toppled, hitting the partition shoulder-first. As he lay there, winded, Bill sprang to his feet, took a light, dancing step forward, and drove his toe into the man's unprotected groin. De Medem gurgled softly, like a baby, and his knees came up into a foetal crouch. Bill kicked him twice more, punting his toe with brutal force into the man's face, and stepped past him.

Bouhila strained to hold Keltum's wrists immobile as her fingers, crooked into talons, sought to tear his face. Blood trickled from parallel scratches on his cheekbone where she had already struck home. She shrieked and raged incoherently as he spoke to her in Kabyle, repeating the same words over and over. Although he spoke to Keltum, his eyes were on Bill, watchful and calm. Seeing Bill step towards him he grinned coolly. Abruptly, he released one of Keltum's wrists, shoving it hard from him, and in the same movement drove his fist in a short, quick hook into her stomach. She gave a single retching cry and collapsed to the floor. Still holding her wrist, he let her hang like a doll.

'You bastard!' Raising his fists, Bill advanced across the intervening space.

With a lazy grin, Bouhila slid a hand into his robe. He drew it out again, swinging his clenched hand out and up, clear of his robe. His thumb moved a fraction as he squeezed a button. Bill heard the distinct, sinister snick of the mechanism as the slim blade of the knife, as long as his hand, sprang into place.

'Remain there, Mister Duvall,' Bouhila told him, conversationally. Dropping his hand, he pressed the flat of the blade against the flesh of Keltum's neck.

Bill stopped as though he had run into a wall. His hands fell useless to his sides.

'Now step back. Do exactly as I tell you.' As he spoke, Bouhila's glance flickered for a fraction of a second to where de Medem lay nursing his groin. 'Can you get up?'

De Medem nodded. Gasping, he pushed himself to his feet. 'I'm alright,' he said, hoarsely, smoothing his hair with the flat of his free hand. 'You know these people?'

Bouhila nodded. He shook Keltum by the wrist as though she were a rabbit. 'This is Bengana's sister. That one's his friend. The American.'

'Ah!' De Medem took a step closer to Bill and punched him hard in the face. The force of the blow dropped Bill to his knees. De Medem gave an ironic bow. 'Pleased to meet you.'

Bill snarled and sprang back to his feet, his fists bunching.

'Be still!'

The edge in Bouhila's voice checked him. He looked across to find that Bouhila had twisted the knife so the edge was against Keltum's neck, indenting the flesh beneath her ear. 'You bastards,' he breathed, letting his fists fall again to his sides.

'Enough of that childishness,' Bouhila said, addressing de Medem in a voice taut with contained anger. 'There's no time for such stupidities. We both have to leave here immediately.'

'What are we going to do about these two?' de Medem asked, scowling at Bill as he continued massaging his groin.

Bouhila grinned. 'Our civic duty. The man's a public danger.

A psychopath.' The dark eyes burned into Bill's. The grin faded, leaving the face totally devoid of expression. 'Kneel down.'

Bill hesitated, looking from Bouhila to Keltum.

The knife bit deeper into Keltum's neck. 'You heard me, Mister Duvall. Kneel.'

De Medem ran his tongue over his lips. 'Ah, I should go,' he said hoarsely. 'If anyone were to find me here, it would, I . . .'

'Go on, get out. Quickly.' Bouhila spoke without taking his eyes from Bill. 'And ensure Khoury is dealt with tonight.'

De Medem took a step back. 'Don't worry. Everything is in place for that.' He wet his lips again and grinned. 'Yes, well, I had better wish you good luck in Algiers, hadn't I? Who knows, we might meet again over there. I rather see myself as Foreign Minister once Vadon's installed. We could, ah, discuss the immigration problem.' He looked at Bill and gave a laugh, that grated in his throat with a dry, rasping sound. 'Yes, well . . .' He turned and walked quickly from the damaged cubicle and up the sloping gangway. Staring in silence at each other, Bouhila and Duvall listened to the man's footsteps grow quicker until they broke into a run. A door slammed and there was silence.

'So, Monsieur Duvall, please come closer, on your knees.'

Bill shook his head. 'You're crazy. Call those two clowns off. The first policeman that comes in here, I'm going to tell him the whole story.' As he spoke he fished the cassette from his pocket. 'I took this off your stooge, Khoury. It's all on there. They'll just cancel Bruckner's appearance and that'll be the end of it.'

A flash of total hatred passed over Bouhila's face. An instant later, it had gone, the face once again a blank. 'Give it to me,' he said softly. 'Throw it over here.'

Bill shook his head. 'Not a chance. Let her go.'

Bouhila's smile faded. 'You're a foolish man, Monsieur Duvall. Give it to me.'

Bill swallowed. 'Not a hope. Unless you let her go first.'

A flash of exasperation flickered behind Bouhila's eyes. He jerked Keltum to her feet and slid his arm round her throat. Her eyes bulged as she gasped for breath. 'I won't tell you again. Throw it down. At my feet.'

Bill took a step back. 'Forget it. I'm leaving. Let her go. For Christ's sake, the girl *idolized* you.'

Bouhila gave a scoffing laugh. 'Do as I say. Throw it down and come over here, on your knees, with your hands on your head.'

Bill moved back another step, half-turning for the door. 'So you can stick me with that thing? Bye.'

He began walking towards the aisle. A tremulous scream made him spin round. Blood poured from Keltum's cheek. The whites of her frightened eyes gleamed bright in the dim light. The knifepoint hovered an inch below them.

'You bastard.' His fists bunched. He shifted his weight, as though about to run at Bouhila.

With a barely perceptible movement, Bouhila twitched the blade again. Blood welled from another cut. 'The cassette. Then on your knees, Monsieur. Now.'

His chest heaving, Bill tossed the tape at Bouhila's feet and sank slowly to his knees.

'Hands on your head. Fingers twined.' Bill complied, his face set. 'Good. Now, over here, please.'

Bill began shuffling across the carpet. As he moved he watched Bouhila step deliberately onto the cassette and grind it under his heel.

Keltum watched him advance, her eyes bulging and her mouth agape as she fought for breath. She moved her feet, groping for some purchase, her toes barely touching the ground. Her foot brushed the shoulder bag that lay there. A new light came into the swollen, frightened eyes. She moved the bag with her toe. At the sound of it, Bouhila jerked her to one side, looking for the source of the noise. At the same time Keltum kicked out wildly, sending the bag skidding across the carpet towards Bill.

'Take the photos, Bill. Run! Let the world know why Ahmed

died.' In the moment of Bouhila's distraction she had prised her thumbs up between his arm and her throat, allowing her to breathe. 'Show them that he did it to *stop* them.'

Bouhila jerked his arm brutally against her windpipe. The point of the knife pressed against her eyelid.

'The photographs?' he hissed, the black eyes on fire. 'Bring them here.'

With his eyes on the knifeblade, Bill reached for the bag and continued shuffling forward.

'No! Run, William. Stop them. For my family's sake!'

The sound of the cry, the voice cracking and shrill, made Bouhila look sharply from the bag down into her face. In that moment, she grasped his knife hand in both of hers and jerked her head forward and down.

For an instant, both Bill and Bouhila remained motionless, frozen with disbelief. Three inches of the knife blade had disappeared into her eye. As they watched, blood flooded from the eye and ran down onto Bouhila's hand. Her body twitched and then slumped, inert against him, suspended from the crook of his arm. With a choking noise he snatched away the knife. For another moment he stood holding onto her, staring as though stupefied at the blade. Then, he opened his arm, letting her body crumple, inert, to the floor, and looked up at Bill.

Bill had recovered himself a fraction of a second sooner. He sprang at Bouhila, pulling the crowbar from inside his jacket. Still numbed with shock at Keltum's action, Bouhila stepped back, slashing belatedly with the knife. The blade slipped past Bill's sleeve as the point of the crowbar caught Bouhila between the knuckles, ripping out a sliver of flesh.

Bouhila cried out and snatched back the knife hand. Bill kept coming, slashing the bar backhand, aiming again for the damaged hand. Bouhila staggered, impeded by Keltum's arm, extended along the floor behind him. Unthinking, not caring about the knife, Bill pressed forward. Bouhila's face, the hooked nose, the thick dark bar of the eyebrows, seemed to fill his vision. The light that blazed in the eyes was different now, the light of rank fear.

Powered by his rage, hardly knowing what he was doing, Bill drew back the crowbar, feinted at Bouhila's stomach and then drove the bar into his face. Bouhila shrieked, a high-pitched, piercing cry, like a wounded bird, and fell back to sit heavily on the carpet. Bill looked at the tip of the bar. A tremor of disgust shook him at the sight of the sticky, transparent mess that glistened there.

Kicking the knife into a corner of the cubicle, Bill knelt and slid an arm under Keltum's head. It lolled back, the head of a broken doll. Tears glistened in his eyes as he gently lowered her to the floor and withdrew his arm.

'Fuck you,' he breathed, and brought the crowbar slashing down on the side of Bouhila's skull.

Turning away, he scooped up Keltum's bag and sprinted up the slope of the aisle.

27

'If you will excuse me, ladies and gentlemen,' the President smiled, handing his empty champagne glass to an alert waiter. 'I think we're being called to our places.'

As the group of people who had been clustered around him moved reluctantly away, shepherded by the anxious stewards, the President reached out and took hold of the sleeve of Pautrat's dinner jacket, holding him back. As he did so, he looked up at the patch of sky framed in the opening that led out to the seating area. 'I hope he isn't going to be late, after all the song and dance.'

Pautrat squinted up into the floodlights, laughing. 'No! He'll be here. He just wants to make an entrance. Vadon was on the line to the embassy a few minutes ago. He was already in the helicopter.'

'M'mm. Have you been observing Vadon, by the way?'

Pautrat looked down at the President, giving him a skewed look. 'How do you mean?'

The President nodded towards the spot where Vadon stood. 'Look at him. Wouldn't you expect him to be holding court?'

Pautrat's eyes followed the President's. Instead of being at the centre of a group, as Pautrat would have supposed, Vadon hovered on the edge of a knot of admirers who crowded round a well-known actor. As they watched, he raised his glass to his lips, making to drink, and then let it fall back with a flounce of irritation, finding the glass was empty. He looked peevishly for a waiter. Attracting one's attention, he swapped his glass for a full one and took a long gulp. As he did so, the knot of people drifted away. Instead of moving with them, Vadon remained where he was, staring out through the opening into the brightly lit compound.

The President frowned. 'That must be the seventh or eighth glass. I hope he's not going to let himself down. He's been jumpy as a cricket all evening, as if he were afraid of something.'

Across the compound, unseen by the President or Pautrat, two technicians in dark overalls strode from the tunnel. They paused for a moment, buttoning their overalls after the body-searches, and then strode purposefully towards the eastern end of the grandstand structure.

As the President looked on, Vadon missed a step, staggering slightly. His free hand flew to his shirtfront, flicking away the spilled champagne. The President grimaced. 'You see what I mean?'

Pautrat chuckled. 'Probably doing it in his pants, afraid Bruckner might not show up, after all. Don't forget he's responsible for tonight. He knows that if anything goes wrong a couple of hundred million television watchers around the world are going to be laughing at him.'

'And, of course, if it goes right . . .'

'He's next for your job,' Pautrat said, his smile fading.

A drone overhead made them both crane upwards. The President sighed. 'And I doubt if there's much *you* can do to stop him, old friend. I'm afraid the man's riding a wave.'

❖

In the cavity at the foot of the tower, working in almost total darkness, the two technicians moved with well-rehearsed precision. By touch, not speaking, they clambered swiftly through the tangles of cable to the heap of drums where Vadon had concealed the bags. One of them lifted the drums carefully aside and set about retrieving the bags from the lower one. The other stepped up to the circle of asphalt exposed by the drum's removal and crouched, examining the ground. The paleness of a chalk mark was just visible on the dark surface. Standing, he lifted a leg and jabbed the heel of his boot hard at the mark.

The asphalt gave very slightly under the blow. He repeated the action, the soft thud of his rubber boot hardly carrying as far as his companion. Again the surface sagged, so that there was now a distinct dip. He braced himself and drove his heel violently into the centre of the depression. The asphalt gave way with hardly a sound. Kneeling, he tore at the sagging edges until he had made a hole wide enough for a man to pass. He turned to see his companion zipping his overalls over the weapon bags. At the sound of the approaching helicopter they paused for an instant to exchange quick, blank-eyed smiles. Then, moving with the same deliberate, unhasty efficiency, they replaced the drum over the hole and began scaling the gantry.

❖

Bill hit the street at a full run, leaving the cashier of the dilapidated supermarket shouting in his wake. He kept running for half a dozen blocks, weaving and turning at random, oblivious now to the possibility of police patrols. At length, panting hard, he paused. Fifty metres away a man waited to get into a taxi, standing back politely as the previous client fumbled with change. Running hard again, he reached the cab as the previous passenger was coming to his feet.

'Sorry!' As he said the word, he sent the waiting man sprawling and hurled himself inside.

'Rue François Premier,' he shouted at the driver, dragging the door closed.

The other man had recovered his balance. He snatched at the door handle, hammering indignantly on the roof. The driver twisted to face Bill. 'Hey, I'm taken. You could see . . .'

Holding the door shut with one hand, Bill wrestled a handful of money from his pocket and dropped it into the cabbie's lap. The objections tailed off as the driver turned back to stare at the money spilling from his knees to the floor. With a shrug at the protesting man, he accelerated sharply away.

'Thanks. Now, rue François Premier. And fast! I've got an appointment to see the parade.'

The driver shrugged again. 'Don't know if I can. The whole centre's a mess.'

'As near as you can.' He pulled more cash from an inside pocket and waved it under the driver's nose. 'There's this, too, if you can do it in time. Watch the lights, though,' he added in an afterthought. 'Too many cops around for that.'

The driver snorted. 'You're telling me! And they've closed half the city down, the bastards.'

'I don't suppose it's personal. Let's drive.'

The dashboard clock was just ticking up to nine when the taxi swung onto the Invalides bridge. To their right, the gleaming gilt horses decorating the Alexander bridge were swallowed by sudden darkness as the city's floodlights were extinguished. An instant later a thousand multi-coloured fingers of light stabbed at the sky, criss-crossing above them.

Bill had a distinct sense that he was hallucinating, as though he were *inside* a kaleidoscope. To their left, the Eiffel tower seemed like part of the dream as its familiar outline pulsed on and off, lit each time in a different combination of colours. Amid his already racing thoughts, the throbbing lights, the intensity of the colours made his head spin, momentarily forcing him to squeeze his eyes closed, regaining his grip on reality.

The car raced across the Seine and turned along the riverside. Craft of all shapes and sizes crowded the river, their occupants out on deck, gulping champagne and gaping at the display. Bill heard himself shouting at the driver, urging him to more speed, spraying more money onto the floor at the man's feet.

They wove among the traffic with total abandon, the driver shouting obscenities into the flashing headlights as he forced oncoming cars to swerve out of their way. They hit the place de l'Alma at speed, accelerating through a changing light, and hurtled up the avenue George V. One more turn brought them into the rue Marbeuf.

Bill was out of the car while it was still moving, sprinting for the steps of the car park. Across the street a policeman watched, tight-lipped, as he disappeared into the stairwell. He leapt headlong down the piss-smelling concrete stairs to the lowest floor. The place was packed, crammed with the up-market cars of spectators come to watch the parade from the invitation-only stands lower down the Champs-Elysées. A sprinkling of latecomers were hurrying towards the exits. Ignoring their stares, he sprinted for the metal door into which Khoury had disappeared the previous day.

The taxi ride had given him time to look again at all his alternatives. Lantier's death finally removed the option of calling in the police. It fitted with everything that had happened since the moment of Ahmed's suicide. It was evidence of a conspiracy on the scale of the Kennedy killing, a web of deceit that reached down from Vadon to every level of the police and security services.

He had considered going to the American Embassy, or to the Israelis. With enough time, and if he had still had the evidence of the tape, he might just have used his own intelligence background to make a case. Without either they would have logged him as yet another of the day's nutcases. To them, he would be the man who had mutilated the prostitute. A madman. They would have let him talk only for as long as it took for the French police to get there and haul him away.

In the end, his decision had made itself. His best hope was to somehow disrupt the whole damned show. At the first sign of trouble Bruckner's minders would get him out. It was up to him to make the trouble, before Bouhila's killers had a chance to do their work. To do it, he needed access to the compound. And he was convinced that the door would give it to him. Somehow there was a connection from there to the VIP enclosure. Khoury's visit could have been nothing other than a tour of inspection, checking out his people's escape route.

Thirty paces from the door he reached into his blouson and pulled the crowbar from his pocket. Skidding on the oily floor, he turned between two cars and ran, crowbar in hand, the last few paces to the door.

'You! Stop!'

He pivoted, the bar raised to strike. The man who had shouted was half out of the passenger door of a Volkswagen parked three bays from the door. His wrists rested on the open door, steadying the gun he clasped in his hands. His companion was clambering out of the driving seat.

'Drop that! Turn around, against the wall.' There was an odd shrillness in the gunman's voice, as though he were trying to quell an uncertainty. The second man, out of the car now, came round the intervening vehicles at a run. He was a metre from Bill, gun in hand, when another shout brought him up short.

A police van was speeding towards them. The policeman who had seen Bill enter the car park hung from a running board on the passenger side. 'Police! Stop!'

The man waved them away. 'Piss off! We'll deal with this. Renseignements Généraux.' He spoke without taking his eyes off Bill.

The policeman jumped from the van, drawing his own gun. His eyes flickered uncertainly from one to the other of them. Behind him, more police were spilling from the wagon. Taking their cue from their leader, they too were drawing weapons.

'Your papers.' The policeman said doggedly, holding out a hand.

The man in front of Bill shook his head angrily, his eyes still unwavering on Bill. 'Piss off, I said. This is a security matter.'

The policeman glanced at the line of men at his back, looking for moral support, and moved closer. 'Your papers,' he repeated, wetting his lips, his eyes fixed on the man's gun.

With a snort of exasperation, the man reached for the zipper of his blouson. He fumbled as the zipper caught the cloth. For just an instant, he glanced down.

Bill swung the crowbar in a short arc, slamming it into the side of the man's head. With a grunt, he staggered against a car. For a moment his body shielded Bill from his companion's gun. As the uniformed policemen stared at each other, not knowing whether or whom to shoot, Bill spun and jabbed the tool into the jamb.

Even as he had hit the man, he knew it was a desperate, hopeless move. He would be shot before he had time to begin forcing the lock. He felt as though he were moving in slow motion, re-living a childhood nightmare, as he dragged at the bar, waiting for the bullet to smash his spine. For what seemed an age but must in reality have been the smallest fraction of a second, he stared in blank astonishment. At the first pressure of the crowbar, a tiny wooden wedge had fallen to the cement at his feet. The door began swinging slowly open under its own weight.

The bullet came, tearing the air by his ear and hitting the metal with a head-splitting whang. Ducking low, he dived into the mouth of the tunnel, dragging the door shut behind him.

Bracing a foot against the frame, he pulled the door tightly shut. As quarrelling voices reached him from beyond the thickness of the steel, he knocked the lever of the lock into place and hammered the crowbar behind it with the heel of his hand, jamming it tight. Turning, he began racing along the tunnel, his way lit by bare bulbs in wire cages set high on the tiled wall.

He knew with absolute certainty now that this tunnel would lead him to Bouhila's assassins. The men in the Volkswagen had been the getaway drivers. Unless . . . He laughed aloud at the sudden realization. Unless they were not there to drive the assassins anywhere. Unless they really were what they claimed, men of the Renseignements Généraux. Vadon's men, there to silence the assassins. He laughed again. It explained the dismay in their faces, and the argument he had heard through the door. They were primed for a private, officially sanctioned killing. The assassins were to come out of the tunnel looking for the waiting getaway car. Instead, each would have been silenced with a bullet in the back of his neck. The unexpected arrival of Bill and his police posse had thrown them completely off balance. His laugh died. If he were too late there was a good chance he would run right into the killers as they made their escape.

❖

The VIP guests who had been crowding onto the ramp from the reception area began moving forward to take their seats, following the instructions of a barrel-chested steward. The man waited until they were all seated before signalling again. The President emerged into the floodlights, his wheelchair pushed by an aide. Daniel Bruckner walked at his side, grinning and waving for the television cameras. To the applause of the seated guests, they took their places at the centre of the podium.

Smiling his hooded smile, the President looked around him. The walls, if Vadon's vaunted armoured resin was all he claimed it was, gave complete protection from the surrounding buildings. Of course, an attack from above was a possibility. But it was a remote one. Bruckner's helicopter, which now stood like a brooding bird at the northern end of the compound, would be the only aircraft to fly low over the city that evening. Air traffic was being specially monitored. If anything moved over the city below ten thousand feet there would be an immediate blackout. He and Bruckner would be inside the specially prepared shelter at the foot of the ramp within seconds. Danger could come only from within the compound. From the reports he had received, independent of Vadon's, nobody could have entered without one of the specially issued passes. His smile widened. Bruckner should survive the night.

Bill ran on towards an elbow in the tunnel, counting steps as he went and going over the path he had taken from the street, trying to work out where he was headed relative to the streets above. The tunnel ran roughly north-east. He reached the elbow, alert for oncoming footsteps. It was a forty-five degree turn, so that he now judged he was running more or less north, towards the Champs-Elysées.

Ahead of him, a massive steel door stood open on its hinges. Slowing to a walk, he moved cautiously forward and peered through the opening. He was looking into the vaulted tunnel of one of the main city drains. An iron ladder led down to one of the walkways flanking the main channel. In the channel itself, water from the recent rain raced past, crusted with a heaving layer of filthy tan foam. Food wrappers and plastic cups littered the walkways, beached there after the last cloudburst had sent the water spilling out of its channel. He paused, re-checking his direction, and then leapt down the steps. He began running again, disregarding the slick layer of silt that lay thick underfoot.

'Here they come.' The speaker, short and wiry, with his overall sleeves rolled tightly over powerful arms, sat with his back against the scaffolding behind the bank of floodlights looking east towards the Louvre. 'Hurry up.'

His companion lay on his elbows on the platform of planks, methodically screwing the barrel to the second of the plastic sniper rifles. 'Relax. I'd never seen these damned things until yesterday. Here.' He tested the fixing and handed the gun to the first speaker, shuffling to sit close alongside him. Together, they watched in silence as the parade approached, headed by a mounted detachment of Republican Guardsmen, the polished leather and brass of their harnesses glinting in the floodlights. As they drew closer, the first speaker changed position, turning to look down into the compound.

The podium was hidden from his view by a striped canvas awning. A short distance clear of the awning, in clear view, was a simple wooden lectern with a bank of microphones sprouting in front of it. The man's eyes were on a thick-set steward in a tight-fitting suit who stood close by the lectern looking from his watch to the approaching parade. As the man watched from his perch, the steward raised his hands in front of him and waggled his fingers towards the podium in a beckoning motion. 'Here they come,' the watcher murmured. As he spoke, the other man threaded the short barrel of his weapon among the skeins of thick black cables. He settled it onto a scaffolding strut, fitted it snugly against his shoulder and bent to squint along the barrel. He gave a soft grunt and lifted his head again. 'Come now. Be ready. In a moment we shall wash away the blood of the women and children of Gaza.'

Bill's chest burned. His leg muscles were dying on him, pushed beyond their endurance by his sustained sprint. Still, at the sight of the name on a wall plaque he quickened his pace, dredging a last reserve of willpower. He was almost under the avenue George V, only a few hundred metres from the compound.

If he could just find the way in, the route the assassins had left clear for their escape, his very appearance, his skin and clothes blackened and rank with the stinking mud, would be enough to create panic. It would need five seconds for Bruckner's bodyguards to have him out of reach. Without slowing, he wiped the filth from his watch and looked at the time. Groaning, he drove his flagging legs to a last effort. Above his head the parade would already be on its way up the Champs-Elysées.

A side channel barred his way, the water boiling past towards the main channel, the roar of the water filling his head. Without pausing, he leapt in.

The rush of water snatched his legs from under him. He went under, his feet scrabbling for a grip in the muddy bottom. Lying almost horizontal, his lungs bursting, he managed to drive a foot deep into the slime, stopping himself from being swept into the irresistible turbulence of the main channel. Leaning at a forty-five degree angle, it took him more than half a minute before he managed to roll onto the far bank, his shoes gone, snatched by the clinging ooze. He lay there for another three seconds, panting hard, and then was on his feet again and running.

The head of the parade drew level with the podium, the perfectly drilled horses leading at a stately walk. The sky exploded in a riot of colour as more batteries of laser lights sprang to life, slashing the low masses of the cloud with fantastical colours and shapes. The President leaned towards Bruckner, smiling. 'Don't worry, Prime Minister. This is just our way of showing off to the world. It will all be over before your speech. For that, everything will be as simple as you asked.'

Bill raced on, his stumbling exhaustion evaporating as he neared his goal. He scanned the walls of the tunnel, looking for what he knew must be there, the way from the surface by which the men planned their escape. Every twenty paces he was obliged to leap another of the narrow side drains that brought rainwater from the service alleys that flanked the main avenue of the Champs-Elysées. The tiled tunnels, the diameter of an oil drum, disgorged their water through thick steel grilles into the central drain. He jumped another of them, skidded to a stop and turned back. The grille was missing. He bent to examine the fixings. The metal was still bright where it had been cut. With a new surge of energy coursing through him, he dropped onto his back and began wriggling his way up the channel, fighting the rush of water that threatened to send him tobogganing down and out into the turbulent main stream.

He had struggled what he estimated was thirty metres up the shaft when his left hand, probing for a purchase hold, slipped and found air. He probed deeper. The tiles had been hacked away to form a side shaft. His senses reeling, he began crawling up the sharp slope of the roughly made shaft, not even feeling the jagged stones of the roof where they gouged the flesh of his back.

The laser lights went out with a suddenness that left them in total blackness. The gunmen closed their eyes, waiting for the flashing colours to stop playing under their eyelids. When they opened them again, the only light was the glow of cigarettes and a single spotlight illuminating the lectern. Abruptly, another bank of spotlights stabbed their beams into the darkness, picking out a group of people in the now stationary parade. They stood facing the compound, men and women whose ages ranged from the middle fifties to the very old. Many were in wheelchairs, pushed by younger companions. Almost all of the men wore skullcaps amid their wisps of hair. A few were blind, their hands held by young girls in simple white dresses. They waited, utterly still, their eyes on the lectern. Bruckner stepped into the pool of light, his hands held up in salute.

Above him, the gunmen mopped away the sweat that ran down their brows and made their palms greasy, and settled lower over their weapons.

On his feet amid a litter of broken asphalt, Bill reached upward. His fingers scrabbled at what felt like wood, perhaps the bottom of a packing case. Flattening his palms against it, he pushed up. The obstruction moved. Curling his fingers round an edge, he heaved it away from the hole. He hooked his arms over the rim, jumped, and swung himself upwards. He was in an enclosed space, lit only by the pale light filtering in from a rectangular opening above him. After the pitch blackness of the tunnel, the paler darkness seemed almost as good as daylight. He began stumbling among tangled skeins of cable, seeking a way into the open.

The gunmen pressed their cheeks against the plastic stocks of their weapons. Below them, Bruckner dropped his arms and leaned forward over his notes, his words booming around them as he began his address. They lay quite still, waiting for him to straighten. He did so, raising his head to look directly at the proud band of camp survivors. As he moved, a pulsating flash of lightning ripped the sky directly overhead. Almost instantaneously, the crack of its accompanying thunder shook the air, leaving their ears ringing. The spotlights went out, casting them into a darkness deeper than before.

'Damn it! Damn, damn, damn!' The leader of the two gunmen reared away from his gunsight, letting his eyes rest. 'Relax for a minute. Give yourself a break. The lightning's blown the power. It won't take them a minute to have it back on.' They eased their positions, flexing the fingers of their trigger hands, and settled to wait.

The momentary brightness gave Bill light enough to see the tarpaulins that formed the outer wall of the cavity. He snatched at the bottom of one and threw himself into the open.

The gantry stood out darker against the sky above him, and next to it the tiered bulk of the grandstand. To his right he could see the silhouettes of vehicles and prowling men, moving in patrols of three. He ran, making for the lower tiers at the front of the grandstand.

The first shout of alarm came before he had run three steps. More followed. He was aware of running footsteps, and then he was leaping onto the raised platform.

The spotlights flooded the lectern with light once again. Bruckner, still standing at the same spot, blinked and shaded his eyes. Clearing his throat, he made to resume his speech.

High above him, the two men settled, taking leisurely aim.

Their fingers were tightening on the triggers when Bruckner swung to his right, leaning to see into the darkness. The men cursed as the sounds of a disturbance reached them. The one nearest to the edge glanced down. A shadowy figure was scrambling across the seating towards the lectern.

'Now! Quickly,' he hissed, turning back to renew his aim.

At the same moment, his companion let out a snarl. Half a dozen burly men had dashed from beneath the awning and thrown themselves on Bruckner, smothering him with their bulk. Crisply shouted commands floated upwards as they ran him out of the spotlight and down the ramp to safety.

Bill was already among the panicking guests when they reached him. The first of them, dinner-jacketed but with the absurdly wide shoulders of a security man, rose from a seat among the guests and dived, taking Bill full in the chest and bringing him to his knees. Other men, running in from the shadows, piled into the fray.

On his knees and gasping, Bill fought to speak. As he opened his mouth something hard slammed into it. He was incongruously aware of the sound of his snapped tooth pinging against the metal of a chair. As his hand flew to his mouth another blow smashed across the back of it, numbing it. He raised his arms to defend his head. Short batons smashed against his undefended ribs. 'Bruckner,' he rasped. 'Get him away! They're going to . . .' His words died as a blow to the temple cut him momentarily adrift from his senses. Clinging to consciousness, he tried to stand, dropping his arms to show them he was offering no resistance. He tried again to speak. A baton struck him across the nose, so that the sound emerged as a sob.

Hands snatched at him, pinioning his arms. He half saw a baton flash through the air, tried to jerk his head aside, and took the blow across the jaw. He heard, rather than felt, the bone snap. He was aware of an authoritative voice, very close by, saying, 'Alright. You can get back to your posts. We'll take care of him,' and then he lost consciousness completely.

* * *

The gunmen watched the brawl in absolute silence, on the edge of panic, sure that they had failed and not knowing whether to run or to remain hidden. They were still wondering when, at a shouted command, the lights were dimmed and the spotlights came on once more, lighting up the lectern, and the ranks of concentration camp survivors. The survivors remained stoically at attention as the dense rain that had come with the thunder, sparkling silver in the lights, drummed down on them.

They stared in stunned disbelief as a man stepped from beneath the awning holding up a brightly coloured umbrella. A moment later Bruckner stepped into the shelter of the umbrella and walked to the lectern. Exchanging looks of sheer, undiluted disbelief, they slid back into firing positions.

Bill was unconscious only a few seconds before the pulsing agony in his jaw nagged him awake. His head lolling, he fought to make sense of his chaotic, nightmarish thoughts. A cry bubbled ineffectually on his lips as his head struck the ground. The fresh, focused pain slicing through him brought him to himself. He opened his eyes to find his head was almost under a car.

The stink of exhaust nauseated him. The shock of realization made him groan. In seconds they would have him in the car. He would be the latest in a long line of people French politicians had found a threat, subsequently discovered floating in a gravel pit, a sad case of suicide. A suicide who had first broken his own jaw.

One of the men dragging him took a hand from his wrist to open the car door. Gathering his will, Bill ripped his hand free and swung a punch at the second man's groin. He was drawing back his arm for another punch, writhing to free himself from the man's loosened grip when a heel crunched down into his face, driving his head back against the road surface. He grunted and fell back. More hands grabbed at him and he was thrown bodily into the back of the car.

Another flash of lightning slashed across the sky. It seemed to stand still for a long moment, a dozen shimmering slashes of light. Sprawled across the seat, Bill stared in stark, impotent horror. Twelve metres above him, backlit by the pale brilliance of the lightning, two men were crouched against the framework, the silhouettes of their weapons clear in every detail.

The lightning faded, leaving the after-image burning into Bill's retina. A voice boomed over the loudspeakers, filling the air around him, speaking in fluent, accented French. Bruckner had begun his address.

The car jerked into reverse, almost toppling Bill to the floor. Instinctively reaching out to save himself, he found he was in a half-sitting posture. The car stopped and leapt forward, causing Bill to lurch back. At the movement, the man sitting next to the driver reached back and flipped his short, leather-covered cosh across Bill's nose.

Bill did not even register the pain. Beyond the windscreen the foot of the gantry rose in a shadowy mass. The driver hauled at the wheel, making for a gate that had been opened up in the perimeter wall. He sat forward, pointing. With a curse, the passenger hit him again.

Hardly aware of it, Bill shoved off from the seat, hurling himself between the two men and into the well at the driver's feet, shouldering the feet off the pedals. Reaching up, he grabbed the steering wheel and hung his weight on it, jerking the car round. With his other hand he jabbed at the accelerator pedal, pushing it to the floor.

Tyres screaming, the car leapt forward and ploughed into the base of the gantry.

The two men murmured to each other, confirming that both had Bruckner's temple at the very point of their crosshairs. Bruckner was quite still, pausing to acknowledge a burst of applause.

'Now!'

As the man spoke the word the tower lurched forward, projecting them hard against the scaffolding. Frantically, they scrambled to regain balance and find a new aim. Leaping and vibrating, the tower rocked back again, shuddered and stopped. At the sound of crashing metal, Bruckner had stopped speaking. He hesitated for a moment and then turned to run.

The gunman who had spoken was on his feet. He raised his weapon, tracking the running figure as it rushed for the protection of the advancing posse of security men. 'For the dead of Gaza!' he screamed. He squeezed the trigger just as the gantry shivered like a stricken animal. The gun coughed softly. A white sliver of wood flew from the platform a foot behind Bruckner. He was steadying the gun for a second shot when the whole structure toppled.

Bill fought his way out from under the wheel. A length of scaffold pole seemed to be sprouting from the driver's chest. Blood ran from the man's mouth. The man who had hit him writhed and screamed, trying to drag free the arm which was trapped by the stoved-in roof. Bill struggled into the back, kicked out the broken rear window and wormed his way out.

He fought through the tangle of twisted scaffold poles, planking and tangled cable, aiming to get out into the crowd, counting on being seen as his best hope of not being shot down like a dog.

He could hear voices in the darkness as people fought to reach the car. Abruptly, light seeped in around him as the floodlights came back on. Exhausted, on the brink of fainting, he dragged himself out into the light. He was standing on the platform amid a jumble of overturned chairs. From all around the compound men were leaping onto the podium and sprinting towards him.

His legs faltering under him, he walked a short way to where the banks of broken lights were strewn among the wreckage. There he stood quite still, looking down at the two broken figures that lay there. He did not seem to see the running men as they formed a tight semi-circle round him, their faces bluish in the light of the sparks from the broken cables that snaked about his feet.

Slowly, he lifted his eyes to look at the circle of faces. Seeing the disbelief in their stares he looked down at himself. He felt an urge to laugh. His clothes stuck to him, streaked and filthy with the mud of the sewers. Blood mixed with the mud. His face, he knew, must be a mask of blood and dirt.

Very slowly, he peeled off his jacket and wiped his face with it.

'It's him! The American! The pervert that killed the woman!' The uniformed policeman, detached himself from the circle and launched himself at Bill, a fist raised to strike.

'Stop that!' The deep, resonant voice, steeped in authority, stopped him in his tracks. The policeman fell back as the circle parted, allowing Vadon into the gap. Fabre, the head of police intelligence was at his side. Signalling Fabre to wait, Vadon advanced alone towards Bill.

'So, Monsieur Duvall,' Vadon said, conversationally. 'You know everything?'

Bill nodded. Very deliberately, he held up the filthy jacket and reached into an inside pocket to pull out a folded brown envelope, soaked and disintegrating. Brushing away the remnants of the envelope he peeled off a photograph and held it out to Vadon.

With a strange, dreamy expression on his face Vadon took the picture from him and looked at it. Bill separated more photographs and skimmed them at the onlookers. Vadon appeared deaf to the gasps that rippled around the circle. He went on staring at the photograph as it sagged and bobbed under the weight of the teeming rain. Gradually, a smile of extraordinary tenderness spread over his face. Very slowly, he looked up at Bill. Tears rolled down his cheeks, mixing with the rain.

'I loved that boy, Mister Duvall,' he said, in faultless English. 'You can't imagine how much.' He took three steps forward, watched in awed silence by the ring of policemen. Still holding the picture, he stooped and picked up one of the cables. 'And, do you know, he betrayed me,' he said, in a high, bereft voice. 'He let that man Bouhila take these pictures. So that he and de Medem could use me.' He waved the photograph at the two men who lay among the wreckage. 'To do this! They *all* used me!' The last words came in a racking sob, as distressing as a child's.

Bill looked at the man, his head bowed, tears dropping at his feet, and shook his head, grimacing as the pain seared him. 'No, Vadon. Not Ahmed. He didn't know. *He* was the one who got the pictures back. They used him, too.'

Vadon raised his head, staring at him, through him, not appearing to hear. Only slowly did Bill comprehend. Vadon could not understand anything he was saying. The snapped jawbone, his mashed lips, swollen to twice their normal size, reduced his words to an incomprehensible blur. Vadon looked down at the cable in his hand.

With an effort at a shout, Bill made to step towards Vadon. His knee gave way, causing him to stagger.

With no change of expression, Vadon opened his mouth and thrust the sparking end of the cable deep into his throat.